THE GLASS FOREST

⋀ *Novel* –

CYNTHIA SWANSON

TOUCHSTONE
New York   London   Toronto   Sydney   New Delhi

Touchstone
An Imprint of Simon & Schuster, Inc.
1230 Avenue of the Americas
New York, NY 10020

First Touchstone hardcover edition February 2018

TOUCHSTONE and colophon are registered trademarks of Simon & Schuster, Inc.

For information about special discounts for bulk purchases, please contact Simon & Schuster Special Sales at 1-866-506-1949 or business@simonandschuster.com.

The Simon & Schuster Speakers Bureau can bring authors to your live event. For more information or to book an event, contact the Simon & Schuster Speakers Bureau at 1-866-248-3049 or visit our website at www.simonspeakers.com.

Interior design by Jill Putorti

Manufactured in the United States of America

10 9 8 7 6 5 4 3 2 1

Library of Congress Cataloging-in-Publication Data
Names: Swanson, Cynthia, 1965- author.
Title: The glass forest / by Cynthia Swanson.
Description: First Touchstone hardcover edition. | New York : Touchstone, 2018.
Identifiers: LCCN 2017027541| ISBN 9781501172090 (hardcover) | ISBN 9781501172106 (tradepaper) | ISBN 9781501172113 (ebook)
Subjects: | BISAC: FICTION / Suspense. | FICTION / Psychological. | FICTION / Literary. | GSAFD: Suspense fiction.
Classification: LCC PS3619.W35945 G58 2018 | DDC 813/.6—dc23
LC record available at https://lccn.loc.gov/2017027541

ISBN 978-1-5011-7209-0
ISBN 978-1-5011-7211-3 (ebook)

To the Brussats and the Fishers—past, present, and future

1

Angie

Door County, Wisconsin 1960

The day started out clear and crisp—a perfect September morning with no foreboding of what was to come. After PJ woke from his nap, I bundled him into a sweater, stretchy knit pants, and a matching cap— hand-me-downs from my sister Dorrie's children. Holding the baby against my hip, I stepped outside the cottage. It had rained the night before, and I breathed in the sultry fragrance, familiar as the scent of my own skin, of swollen lake water and sparse Wisconsin woods.

My feet crunched across our sand path over the unpaved road to North Bay; like all residents of North Bay Drive, Paul and I had created a path of sand across the gravel-and-oil road, to curtail oil sticking to our shoes. I made my way down the rickety wooden staircase to the bay, careful of the mud that always stuck to the stair treads after a hard rain. At the bottom, I squelched through the tall, mucky grasses to the edge of the water and with one hand turned over the lightweight canvas canoe my grandfather handcrafted decades ago. Over the weekend, Paul had fashioned a small wooden seat for PJ, padded and reclining, across the canoe's middle bench. I was eager to try it out.

Humming softly, I fastened the baby with leather straps that Paul had hammered into each side of the bench. I was thinking about the night before. I remembered how rain had pelted the tin roof of the cottage, pounding into my ears as Paul and I rocked together in tangled sheets, our limbs entwined. At the end, I'd cried out Paul's name, my voice raised above the sound of raindrops lashing against the window-panes. Afterward we were still, listening to the occasional rumble of thunder as the storm moved eastward over Lake Michigan. Gratitude—for my marriage, my life, my future—wrapped itself around my heart as securely as Paul's body encircled my own.

Now, twelve hours later, my breath caught at the memory. I paddled onto the bay, which PJ and I had to ourselves, save for a gathering of ducks floating serenely near the shore and a pair of gulls farther out. All the gnats and most of the mosquitoes were gone for the season. Only the occasional dragonfly buzzed over the water, its wings shimmering purple and blue in the sunlight.

I put up the paddle and let the canoe drift. Lulled by the gently rocking craft, PJ babbled cheerfully as he watched birds flying overhead.

I looked up, shielding my eyes from the sun, and as I did, a burst of splashing water erupted to my right. I whipped my head and shoulders around in time to see a trout shooting out of the bay, sending ripples across the surface when it plunged back in.

Pulled off balance by my sudden shift, I felt the canoe tipping sharply. PJ let out a wail. I twisted and saw the baby roll to the side and the top of his head touch the water. His shoulders and torso followed. The leather straps had come loose from the bench—Paul must not have hammered them in securely enough.

I grappled forward and snatched the baby by his ankles just before he went fully underwater. The canoe tilted and I sat down hastily, grinding my hip into the bench as I restored myself upright.

The baby wailed with surprise, his hair soaked, lake water dripping into his eyes and mingling with his tears. I hugged him to my chest and ran my fingers across his drenched head. "It's okay, my little one," I murmured. "You're safe."

I kissed PJ's brow, tucking his head against my breast, and with my free hand crossed myself. *Thank you, Virgin Mother*, I silently prayed. *Thank you for watching over us.*

The wooden paddle drifted nearby. Shaking, I stared at it. I snuggled the baby under my left arm, dunked my right forearm into the water, and propelled the canoe by hand until I reached the paddle. I retrieved it and tucked the baby more tightly against my body. Awkwardly, one-handed, I paddled toward the shore—graceless but steadfast.

I was just walking in the door when the telephone began to ring—the two short rings signifying the call coming over the party line was for my household. Still trembling, I slipped off my muddy galoshes. I dashed to the bathroom, wrapped the baby in a towel, and placed him on the davenport.

I crossed the cottage's diminutive living room and picked up the telephone receiver on the desk, turning down the radio volume with my other hand; I'd neglected to shut off the radio before I went out on the bay. Throughout the morning on WDOR, the announcers had been discussing last night's presidential debate. They said that while Vice President Nixon came off favorably over the airwaves, those who'd watched the televised version felt Senator Kennedy won by a landslide. The first time I heard those words, earlier that morning, I'd raised my fist in a little cheer. In less than two months, I would be voting in my first presidential election. The senator from Massachusetts had my full support.

"Aunt Angie?" The female voice on the other end of the line was unfamiliar. I have more than a dozen nieces and nephews—I'm the youngest of six, and all my siblings have several children apiece—but only a handful of those children were old enough to make telephone calls. And of those few, none had a mature voice like this. Not quite the intonation of an adult, but surely not a child, either.

Only one person might call me *aunt* in that type of voice.

"Ruby?" I asked. "Is that you? Are you all right?"

There was no answer. I glanced across the room, watching PJ burble to himself as he swatted the loose threads on a sofa pillow. Considering what he'd been through on the bay, PJ was terrifically calm. How lucky I was to have such an agreeable baby, when all I heard from my sisters and sisters-in-law were gripes about colic and crankiness.

"We got us a winner," Paul said whenever I marveled at this. "The boy's a winner, Angel."

And I would smile, both at his words and his pet name for me. *Angel*.

There was an almost inaudible sound on the line—not spoken words and not quite the clearing of a throat. I hoped it was Ruby, but I suspected it was old Mrs. Bates from down the road, using the party line to snare gossip like catching a weasel in a baited live trap.

"Ruby?" I said again. "Are you there? Are you all right?"

"No," Ruby answered in that restrained voice of hers, devoid of emotion and cool as the water in the bay. "No, Aunt Angie, I am not all right."

There was another pause, and then Ruby said, "Aunt Angie, my father is dead. And my mother has run away."

2

Ruby

Stonekill, New York 1960

"My mother left a note," Ruby says to Aunt Angie on the telephone. "Explaining to my father and me that she was leaving." Her voice lowering to a whisper, Ruby goes on. "She said she was sorry. But life is too short to wait."

"That's awful, Ruby," Aunt Angie says. "Just awful."

Ruby doesn't answer. After a moment, Aunt Angie asks, "And your father . . . ?"

Winding the telephone cord around her thumb, Ruby tells Aunt Angie the rest of the story: her father's body was found slumped on the forest floor, just a few feet into her family's woods behind their house. "He was at the base of an oak tree. There was an empty teacup nearby," Ruby says. "They're testing the cup for poison. The police told me the coroner will likely rule it a suicide."

Ruby's voice is matter-of-fact. Because these are the facts, after all.

"Oh, my goodness," Aunt Angie says. "I'm so sorry." She pauses, and then adds, "Where are you now, honey?"

Ruby is silent. She is taking in the word Aunt Angie used. *Honey*. Nobody calls Ruby anything like that. Not anymore.

"I'm at home," Ruby says. "Would you have Uncle Paul call me as soon as he can?"

After they hang up, Ruby turns and opens the patio door. She steps off the patio, crosses the backyard, and enters her family's dense forest.

All she hears are birds and insects and the occasional squirrel scurrying through the underbrush. Passing a thick-trunked oak, she taps it gently, then moves on.

Ruby tramples along the narrow, barely perceptible path. She presses her threadbare gray-white tennis shoes into supple earth and soggy fallen leaves.

Eventually she comes into a small clearing. She sits on a rock. A heavy, rut-topped boulder, two feet in diameter, two feet tall. A rock that's slick with dew, embedded quartz chips sparkling in the late-morning sunlight that filters through the treetops.

The rocks are the earth; everything around them is temporal. These rocks were here before the Algonquians, who in their turn inhabited this forest long before the Dutch settled New York State a mere three hundred years ago. Boulders like the one Ruby perches on have seen trees, animals, and people come and go. They've known the nearby oaks and pines for fewer years than the life span of a tortoise.

She crosses her left ankle over her right knee. Gently, she picks at the little blue rubber tag on the heel of her left shoe. The one that once said KEDS but because she's picked at it so much now only reads KE.

Ruby lowers her fingertips, anticipating the cold chill of rock.

And then—quickly—she pulls her hand away. Because instead of hard stone she felt something rippling and leathery.

She looks down. Coiled on the rock, not six inches from where she sits, is a solitary, thick-middled snake.

It hisses and she jumps up. She moves away, staring. The snake glowers, its beady eyes gleaming, its forked tongue flicking. Its flesh is mostly dark green—the color of the forest—with narrow stripes of yellow running the length of its body.

To prove she's not afraid, Ruby extends her hand.

The snake hesitates. It elongates and then recurls itself.

She wiggles her fingers.

That's all it takes. The snake pulls back its head to gather strength and momentum. With a vulgar hiss, it flings its open mouth toward her outstretched hand.

She could scream. But no one would hear her if she did.

3

Angie

I deposited PJ in his crib, put my galoshes back on, and flung myself out the door. I sloshed across the mucky yard as fast as I could.

My mind raced, taking in what Ruby had said. Suicide—what an awful thing. I couldn't imagine how I'd find the words to tell Paul this news about his brother. He was going to be crushed.

And Ruby! What a situation for a young girl to be in. Abandoned by her mother. And her father, too—brokenhearted, obviously, and had killed himself rather than face reality. How could parents do such things to their child?

I thought about the pet name I'd called Ruby, and how she clammed up when I said it. *Honey*. It was the term of endearment I used for all my young nieces and nephews, and it had come out spontaneously.

But Ruby was seventeen and I was twenty-one. Ruby would not consider herself my *honey*. I should have known better.

At the edge of the forest, I picked my way along the wide, muddy path to Paul's studio. Dappled sunlight fell on my shoulders through the thin stands of cedar and birch. After clear-cut logging in the late 1800s, the woods of Wisconsin's Door County peninsula were only now beginning to fill with maturing trees. The sparse forest provided the odd effect of simultaneously exposing and enfolding me.

The property—two acres on a gravel road facing North Bay, on the eastern side of Door—once belonged to my paternal grandparents. Paul and I had been living in the cottage on this property since our wedding the year before. Paul's studio, set back in the woods about ten yards behind the cottage, was doll-size. In the past, my grand-parents used it as a storage shed.

"Paul," I called, banging open the studio door.

Paul looked up from the half-painted linen clipped to his easel. The table next to him was littered with boxes of watercolor paints, brushes of various sizes, water pots, and a couple of rags. On a chair rail that Paul had mounted to the shed's walls were paintings in various stages of completion—scenes of North Bay, Lake Michigan, and the sunset over Green Bay on the other side of the peninsula.

"What is it, Angel?" Paul stood, facing me.

"I don't . . . I don't even know how to tell you this." I walked into the studio. "It's Henry. And Silja."

"What about them?"

I swallowed hard. "Ruby called. She said . . . oh, Paul." I put my arms around him. "Henry is . . . dead."

Paul extracted himself from my embrace and sat down heavily on his stool. "I don't understand."

"Me, neither, really," I said. "But Ruby says . . ." I bit my lip. "She says Henry was found in the woods near their house. His body, I mean. The police are expecting it to be ruled a . . . a suicide." I felt tears stinging my eyes. "And Silja is missing." I hesitated, and then added, "Ruby said Silja has abandoned them."

I told him about the note Silja had left. And then I trailed off, letting him put the pieces together for himself.

Paul didn't say anything. Then he asked, "Are you sure? You're sure that's what she said?"

I nodded. He looked out the studio window, blinking, then turned back to me.

"Tell me everything," he said. "Word for word, Angel, repeat exactly what Ruby said."

Paul's brother, Henry, lived in New York State with his wife, Silja, and their daughter, Ruby. I had met them only once, when they came to Door County the previous September for our wedding.

Henry and his family were scheduled to arrive late the evening before the wedding. By the time they made it to Door County, I had long since bid Paul good night at my parents' doorstep and gone up-stairs for my last night sleeping in my childhood bedroom. The next day I didn't see Paul until I walked down the aisle at St. Mary of the Lake and joined him at the altar, where Henry stood beside him.

As the priest intoned words of welcome, I glanced sideways at Henry, struck by his overwhelming resemblance to Paul. I look like everyone in my family, too—all six of us, from my oldest brother, George, on down through me, have mousy brown hair, freckles across our noses, and round blue eyes under arched brows. But Paul and Henry—both of them tall, thin, with narrow faces, a shock of dark hair, and sparkling, chocolate-brown eyes—looked as if they could be twins.

They practically were, Paul had told me on our first date. Only a year apart in age, the brothers had been inseparable as children. "We didn't have many friends," Paul said. "We didn't need them. We had each other." They'd grown up in California wine country. Their parents had been caretakers at a vineyard, and Paul and Henry were raised among the vines, helping tend the delicate plants, harvest the grapes, process them into wine.

"Did you squish them with your feet in a big wooden vat, like the Romans?" I asked him, angling myself forward to reveal the tops of my breasts protruding from the neckline of my favorite polka-dot dress.

"Every fall," Paul assured me with a grin. I felt my heart go pitter-patter.

Well, who could blame me? With his broad smile and twinkling eyes, he looked just like Cary Grant. I'd been powerless against the charms of Paul Glass—this beguiling, almost middle-aged artist who'd shown up in Door County seemingly from nowhere.

When I met him, I had just begun my annual summer job at Gordon Lodge as a cottage girl. It was sweaty, grueling work, cleaning the guest cottages and lodge rooms while wearing the nylon turquoise dress and the stockings that management required of its cottage girls. After my shift one afternoon, I wandered into the Top Deck, Gordon's lounge, for a drink of water. A bartender I didn't know was washing glasses and whistling. The top two buttons on his shirt were undone, and a St. Christopher medal peeked out from the nest of dark hair on his chest. As I sat down at the bar, I had an almost irresistible urge to reach out and touch the medal. The bartender smiled at me, flashing his dark eyes and placing a tumbler of ice water in front of me before I even asked for it.

That same night, we went on our first date—which actually consisted simply of me going home, showering and changing, then heading back to the lodge to sit at the bar and wait for him to close up.

Paul told me that both he and Henry had fought in the war; every young man did in those days, as I was aware, although I was only a toddler when the Japanese bombed Pearl Harbor. Paul went to the Pacific, and Henry was assigned to the European front. Before shipping out, Henry's company had leave in New York, where he met Silja.

"What kind of name is Silja?" I asked Paul. "Is it Italian, like Saint Cecilia?"

"No. It's pronounced like that but spelled differently," Paul replied. "*S-i-l-j-a*. It's Finnish. Silja grew up in some little Finnish socialist cooperative in Brooklyn. All for one, one for all—that sort of nonsense." He scoffed. "But she doesn't live like that anymore."

"How does she live now?"

Paul grimaced. "Opulently," he told me. "Silja lives opulently."

That first date led to a summer of nights together. Daytimes, too, when I'd slip away to the room Paul rented in town—glancing around furtively before entering the building, making sure no one saw me who would report back to my parents or brothers. I'd never done such a thing before—but I'd never known anyone like Paul before, either. He was as different from the boys I grew up with as a peacock would be among the multitudes of gulls that swarmed outside the lodge begging for scraps of food.

It wasn't just his charm; it was also his maturity. He'd been everywhere; he'd seen everything. Nothing fazed him—a turn of the weather, a harsh word from a demanding customer, a flat tire on a deserted road. His hands were more capable than any other man's—with the exception of my father, of course. I could trust Paul with anything.

Marvelously, it turned out he was as enamored with me as I was with him. When he smiled at me, I felt like a beauty queen. So it was no surprise, really, that a wedding took place only three months after we met.

It wasn't until our reception in the Top Deck that I got a good look at my new sister-in-law. Silja was sensuously plump: large-chested, round-bottomed, and tall. An emerald-green strapless dress accentuated her curves. Her ash-blond hair was upswept in back, styled low on her forehead in front. Her face was not especially pretty; she had a large, rounded nose that overshadowed her other features, in particular diminishing the exquisite hazel color of her eyes, which were hidden behind cat's-eye-shaped glasses.

Silja told me that she had a prominent job in New York City, managing food operations at the Rutherford Hotel. "It's not the largest hotel in New York by any means," Silja said. "Nor the most famous. But we have a reputation for impeccable service, particularly in our restaurants."

I nodded absently, looking around the room for Paul. He was behind the bar, mixing drinks and laughing with the guests seated across from him. The jovial bartender, even at his own wedding.

"So we're sorry we can't stay longer," Silja was saying, and I reluctantly turned my gaze back to her. "But I'm needed at work on Monday."

Silja reached into her handbag with manicured fingers, pulling out a gold cigarette case and matching lighter. She lit her cigarette, taking a long drag and regarding me. "And you, dear?" she asked. "What do you do?"

I clutched my handkerchief—something blue, just like the poem says you're supposed to carry. "Well, I was working here at the lodge over the summer," I said. "But now . . . with being a married woman and all . . . "

I closed my mouth, uncertain whether to say more. No one except my family and my closest friends knew the big secret—although once it became obvious, there would be little surprise, given how hastily Paul and I married. I was barely showing, my rounded belly easily hidden beneath the full skirt of my wedding gown—which, not many years before, had been my sister Carol Ann's wedding gown. Carol Ann was a size larger than me; hiding my expanding waistline wasn't a problem in the abundant yards of satin and lace. Still—this was Paul's sister-in-law, after all—*his* family. Had Paul told Henry about the baby? And if so, had Henry told Silja? I wasn't sure.

Silja nodded. "Marriage is work," she said faintly. "Marriage is . . . " She smiled wistfully. "Well, what do I know about it, right? No more, nor less, than any other wife." She inhaled cigarette smoke, then blew it away from me. "Every wife has her own story."

"Yes," I agreed. "I'm sure that's true."

Silja tilted her head, regarding me thoughtfully. "I can see how much you adore Paul. It's very sweet." She smiled again. "It reminds me of how I felt about Henry when we met. I was just about your age then." She turned away, staring contemplatively past the crowd of wedding guests toward the lake outside the Top Deck's wide window-panes. "That was such a long time ago."

A clinking sound filled the room—people tapping silverware against wine and beer glasses, signaling that they wanted the bride and groom to kiss. Paul met my eye and beckoned me over.

"Excuse me," I said to Silja, and scurried across the room. Leaning over the bar, I received Paul's warm kiss and our guests' enthusiastic applause.

4

Silja

1942

In Brooklyn, love at first sight only happened in one place: the movies. It happened every Saturday afternoon, to girls who spent their pin money each week to sit in velveteen seats in the Sunset or the Coliseum, contemplatively munching popcorn and watching as Barbara Stanwyck fell hard for an affable Henry Fonda, Vivien Leigh stared hypnotically into Laurence Olivier's eyes, Irene Dunne found herself defenseless against Cary Grant's charms.

And then the girls went home through the blustery, littered streets—home to their overworked mothers, silent fathers, and hordes of little brothers and sisters. The starry-eyed girls scribbled things like "Mrs. Emma Olivier" in their school notebooks, imagining what would happen if dreamy Laurence showed up on the doorstep. For surely he would forget Vivien in an instant, if he had her, Emma, to love instead.

That girl was Silja Takala. Twenty years old, bespectacled, and untarnished as a new copper kettle yet to feel the heat of fire, Silja was a girl whose only knowledge of love was through the movies.

But then real love *did* happen. Just like in the movies.

She met him at a bus stop. She was on her way to visit her friend Johanna. It was Friday, Silja's short day at Hunter when she only had morning classes. She had loads of homework to do over the weekend, but she hadn't seen Johanna in months, not since Johanna's family moved from Brooklyn's Finntown to New York's other Finntown, the one in Harlem.

As she waited for an uptown bus, a tall young man, thin as a cane and dressed in uniform—so many young men were in uniform these days—hesitantly tapped her shoulder.

"Hi-de-ho, miss." He grinned sheepishly. "I'm trying to get to the Bronx Zoo. Is this the right bus?"

"The zoo? Why do you want to go there?" She couldn't take her eyes off him. With twinkling eyes and an inviting smile, he was Cary Grant's double.

"I'm only in New York for a few days. I thought I should see the sights." He looked up at the bright, sunny sky—remarkably cloudless for the first Friday in March. "And it's a nice day for the zoo."

Such a peculiar thing for a GI to do on leave. There were burlesque clubs and taverns lining every side street in Manhattan. There were jazz joints and dance halls and any type of restaurant you could want. There were pleasures galore that a young man on his way to an uncertain future should surely enjoy while he could. What nutcase—especially such an attractive one—would choose the Bronx Zoo?

"I'm Henry," he said, almost as if she'd asked.

"Silja," she replied. The bus roared up next to them, spitting diesel fumes. "This is your bus," she informed him. "Mine, too."

Silja never made it to Johanna's. She arrived home well after supper time, her neatly rolled hairdo ruined by the wind at the zoo. She and Henry had strolled past the lions, the seals, the monkeys rattling their cages. Though Henry had claimed he wanted to see the sights, he seemed not to notice the animals. His eyes were on Silja.

They caught a downtown bus just before dark. Sliding into a seat near the back, Henry put his arm around Silja's shoulder, which she found both unsettling and exhilarating. She'd never before been the object of anyone's affection in public. But with the war on, boys in uniform—and the girls accompanying them—could get away with nearly any degree of necking. When Henry leaned in to kiss her, no one around them batted an eye. He pressed his mouth against hers softly but persistently, his tongue only scarcely flicking between her lips. Her heart was pounding when they broke apart.

"I have to see you again, Silja," he said. "Can I call you?"

Could he call her? What a question! She got off at Sixty-Eighth Street near Hunter and headed for the subway, leaving Henry on the bus holding a slip of paper with her number.

At home, her mother glared and asked Silja where she had been.

"I'm sorry, Äiti," Silja told her. "The subway trains were running late." She bowed her head so her mother couldn't see her faint smile.

Love at first sight? Silja asked herself that night as she fell into bed. She reached inside her nightgown, absently stroking her breasts. But love at first sight isn't real, she reminded herself, squeezing her nipples, feeling them stand erect against the thin cotton of her gown. It only happens in the movies.

Perhaps, she thought, lowering her hands. And perhaps not.

They met the next morning at Vic's, near Hunter on Sixty-Ninth Street—a spot Silja selected intentionally, hoping some of her classmates might see her with this dreamboat of a GI. But she saw no one she knew in the café.

"New York is *my* town," she told Henry as she sipped coffee and he drank black tea. "I can show you anything you want. I've lived here my whole life. I know everything about this city."

Henry chuckled. "Is that so, hotshot? We'll see."

He professed an interest in abstract paintings, so she took him to the newly opened Museum of Modern Art. As they wandered the galleries, Silja admired the Kandinskys and the Picabias. But Henry scoffed. "I'd hardly call this abstract," he said, waving at a Kandinsky woodcut. "Where's the daring? Where are the guts?"

Overhearing him, a fellow nearby butted in. "Do you know of the Riverside Museum?" When they shook their heads, he handed them a pamphlet. "They're having a swell show of American abstract artists. It's worth your time."

So they headed uptown. "This is more like it," Henry said as they took in the works of Rothko and Gottlieb and others. "These Americans, they know how to cook with gas."

He knew what he liked; she had to give him that. On Saturday, she'd worn a clingy green sweater with pearl buttons and a matching pencil skirt. Henry remarked how swell the outfit looked on her. "You should always wear green," he told her, eyeing her up and down. "It brings out the color in your eyes."

But he wasn't looking at her eyes when he said it.

Silja smiled and thanked him. On Monday, when they met again at Vic's during her lunchtime break, she was in a loose-cut pink blouse and a gray wool circle skirt. It was one of her favorite outfits and she thought he'd like it. But when he saw her, Henry frowned and asked sharply, "Where's the green?"

"I forgot," she said.

"Don't forget next time, baby doll." He escorted her to a booth in the back of the café.

She resolved she would go out of her way to include something green in her ensemble—a scarf, a hat, jewelry—every time they got together. After all, she told herself, Henry is a GI about to put his life on the line for everyone in this country. It was peanuts, what he asked of her. It was the least she could do.

She was never sure exactly when she'd see him. His troop was stationed at Camp Kilmer in New Jersey, and there was a snafu with their orders—one she didn't understand but knew wasn't unusual. President Roosevelt had declared war only three months ago; the army was trying to sort it all out and get troops trained and moved into service efficiently. But it took time.

Silja, who before she met Henry had all but lived in the Hunter campus library, took to studying in the apartment she shared with her mother, Mikaela, in the *Alku*, their Finntown co-op. Mikaela frequently went out in the evenings—she was one of a small group of Finntown female air raid wardens—so she wasn't there on the nights when the telephone rang and Silja grabbed it, a broad smile on her face if it turned out to be Henry calling to say he was in Manhattan.

"Can I spring you from that gloomy prison of yours?" he'd ask over the line. "Take you to some ritzy joint and get our kicks, Silja, how about that?" She never knew whether he was kidding or if he truly believed what he said about the Alku, which he'd never seen. A prison? Hardly—their apartment was light filled and pretty. Either way, she always replied yes, she'd be there in thirty minutes.

As she emerged from the subway and into his welcoming arms, her heart thudded. Whenever he touched her—even small touches like helping her into her coat after a restaurant meal—she felt her body flush and warm all over.

She half hoped, each time she saw him, that he'd suggest getting a hotel room. She had never been a type of girl to think such things. Previously, her sexual notions had been foggy and vague, mostly centered on kissing some shadowy, indistinct male.

But that was before Henry. Now, alone at night in her bed, when she closed her eyes she saw his face and imagined his kisses raining onto her. She felt Henry's warm hands when she touched her own bare skin.

On the third Monday in March, when they'd known each other exactly ten days, they strolled through Central Park on a warm afternoon. As they rounded Bethesda Fountain, Henry took Silja's left hand. He placed a modest diamond solitaire on it.

"Marry me now," he said. "Marry me, Silja, and after this war is over, I'll come back and we'll make a life together. A life beyond your wildest dreams." He gently squeezed her hand. "I'll be yours forever, if you'll be mine."

Silja was speechless. Was this really *her* he was speaking to? Silja Takala, pleasant but ordinary girl from Brooklyn? The girl who was valedictorian of her high school class, went on to study at Hunter, and was the pride and joy not only of her mother but also of everyone in the Alku? How could she, of all people, be the one receiving this ring, accompanied by this illogical but madly romantic proposal? It was the stuff that Hollywood movies were made of.

She could barely believe it when she heard her own voice responding yes.

5

Ruby

She'd thought no one would hear her if she screamed, but it turns out she might have been wrong. Because glancing to her left, Ruby sees Shepherd parking his car in the cemetery beyond her family's forest. He gets out, closing the car door softly, and looks up to see her watching him. He weaves through the gravestones, steps over the stone wall, and stands beside her, next to the rock.

The snake has slithered off into a thicket. It didn't bite her. Ruby is too fast to let that happen—and besides, garter snakes usually don't bite or even lash out. They generally keep to themselves and mind their own business.

That one, though—Ruby thinks it was a crank. It had to have been a crank, to get so riled up about a finger or two wiggling in its face.

"You shouldn't be here," she tells Shepherd. "The cops were here an hour ago, taking measurements of the oak tree and talking and writing notes. I saw them but they didn't see me. They're gone, but what if they come back?"

He nods. "But *you're* here, Ruby. Are *you* supposed to be here?"

"Not really," she admits. "I'm supposed to be at Miss Wells's apartment. She said it was okay for me to stay home from school and call my uncle whenever I was ready to talk to him. And then she left for school." Ruby shrugs. "I didn't want to be there alone," she says. "And I didn't want to run up Miss Wells's telephone bill. So I came back here. I tried to reach my uncle, but I had to leave a message with his wife."

Shepherd nods again. "I thought you might be here," he says. "Want to go for a walk?"

Ruby knows she should go back to the house and wait for Uncle Paul to return her call. But looking into Shepherd's eyes—which are cloudy despite the brilliance of the day—she can't refuse.

"Just for a few minutes." She turns into the woods and Shepherd follows her.

Silently—because what is there to say?—they single-file walk, with Ruby leading the way. Sunlight filters through trees brilliant in reds, yellows, and oranges. Leaves crunch under their feet. It's the exact kind of day that makes people say fall is their favorite season.

They walk west, then north. There are no fences or markers separating these woods, but Ruby knows where her family's property is divided from the Burkes' on the north, the Powells' on the south. The old, abandoned Dutch Reformed Church cemetery—the one nobody ever gets buried in anymore, the one where Shepherd parks when he visits—is to the east.

They sit on a fallen black birch, its rotting core soft and crumbly to the touch. She sifts the broken pieces through her fingers. Heart rot, that's called—when a tree decomposes from the inside. Shepherd taught her that.

He puts his hand tentatively on her shoulder, and she raises her face to his. His eyes hold sorrow like buckets hold water.

"Do you want to talk about it?" he asks.

She shakes her head. "Let's talk about something else."

And then she tells him a story.

"When we first moved here," Ruby says, "the summer after I turned ten, I used to lure the neighborhood kids into the forest after dark. I wasn't scared, because nothing out here is more harmful than what's inside everyone's houses. Like the television—even back then, I knew television was doing those kids more harm than anything they'd encounter at night in the woods."

He nods because he knows it's true.

"This is what I'd do. I'd sit on a low tree branch behind the Burkes' house next to ours, where they were all playing in the backyard, and I'd give a soft hoot. I'd be in my navy dress because it was my favorite, I wore it long past the time I outgrew it, but I loved it because if I wore it with dark tights, it made me look more like a shadow than a girl. I'd tie a black scarf over my head to hide my hair. I'd pretend that instead of being blond like my mother, my hair was dark like my father's."

"So you wanted to look like your father?" Shepherd asks. "More than you wanted to resemble your mother?"

"No," Ruby explains. "I didn't want to look *exactly* like my father. But dark hair would have come in handy for this situation."

"Ah," he says. "I see what you mean."

"The kids would hear the hoot, and the talk would stop and I'd do it again and someone would say, 'Did you hear that?' And someone else would answer, 'That's just some old hoot-owl; it can't hurt you.' And someone would say, 'Let's go find it.' So they'd trudge near me but before they could get close enough to see me, I'd run to another tree and do it again. And they'd stand where I originally was and someone would say, 'It flew off—we're not going to find it,' and someone else would say, 'Wait, be quiet!' And they'd all be quiet and listen and sure enough that hoot would come again, and someone would say, 'This way!' And they'd all tramp near me, breaking branches and making a hullabaloo and I'd wonder, do they not understand that if I really was an owl, I'd want nothing to do with all that racket?"

Ruby can hear in her own voice that she's become caught up. Telling a story makes her feel less sad. Not long ago, Ruby's mother made the observation that once you got her going, you'd never guess she was a quiet girl. "Put you with the right company, Ruby," her mother said, "and you're a different person."

"I'm sure you can guess how this goes. By the time we'd been through the routine a few more times, we were so deep in the woods nobody except me knew the way out."

She reaches for Shepherd's hand. He hesitates not even a second before clasping hers. This is the sort of thing she loves about Shepherd—how he never hesitates.

They stand and begin to ramble through the underbrush, Ruby savoring the feel of his dependable hand in hers.

"Those kids were so stupid," she says.

"They were just kids, Ruby," he replies, and she worries he might let go of her hand. But he doesn't.

"I know that," she says. "But I couldn't help myself. By then I'd have tired of the game and stopped hooting, but nobody knew how to get out of the woods. Somebody would inevitably cry. Somebody else would say the first somebody was being a baby. Then there'd be arguments about what makes someone a baby and what doesn't. Some kid would say that anyone who wasn't scared was stupid.

"Eventually, after they'd turned in circles for a while, the streetlights would come on over on Stone Ridge Road, and someone would notice, and with shouts of relief they'd make their way out. There'd be cheering and rejoicing. There'd be slapping of mosquitoes on bare arms and legs. And then the mothers would start hollering for kids to get on home and soon everything would be quiet.

"That," Ruby concludes, "is when I would finally make my way out of the woods."

He looks at her. "I can picture it. You're a good storyteller, Ruby."

She says thanks and then reminds him she has to get back and wait for her uncle's call.

They turn left and approach a narrow space between the wide trunks of two elms. They drop hands to pass through, but he stays right behind her and she can feel his breath on her neck.

"I did that at least once a week all summer long," she tells him. "But I wonder if those kids recall it differently. 'Remember that old hoot-owl in the summer of fifty-three? Remember how we never found that thing, no matter how many times we looked?' "

"Nineteen-fifty-three," he murmurs. "So long ago."

She turns to face him. "Do you think it was wrong, leading those kids on?"

Shepherd tilts his head thoughtfully. "I suppose in some ways it was," he says. "But it's not your fault you were smarter and braver than them, Ruby."

"No," she agrees. "It's not my fault."

Ruby never asked to be Ruby.

6

Angie

Paul followed me to the cottage and picked up the telephone. While it rang on the other end, he glanced at me.

"Angel . . . would you mind . . . I need a little privacy here."

I felt my mouth pucker into a frown. What did he have to say to Ruby that he couldn't say in front of his wife?

Paul didn't notice me scowling. He was hunched over the desk, his hand cupped around the receiver. His voice was low, offering soothing whispers over the line.

I took a few steps back, but I didn't leave the room. Instead, I hovered in the shadows, straining to hear what Paul said to Ruby.

As he hung up I ducked back by the bedroom door. I hadn't realized that I'd been creeping forward, step by small step, in an attempt to overhear him. I hadn't caught much of anything—just a few mumbles of "Yes, sweetheart," and "Don't worry, Ruby," and other such platitudes.

I moved into the living room. "What did she say?"

"Probably the same thing she told you." Paul reached for the yellow pages on the bookshelf next to the desk. "I have to get out to New York right away."

"Yes. We all do."

Paul turned to me. "All? What do you mean?"

"You, me, and PJ, of course." I couldn't believe he'd consider going without me. We were a family, after all—and during a crisis, families stick together.

Paul sighed. "I don't know what it will be like there," he said. "I don't know what will be expected of me, and how Ruby will be. On the phone, she sounded . . . well, you talked to her. Not like her true self."

I had no answer for this. I'd met the girl only once. I had no idea what Ruby's true self was like.

I thought about my first glimpse of Ruby at my wedding reception. I recalled Ruby's lanky, awkward body, her chest flat as a board and her long legs sticking out uncomfortably below the knee-length hemline of her blue taffeta dress—its length too long for a schoolgirl, too short for a woman. Ruby wore low heels that matched her dress, and I wondered if it was her first time wearing them. I remembered how Ruby's face lit up when she spotted Paul, and how, despite the heels, the girl had quickened her steps toward her uncle.

"Ruby!" Paul had cried. He left my side, striding across the dance floor to embrace the girl in a bear hug.

I recalled my sting of jealousy—and how I had chided myself about it. For heaven's sake, Angela, I thought, this is your husband's only niece. Of course they adore each other.

It won't be long, I assured myself, before he feels that close to my family, too.

Remembering it now—a year later—I tilted my head tenderly at Paul. "You shouldn't go to New York alone," I said, touching his sleeve. Through the fabric, I massaged his upper arm, feeling the muscles underneath. "We should be together."

"Angie, I really don't think it's a good idea." He shook his head. "I'll have to focus on Ruby's needs. I'll have to . . . grieve, I guess would be the right word. I can't do that if I have to think about you and PJ, too."

"Of course you can," I said. "PJ and I won't be in the way. I'd be there to *help*." My hand lingered on his arm. "You and I—we're in this for better or for worse, right? Mine is the shoulder you can cry on, Paul."

He smiled tenderly. "It's a long way down to your little shoulder, Angel." He looked out the front window toward the bay.

I reached up and turned his face gently toward mine. "If you don't take me," I said, forcing him to look me in the eye, "I'll buy my own ticket and follow you there."

Annoyance flickered across his face but quickly disappeared. "I wouldn't put it past you, Angel."

I slid my arms around his neck and pressed the length of my body against his. "Trust me, Mr. Glass," I whispered. "You won't regret it."

7

Silja

1942

In the few days between accepting Henry's proposal and their wedding, Silja experienced frequent moments of panic and self-doubt. But she kept them to herself. All brides-to-be are nervous, she told herself. It would be fine.

More than fine. Beyond her wildest dreams—just like Henry said.

They were married at the city clerk's office in Manhattan. Silja wore green. Her friend Johanna, who had forgiven Silja for their missed date and was caught up in the romance of it all, agreed to be Silja's witness. One of Henry's buddies from his company, a fellow named Bill Something-or-Other, stood next to him.

They did not invite Silja's mother. In fact, as of yet Silja had failed to mention Henry to her mother at all.

Following the ceremony, they parted from their friends on the street corner—replete with warm wishes from Johanna and cries of "Hubba hubba!" from Bill. And then they took the subway uptown to the Hotel Seville, where Henry had booked a room.

It was what she'd been waiting for, Silja told herself as she undressed in the hotel room's bathroom. She put on the rayon negligee she'd bought at Woolworth's for three dollars, using money her mother gave her for incidentals. As she slipped the matching bed jacket over her shoulders, Silja was certain this wasn't the type of incidental her mother had in mind. The negligee was mint green with a lacy bosom and a midthigh hemline. She hadn't worn anything so short since childhood.

This was what she'd dreamed of, at home in her lonely single bed. And those times she sat on the subway, her eyes closed, her knees pressed tightly against one another. So why was she scared? She couldn't say. But her legs felt shaky as she opened the bathroom door and peered into the room.

Henry lay on the bed, the lamp beside him dim. He was shirtless, only a sheet covering him from the waist down. When he saw her, his face broke into a smile. "Come here," he said, sitting up.

Silja walked across the room, her heart pounding. At the bedside, he placed his hand just above her left breast. "Your heart is racing," he said. "It's okay, baby doll. Calm down and come on in."

He threw back the sheet and she saw that under it, he wore nothing.

She'd never seen a naked man before. Fatherless and brother-less, Silja lived in an intimate world inhabited only by her mother, herself, and the Finnish immigrants— only females, of course— welcomed by Silja's mother as others had once welcomed her, boarding with the Takalas until the young women got on their feet in the new country.

During the summers, on hot Brooklyn evenings, the Alku men would gather in the courtyard in their undershirts and carpenter pants, their broad backs glistening with sweat as they smoked and drank beer. As the boys Silja's age matured, they joined the men. Sitting on the fire escape above, Silja and the other Alku girls would giggle, whispering about Tavho's sleek, muscular shoulders, about Olavi's puny build, which all the girls agreed would look better with a work shirt covering it.

Henry was the first man Silja had ever seen with no clothes at all. His legs were long, his torso narrow but powerful, his stomach flat. His erection, emerging from a mound of dark pubic hair, took Silja by surprise. She'd never seen one before, not even in pictures. She'd had no idea it would be so veiny and red, as if all the blood in his body was concentrated in that one area.

"That's quite a pretty outfit," Henry said. "Now take it off."

Her hands shaking, Silja let the jacket and gown fall to the floor.

She'd long ago accepted the fact that she didn't have an especially attractive face. She thought of her looks as simply a fact of who she was, no different from her smart brain or her Scandinavian heritage. But her body, she knew, was just right—full in the bosom and hips, nipped in the waist. Not that anyone saw that usually; the green pencil skirt and matching sweater she'd worn the day she and Henry had their first date was the tightest outfit she owned. And no one, save her mother when Silja was a small girl and needed help bathing, had ever seen her fully unclothed.

But now she was married. And being nude in front of each other was what married people did.

"Hot damn." Henry let out a soft whistle. "You are one sexy cookie."

He reached out a hand and drew her onto the bed. She took off her eyeglasses, set them on the bedside table, and turned to face him.

She tried not to worry about what might happen next. She knew it might not be easy, that it didn't always work out the first time. She'd heard such things whispered at Hunter, had overheard conversations among girls who had done it. Girls who were married like Silja was now, or engaged and pressured by a fiancé to go all the way before he shipped out.

And then, of course, some girls were simply fast. They saw no reason to save it for one particular boy; they moved from boy to boy like changing hats or gloves. In another life—a life in which she didn't have a bright and tenacious mind, not to mention a mother's encouragement to better herself—Silja knew she might have become such a girl herself.

If it's not going in, the girls would murmur to one another at Hunter, use Vaseline. So Silja had a little jar in her pocketbook. When it turned out just that way—Henry pushing, Silja trying to relax—she hesitantly suggested it to Henry.

"I've never heard of that," he said. "But if it will help, let's try it."

Silja slipped out of bed, retrieved the Vaseline, and asked him to turn his head. When she got back in, they tried again. Henry's girth startled her; it seemed impossible that such a thing was designed to fit inside her. But the girls were right; the Vaseline did help. Henry found a rhythm; Silja heated up and moistened, responding to his thrusts. She clung to his back and pulled him tightly against herself. She felt sweat glistening on his body where it met hers.

Silja had never felt so close to another person in her life. She was shocked that the act made not just her body but also her entire being feel interwoven with Henry.

She wanted it to go on forever, but then he was done, crying out so loudly she wondered—but didn't care—if the people in the next room heard them. He collapsed on top of her and then rolled to the side. "My baby doll," he whispered.

Silja snuggled against him, wrapping both of them in the top sheet and cocooning her body against his. She knew he had to rest. She breathed slowly in and out, calming her own racing heart.

She couldn't wait to do it again.

After their wedding, instead of sharing meals or going sightseeing as they'd done when they first met, when he came into Manhattan they rented a hotel room. Henry paid for the rooms and signed the registers, "Mr. and Mrs. Henry Glass," in his block-shaped penmanship. The clerk would smile at Henry in his uniform, nod toward Silja beside him with her ring flashing on her finger, and tell them to enjoy their stay—which Henry assured him, they certainly would. Riding the elevator, they held hands.

And every time was as good as the first. She adored running her hands all over his skin, touching every part of him. Feeling the hair on his arms, his chest and legs. She even enjoyed the feeling of his penis as she held it. The first time she reached out tentatively to stroke it, she was astounded by his reaction, as if her hand gave him as much pleasure as being inside her did.

He moaned and slid closer to her. He placed his hand around hers so they were both holding his pulsing member.

"Put it in your mouth," he directed her.

She stared at him, astonished by the request. His eyes softened. "Do it, Silja," he said. "Please. I'll do anything for you if you do."

He placed one hand on the back of her head and gently pushed her face toward his lower body. She drew a breath, then put her lips around him. Grasping her hips, he turned her so she was lying below him. On his hands and knees, he thrust his mouth toward her lower lips. She was shocked at how it made her feel—like a jolt of electricity coursing through her. They fell into a rhythm, tongues and fingers moving until both of them were spent.

Silja was amazed at herself. She'd been unaware that people even did such things. And here she'd done it as if it were the most natural thing in the world.

Well, she was married now. Henry—beautiful, perfect Henry— belonged to her and no one else. She had rights to his body that no other woman ever would; nor would any man besides Henry ever lay claim on hers. Not for the rest of their lives.

"I'll never regret this," Henry whispered as they lay together, slack with fulfillment. "Baby doll, marrying you was the smartest thing I've ever done in my life."

8

Angie

My first view of New York City was through the window of a 707. The day was clear, the sky a bright blue. "A perfect afternoon for landing in New York," the pilot said over the intercom. "Look out the left side of the airplane, folks, for a wonderful view of the Manhattan skyline."

I peered through the tiny oval-shaped window, unable to wipe the grin off my face. Flying was every bit as exciting as I'd always imagined it would be. I easily picked out the Empire State Building rising above the other buildings in the center of the city, and I thought it was probably the Statue of Liberty that I was seeing on its own little island in the distance.

I fastened my safety belt, as instructed by a stewardess over the intercom. Snuggling PJ to my chest, I pointed out the sights to the baby as the plane descended. I kept my voice low so I wouldn't disturb Paul, who had been reading magazines and chain-smoking during the entire flight. Out of the corner of my eye, I watched as a leggy, pouty-lipped stewardess came through the aisle and gently reminded Paul that all smoking materials needed to be extinguished for landing. Paul stubbed out his cigarette in the armrest ashtray and gave the stewardess—who, despite the curves inside her form-fitting uniform, had the chubby-cheeked, fresh face of a twelve-year-old—a warm smile.

I frowned, then turned back toward the window, reluctant to let Paul see my jealousy.

✿   ✿   ✿

No one was meeting us at LaGuardia Airport. There was no one who could meet us, because who did we know in New York except for Paul's family? No one, that was who.

I knew Paul had flown commercially only a few times himself, but he handled the experience like a seasoned traveler, knowledgeably reading the terminal signage and leading me to the baggage claim. After we fetched our luggage, he said he'd see about renting a car. I sat with the baby on my lap, looking around. Everything at LaGuardia—from the fast-moving luggage conveyor to the orange molded plastic seat I sat on—was modern, bright, and hard. I felt as if I'd landed in another country entirely, not even in America anymore.

And this was just the airport. Who knew what I'd find in Stonekill? What an odd name for a town.

"'Kill' is Dutch for creek," Paul had told me when I mentioned how peculiar I found the name of the town where Henry and Silja lived. "So it's Stone Creek, if that seems less strange to you."

It did seem less strange, but only slightly so. A creek is called a crick at home. Depending on where they're from, tourists say the same thing, or else they use the word creek.

I'd been a cottage girl at Gordon's for four summers—every year since I was sixteen, except the past summer, when PJ was a newborn. With all my experience, I thought of myself as rather worldly. I'd cleaned rooms for people from as far away as Philadelphia, Washington, DC—and yes, New York. I even saw Californians one time, a group of three childless couples who took rooms in the lodge and sat in the Top Deck drinking tequila shots into the wee hours.

But none of those tourists—and tourists do all kinds of crazy things—ever did anything as odd as calling a crick a kill. Although I was trying to keep an open mind, I found the name of the town sinister.

The drive to Stonekill in the turquoise Ford Fairlane Paul rented took over two hours. Paul got lost twice, missing the exit onto something called the Bronx River Parkway, and then missing the exit onto another road that led into Stonekill. He handled these inconveniences with fortitude—neither flying off the handle like some people would, nor getting flustered as I surely would if I had to drive on these narrow, congested roadways and make split-second decisions about when to turn. When he got it wrong, Paul took the next exit and pulled over to consult the map the rental car agent had given him. Once satisfied that he knew how to get back on track, he said nothing and continued on.

It was almost seven when we pulled from Stone Ridge Road into the driveway of Henry and Silja's home. "Ruby said she wouldn't be here," Paul told me. "But she left a key under the doormat for us." Ruby, Paul explained, was staying at the apartment of a Miss Wells, her English teacher, who lived alone on the other side of town.

I thought that odd. Surely Ruby would be better off staying with a family, in a house with a mother and father. "Doesn't she have any friends her own age?" I asked Paul. He shrugged.

I shook my head fondly at him. A man can't be expected to understand such things, but every girl should have at least one close girlfriend. I thought of the girls I'd grown up with. Besides my sisters Dorrie and Carol Ann, there are Joyce Lang and Alice Solberg, whom I've known since first grade. The Three Musketeers, we were back in school. Joyce still lived in our hometown of Baileys Harbor, just down the road from North Bay. Alice was a couple miles south, in Jacksonport. We saw each other most Sundays after church. We went to our parents' homes for Sunday dinner, and we'd generally gather at one house or another for part of the afternoon, toting our babies along. The other girls had married local boys; they found my relationship with Paul wildly exotic and were always pressing me for details about his painting, our home life, and even our romantic moments. I laughingly measured out such details only in minimal doses.

I usually didn't see the girls during the week; none of us had her own car and we all had limited use of our husbands' vehicles. But I couldn't imagine a day going by without speaking on the telephone with at least one of my friends or sisters.

I didn't see how it was possible that Ruby had no one her own age to rely on. The poor girl clearly needed a woman in her life—someone besides a teacher. Perhaps, I decided, my role in Stonekill was to stand in as both mother and friend to Ruby.

It was fortunate I'd convinced Paul to bring me along. It would be a disaster if Paul were there without me.

Henry and Silja's property sat on a winding, thickly wooded residential street. An expansive lawn sloped gently toward the road. On either side of the house, stands of thick pines, oaks, and elms separated the home from its neighbors. The country location surprised me; despite Ruby mentioning that Henry's body was found in the woods, I'd been unable to let go of my lifelong mental image of New York as consisting only of skyscrapers and asphalt.

The house was modern, one story, with dark wood siding on the right half and a wall of glass on the left. The setting sun's rays reflected off the glass. The roof was composed of several zigzagged peaks and valleys. It reminded me of an article I once saw in a movie magazine about stars' houses in Palm Springs, California. In the magazine spread, such houses fit right in, their peaks mimicking mountain ranges, with scant desert foliage around them and the bright blue western sky as backdrop. But here, set into dense woods, the overly modern house felt out of place. It looked as if it had been constructed here by mistake.

Paul told me that Silja and Henry had the house built about seven years earlier. "Silja wanted something contemporary," he said, pulling suitcases from the trunk of the Fairlane. "Their last house dated from the 1890s. Big Victorian place with gingerbread trim work and a creaky front porch. It was in the center of town, near the train station. In the old days, I'd arrive here from Grand Central and Henry would meet me at the station. We'd walk back to their place." Paul looked toward the road, squinting into the setting sun. "Henry loved that old house. He was constantly remodeling and repairing. But Silja complained about things breaking all the time—no matter to her that

Henry fixed them right away. She wanted a brand-new house, one that no one had ever lived in except them." He slammed the trunk shut. "Well, she got what she wanted."

I didn't know how to answer. I cradled the baby to my chest and followed Paul up the steps to the fancy house.

As Paul was unlocking the front door, a female voice behind us called out a greeting. I spun around to see a woman climbing out of a Chevrolet parked at the curb beyond the sloping lawn.

"Yoo-hoo!" the woman exclaimed. "Might I have a word?"

Paul set down the bags, then strode the length of the driveway with swift, firm steps. I hurried behind and caught up as he reached the woman. "Can I help you?" Paul asked, his voice cool.

I inspected the woman. She had short, frosted-brown hair and looked to be in her early fifties. Her legs were slender, but she had the thickset middle common to women her age; I had seen it happen to my mother and prayed it wasn't my own fate.

The woman held out her hand to Paul. "Jean Kellerman, *Stonekill Gazette*." She paused and then added, "Surely you remember me, Mr. Glass."

"You have the name right," Paul said, without taking her hand. "But no, I don't remember you."

Mrs. Kellerman raised her eyebrows. She glanced at me, then back at Paul. "Fine," she said. "Maybe a few questions . . . ?"

"Mrs. Kellerman," Paul said. "This is a time for us to mourn and give our attention to family matters. We'll thank you to leave us in peace. Come on, Angie." He took my elbow and steered me up the driveway.

At the front door, I glanced back and saw that Mrs. Kellerman was still observing us from the street. After we stepped inside, I peered out the narrow window next to the door. I watched as Mrs. Kellerman slowly drove away.

9

Ruby

Miss Wells is so good to Ruby. She serves a healthy dinner with all four food groups represented. Meat, milk, bread, and a vegetable. Just like Ruby's mother would want her to eat, if she were there.

Ruby wishes her mother were there.

She drinks her milk like a little girl, gulping it down and using a paper napkin to wipe the mustache from her upper lip. As they clear the table Miss Wells tells Ruby she has homework to grade. Ruby assures her she'll be quiet as a mouse in Miss Wells's spare bedroom, read a bit, and then go to sleep.

Miss Wells asks, "You'll see your uncle tomorrow, is that right?"

"Yes," Ruby says. "That's right."

She truly does intend to go to sleep. She doesn't put on her nightgown—she stays in the dungarees and sweater she's worn all day—but she crawls onto the bed. She has *To Kill a Mockingbird* with her, such an excellent book; she's read it three times since it came out in July. She curls up with Miss Harper Lee, looking forward to reading until she gets tired. Reading takes Ruby to other worlds so she doesn't have to think about her own. She opens the book to part one, chapter one, in which Scout and Jem argue about what started the cascade of events leading to Jem's broken elbow.

But it's lonely in that room, with Miss Wells so far away at her kitchen table, quietly penning comments on Ruby's classmates' papers, Jimmy who Ruby knows will get a D because he doesn't give a shit and Glenna who'll get an A but not because she's a reader like

Ruby, only because she's a Goody Two-shoes who does her assignments the way the teachers want.

Since this is Ruby's fourth reading of *To Kill a Mockingbird*, she
already knows what will happen. She starts thinking about Boo Radley
and how he went around Maycomb without anyone noticing him. She
starts thinking about how handy it can be to feel invisible, like Boo.

She slides the novel into her pocketbook. It's a cloth bag her mother
bought her in the city, patchwork with a long leather strap that goes
over one shoulder and crosses the body. It's nice and roomy, allowing
Ruby to keep everything important with her at all times.

Because you never know.

Ruby carries the pocketbook and her shoes to the apartment's
front door and slips through without Miss Wells spotting her. It's a
long walk, but it feels good to have cool air on her face.

10

Angie

Paul turned on the overhead lights and we stepped into the open, wide space. Separating the kitchen from the living and dining areas was nothing but a bar-height countertop with three backless chrome stools topped by black leather seats lined up below it. There was a massive stone fireplace on the wall opposite the kitchen, with a davenport and two easy chairs arranged companionably around it. Wall-to-wall carpeting in a faint chevron pattern, beige mixed with brown, was everywhere except the tiled kitchen floor. A teak dining table with a view to the backyard had seating for eight. The ceiling, accentuated with lustrous teak beams in the exact hue of the dining table, mimicked the hills and valleys of the home's roofline. The expansive, thick glass windows—both front and back, with no draperies—made me feel like I was inside a fishbowl.

I sniffed the air and wrinkled my nose. The house had a smoky, stale smell. I wanted to open a window, but I didn't see latches on the tall window frames.

I fixed a bottle for the baby, and Paul found some crackers in an upper cabinet and a jar of Cheez Whiz in the refrigerator. After we ate, Paul stood up from his barstool. "Come," he said. "I'll show you the rest of the house."

Down the hall, he opened the door to the master bedroom, which featured a king-size bed, a dresser, and a large, glossy oak desk on spindly metal legs. And, thankfully, drawn-shut drapes. "We can sleep in here," Paul said, dropping our suitcase on the floor.

I swallowed nervously at the idea of sleeping in the bedroom of a missing person. What if Silja came back in the night and found us in her bed?

But Paul would be right next to me, his arms wrapped around me. It would be all right.

I followed him into the hallway. He opened the door to Ruby's room, which faced the woods behind the house. It was a typical girl's room, with posters on the wall of Elvis and James Dean and Frankie Avalon. A messy, unmade single bed. Piles of unwashed clothes on the floor. Books in a haphazard heap on the bookshelf.

There was one more bedroom, also facing the rear of the house—smaller than the master or Ruby's, with a modest dresser and full-size bed neatly made up with a navy bedspread. "We can put PJ in here," Paul said, setting down the baby's luggage. While I got PJ ready for bed, Paul fashioned a makeshift crib by pushing the bed into a corner and arranging several of the tall dining room chairs on the other side of the bed, facing outward. "He'll be fine," Paul assured me, apparently reading the worried look on my face. "He's exhausted, Angel . . . he's going to sleep and sleep."

I smiled gratefully at my husband. I ran my fingers lightly over the baby's cheek, and he closed his eyes.

"I'm fixing myself a drink," Paul said. "Want one?"

I nodded. Paul disappeared toward the kitchen, and I took a few moments sitting next to the baby, rubbing his back until he fell asleep.

In the main room, Paul carried icy tumblers of Scotch and soda from the kitchen to the living area. We sat on the davenport, which was long and spare, upholstered in stiff tawny leather. Paul handed a glass to me.

"To life ended too soon," he said, clinking his glass against mine. "To Henry."

"To Henry," I echoed, raising my glass to my lips.

I sipped the Scotch, my eyelids heavy. The day had started out as an adventure—the airport, the plane ride, seeing New York for the first time. But now I was drained. I couldn't remember a time when I'd felt this tired—even the day PJ was born. When I gave birth, my body took over. Though I'd been physically spent after PJ's birth, I didn't remember much of the actual experience—partly because of the drugs I was given, of course, but also because my body knew what to do. My brain hadn't been in charge that day; it merely followed my body along.

This was different. Here, I would be expected to act in certain ways. To say the right things, do the right things. Be an adult.

Well, I *am* an adult, I reasoned. A married woman with a child. I was there to act as surrogate mother to my niece.

It was the sort of thing adults did.

I set my drink on a coaster. "I need to turn in," I told Paul. "I'm sorry . . . I can't keep my eyes open another second." I reached out, putting my arms around his neck. "Will you come in soon? Please?"

Paul gave me the warm look I loved so much. But then he gently drew away from me.

"You go on and get ready for bed," he said, staring contemplatively into the cold hearth. "I'll be there soon."

11

Ruby

It's dark and when it's dark no one can see outside. Inside, the lights are on and Ruby can see everything. She watches them moving around and her breath catches because she hasn't seen Uncle Paul since he got married and stopped visiting Stonekill.

He has other people now. Aunt Angie and an infant son. But he still loves Ruby, too. If he didn't, he wouldn't be here, right? That only makes sense.

Ruby knows what makes sense. She's not stupid.

Kids at school think Ruby is stupid because around most people she doesn't talk much. But that's not the same as stupid. Miss Wells once told her, "You're still waters that run deep, Ruby."

She stands outside, behind one of the ash trees in the front yard. They can't see her but she sees them inside. She watches them eat, sitting at the counter. They do things that look ordinary, as if they are the people who live there now.

Ruby sneaks around the back and she's there when they turn on the overhead light in her room. She's glad they don't stay in her room for long. She tries to read the expression on Aunt Angie's face, but she's not sure what her aunt is thinking.

After Aunt Angie goes to bed, Ruby watches Uncle Paul alone by the cold hearth, sipping first his own drink and then, once that's gone, the drink Aunt Angie abandoned. Ruby thinks maybe he's crying but she can't tell for sure.

She wishes she could go in and take the seat beside him. Just sit beside him and not say a word.

12

Silja

1942–1944

Henry and Silja had two short weeks of wedded bliss. And then, with only a hasty phone call to tell Silja good-bye, Henry, along with his company, departed Camp Kilmer. The company began moving frequently, stationed up and down the East Coast in various camps from the Carolinas to Maryland. They continued training, Henry told her in his letters, while also protecting the coastline from potential German U-boat attacks. Henry wrote to her:

> *We expect to ship out any day. Where and when nobody can say. Sergeant claims we're headed to the Pacific but we hear rumors of going to England. Nobody tells us dogfaces nothing.*

Silja read and reread his letters until the pages wore thin in her hands. If not for the letters and her ring, she might have thought her marriage something she'd imagined. She kept the ring with her at all times, but rarely on her hand; she stored it in a velveteen bag on a satin string around her neck. Alone in her room at night, she placed it on her finger, looking in the mirror over her dresser with her hand next to her face, where she could see the sparkling diamond beside the twinkle in her eyes.

A few weeks after he left, she missed a period, which she attributed to nerves over midterm exams. Until, a month later, she missed another one.

She was overcome with anxiety. She wanted to be with him forever, but she'd assumed they'd wait to start a family until he got back. How foolish she'd been to throw caution to the wind. Why in heaven's name hadn't they used rubbers? So dazzled had she been with the notion of being his wife and lover, she hadn't given it any thought. And Henry never brought it up.

Well, there was nothing to be done now but face the music. Silja cried privately and quietly. Then she wiped her tears and resolutely wrote to Henry. She waited nervously for his reply, rushing to the mailbox in the lobby of the Alku every evening when she returned from classes.

Finally, she heard from him. In his typical jolted writing style, Henry's letter ran:

This, it's wonderful news. These things, it's the start of our life together. What better way to seal ourselves to one another forever than a child?

She read his letter over and over. She whispered to herself, "A child seals you forever."

She ignored the voice in her head reminding her that a child hadn't sealed her own parents forever. Her father, who had made the trip from Helsinki to New York with his pregnant bride, had deposited Silja's mother at the Alku with a family they'd met on the boat, promising to send for her when he found work. He disappeared somewhere into the interior of the United States, and they never heard from him again.

At three months along, Silja knew she couldn't hide it from her mother any longer. Her skirts were getting tighter; her already full breasts were even larger. She had morning sickness a few times but had passed it off as a stomach flu; it was going around Hunter, she told her mother.

One warm night in early July, as they started the supper dishes, Silja slipped her ring on her finger and said, "Äiti, look here."

It took her mother a moment to figure out the meaning of the ring. "You're engaged?" she asked. "You're marrying some boy? Is he a Finntown boy?"

Silja shook her head. "No, Äiti, no one from Finntown." Gently, she took her mother's hand and led her into the dining room, sitting beside her at the familiar oak table. "You'd best sit down for this."

As she spoke Silja watched her mother's face carefully. Mikaela would soon turn forty, but looked ten years older. The combination of her small stature, the extra weight she carried, and the brightly patterned blue and green shawl she so favored made her look like a powerful little version of Earth with a head on top. Her graying hair, pulled back in a bun, wasn't something she gave much thought to. But behind her glasses, her hazel eyes had a light to them, as if illuminated by everything that went on in her sharp mind.

In 1921—a newlywed, pregnant and fresh off a steamship from Helsinki—Mikaela Takala had not let her husband's desertion get her down. She'd given birth to her child, found work in a dress factory, and relied on the generosity of the co-op to help raise her daughter. Their stalwart little party of Finnish socialists believed passionately in Marxist philosophies and improved living conditions—sanitation! heat!—not just for New York Finns but for everyone. Mikaela took meeting notes and created leaflets. She designed signs that party members held when they stood next to striking sweatshop workers protesting low wages and poor working conditions. During the Depression, when the Nylund family sold out and moved to Pennsylvania in hopes of making it on a farm, they sold their co-op shares to Mikaela. The Takalas moved into the third-floor, street-view apartment and began taking in boarders of their own. Soon afterward, when her employer's dress factory shut down, Mikaela found a job in a laundry, washing sheets and towels for Manhattan hotels. Just a month ago, she'd quit the laundry for more lucrative work sewing GI uniforms.

After she'd said all there was to say, Silja showed Mikaela the photograph Henry had sent. He wore his uniform, holding his M1 semi-automatic and standing in front of a barracks.

"This is a very handsome boy," Mikaela observed, fingering the photograph.

She turned it over. On the back, Henry had written: *For Silja— forever my love, H.*

Mikaela looked at her daughter. "Silja, we need a plan."

It would be best to take the next year off from school, Mikaela said, to ensure a safe and healthy pregnancy, as well as a period for connection with her newborn. But after that, Silja would return to Hunter.

Mikaela went into the kitchen and came back with coffee for both of them. "You need to get as much schooling as you can," she said, picking up the creamer and filling her cup to the brim. "No matter what happens, Silja, you *must* have an education."

She said no more. But Silja knew what her mother was thinking. She believed Silja would end up raising the child on her own, like she did.

Silja nodded her head, implying agreement; it would be useless to argue with her mother. We'll see, she thought.

She could envision exactly how her life would unfold. Henry would come home and get a job—doing what, Silja didn't know, but something lucrative and fulfilling. They'd move to the suburbs. Silja would have more babies. She'd have no need for the bachelor's degree she was pursuing.

Silja hoped the baby was a boy. She wanted a big, strong boy— one who looked just like his father, with Henry's glowing smile and dreamy eyes.

She'd be happy either way, she told herself—but she was keen on baby blue.

Henry wrote frequently and called whenever he could. One humid afternoon when she answered the telephone, he told her he was in New York. "I'm at the cruise ship terminal," he said. "They've turned the *Queen Mary* into a troopship; we're going to England. Come down right away. I hope I can see you, but they tell us there's not much time."

She hurried to the subway and headed for the terminal in Manhattan. When she got there, she was told that all soldiers had embarked and could no longer return to the pier. "Just wave your handkerchief," said a man in uniform—one of a group of soldiers forming a line that held Silja and the other well-wishers back.

Silja waved, shouting Henry's name. Men leaned over the *Queen Mary's* railings waving back to the crowd, but she couldn't pick out Henry. It was agony—being this close but not being able to see him; knowing that he was on the ship but had no way to contact her. Knowing that he must have hoped—but couldn't be sure—that she was among the throngs on the pier.

Finally, the ship's engines came to life. Her mooring lines were cast off and tugboats guided her into the river. Silja expected her to head south toward the sea, but the *Queen Mary* sat in the middle of the river, tugboats lined up beside her gently keeping her bow and stern in line.

"What are they waiting for?" Silja asked a woman beside her.

The woman shrugged. "Who knows?" she said. "Word from some muckety-muck that they're cleared to go, I suppose. They'll get it, but who knows when. I wouldn't hold my breath for your man coming back ashore anytime soon, miss."

"Hurry up and wait" was how Henry described army life in one of his letters. During the long hours she stood on the pier, Silja saw firsthand what he meant.

"They'll likely leave overnight," the guards told them. "No saying exactly when. You may as well go home now, ladies."

The sun went down; the hour grew late. Silja's stomach rumbled with hunger. One by one, girls and mothers and families left the pier. Eventually Silja turned away and walked to the subway, heading for home.

In the dark, early hours of the first day of 1943, Silja's child was born. When she awoke from the anesthesia to learn the baby was a girl, Silja was stunned. Over the course of her pregnancy, she'd convinced herself she was having a boy. Henry Junior, she called him—sometimes aloud as she affectionately patted her abdomen.

She had a hard time believing she'd given birth to a female instead. After the nurses and Mikaela left her alone in the new mothers' ward, she furtively unwrapped the child's diaper, checking the baby's genitals to confirm what she'd been told.

She mourned for little Henry Junior. But the baby girl was beautiful—no hair to speak of, but she had Henry's stunning dark eyes. And she was healthy, with a good set of lungs and a strong heart.

There would be other babies, after the war. She and Henry would have their boy—at least one. And many more, she hoped. Boys who would, no doubt, torment their big sister endlessly.

Silja named the baby Ruby Mikaela Glass. Mikaela for her mother, of course. And Ruby because Silja loved the simplicity and Americanness of the name.

Ruby is a very good name, Henry wrote to her—from north Africa now; his company was thick into the fighting there. *A pretty name and I am sure a pretty girl that her dad can not wait to meet.*

For eight months Silja stayed home with Ruby. She got used to a routine of feeding, diapering, rocking Ruby to sleep before dozing off herself. Ruby was a colicky baby—fussy and quick to change her moods, a restless and inconsistent sleeper. Silja despaired that the child would always be difficult, but Mikaela assured her that Ruby's behavior was normal for one so small. "Just give her time to grow, *pikkuäitini,*" Mikaela said.

Silja scoffed. She didn't feel like a "little mother." She felt like a cow. Her enlarged breasts leaked, staining blouse after blouse. But it would be wasteful to buy formula, when Silja had such a plentiful supply that cost nothing beyond her own dignity.

And then, magically, Ruby *did* grow out of her difficult stage. Her smile became a sign of genuine happiness, not just of gas. She ate oatmeal and pureed fruit. She sat up on her own. She slept for six hours each night. Silja fell in love with Ruby's toothless grin, her rosy cheeks, her burbled language. She couldn't get enough snuggling with her child, darling and cuddly as a teddy bear or a favorite pet.

Then it was time to reenroll at Hunter. Mikaela changed to working nights at the uniform factory, allowing her to be with Ruby during the day while Silja was at school. "You get back to your studies," Mikaela told Silja. "The baby and I will manage. The important thing is your education."

They fell into a rhythm—Mikaela and Ruby spending their days together, Silja remaining at Hunter for classes and to study in the peaceful, hushed library. Each evening, Silja arrived at the Alku in time to have supper with her mother and Ruby, then put the baby to bed herself after Mikaela left for her shift at the factory.

Silja missed being with Ruby terribly. At Hunter, it was hard to concentrate on her schoolwork. More than once she considered quitting. What was the worst that would happen? She'd have to contend with Mikaela's disappointment, but her mother would hardly throw Silja out on her ear.

If only the damn war were over, then Henry would come home and take care of them. That would solve everything. But it dragged on, with no end in sight. At least he wasn't seriously hurt—or worse. In his letters from Sicily and later mainland Italy, Henry told her the names of his buddies who were gravely wounded or killed. He was grateful, he said, to have suffered only minor injuries. *Nothing to keep me off the front lines,* he said. *Guess I'm a lucky duck. Right, baby doll?*

Despite spending so little time with her, Ruby gravitated toward Silja. Mikaela reported that Ruby began looking for Silja as soon as the shadows lengthened each afternoon; it was as if the tiny girl could sense her mother's presence simply by the change in how light played across the living room walls. When Silja opened the apartment door, Ruby's eyes lit up and she crawled enthusiastically across the floor to greet her mother. She climbed into Silja's lap for supper, crying out in protest if they tried to put her in her high chair.

Silja was surprised that Ruby was still so attached to her. But Mikaela nodded approval. "Babies *should* love their mothers more than anyone else," she said. "That's the natural order of things."

By June of 1944, when Ruby was eighteen months old, Silja was ready for another break from school. She usually worked summers to earn extra dough, but Mikaela agreed she should stay home this year. "We don't need the money," she said. "I'm making plenty these days. You rest up, get ready for your senior year, and enjoy being with your daughter."

It was a swell plan—but ironically, despite her happiness at finally being home for a stretch, Silja found it hard to concentrate on Ruby. The papers were full of articles about the Allies' invasion of Hitler's Atlantic Wall on the northern French coast. Tens of thousands of soldiers were involved in the battles, which took place mostly in a town called Caen and on the surrounding beaches.

She knew Henry had returned to England and that he'd been waiting for something important to happen—something he didn't talk about specifically, though he alluded to it in his letters. The last one he'd sent was full of mystery:

> Baby doll, things are looking grim. We wait in agony, we don't know what to expect. It will be big is all they say. Think of me and my pals and tell everyone at home to say prayers.

Then the letters abruptly stopped. She heard nothing for weeks.

She made a million calls, but no one would tell her anything. "The status of specific soldiers is pending," is what she heard each time she telephoned. "When there's word about your husband, ma'am, you'll be informed."

So she waited, played with her child, cooked, and cleaned to make it easier on her mother when she got home from the factory after a night hunched over her sewing machine. Silja took lengthy, meandering walks through the scorching Brooklyn summer, the baby buggy heavy and awkward to push, the humidity drenching her skin. While Ruby napped, Silja sat in the Alku's courtyard, reading novels she checked out of the library. But Agatha Christie and Saul Bellows and W. Somerset Maugham couldn't take her mind off Henry.

She wondered whether to contact Henry's mother. He'd spoken little of his mother when he and Silja had met, and hadn't once mentioned her in his letters. She knew the mother lived in northern California, where Henry and his brother had been raised.

"We both left home shortly after our father had a heart attack and passed," Henry had told her in the spring of 1942, before he left New York. His voice was flat, matter-of-fact. "Paul and I traveled together for a while, working odd jobs. And then I wanted to see more of the country. Paul stayed in the West, and I moved eastward." He shifted in his seat. "Last year I enlisted. I knew Roosevelt would get me eventually anyway—and besides, I didn't have anything better to do." He shrugged. "Paul's registered for the draft, of course. So far his number hasn't come up, but I expect it's only a matter of time. Until then, my little brother is still drifting around." Henry smiled fondly and shook his head.

"And neither of you ever went back home?" Silja asked. "You haven't seen your mother since?"

Henry shrugged again. "She didn't need us," he said quietly. "And it seemed like she didn't want us around."

"Your mother didn't want you around?" Silja couldn't fathom it.

They were riding a Lexington Avenue express train, heading toward Battery Park because Henry wanted to see the tip of Manhattan. Silja watched as they passed through Canal Street station, the train barely slowing down before speeding up again.

"She had other concerns, that's all." Henry squeezed Silja's knee through the flannel of her skirt, his thumb sliding partway underneath the fabric. "And anyway, if she hadn't, maybe I'd still be there, working those vineyards in Sonoma instead of riding in a New York City subway car with a looker like you."

Henry never spoke of his mother again. Silja supposed he'd written to tell his mother about Silja, about Ruby—but Silja never heard from the mother and had no idea how to contact her. Since they'd married, the army had considered Silja to be Henry's next of kin; information about his condition or whereabouts would come to her.

Nonetheless, Silja worried. Suppose some mistake was made? Suppose his mother had received communication that Silja hadn't?

At last, toward the middle of August, a letter arrived. It was from Henry, but not in his hand. In beautiful penmanship at the top of the page, a nurse noted that Henry had dictated the letter to her.

Dear Silja,

I'm alive and in an army hospital in England. I was hit pretty bad and they did not think I'd make it, but here I am. Doc says they'll send me home when I'm well enough to travel. Next time I write, I'll provide details about what happened. But now I'm tired and need to rest.

Love,
Henry

Silja breathed a sigh of relief and immediately dashed off V-mail to Henry. She told him how thankful she was to learn that he was all right.

I can't wait to feel your arms around me. I think of nothing else. I dream of us together again.

Henry's response was delivered two weeks later. Holding the thin paper, reading his words, Silja's hands shook. The truth sank in for her, and for the first time she began to understand what their future might hold.

13

Angie

Without meaning to, I slept in the next morning. Going to bed the night before, I'd expected to toss and turn in the unfamiliar room. But I found Silja's bed unexpectedly comfortable; I slept soundly all night.

Facing west and with the drapes drawn, the master bedroom stayed dark even after daybreak. When I opened my eyes, I was surprised to find the little round-faced clock on Silja's bedside table showing almost eight. I reached for Paul, eager to touch his skin before I arose, hungry to feel his mouth on mine. But his side of the bed was empty.

I opened the drapes, releasing dust that made me cough. Now that I was more awake, I noticed that the room had a musty feel to it, as if the carpeting could use a thorough vacuuming and possibly a shampoo. In the large, fancy bathroom, I noted that Silja's fixtures didn't gleam the way they did in the tiny bathroom in my cottage on North Bay. Silja's tiled bathroom floor was gritty with dirt and long strands of hair. I prided myself on being a meticulous housekeeper; I cleaned our bathroom twice a week, scrubbed all our floors at least once a week, and washed every window monthly. I loved the fresh, lemony scent of a clean house.

Silja's house could use a good scrub-down, I thought. Maybe I'd have time to give it a going-over while we were there. I hated thinking of myself as a cleaning lady, but I loathed the idea of staying in a dirty house, too.

Passing the guest room, I peered in and saw that PJ was still snoozing. In the chic, modern kitchen with sunlight streaming in from the east, I found Paul standing in his robe and pajamas in front of the sliding door, hands on hips. He was staring into the woods behind the house. I wrapped my arms around his waist from behind. He turned, pulling me against him. I nuzzled my face against his chest, my forehead resting on his St. Christopher medal while he continued looking outside.

The shrill ring of the telephone interrupted us. Paul broke away from me and dove for it, grabbing the kitchen wall phone's receiver.

He listened to the caller introduce himself, then said, "Yes, I'm his brother, in from Wisconsin." He was quiet again as the other party spoke. "I understand. Yes." He reached for a pad of paper and a pencil sitting on the kitchen counter. I watched him scratch down some words I couldn't make out. "All right," Paul said. "Thank you."

He hung up the phone and turned to me. "It was the police," he told me. "Said they've finished taking all the samples they need, and . . . the . . . the body has been moved to a local funeral home." Paul ran his hand through his thick hair and shook his shoulders. "Jesus, what a thing to be saying about my own brother." His look was grim. "Cop gave me the name of the place, but he forgot to give me the address or phone number." He took a telephone book from a shelf on the lower end cabinet and laid it on the counter, opening the pages.

I got coffee on and started a bottle warming on the stove. I was looking in the refrigerator for breakfast items when I heard the baby start to wail. I poured a cup of coffee and set it down in front of Paul as he picked up the telephone receiver. I headed to the guest room with the warmed bottle.

When I returned, Paul told me he had spoken to the funeral director and to Ruby. He was going to fetch Ruby at her teacher's house and then go to the funeral home.

Baby on my hip, I followed him down the hall toward the master bedroom.

"I told Ruby we could wait a bit," Paul said. "We could hold off on making any . . . decisions . . . until Silja returns." He shook his head. "But Ruby is adamant. She wants to have a funeral as soon as possible."

I furrowed my brow. "Surely, she doesn't get to make that decision," I said. "She's a child, Paul."

At the bedroom threshold, he gave me a long look. "Ruby is almost eighteen, Angie. She *does* get to make that decision."

I bit my lip. I wanted to say more, but I knew it wasn't a good idea.

Paul pulled on pants and a checkered shirt. After he finished tying his tie, he turned to me. "Do I look all right?"

"You look quite handsome." I stood on my toes to kiss him. "You don't want to eat breakfast first?"

He shook his head. "No, I should go." He brushed a lock of hair from my face. "Ruby and I will be back soon," he said. "I don't know how long it will take, but I wouldn't think more than a couple hours. See if you can rustle up something for lunch, would you?"

After Paul left, the first thing I did was find the vacuum cleaner and run it quickly around the living and dining rooms. The carpeting needed a more thorough going-over—everything in the house did— but it would do for now.

Next, I rummaged in the linen closet, looking for a blanket that the baby could sit on while he played. Though I found no blankets, there was a blue and green shawl on the middle shelf, made of soft wool elaborately crocheted in a wild pattern of swirling, sweeping color. I spread the shawl over the carpeting in front of the fireplace, then placed the baby on it. PJ was just mastering sitting up, and he settled solidly on his bottom, happily surrounded by the playthings I found for him in the kitchen—a couple of metal measuring cups, a plastic mixing spoon, and a small plastic bowl. "Knock yourself out," I told him and made my way back to the kitchen. I had to admit the layout of the house was clever; I could glance across the kitchen counter and check on PJ as he played in the sunlight coming through the big windows.

Yes, it was pleasant in the daytime. True, the windows looked as if they hadn't had a good cleaning for several seasons, and the kitchen countertop was grimy; I set about scrubbing it with Ajax as soon as I finished my coffee. But I didn't get the sensation, as I'd experienced the evening before, that someone could be looking in. In daylight, the glass-walled house—while nothing like my cottage at home—wasn't as disturbing as it was at night.

Though the day was chilly, I opened the sliding door to the backyard, leaving the screen door in place. Fresh air would do the house wonders—get rid of that smoky stink that seemed to permeate every surface.

I longed to call one of my sisters, or Joyce or Alice, and talk about everything that had transpired. I wanted to tell them about the flight, the busy airport, how easy it was to get lost in New York. Most of all, I wanted to describe Silja's house. I wanted to chew over why anyone would live in such a fancy place yet fail to take care of it. But I was hesitant to make a long-distance call. I should have asked Paul before he left if it would be all right. I thought he would have said yes, but I wasn't sure. And I had no place charging up Silja's telephone bill without getting the green light from Paul first.

I was sniffing an opened jar of mayonnaise, trying to determine whether it might be spoiled, when I heard the doorbell ring. I ran to the door and peered through the side window.

It was the reporter from the night before. Jean Kellerman. I opened the door.

"Hello." She held out her hand. "We didn't get to meet last night. I'm Jean Kellerman, *Stonekill Gazette*."

"Yes," I said. "I remember. I'm Angie Glass." I took the woman's hand in my own. Mrs. Kellerman's hand was paper dry. She smelled of lavender.

"You're Paul's wife?" the reporter asked.

I nodded. Mrs. Kellerman seemed to be waiting for an invitation to come in. I hesitated a moment, then ushered Mrs. Kellerman inside.

"What a lovely place." The reporter took in the beamed ceiling, the stone fireplace, the modern furniture. She cooed at PJ, still playing on the floor.

"Yes, it's very . . . " I didn't know what to say. "Please have a seat, Mrs. Kellerman."

"Thank you. You can call me Jean. Is it all right if I call you Angie?"

I nodded as we both seated ourselves. I picked up the baby from the floor and snuggled him close. Jean reached in her handbag for a pad of paper and one of those newfangled ballpoint pens. She regarded it fondly as she uncapped it, then glanced at me.

"'Writes first time, every time,'" I said, parroting the slogan from magazine ads.

"Indeed," Jean said. "And so much more convenient than carrying a fountain pen. I can't tell you how many pocketbook linings I've ruined with ink spills."

"How many what?"

"Pocketbook linings."

I shook my head. "What's a pocketbook?"

Jean held up her purse. "This."

I smiled. "Oh, of course," I said. "At home, we'd call that a purse or handbag."

Jean nodded and looked down, putting pen to paper, then back at me. "Let me get to the point, Angie. I broke the story a few days ago about Henry's death and Silja's disappearance. I know the coroner is likely to rule Henry's death a suicide. I have sources in the police department, and numerous facts for a follow-up story."

I was impressed but tried to hide it. I kept my eyes downcast.

"What I was looking for from your husband, and what I'd love from you, would be the 'heart' of the story. A father is deceased. A mother has abandoned her young daughter. That unfortunate daughter must carry on—and luckily, she has a loving family to comfort her."

Jean sighed as she observed the baby in my lap. "I can see what a motherly person you are, Angie. I'm sure Ruby needs that right now. At a tragic time like this, a girl needs mothering. It's such a blessing you're here to step into that role."

Despite myself, I smiled gratefully at Jean. This woman understood my place exactly.

Jean leaned forward. "Tell me," she said. "Where do you think Silja went? Why would she run off at a time like this?" Her voice lowered. "Do you think Silja is responsible for Henry's death?"

"Well, clearly he was heartbroken that she'd left," I replied. "That's why he took his own life."

Jean's expression was dubious. "Do you think there's a chance that someone else—perhaps Silja—set it up to look like Henry committed suicide?"

I leaned back, shocked at Jean's revolting guesswork. "No! I can't imagine that." I shook my head. "I didn't know Silja well. I only met her once. But no mother . . . "

I trailed off. Jean waited, and then asked softly, "What were you going to say, Angie?"

I trembled. I hugged PJ close.

"Just that no mother . . . that I can't imagine a woman . . . a mother . . . " I blinked. "Could intentionally do something like that. Not to the father of her child." I shook my head, then whispered, "I just can't imagine such a thing."

It was only after Jean left—after she gave me a business card and urged me to telephone if I thought of anything else, after she'd gotten in her Chevrolet and drove away on hilly, winding Stone Ridge Road—that I recalled something from the encounter with Jean the night before: the reporter had asked Paul if he remembered her, and he'd said he didn't.

I was sure Jean didn't believe him. I wished I'd thought of it while Jean was at the house in the morning. I could have asked about it. I could have used it as a bargaining chip before agreeing to speak with her.

Tell me how you know my husband, Jean. Then—and only then— will I answer your questions!

Too bad I only remembered when it was too late.

14

Ruby

Uncle Paul doesn't think they should have a service for Ruby's father this soon. On the drive to the funeral home, he tries to talk her out of it. "It's not necessary," he says. "We can wait a bit, see if your mother turns up. There's no rush."

"There is a rush," Ruby tells him.

Uncle Paul doesn't press the point. Instead, he asks, "And who exactly do you think will come to this proposed service? Only the morbidly curious and the entirely unsuitable. You know that, Ruby."

"Of course I know that."

But here's the thing (she doesn't tell Uncle Paul this): one time, not long ago, her father told her exactly what his wishes would be when he died.

"No funeral," her father had said. "No fanfare, no grave, no burial. Just have them cremate me and toss the ashes somewhere, anywhere. The garbage heap, for all I care."

Ruby isn't sure if her father ever told anyone else—her mother, Uncle Paul—these wishes. She hopes he didn't.

Because it doesn't seem right to her, what he said he wanted. Ruby thinks when a person dies, his death should be acknowledged.

When she met Shepherd in the woods on Tuesday, she told him she wanted to have a funeral for her father. "A public recognition that he's—well, gone."

Shepherd had shrugged. "That's up to you," he said quietly. "If you want to recognize his death, I think you should do so, Ruby."

Shepherd agreeing with her—or, at least, not disagreeing—sealed it for Ruby. So now, in the car, she tells Uncle Paul they should have a service for her father right away, and then get him in the ground. "There's a nice Catholic cemetery not far from Stonekill," she said. "I know he wasn't practicing anymore, but in the end, he'd surely want to be there."

Uncle Paul comes to a stop at a red light. He shifts his shoulders toward Ruby.

"Sweetheart," he says. "I need to ask you something."

She waits, her mouth shut.

Uncle Paul frowns and then he says, "Ruby, do you know where your mother is?"

She stares at him.

The light turns green.

15

Angie

I heard the car pull into the driveway at eleven forty-five. Two car doors slammed. I hurried to the front steps to greet my husband and niece.

The girl who emerged from the passenger side of the Ford seemed less gangly than I remembered from my wedding the year before. Ruby was still lean, but she had grown into her height, with shapely legs and supple arms. Her blond hair was pulled back from her face with a navy-blue headband. Draped across her body was a large cloth purse, patchwork-patterned like a quilt. Ruby's eyes were downcast, but as she approached the steps, she looked up, and I saw the blazing dark brown that was the same as Henry's and Paul's eyes. And PJ's.

"Ruby." I held out my arms, and the girl allowed herself, stiffly, to be enfolded in my embrace. "I'm so sorry," I whispered.

Ruby nodded and stepped back, brushing past me and going inside the house. Disappointed, I watched the girl's back as she retreated down the hallway toward her bedroom.

Paul came up the steps. "How did it go?" I asked him.

"It went all right," he replied. "Everything is arranged. We just need to provide a suit for . . . for Henry to wear." He shrugged. "There were all these things that had to be decided. Casket, flowers . . ." He rubbed his eyes. "I had no idea."

"Didn't you have to decide that sort of thing when your parents passed?" I knew both of Paul's parents had died—his father when Paul was a youth, and his mother just a few years ago.

Paul's expression became dark. "Those were entirely different situations," he said stiffly. "Nothing like this." He swept past me into the house.

I chided myself inwardly for my impulsiveness. "I'm sorry," I said, following him inside. "I didn't know."

Paul's look softened. "And I'm sorry I snapped at you." He took off his jacket and we crossed the big room toward the kitchen. "Having to make these choices when I'm at my worst . . . it got to me. It affected Ruby, too. But the funeral director—his name's Wagner—he was helpful. Got us through it."

I nodded. "Did you meet the teacher when you picked up Ruby?"

"No. She was at school." Paul sat down on a barstool and put his head in his hands.

I touched his shoulder. "Paul," I said softly. "I'm so very sorry. About . . . everything."

He looked up. "How could this happen?" he asked. "How could he have taken his own life?"

I had no answer for that. I thought about what Jean Kellerman said—how she speculated that Silja might be involved in Henry's death.

I didn't believe that for a minute. And even if I did, I'd never mention such a thing to Paul.

Paul shook his head. "I don't understand this at all." He stood. "All I know is there's a young lady who's left to pick up the pieces. She's so heartbroken, Angie, she—"

He broke off. I waited. I followed Paul's gaze as he glanced across the room toward the hearth. After PJ's morning nap, I had deposited him back in his new favorite location on the blue and green shawl, and he was happily chewing on the plastic bowl.

"This is hard, Angel. Really hard." He paused a moment before adding, "Ruby's a swell kid. Always has been. Smart as a whip, just like Henry. And resilient. She's had to put up with a lot." His look became bitter. "Especially from Silja."

"What do you mean?"

Paul shrugged. "Silja has never been easy to get along with, that's all." He shook his head, his eyes still on PJ. "Not like you, Angel. You're a great mom. You're warm and loving, and that's what children need."

I smiled gratefully. It was similar to what Jean Kellerman had said, but it meant more coming from Paul. "Do you think Ruby will eat some lunch?"

"I'll go ask her."

We sat at the countertop, on the backless stools. I fashioned a high chair for PJ using one of the dining room chairs, a phone book, and a dish towel tied around the baby's waist. I leaned over to feed him small bits of bread from my sandwich, which he gummed happily.

Paul sat at the far end of the counter, his stool facing toward the forest. He contemplatively chewed his meal as he studied the woods through the sprawling back windows of the house.

Ruby nibbled her tuna fish sandwich and said nothing. I noticed that she kept glancing at PJ, then hastily turning her gaze away, as if she didn't want me to catch her looking at my child.

"After lunch, you can give the baby his bottle if you want," I offered to the girl. But Ruby shook her head.

I stood and went to the stove, turning on the burner to warm a bottle. "I'm going to need a trip to the market," I announced, reaching for the can of powdered formula I'd brought from home. "For milk and eggs and bread. Fresh fruit would be a good idea, too."

Paul turned toward me and nodded. "I'll take you this afternoon."

After we finished eating, Ruby retreated wordlessly to her room. I glanced at Paul, who shrugged. "What do you expect?" he asked.

Paul cleared the countertop of dishes while I filled the sink with soapy water. There was a dishwasher, but I didn't know how to use it, so I just washed up the regular way. As I was rinsing the plates, Paul told me the funeral would take place the next morning.

"No wake?" I asked. Every funeral I'd ever been to at St. Mary's had been preceded by a wake the night before.

Paul glanced away. "Given the . . . circumstances . . . we decided not to have one. It would only attract a lot of lookie-loos, rather than genuine mourners." He picked up a dish towel and began drying the plates I stacked beside the sink.

I nodded. I'd never before known anyone who committed suicide. But it made sense that—even if the person was Catholic like Henry— the survivors of a suicide wouldn't go through typical Catholic bereavement rituals.

Personally, I believed Henry was in hell, making eternal payment for what he'd done. I felt terrible about it—especially since Henry must have killed himself because of heartbreak caused by Silja's abandonment. It didn't seem fair, really, but that's how things were. Suicide meant the soul went to hell. It said so in the Bible, it was said in the Church. It shouldn't come as a surprise to Henry. It wasn't as if he hadn't been forewarned.

I headed down the hall, baby on my hip and Paul following close behind. I turned to face him. "Let me put PJ down for his nap, and then I can help you pick out a suit for Henry," I said. "You go on and start looking in his closet. I'll be there in a minute."

Paul hesitated. Then, his voice low, he told me, "Henry's clothes are in the guest room."

I stared at him. "Why?"

Paul shrugged. He looked down at the carpeting. "Henry and Silja haven't shared a bedroom in years."

I raised my eyebrows. Paul sighed. "Angie, it's none of our business," he said. "Other people's marriages have nothing to do with us." He turned and went into the guest room.

"But . . . " I protested to his retreating back.

He turned to face me. "But what, Angel?"

I didn't know what to say. There *was* nothing to say. Paul was right; Henry and Silja's marriage was none of my business. I followed Paul into the guest room.

He pulled several suits from the closet and laid them on the bed. The suits looked costly and as if they'd rarely, if ever, been worn. Some of them still had store tags attached. But they also seemed behind the times. I was from a small town, but I read magazines and watched television; I knew men were wearing their lapels thinner these days than they did ten years ago.

Paul held up two suits for my inspection. "What do you think? Brown or blue?"

"Blue." I touched the fabric. The suit was finer than anything Paul owned.

He nodded and hung the other suits back in the closet. "I brought a suit from home for the funeral, but I guess I didn't need to," he said. "I could've just borrowed one from Henry."

Was he serious? What a spooky notion—wearing a dead man's clothes to that man's funeral. I looked at Paul in shock, and saw that he was smiling grimly. He clearly hadn't meant it.

Still—what a strange thing to say.

"I'm going to run these things to the funeral home," he told me, adding a tie, shirt, and shoes. "You go ahead and put PJ down. When I get back, maybe he'll be awake and I can take you to the market."

I set the baby on the bed and put my arms around Paul's neck. "Kiss me before you go."

He did—long, lingering, and throaty. I pushed his mouth open with my tongue and explored inside, feeling the lower half of my body warm up. "Let me get PJ down and meet you in the . . . the other bedroom," I whispered. "I can have the baby asleep in minutes. And Ruby doesn't care what we're doing."

Paul sighed. "Angel," he said, pushing me gently away. "I want to . . . I do . . . but you know this is not the time."

Hurt and surprised, I stepped back. Yes, the timing was unusual, but still—he'd never refused me before. Not once since our first time together.

He softened his gaze and reached out to touch my cheek. "Later," he promised, then spun on his heel and left the room.

I got PJ ready for his nap, listening with one ear to Paul leaving the house. After PJ was down, I started back toward the kitchen. I could get to work scrubbing that floor, I thought—it needed it.

And then, curious, I reversed direction and went into the master bedroom. I closed the door behind me and peeked into Silja's closet.

I glanced at a neat row of shoe boxes on the upper closet shelves. I rifled through hangers on the rack—Silja's smart business suits, her sumptuous dresses, her casual but expensive-looking weekend wear. I found the strapless emerald sheath Silja had worn at my wedding. She seemed to have a lot of green in her wardrobe—she must favor it, I thought.

I closed the closet door. Turning, I spotted a large leather jewelry box on the dresser. I crossed the room and, glancing once toward the door, lifted the hinged top.

Everything was meticulously arranged: earrings in small square sections at the top, bracelets below, and at the bottom, a tray of necklaces that came out to make selection easier. I removed the tray and fingered the fine gold strands, the string of pearls, the heart-shaped locket on a tarnished silver chain. I opened the locket to find tiny black-and-white photographs pasted into both sides: a teenage girl in old-fashioned clothing on the left and a solemn-looking, dark-eyed toddler on the right. Silja and Ruby, I guessed, of years past.

I was about to place the necklace tray back in the jewelry box when I noticed an envelope tucked into the bottom of the box. The paper was heavy and cream colored; the front was blank.

I reached for the envelope. What was in it? A letter to Silja? From whom? And what did it say?

I was itching to find out.

As I put my fingers on it, I heard the bedroom doorknob rattle. I let go of the envelope, shoved the necklace tray into the jewelry box, and slammed the lid shut. "Ruby?" I called, whirling around. "Is that you?"

There was no answer. I stepped to the doorway, but the hall was empty. Ruby's bedroom door was open, and I could hear music from within. I went down the hallway and peered into Ruby's room.

The girl, propped on her bed scribbling in a notebook, stared at me with hooded, inquisitive eyes. "Yes, Aunt Angie?"

I shook my head, flustered. "It's nothing," I said. "I'm going to just . . . " I waved toward the open part of the house. "I thought I'd wash the kitchen floor," I said weakly.

Ruby nodded and turned her attention to the notebook in her lap.

I couldn't think of anything else to say. I backed into the hall and headed for the kitchen.

16

Silja

Henry weathered the initial fighting in Normandy but was severely injured a few weeks later as Allied troops penetrated France. In a skirmish near Cherbourg, he took five German bullets—one in his stomach, one in his right hip, and three in the groin. He lost so much blood they didn't expect him to survive. *But others near me, they were quick to action*, his letter said. *Nobody snapped his cap. Those medics saved my life.*

He was transported to a field hospital, and then to a station hospital in Cheltenham, England. His wounds healed, but for weeks he was unconscious, the nurses keeping him comfortable and waiting for the end. Then one morning he opened his eyes and spoke. *This is not in my memory but they say I asked where I was and for water.*

He didn't mention if he'd asked for her, Silja. Well, it was no matter. He slowly gained strength and eventually was moved to a convalescent hospital in Warwickshire. In the fall he was put on a carrier headed home.

Silja had dreamed of Henry's homecoming almost since he'd left. She'd pictured how his eyes would blaze with adoration for her. How he would enfold her in his arms, bury his face in her hair, breathe her perfume. "Oh, baby doll, how I've missed you," he'd say, while her eyes brimmed with tears.

His ship arrived on a blustery November day. Silja knew he wouldn't be able to go home with her right away; he'd have to go to a disembarkation center for processing, which could take days. Still, she took Ruby and Mikaela to the pier, hoping for a glimpse of him. It felt as though they waited hours. Unable to stand still, Silja stepped back and forth, her feet on the rough concrete pier as spirited as an auditioning dancer's on an oak-floored stage. Ruby toddled about chasing seagulls, with Mikaela lumbering after her. Finally, the ship's portal opened and men started down the gangway.

She scanned for Henry in the line of hobbling soldiers. When she saw him—limping, supporting himself with a cane—she screamed his name and held up their daughter. He turned his head, gave her a slight wave, then followed the line of men toward waiting buses.

Two days later, he arrived at the Alku. Silja had offered to come and fetch him on the subway, but he declined. "I can get there myself," he said over the telephone. "Keep an eye out for me in the afternoon."

When Silja saw him shuffling down Forty-Third Street, cane in hand and duffel bag over his shoulder, she sprinted down the hall staircase and burst outside. "Henry!" she called, meeting him on the sidewalk.

He gave her a peck on the cheek and a one-armed hug around her shoulders. "Hi-de-ho, Silja." It was his jovial expression from the old days, but his weary voice masked the sentiment's cheeriness.

She wrapped her arms around his back—in her excitement, she wasn't thinking about his weakness. He began to topple and she stepped away, releasing him. Leaning on his cane, he righted himself. Their eyes met.

"I'm sorry," she whispered.

He didn't reply. He stared at her as if he didn't know who she was.

Mikaela appeared on the doorstep, Ruby in her arms.

"Meet your daughter," she said. "And my mother, Mikaela."

Mikaela held out the child for his inspection, and Silja felt a ray of hope. She saw his eyes widen with pleasure as he took in their pint-size daughter. "She's beautiful," he whispered. "Hi-de-ho, beautiful Ruby." He clucked the girl under her chin. Ruby giggled.

He awkwardly held out his left hand to Mikaela, his right still gripping the cane's top. "Ma'am."

She nodded, shifting the child in her arms and clasping his hand.

"Let's get you inside, Henry." She let go of his hand, turned around, and started up the steps. Henry and Silja silently followed.

That night in bed, Silja tried to get him to talk. "Tell me what happened," she whispered. She sat with her nightgown wrapped around her knees as he lay on his back staring at the ceiling. "Tell me exactly where you were and what you were doing when you got hurt."

In the half-light from the window, he turned toward her.

"Silja." His voice was even and firm. "I'm going to say this once. I won't say it again." He sat up, facing her. "I don't want to talk about what happened over there." He looked out the window. "Don't ever ask me again."

Silja put her hand on his hip. "All right," she said. "We don't have to talk." She reached forward, her hand crawling toward the buttons on his pajama bottoms' fly—the new satin pajamas she'd splurged on for his homecoming night. "There are other things we can do."

He pushed her hand away and shook his head angrily. "We can't," he said. "We never will again."

"Never . . . will again?" Silja shook her head. "What do you mean?"

Henry grimaced. "You know where . . . on my body . . . my injuries occurred." His mouth was a thin, irritated line. "I was told that you'd be informed about what to expect. And you were informed, weren't you?"

Silja frowned. She'd had a rather awkward telephone conversation with a stateside army nurse who'd explained what Silja might anticipate. "He should be fine by the time he gets home," the nurse had assured her. "Or if not right away, then certainly with time, recuperating at home . . . everything will be okay."

"I understand." Silja had held the receiver close to her ear and watched Ruby, who was calmly stacking alphabet blocks on the living room rug.

"You just be patient with him, dear," the nurse's motherly voice went on. Silja could almost imagine the woman patting her hand through the telephone line. "Give him your devotion and love. That's all it takes for these fellas to get back to their old selves."

Now, sitting in bed next to Henry, Silja said, "They told me it would be okay."

But that *wasn't* what they told her, was it? She'd discounted the nurse's warning about time and recuperation. She'd been certain everything would be wonderful the moment he was back in her arms.

"I'm sorry I rushed you, Henry," she told him. "I shouldn't have done that." She looked at him hopefully. "But maybe . . . another night . . . soon?"

Henry lay back against the pillow. "Silja, I'm beat," he said. "I don't want to talk about this anymore. Good night."

He turned away from her.

Silja did what she should have done in the first place—gave him time. She didn't bring it up again for weeks. She demonstrated her affection but kept her advances small—a peck on his stubbled cheek when she returned from school in the evening, a good-night squeeze of his shoulder as they settled into bed for the night. His rejoinders were stiff and indifferent. He never responded in kind, nor initiated such actions himself.

Each night they slept chastely next to each other. Sometimes he had nightmares—calling out names in his sleep, names she didn't know: *Walters! Channing!*—and broke out in a sweat, his shoulders lifting off the mattress as he threw himself from side to side. Silja would gently shake him until he woke and stared at her blankly.

"It's okay," she'd tell him softly. "You're home, Henry. You're safe."

She longed to throw her arms around him, squeeze him tightly and comfort him as she would a child who'd scraped a knee on the sidewalk. But when she reached for him, he said hoarsely, "I apologize. I'm all right. Go back to sleep, Silja." He turned his back to her and pushed himself to the edge of the bed, as far from her as possible.

Holding on to the nurse's words, treasured as if they were rare coins, Silja assured herself it would get better over time. As fall gave over to winter, as sidewalks became slick with snow that puddled and froze, as reports came from the front that Hitler's army was collapsing, Silja waited for Henry to initiate physical contact with her. Eventually, he would—she was certain—snuggle next to her in bed and hesitantly take her hand, guiding it toward him, asking in a whispered voice if she was ready to try, because *he* was . . .

But it never happened. When finally she brought up the subject again—asking him one subzero January night if "things were getting better for him"—his mouth turned sour.

"It's *not* better," he said. "If it were, I would tell you. If I don't say anything about it, Silja, the subject is closed." He turned away and pulled the blanket over his shoulder.

She couldn't believe he didn't even want to discuss it. After the passion they'd shared before he went to Europe—the passion she'd dreamed about since—she couldn't believe Henry would allow it to simply dissolve.

Were his injuries that encompassing? And even if they were, he had been the one to teach her that intimacy came in many forms. She knew war changed men, but she hadn't expected so drastic a change.

Had he fallen out of love with her? Perhaps. But if he didn't love her, why had he returned to her at all?

When she asked him this question, he sighed, as if she were a dim-witted child. "You're my wife," he said. "You're the mother of my child." He glared at her. "Do you know how many pretty English girls I met? Do you realize how tempted a man becomes over there? Do you know how many fellas filed for divorce from overseas? I'm not going to do that, Silja, no matter what happens. Marriage is forever."

"Of course," she agreed. "Of course it's forever, Henry, and I'm so glad to hear you say so—"

"And not only that," he interrupted. "Think about how many men came home in body bags." He grunted. "You, Silja, got a real, live husband returning to you. Yet all you do is complain."

"I'm not complaining," she replied. "I just want . . . " She trailed off.

His look was challenging. "You want *what*, Silja?"

"I want . . . us to be happy," she said in a small voice. "Like we were before you went over there."

"If you want to be happy, you can start by not bellyaching so much," he said. "Be grateful for what you have, Silja."

✿   ✿   ✿

The two-bedroom apartment in the Alku, which had always seemed spacious to Silja, felt crowded with Henry there. When Henry came home, Mikaela moved her things into the smaller bedroom that once had been Silja's, sharing it with Ruby. Silja and Henry took over the larger bedroom that previously belonged to Mikaela. Silja kept up her studies, throwing herself into her work at Hunter. She got straight A's in every class and began looking forward to graduation, which would take place in a few months.

Initially Mikaela worked nights, as she'd done before Henry's homecoming. But within a few weeks she changed her schedule. She said it was because the factory was reducing the night shift; demand for uniforms was slowing down. That might be true, but Silja suspected her mother also was uncomfortable being alone with Henry during the day while Silja was at Hunter.

Silja knew Mikaela hoped that when Henry found work, she could quit the factory and stay home with Ruby full-time. But Henry appeared in no hurry to look for a job. He collected his unemployed veteran's pay, going once a week to the VA office in Manhattan to pick up his twenty-dollar check. But he did nothing about seeking paid work.

She encouraged him to think about his future. The GI Bill had been passed in June; the government was providing boatloads of assistance for returning servicemen. College, starting a business, going to trade school—the world was Henry's oyster. For Silja, who still felt like an oddity as a working-class coed, the bill seemed like an amazing opportunity.

But Henry said there was no rush; he was content to convalesce and spend time with their daughter. "You carry on, Silja," he told her. "Finish that fine education. That degree they're going to give you— that's the ticket to any job you could possibly want, isn't it?"

Silja watched as he set a bowl of rice on Ruby's high chair tray and pulled up a seat in front of her. He placed a child-size spoon in Ruby's hand and helped her wrap her fingers around it. Ruby looked at Silja—a questioning gaze, as if she sought Silja's approval before doing what Henry asked of her. Silja nodded. The child placed her other hand in the bowl, pushing small clumps of rice onto her spoon and bringing it to her mouth. Silja smiled, and the girl smiled back before attempting another spoonful.

Henry was so engrossed in watching Ruby's activity, Silja began to wonder if he'd forgotten she was in the room. But he surprised her by speaking. "I'll take care of Ruby," he went on, without looking at Silja. "You don't need to worry about us."

It was hard on her mother. Mikaela, who had never needed a man around, now had to endure a man taking over the job she most adored: caring for her grandchild.

"He should be working," Mikaela badgered Silja. "What kind of man sits around all day minding a child?"

"Hush, Äiti," Silja chided her. "Henry has been to war. He was injured. He needs time."

Silja loved her mother; nonetheless, she dreamed of moving away from Mikaela and the Alku. She dreamed of the suburbs, of three-bedroom, two-bathroom houses smelling of green pine boards, unblemished paint, and wall-to-wall carpeting. She thought about bright schoolrooms full of charming, fresh-faced students. Children who would become Ruby's playmates, her lifelong friends.

But they couldn't move—not now. They were stuck. Because in the spring of 1945, Silja began to suspect something was terribly wrong with her mother's health.

She didn't know what it was. Mikaela coughed all day long. She said it was residual from her years of working in a laundry. "It was the chemicals and bleach. Everyone there developed a cough," Mikaela said. "You shouldn't concern yourself over it."

After much cajoling, Silja convinced her mother to see a doctor, and her fears were confirmed. Mikaela was diagnosed with lung cancer.

Silja's last few weeks of school were a blur of worry. On graduation day, Mikaela struggled onto the subway, coughing so much other passengers took seats on the opposite side of the car. Ruby nestled onto her grandmother's lap. Mikaela petted the child, smoothing her hair back, kissing the top of Ruby's head. Going up the subway stairs, Mikaela gripped Silja's arm and stopped three times to catch her breath before they emerged onto Sixty-Eighth Street.

After the ceremony, they had a small party at the Alku, with the neighbors and some of Silja's classmates. They had champagne, something they'd never had in their apartment before—like so many Finns, Mikaela and Silja preferred beer to other alcoholic drinks. Henry kept a bottle of Old Crow rye whiskey in the kitchen cabinet, but he was the only one who drank from it.

After the guests left and Mikaela and Ruby went to bed, Silja cleaned the kitchen. Glancing into the living room, she saw Henry sitting in the darkness, in the easy chair that faced the window, looking out onto Forty-Third Street. On the table next to him was the last, half-empty champagne bottle. He was draining it, pouring glass after glass and methodically, silently drinking.

Silja watched his shadowy figure. She longed to go to him. She longed to sit in his lap, put her arms around him, and ask him to pour her a big glass of champagne. She wished he would clink his glass against hers and her heart would skip a beat, the way it used to before he went to war.

No. What she really wanted was a life utterly dissimilar from the one they had.

She didn't want to just drink champagne with Henry. She wanted to bathe in it with him. She wanted to splash naked in bubbles and candlelight, playful and carefree as puppies. She wanted to touch him all over and feel him touch her—nothing held back and nothing off-limits, the way it was before he left for Europe. She wanted to stay up all night, rocking her hips with him inside her—time and again until they were spent, until they could only hold each other and close their eyes, never wanting to break apart.

It was, she thought as she wrung out the dishrag, the only hope she still had.

Mikaela weakened with alarming speed. Within months, her bulk reduced until she was little more than saggy skin. She stopped eating and barely drank the broth and water Silja urged on her. She lay in bed, Ruby beside her, stroking the child's hair until they both fell asleep.

The morning her mother died, Silja was with her—only Silja, because she knew the end was imminent. A few hours earlier she'd knocked at the next-door neighbor's and asked her to come over. When Agatha arrived, she asked, "Do you want me to sit with her, Silja?"

Silja shook her head and said, "No, please—just take care of Ruby. Let Ruby say good-bye, and then take her away."

She couldn't depend on Henry. When he'd glanced in on Mikaela that morning—when he'd seen her gray face and heard her slow, irregular breath—he told Silja he was going out. He put on his hat and walked out the door without another word.

Now Agatha and Silja stood beside Mikaela's bed. Ruby, seated on the bed holding Mikaela's hand, looked at Silja questioningly.

"Kiss Grandma," Silja told Ruby. "And tell her good-bye."

The small girl—not quite three, but wearing a solemn expression that made her appear years older—leaned over and put her lips against Mikaela's pale cheek. "Good-bye," she said obediently, and then added, "All better soon, Grandma."

Agatha led Ruby from the room. Silja sat next to Mikaela, listening to her shallow breathing.

"You can go now, Äiti," Silja said softly. "Take your rest." She kissed the dying woman's ashy forehead. "We're going to be all right."

Silja closed her eyes, then opened them again, looking at Mikaela's face—the face she knew better than anyone's. "Go peacefully, Äiti, and know that I'll be all right. Ruby will be all right."

As if she understood, Mikaela drew in a final breath. Silja waited, but her mother didn't exhale.

"*Lepää rauhassa,*" Silja whispered. "Rest in peace."

17

Ruby

Ruby stares through the darkened panes of her bedroom window toward the forest. With the lights off in her room, she can see into the blackness, can see the congregations of pine trees, the thick-trunked oaks. She knows there are foxes out there and raccoons. If she were out there, she would see them, as they would see her.

"Animal eyes," her father used to tell her. "Ruby, you have night vision like a wild animal. You get that from me."

And then her father would add something like, "Your mother can't see a damn thing in the dark. Or in the daylight either, for that matter."

The scorn in his voice made Ruby cringe, but he did have a point.

In Finnish, *Silja* means "blinded." Not so very long ago, Ruby asked her mother about her name, and she told Ruby its meaning. "I don't know why Grandma named me that," Ruby's mother said. "Maybe she just thought it was a pretty name."

In the unlit bedroom, Ruby thinks about how she despises this house. It isn't a house people should actually live in. It brings to mind a movie set, nothing out of place unless the scene requires it. She knows that's how her mother designed this glass house—to be as near as she could get to living inside the glamorous, fake world of the movies.

But that's not how Ruby thinks of the house. It reminds her of the glass display cases in the pet store in downtown Stonekill—a store that Ruby and her mother used to browse, particularly to visit the puppies.

The birds were housed in thick-walled glass cases—parakeets in one case, finches in another, and in the third, a solitary, nonverbal parrot with a green and turquoise head. Nobody bought the parrot or even gave him much attention. He sat silently on his perch behind the glass for years until one day when Ruby went into the shop, he was gone. She didn't ask but assumed he'd died of old age or sadness, or maybe both.

The parrot didn't move much, but the finches and parakeets flew madly around their cases, fluttering near the glass walls and ceiling of their prison cells. They'd zoom up and around and down, but there was no way out unless somebody bought them and took them home.

The birdcage Ruby lives in feels like that, too. It isn't a house with a soul, like their old house in town was. Thinking about the old house makes Ruby feel so sad she has to change her thoughts, like changing out of a wet blouse when you come inside after being unjacketed on a rainy day.

There's only one thing Ruby likes about this glass-walled birdcage: it's on one level. Unlike the pet store cases with their lack of escape route, Ruby's room has a wide casement window that opens effortlessly. She climbs out, hops onto the soft dirt a few feet below, then closes the window almost but not all the way, so she can get back in when she's ready to return to the aviary in the woods.

And off she goes. Free.

She reaches into her sweater pocket and takes out her Camels and the Zippo her father gave her last year because he said everyone should have a dependable lighter. This one was his during the war. It's embossed with an American flag she can barely see because it's so worn down, but she knows it's there.

She lights a Camel and walks, inhaling and exhaling, thinking and not thinking. There's a rustle nearby, and a raccoon trots out from the trees, onto the path in front of Ruby. They exchange glances before going their separate, perpendicular ways.

She could live out here. She could disappear into the forest.

The Shelter is back here. A person would have to know where it is—at the back end of the property, near the cemetery wall—and would have to roll a heavy boulder to the side; no small feat. The person would need to brush dirt away, then twist the big round metal door in the ground—it takes both hands and all one's strength to turn and lift it. Only then could one descend the iron ladder rungs into the dark.

For someone not used to it, being that far underground might feel unnerving. Ruby herself has been inside the Shelter many times, and it's never particularly bothered her. Still, she has no intention of going down there tonight. Even a passing thought of using the Shelter as a hiding place is absurd. She wouldn't feel safe there.

Her father, if he were here, would beg to differ. "The safest place on earth," he used to say about the Shelter.

Well, it wouldn't be the only thing Ruby and her father disagreed about.

Few people are aware of the Shelter. Certainly not the police—when they were in the woods the other day, they didn't go anywhere near it. Why would they?

But Uncle Paul knows about it.

Why did Uncle Paul bring his wife and baby to Stonekill? Everything would be so much easier if they weren't here.

Even so, Ruby admits that PJ draws her in—which isn't something she would have expected from a baby. She's been running it over and over in her head, searching for understanding.

As she walks she decides it's because PJ reminds her of baby pictures of herself. Her mother used to show them to Ruby. Her mother kept photographs in a shoe box in her closet. Most of her photographs were of the glass house; she started taking pictures when construction began, and continued until the house was finished and all the fancy new furniture was moved in. But among her pictures, she had a smattering of family photographs from over the years.

In Ruby's favorite photo from when she was little, she's sitting on her *isoäiti's* lap. It's one of the few Finnish words Ruby knows: *isoäiti*. It means "grandmother"—but Ruby never called her grandmother Isoäiti, or even the more familiar Finnish term for grandmother, which is *mummi*. Instead, Ruby just called her Grandma. She thought her grandmother would have liked to be called Mummi—she sometimes called herself that when she talked to Ruby. But Ruby's mother said they were Americans, and they should use the American word.

Another Finnish word Ruby knows is *Alku*, where they lived when Ruby was a little girl. It means "beginning." The Alku was called that because it was the first co-op built in Finntown. But for Ruby's family, the Alku was more like an ending.

Ruby was just shy of three when her grandmother died, but she remembers everything about her. Before she got cancer, Grandma was soft and round as a ball of yarn. Her skin always felt warm, even on the coldest winter days.

In the photograph, Ruby's grandmother has her arms wrapped around Ruby, and Ruby is curled up against her chest. Grandma is smiling and Ruby is not. But that doesn't mean Ruby was unhappy. Just because a person isn't smiling doesn't mean she's troubled.

She thinks about the last time she saw her grandmother alive. Ruby told her it would be better soon. "You were such a sweet little thing," her mother has said about this. "You thought Grandma was going to get better. You thought she would get out of bed and be well."

Ruby's mother didn't need to recall this moment for her, because Ruby is pretty sure she remembers it.

Why would she have said such a thing? Did she truly think her grandmother was going to get better? Even now, Ruby doesn't think that's what it was.

Instead, Ruby believes her small self had some innate sense of what was to come. She knew Grandma would feel better once her ragged breathing stopped.

For some people, there comes a point when things get better simply because the breathing stops.

Today at lunchtime, when Aunt Angie offered to let Ruby give PJ his bottle, she was tempted. But she knew he wouldn't find her warm and comforting like she used to find Grandma. If PJ were in her arms, he would feel like he was being held by a prickly, oversize insect. What baby would want that? He'd surely cry. So she shook her head no.

She's reached the rock, that ancient rock with all its secrets. She stubs out her Camel against it, taking care to make sure it's fully extinguished before she tosses it. Her father taught her to pay attention back here. "Have respect for the land, Ruby," he told her. "The land will take care of you when people no longer do."

She moves on, crunching through the underbrush. Reaching into the neckline of her blouse, she pulls out her mother's pendant. She can't see it in the pitch-black of the forest—even her animal eyes aren't that sharp—but she knows how stunning it is: a large, teardrop-shaped sapphire on a long, heavy chain.

This necklace simply showed up one day, but it quickly became her mother's favorite piece of jewelry. Ruby's father never asked where her mother got it. He assumed she bought it for herself, the way she'd bought herself so many presents, big and small, over the years.

Ruby winds the chain of her mother's necklace around and around her fingers. She stops walking and pulls the photo of her mother, the one she carries everywhere, out of her pocketbook. Using her father's lighter, she takes a good look at it.

Not all of her mother's photographs were stored in the shoe box. Some came from other places, and this is one of them. Ruby studies the background and thinks about places that are perpetually sunny, places as warm in her memory as a melting ice-cream cone.

She runs her hand over the image of her mother's fine, soft hair. She remembers her mother being happy, the way she looks in this picture.

18

Silja

1945–1947

A month after Mikaela went to her grave, the one-year anniversary of Henry's homecoming was upon them. Though they did nothing to mark the occasion, when Silja noted the date on the kitchen calendar it gave her pause. Since his return from Europe, Henry had done nothing except brood, care for Ruby, and take walks, which he said he did to improve his health. It did improve—over time the limp all but disappeared—but he still showed no interest in finding a job or going to college. Nothing had changed in the bedroom, either.

Other veterans weren't like Henry. They came back from Europe and Japan determined to better themselves. Get an education, begin careers. Take care of their families.

Silja felt cheated. And yet she still loved him with all her heart. Why is that? she wondered. What makes me love a man like this?

He was still so beautiful. Saying that made her feel shallow, but it was true. She was someone who could look at her husband and think, Cary Grant—and that made it all better. She could pretend he was someone different inside.

She began to suspect his problems had more to do with his head than his body. She read about a program initiated in early 1944 at Mason General, a Long Island psychiatric hospital, for returning vets with nervous conditions. Most were selected for the program before they got off their transport ships. They were transferred directly to Mason General. They spent weeks in therapy—one-on-one with doctors, in groups, learning new skills and how to adapt to stateside life.

Why hadn't Henry been offered this program? Surely, he'd have qualified. How had the army missed it?

Silja attempted to make inquiries, but that got her nowhere. "Your husband can speak with his veterans' affairs office," Silja was told. "But he'll have to make the call himself, ma'am."

One winter evening after Ruby was in bed, she tried to show him an article she'd clipped from the *Brooklyn Eagle*.

Plan Three-Day Court
Play for Mason Patients

Basketball tournaments are a dime-a-dozen during February and March, but when one of them is listed for December, that's news, brother. But there's a darn good reason why this one is being held so early in the season. Fifteen hundred reasons, in fact.

For that's the number of "battle fatigue" patients recuperating at Mason General Hospital at Brentwood, L.I. When the weather was warm, most of the GIs entertained themselves with a bit of softball and volleyball, but they can't do too much nowadays. So Lt. George Menarick conceived the idea of a three-day hoop event, which will find the leading service teams of the area competing tonight, tomorrow, and Wednesday. A handsome plaque and gold basketballs will be the winner's reward.

"You see, there's fun and games, too," Silja said to Henry. "They do the hard work necessary to convalesce, but they also get to blow off steam."

Without a glance, Henry pushed the paper away. "That's ridiculous," he said. "I don't need a shrink, Silja. I'm fine."

"No, you're not." She nudged closer to him on the davenport. "Admit it, Henry. You're not yourself—and you haven't been since you came back."

Abruptly, he stood, towering above her.

"This is none of your business," he replied, quietly but firmly. "My choices have nothing to do with you."

"But they do," she countered. "They have everything to do with me. You said yourself—you said it, that I'm your wife forever. So what kind of future do you want us to have, Henry? Whatever we want, we have to make it so. It's not going to come from you moping all day."

Even as she spoke, she knew she'd said too much. His face reddened and a vein popped out on his forehead.

"What makes you think you can tell me what to do?" he yelled. "You weren't there. I repeat—because obviously I need to say it again and again—you were *not* there. You have no idea what it was like. And you have no place telling me how to run my life."

He leaned over her—one arm on the davenport's back, over her head, the other grabbing her shoulder. His grip wasn't tight—he still didn't have the strength he'd had before he left for Europe—and yet, he overpowered her physically.

She tried to stand, and he pushed her down. Her head snapped against the davenport's tall back.

She stared up at him. Neither spoke.

It wasn't as if he'd hit her, she told herself. He'd simply prodded her. Just a little.

"Henry," she pleaded. "I love you. I've always loved you. I want what's best for you. What's best for our family." She felt tears stinging her eyes, and she wiped them away.

Her actions, her words, seemed to still him. He took his hand off her shoulder and fell onto the sofa next to her.

"I'm sorry," he said hoarsely. "I know this isn't easy for you, either."

He looked away, toward the window. "You just have to trust me," he said. "You have to let me figure this out for myself."

He bit his lip, and she could see the clash of emotions in his eyes. "You figure out your life, Silja," he said. "And I'll figure out mine."

He put his hand on her shoulder again—gently this time. "Trust me. It will work out."

After that night, the tension between them slackened. Henry's voice was gentler when he spoke to her. He thanked her for making breakfast, for taking a load of laundry to the washroom in the Alku's basement. One day he brought home an iced cake from the local bakery and they had it for dessert, much to Ruby's delight.

Silja didn't ask him for anything. She didn't bring up the psychiatric hospital again.

He wanted time; he wanted to be left alone to figure it out—well, fine. She would give him all the time he needed.

She would do whatever it took to set their world aright.

Taking her focus off Henry, Silja set upon the task of finding herself gainful employment. She contacted her favorite professor from Hunter, Dr. Elizabeth Franck. When she'd graduated with the highest honors, Dr. Franck assured her that with all her business contacts, she knew companies that would clamber to hire Silja. "You're the smartest girl I've ever met. And the most conscientious," Dr. Franck once told her. "Any employer will see that and value it."

What she didn't say—didn't have to say—was that Silja was a plain-featured girl. Silja thought it must have been the same for Dr. Franck when she was younger. Like Silja's mother, Dr. Franck was of the generation that changed the way women worked and thought and lived. The generation of females who started the twentieth century with modern ideas and brave plans—college! voting!—ideas that must have shocked their own mothers.

And which females had those valiant notions? The plain ones, Silja thought. It was, and always had been, plain girls who moved mountains.

She knew, although Dr. Franck never came right out with it, that when she said employers would value Silja, she meant companies prefer to have plain girls around. At the reception desk, sure—you want a pretty girl. But back in the trenches, you want plain girls who will devote themselves to the company.

With Dr. Franck's help, Silja found a job with Littleton Foods, an outfit that supplied foodstuffs to restaurants and hotels. She was hired as a field representative in the frozen foods division. To her surprise, she enjoyed it. Over time, everyone—her boss, her fellow reps, and her contacts in the field—came to respect and appreciate her. Silja could walk into a restaurant's kitchen and take a seat in the manager's office, opening her portfolio of product descriptions and sketches, and work with the manager to create a custom order. They concentrated on the job, the way two men might. She took up smoking—everyone in the restaurant world smoked, and it was diplomatic to join them, so she littered the managers' ashtrays with lipstick-stained butts. She dressed conservatively, never showing off the curves that had softened and become even more generous after Ruby's birth. She and the manager shook hands at the end of their meeting, and the next day a truckload of exactly what he required showed up on his loading dock. By that evening, guests were raving over the sumptuous fare in front of them.

"You keep our biz in business," the manager at one midtown hotel said to her. "You're one smart dame, Silja."

19

Angie

That night, with PJ and Ruby both sleeping soundly in their respective rooms, I took Paul's hand and nodded toward the hallway and the master bedroom. He sighed and followed me, closing the bedroom door softly behind us.

I felt as if I'd been waiting a lifetime for this. Watching his face, I slowly undressed, button by button on my blouse. I turned around and looked at him over my shoulder as I reached behind myself to unfasten my skirt, tooth by tooth on the zipper, finally letting the loosened material fall to the floor.

I stepped out of my slip and underthings as Paul took off his own clothes. We stood naked and clinging to one another, our kisses long and deep, his hardness unyielding against my thigh.

Paul groaned. "What you do to me . . ." he murmured, and pulled me toward the bed.

I glanced apprehensively at the neatly made coverlet. As desperate as I was to make love with Paul, I didn't want to do it in Silja's bed.

Paul read my thoughts. He grabbed the coverlet and spread it out over the carpeting.

"Come down here," he said, lying on the floor. "I'll keep you warm, Angel."

I dropped to my knees, then on top of him, my legs on either side of him. He slid his hands across my bottom, gently squeezing my buttock cheeks. He lifted his head and took one of my breasts and then the other into his mouth, kissing my nipples. I looked down, enjoying how round and full my breasts were against his lips.

I loved his body heat, the way his skin smelled like fresh air after a rain shower, how his chest hair tickled my ribs when I leaned over him. I adored everything about him. But there was more to our love-making than that.

I wanted another baby.

Not long after PJ's birth, I'd been fitted for a diaphragm. Since I never nursed PJ, I knew the possibility of getting pregnant again right away was very real. And in the first few months, when PJ was tiny, I'd been keen to prevent it.

But now PJ was six months old and such an easygoing baby. There was no reason we shouldn't start trying for a second. I'd always wanted a big, tight-knit family, like the one I grew up in. Babies year after year, like my mother had.

I knew Paul thought we should wait, but I figured once I was pregnant, he'd get used to the idea—and even, I hoped, become enthused. After all, look how close he and Henry had been. Wouldn't he want the same for his own children?

"What about your diaphragm, Angel?" Paul asked me.

I hesitated a moment and then said, "Thanks for reminding me." I went into the bathroom, closing the door behind me. I opened Silja's vanity drawer, where I'd stored my plastic diaphragm case when I unpacked the night before.

Reaching into the drawer, I was surprised to feel two such cases. I had to take them both out to determine which one was mine—the yellow one; Silja used a white case for her diaphragm.

I stuck Silja's case back into the drawer and opened my own. I regarded the rubber half-moon, pushing it with my index finger, watching it spring back to shape.

Paul was just nervous, I decided. All men were, when it came to pregnancy and babies. That didn't mean they didn't want a family.

I looked at my reflection in the mirror. I imagined a giggling baby girl. A beribboned, pink-clothed girl with half my features and half Paul's.

I took one more look at the diaphragm in its case, and then resolutely closed the clasp. I returned to the bedroom and lowered my body once more on top of Paul's. Reaching between my legs, I took him in my hands and guided him inside me.

"Now," I said, settling my weight onto his until I was crushed against him. "Now, Paul, and don't ever, ever stop."

The next morning, I sighed in contentment as Paul and I sat on the barstools drinking coffee. I leaned toward him and blew hot breath into his ear. "You're magic to me," I whispered. "I love every second I spend with you."

Paul smiled and finished his coffee. He rose from the barstool. I stood, too, and went around the counter. I opened the packet of bacon I'd bought yesterday at the market. I fiddled with the knobs on Silja's fancy electric range, trying to determine which setting I should use to cook the meat.

I turned to watch as Paul crossed the room, opened the front door, and bent down to retrieve the newspaper on the stoop. He flapped it open and began to read. Remembering Jean Kellerman's visit, my hand trembled as I pulled a carton of eggs from the refrigerator. When I closed the door and turned around, Paul was standing over me, fuming.

"What the hell is this about?" he shouted, slapping the newspaper on the counter in front of me.

My heart racing, I set down the eggs and picked up the paper.

No Mother Would Do Something So Violent

By Jean Kellerman, Special to the *Stonekill Gazette*

While the coroner's office confirmed that Stonekill resident Henry Glass, 39, perished from suicide via poison, the dead man's sister-in-law agrees with officials that Mr. Glass's missing wife could not be involved.

"I can't imagine a mother could do something so violent to the father of her child," Angie Glass told this reporter in an exclusive interview.

Mrs. Angie Glass concedes that she does not know Mrs. Silja Glass, 38, very well. "I only met her once. But no mother would do something like that."

But would she? On Monday, Silja Glass left her family a note indicating she was leaving them. The note has been placed in evidence, and reporters were not permitted to view its contents.

Was the note a ruse? Did Silja stage an abandonment to cover up something more sinister?

No one seems to know. A prosperous businesswoman in the New York City hotel industry, Silja was last seen leaving her Manhattan office Monday after work. She reportedly maintains an erratic evening schedule, sometimes commuting home at rush hour but other times later in the evening. She drives a silver-gray 1958 MGA sports coupe back and forth from the Stonekill station to the couple's glamorous home on Stone Ridge Road. Her MGA was found at the station late Monday night. Police have since towed and impounded the vehicle.

On Wednesday evening this reporter interviewed passengers exiting the rush hour trains to determine if anyone remembers seeing Silja. "I know the lady you mean, but I can't say whether I saw her on Monday," said Mr. Bert Meyer of Albany Post Road, Stonekill. "She keeps irregular hours. Sometimes on the train, sometimes not." He added, "Besides, I'm usually too fixated on getting home for dinner to pay attention to folks getting off the train."

Other commuters echoed Mr. Meyer's sentiments. Police were also observed interviewing passengers, presumably asking similar questions.

It's probable, therefore, that Silja Glass did not return to Stonekill on Monday evening. The couple's seventeen-year-old daughter found her father's body in the woods just behind the family home, with a poisoned teacup by his side.

Mrs. Angie Glass, a maternally minded individual hailing

from Wisconsin, asserts that she will see her niece through this catastrophe. "At a tragic time like this, a girl needs mothering," the young, fresh-faced Mrs. Glass said. "I'm lucky to be here so I can step into that role."

This is not the first time the Glass family has come under scrutiny in our humble hamlet. In 1951, Mr. Glass's brother, Paul,

[Continued on page 3]

I shook open the paper to turn to the inside pages. Paul, hovering behind me, smacked it out of my hand. He picked it up from the floor and folded it, tucking it in the back pocket of his pants. "That's enough," he said gruffly, glaring at me. "You don't need to read the rest."

Fearfully, I raised my eyes to Paul's. "Half those things, I didn't even say," I told him, my voice wobbly. "She—the reporter—put words into my mouth."

"Of course she did!" Paul slammed his fist onto the counter. A vein stood out on his temple. I had never seen him so angry. I stepped back.

My action seemed to give him pause. He took a deep breath and regarded me carefully. "I'm sorry," he said hoarsely. "I shouldn't have lost my temper. But please, Angel, please—" He reached forward and gently took hold of my shoulders. "Promise me you won't talk to her—or any reporter—ever again." He tilted my chin so our eyes met. "Promise me."

"I promise," I said, weak with relief that his anger was subsiding.

He released me. "That's my girl." He leaned over and inspected the bacon on the stove. "Smells wonderful," he said. "I'm going outside for a bit of fresh air. Call me in when it's ready, would you?"

I grabbed his arm as he started to walk away. "Kiss me first," I pleaded. "Tell me you love me."

I closed my eyes and waited, and after a moment, I felt his lips, warm against my own.

When he moved away from me, I opened my eyes. He glanced toward the stove. "Don't let that burn, Angel." He turned and opened the sliding glass door, stepping outside. I watched as he opened the paper and held it before his face. I removed the bacon from the pan to a plate covered in paper towels, then cracked eggs in a bowl, added milk, and contemplatively began whisking with a fork.

I wanted desperately to call Dorrie, Carol Ann, or one of my friends. I longed to hear a familiar voice. I wanted to report the events in New York and get an outsider's take on the situation. I stared at the telephone mounted on the kitchen wall, my fingers itching to pick it up and dial one of the well-known numbers.

No. More than talking to my sisters or friends on the telephone, I wanted to go home. That's what I wanted, really—simply to go home.

Well, I had no one to blame but myself. Paul had been right. He should have come alone. He could have taken care of things in Stonekill. He didn't need my help making the arrangements, nor my presence at Henry's funeral.

In addition to supporting Paul, I had expected my role to be that of Ruby's caregiver—to provide a sympathetic ear, a shoulder to cry on as the girl struggled to understand why her mother had left her. But I could tell Ruby had no desire to confide in me. Ruby probably saw PJ and me as decoration at best. A nuisance, more likely.

I would have been better off staying home. I could have stayed in Door County with the baby, blissfully unaware of what it was like in Stonekill. From afar, I could have grieved for Henry. I could have gone to St. Mary of the Lake on Sunday morning and said prayers for his soul. I could have spoken on the phone with Paul, asking if there was any more news about Silja. And after we hung up, I could have headed to my parents' house for Sunday dinner, where there would have been polite questions about Paul's family before the talk turned back to UW-Badgers and Green Bay Packers football, as it always did on autumn weekends in my parents' household.

I could have stayed home in my normal life, with my normal family. And yet, the decision to be in Stonekill, to be a part of this peculiar experience, was entirely my own. I had no one to blame but myself.

The phone I'd been staring at rang, interrupting my thoughts. Startled, I reached over and grabbed it. "Glass residence."

There was no response. "Hello?" I said. "Is anyone there?"

After a moment, I heard a woman's voice, one I didn't know. "Mrs. Glass?"

"I'm sorry," I replied. "Mrs. Glass isn't here right now. She . . . "

I trailed off, not sure what to say. Not sure how much the caller, whoever she was, knew about Silja's disappearance.

"Is this Mrs. Paul Glass?" the caller asked.

"Oh," I said breathlessly. "Yes, that's me. This is Angie Glass. I'm Paul Glass's wife."

There was a pause, and then the woman said, "This is Mrs. Hawke, the principal at the high school. I was just calling to check on Ruby."

"How kind of you." I glanced outside. Paul was still standing on the patio. He had finished reading the paper and was smoking, his back to me. "Ruby is . . . she's doing her best, Mrs. Hawke. She won't be at school today. It's the day of her father's funeral."

"Yes, so I've been informed," Mrs. Hawke said. "One of my teachers will be attending to represent the school."

"That's very thoughtful of you." I stirred the raw eggs in the bowl, reluctant to put them on the stove—I didn't want to overcook them—until the call was finished.

"Well." Mrs. Hawke's voice was crisp. "We're all very sorry here at the school, Mrs. Glass. Please accept our condolences." She paused again. "And, as well, please pass them on to . . . *Paul.*"

I wasn't sure, but I thought I heard the principal's voice bristle when she said Paul's name.

I looked outside again. Paul sank into a patio chair, his back hunched. I watched him with sadness. Poor fellow.

"I'll do that," I said. "Thank you for the call, Mrs. Hawke."

20

Ruby

Today her father's body will be put in the ground.

Ruby is in her room in the birdcage with the door closed. She stands by the window, looking out. She's watching Uncle Paul, who is on the patio reading a newspaper and smoking. He looks agitated, like somebody waiting for a train that's fifteen minutes late.

He grinds out his cigarette and folds the paper, putting it in his pants pocket. He stares into the forest, then hunkers down on one of the metal patio chairs, his head lowered and his hands on the back of his neck.

Ruby has never seen Uncle Paul curl up his long body this way. His posture reminds her of atomic bomb drills at school. They still do the drills a couple times a year. In elementary school, they watched a short movie featuring a turtle hiding in its shell. Then they practiced hiding themselves. In high school, there's no movie, but they still practice what to do. Duck and cover. That's what Uncle Paul looks like he'd doing on the patio—ducking and covering.

During the drills, you were supposed to duck and cover under your own desk, but the girls sometimes crawled over to be with their neighbors. If the teacher reprimanded them after the drill, they said they didn't want to be alone. They felt safer ducking against each other.

In the cafeteria after the first drill this school year, a few boys said the girls could come under the boys' desks if they wanted protection. "I'll keep you safe . . . and warm," Jerry Krouse told Emily

Bruno. He made motions like he was feeling up the air, and all the boys laughed.

"Gross, Jerry. I'll stay with my friends, thank you very much." Emily pranced off, her ponytail bouncing behind her.

Ruby understood how Emily felt. She wouldn't want to duck and cover with any of those disgusting boys either. She wouldn't mind the company of a girl, though.

She wouldn't mind having a friend.

Except Ruby knows none of the girls want to be near her. "The girls at school think I'm weird," Ruby once told her father, explaining why she didn't bring friends home. He hadn't asked, but they were talking about friends—her father said Uncle Paul was his best friend, always had been. "All they talk about are boys and clothes," Ruby said. "And I don't know how to talk about that stuff. If I try starting a conversation about anything else, they look at me like I have two heads."

Her father shrugged. "You don't need friends," he replied. "You just look out for yourself, Ruby, and you'll be fine."

Looking back—that conversation was more than six months ago—Ruby realizes it's the last heart-to-heart talk she had with her father. That is, if you can call it heart-to-heart—the sort of discussion where her father, based on his own experience, told Ruby how to feel and what to do. Her father gave a little piece of himself. And back then Ruby thought that meant they were talking heart-to-heart.

But now she sees it differently.

Uncle Paul steps into the kitchen. Once he's gone, Ruby opens the window and leans out. She smells the earth in the backyard.

She thinks about dirt and what it would feel like to be six feet underneath it, in a tiny little box. One you can't stand up in, can't move around in. It would be even more confining than being under those little desks at school.

Of course, she knows her father won't feel that. He won't feel anything ever again.

But still, she imagines it. What it would be like if her father woke up. If he felt the darkness around him, the enclosed space. If he raised his hands and pushed against tufted, satiny material—nothing but the best—and felt the hardness above it, the wooden box. And then he'd know, surely, that above the box was earth, shovelful after shovelful. And no matter how hard he beat his fists and how loud he yelled, he'd never get out.

His world has been reduced—smaller by far than it's ever been. And now he'll never escape that pitiful, circumscribed den.

21

Angie

As I was hanging up after speaking with Mrs. Hawke, Paul turned around to stare at me from the patio. He rose and stepped inside. "Who were you talking to, Angie?"

His low, stern voice told me it would be best to lie. "It was my mother," I said, crossing the kitchen and turning on the stove. "She was just calling to check on us." I melted butter in the pan and added the raw egg mixture, then turned to him and smiled. "Breakfast in just a minute."

Paul, apparently accepting my explanation, sat at the bar and waited for me to put a plate in front of him.

The service for Henry, he told me as we ate, was to be held at the funeral home. "They weren't religious," Paul said. "Henry was never all that serious about Catholicism, even back in California when we went to Mass every Sunday. And Silja grew up in some Finnish church—I can't remember what it's called, but from what Henry's told me, everyone went to the same church. Religion is pretty much the same thing as heritage, I guess, if you're Finnish." He shrugged. "Anyway, after Silja's mother died and they moved away from Brooklyn, I don't think Silja ever went to church again."

I couldn't fathom this latest information. Like so much in Henry and Silja's world, a dearth of religion in the home was something with which I had no experience.

"What about Ruby?" I asked. "She's never gone to church?"

Paul glanced toward the hallway, but there was no sign of Ruby;

she hadn't come out of her room for breakfast. "Maybe when she was small, back in Brooklyn," he said. "But to my knowledge, not since." He stood up from the bar and popped the last piece of bacon into his mouth. "So it seemed simpler to do the service at the funeral home."

In the car, I held the baby on my lap and gently rubbed his back. Ruby curled into the corner of the backseat and said nothing, as usual. As we drove along the narrow, hilly streets into the center of town, I glanced at the homes and small stores. We passed bakeries and stationers, tailor's shops and cobblers. The businesses were stuck into small, squat buildings with dusty looking display windows and dingy signs advertising their names. Most of the houses were narrow frame structures, two or three stories high, in need of fresh paint and roof repair. They had steep pitched roofs, gingerbread trim along the gutters, and sagging front porches.

"Up that street, that's where Henry and Silja used to live," Paul offered quietly, nodding in the direction of a side street. Its sign read LAWRENCE AVENUE.

Ruby did not turn her head.

Near the train tracks and the Hudson River, we turned onto a main road and Paul sped up. As we passed into the next town south, I looked out the side window at the river. Row upon row of ships—dozens or more—were anchored in the distance near the other shore.

"What are those ships?" I asked Paul.

"Reserve warships, mostly," he said. "Government uses them for grain storage and the like, then puts them into service when they're needed." He slowed for a curve in the road. "The locals call it the Mothball Fleet. People take their speedboats up and down between the rows, pulling water skiers. It's less choppy in there, compared to the open water of the river. Smooth as glass in between the ships, from what I understand—perfect for waterskiing."

I nodded, twisting my neck to keep looking at the ships as we drove by. Out of the corner of my eye, I could see Ruby leaning against the car door. Her head was ducked and her eyes were closed.

I stared at the vast river. Though I knew it was significantly smaller than Lake Michigan, somehow the Hudson felt larger than the lake I was so accustomed to. The river seemed disconnected from its shores, like a distant relative one has heard of but never met.

Maybe, I thought, it was just because I was in a car. Perhaps if I stood on the banks of the Hudson, dipped in my toes the way I'd so often dipped into Lake Michigan, shielded my eyes as I looked across the water at that silent, distant fleet—perhaps then the river would feel as safe and familiar as my lake at home did.

I shook my head. I didn't know if the river had sandy banks anywhere, if it had parks or beaches, places for picnics and games. Nonetheless, I couldn't shake the disconcerting feeling that if I touched a foot into that river, I'd fall in headlong and drown.

There were about a half-dozen cars in the funeral home lot. Right away I spotted Jean Kellerman's Chevrolet. Uh-oh, I thought as I stepped out of the Ford.

The funeral director met us at the door. "I'm sorry there are . . . intruders," Mr. Wagner said to Paul. With his small eyes darting about, he reminded me of a nervous rabbit. "I can send for the police, if you like. They could keep a watch on things and escort anyone you don't want to be here off the premises."

Paul shook his head, his eyes steely. "Let them do what they want," he said to Wagner. "They can't hurt us."

Cradling PJ against my body, I followed Paul, Ruby, and the funeral director inside.

A small crowd had gathered, mostly men but also including Jean Kellerman, who tried to meet my eye; I looked away. As one, the group approached Paul with murmured sympathy, followed by requests for, "Just a few words, Mr. Glass." Most had notebooks like Jean's, pens poised. Two men held up cameras, but Mr. Wagner stepped in front of us just as their flashbulbs went off.

Paul took my elbow on one side, Ruby's on the other, and brushed past the reporters and photographers. Mr. Wagner hastily accompanied us into the main room. He spoke sharply to the people in the vestibule, then shut the door.

Paul strode to the front of the room and glanced at Henry's casket, nodding his approval to Mr. Wagner. He moved to the back of the room and lit a Lucky Strike. Mr. Wagner stood next to him, and the two spoke in hushed tones, heads bowed toward one another.

Babe in arms, I walked toward the casket, which was placed on a raised dais with a large mixed bouquet of flowers on a pedestal to the side.

I peered inside the coffin. PJ, curious, tried to push himself out of my arms, reaching toward Henry's lifeless body. I recoiled and pulled the baby back, snuggling him against my breast. He became interested in the floral bouquet, and I shifted so he could just touch the tips of the tiger lilies and sprays of baby's breath.

I studied Henry, laid out in the mahogany coffin lined with ivory satin. In death, Henry's resemblance to Paul was not as strong as I remembered. Henry's coloring was off, more orange than ruddy-brown, and his hair was parted crookedly on the right. Still, his lanky body in the blue suit was identical to Paul's. Same thin frame, same long legs and arms.

I had a sudden image of Paul without clothes on. At home, when it was just the two of us in the cottage—not counting the baby, because he was a baby, after all—I adored looking at Paul undressed. During the warmer months, late the previous spring and through the summer, he'd often walked around the cottage naked. He would move from bed to shower with no clothes on, and then, when he was done, he'd dry off and come into the tiny kitchen, not even a towel wrapped around his hips, to accept the cup of coffee I had ready for him. He'd stand at the living room window, sipping his coffee as he looked at the bay, his perfect hips and buttocks in full view from the kitchen, where I was cooking breakfast. It was hard to concentrate on making toast and eggs; I found it nearly impossible to draw my eyes away from his exposed backside.

Holding the baby, standing beside Paul's brother's casket, I felt my face redden at my improper thoughts. I turned my back on Henry and scanned the room for Ruby. I expected the girl to come forward and inspect the casket, as Paul had.

But Ruby did not approach the dais. Instead, she stood near a side wall, far apart from Paul, Mr. Wagner, and me. Her patchwork purse was slung across her body and rested against one hip. Her arms were crossed over her chest and her face was blank, as if she were deliberately trying to clear her mind of all thought and emotion.

I walked over to the girl. "Ruby?" I said softly. I wanted to reach out and touch Ruby's sweater sleeve or brush her hair back from her face—anything to have physical contact. But Ruby's eyes, staring straight ahead and refusing to meet mine, told me to keep my distance.

"Can I get you something?" I asked. "A cup of water, perhaps?"

Ruby shook her head and looked down at her shoes.

I didn't know what else to do. I crossed the room and stood next to Paul, ready to greet mourners as they came into the room.

22

Ruby

In that stifling space, staring straight ahead of her, not at the front of the room where there's a coffin and not at the back of the room where there are living people, Ruby tries not to think about anything. But it's impossible, of course, to stop the mind from wandering. To stop thoughts from creeping in.

She doesn't believe in a conventional heaven, but she knows dead people are present. If you think warmly about the dead, they can be a comfort—it's almost as if your warm thoughts give them a live, warm body again. When you think pleasant thoughts about the dead, it feels like they're right next to you, breathing the same air you breathe. It's something Ruby has done with her grandmother for years. It's something she could do with anybody she loves who has died.

She could imagine her father now that he's dead. But she doesn't.

Instead, she thinks about Grandma's funeral, which was held at the Finnish Lutheran Church in Brooklyn. Ruby's grandmother had a locket she wore every day, a silver one with photographs of Ruby on one side and Ruby's mother opposite. Before they shut Grandma's casket, the pastor asked Ruby's mother if she wanted the locket.

Her mother shook her head no. The pastor gently touched her arm. "*Tytär,*" he said. "I would advise you to take your *äiti's* jewelry. It does her no good in the ground, but it's a keepsake for you and your own little *tytär* —" and here he looked at Ruby with sympathetic blue eyes. "If you don't take it, Silja," he urged, "I believe you'll regret it later on."

Reconsidering, Ruby's mother nodded. The pastor removed the

locket from Grandma's neck and handed it to Ruby's mother, who put it in her pocketbook.

In all these years, Ruby has never seen her mother wear that locket. It rests untouched in her jewelry box. Nonetheless, Ruby thinks the pastor was right. She's glad the locket is still around.

How sad her grandmother would be—not about the locket sitting in a jewelry box; Ruby knows Grandma wouldn't care about that—but by this recent turn of events in the family.

If there was a heaven, Grandma would be there, because she never did a bad deed in her life. In Hebrew, a bad deed is called an *aveira*. When Ruby lived on Lawrence Avenue, one of the neighbor girls told her this. The girl's name was Sarah and she was the only kid in the neighborhood who was Jewish. Ruby and Sarah got along because neither had siblings and because Ruby was the only kid who was half Finnish, which in that neighborhood was almost as kooky as being Jewish.

"An *aveira* is kind of the opposite of a *mitzvah*," Sarah told Ruby. "But not exactly, either, because a *mitzvah* can be anything good that you do, but an *aveira* is a specific sin."

"Like what?" Ruby asked. "What specifically?"

"Oh, things like withholding charity from the poor," Sarah said. "And silly things out of the Bible. Things people don't even do anymore. Like building an altar with stones cut by metal."

Ruby thought about that, and then she asked, "What about murder? Would murder be an *aveira*?"

Sarah nodded and said yes, of course it would.

Sarah moved away from Lawrence Avenue before Ruby did. Her family moved to New Jersey. Sarah and Ruby promised to write to each other and maybe even visit, but they never did. Which is unfortunate, because since then Ruby hasn't made a single other friend her own age.

If Grandma had been Jewish, she wouldn't have been the *aveira* type. She surely would have been the *mitzvah* type. She would be in heaven, looking down on all this with sadness.

What about Ruby's father in heaven?

Nope. Not a chance.

23

Angie

I stood slightly behind Paul, holding the baby, smiling shyly at the mourners as they came into the room. They nodded politely in my direction but failed to speak to me. I heard more than one whisper to a companion, "That's his young wife," or other similar lines.

Paul didn't introduce me to anyone. It was almost as if he'd forgotten I was there. I felt resentment building, but—hearing my mother's voice in my head—I reminded myself that peevishness was not appropriate, nor was it becoming.

The reporters and photographers weren't permitted inside. But others came in—primarily men, but there were a few women, too. Most were middle-aged or older. They wore dark suits or dresses; the men took off their hats and held them humbly in front of their middles. Paul shook hands, nodded, spoke a few quiet words to some of them. Words that I didn't catch.

Once in a while, someone would walk in and Paul was less friendly. I saw how he stiffened at the sight of one man who looked about Paul's own age—a burly, balding fellow with dirty fingernails and scarred hands who seemed uncomfortable in a suit and tie. The man, who was alone, didn't hold out his hand to Paul. He merely brushed his way inside, finding a seat toward the middle of the room.

After that, Paul turned to me—so he *did* realize I was there, after all—and told me to go sit down. "That front row, sit there. It's reserved for family," he said. "Go get Ruby and tell her it's time for her to sit down, too."

I obeyed. Ruby, saying nothing, followed me to the front row. We sat in silence, except for the baby babbling to himself and playing with my rosary.

At ten o'clock, Mr. Wagner closed the double doors to the room, and he and Paul made their way forward. Paul took the seat next to me. Mr. Wagner, at the front of the room, cleared his throat. "Thank you for being here," he said to the gathering—about twenty-five people, I estimated.

And then he stopped talking.

I followed his eyes to the back of the room. A young Negro woman softly closed the double doors behind herself as she stepped inside. She came down the center aisle, her footsteps light across the carpet. All heads turned as she made her way toward the front of the room. A murmur went up from the crowd. I caught snippets of conversation:

The English teacher.

There's the Negro that Mrs. Hawke hired.

I hear she's close with the Glass girl.

Ruby stood and approached the woman, who held out her arms. "Dear girl," the woman said as she and Ruby embraced—a close embrace, not just a slight-touch sort of hug. They stood in the aisle, arms wrapped around one another.

Finally, the embrace broke and the woman walked with Ruby toward Paul and me. She held out her hand. "I'm Nancy Wells," she said. "I'm Ruby's English teacher. It's nice to meet you, although I'm sorry for the circumstances."

Paul stood. "Miss Wells," he said stiffly. "I'm Paul Glass, and this is my wife, Angie, and my son, PJ."

I noticed that Paul did not shake the teacher's hand. Miss Wells noticed, too—I was sure of it. The teacher's face tightened and she dropped her hand to her side.

Miss Wells turned toward me. "Ma'am."

I had a moment of panic, unsure what to do. And then—with my eyes deliberately on Miss Wells, willing myself *not* to glance at Paul— I stuck out my hand toward the other woman's.

Miss Wells reached forward and took my hand in her own. Miss

Wells's skin was warm and soft, as if she were a frequent user of hand cream. Her grip was firm.

I had never, in my whole life, touched a Negro. At home, I'd seen black people working in the cherry orchards during the yearly harvest; most of the migrant pickers in Door County were black, Indian, or Mexican. They arrived each July with their families, living in the bunk-houses on the orchard lands—men, women, and children as young as eight doing the picking, the smaller children spending their days near the bunkhouses, with elderly or infirm relatives minding them.

Even with migrant workers, there never seemed to be enough hands for the harvest. My brothers, like many Door County boys, earned extra dough by picking cherries every summer. But our parents forbade Dorrie, Carol Ann, and me from doing that type of work. "There are more dignified ways for a girl to make money," they said—which is how I ended up being a cottage girl at Gordon's, cleaning toilets and emptying wastebaskets for vacationers in the summer.

But sometimes, on our days off, my friends and I went cherry picking for our mothers, bringing home bushels for jam and pies. The orchard owners set us in a separate section from the migrant workers, across the orchard. Occasionally, I'd catch the eye of a passing worker; I'd smile and wave, and the worker would wave back amenably. Until today, that was as close as I'd ever come to a Negro.

After Miss Wells and I dropped hands, she cooed at the baby, which made me smile proudly. The teacher then moved to take a seat behind the family.

"Please, Miss Wells," Ruby said. "Sit here beside me."

I could feel my mouth hanging open in shock. It was the first full sentence I'd heard Ruby speak since Paul and I arrived in Stonekill.

Miss Wells nodded and seated herself beside Ruby.

Mr. Wagner resumed. "Again, thank you for being here," he said. "We're here to mourn the passing of Henry John Glass . . ."

He trailed off. I followed his gaze, which was once more fixated on the aisle. Another latecomer had stepped into the room; he stood in the center of the aisle, near the back row, straight-backed and silent. He was not very tall and was dressed in a fawn-colored suit with a blue-and-brown-striped tie. His felt hat was positioned low over his forehead.

Mr. Wagner seemed to be waiting for the man to sit down. When he didn't, the funeral director called out loudly, "Do you need help finding a seat, sir?"

The man walked up the aisle to the front of the room. "No, thank you," he said. "I'm here because Miss Ruby Glass asked me to perform this funeral service."

A murmur went through the crowd. One mourner stood up and said, "His kind does *not* belong here! Not at Henry Glass's funeral, for God's sake. Throw him out!" Others took up similar words and half-stood in their seats.

Mr. Wagner turned toward Ruby. "Is this true, young lady? Did you invite this man to perform your father's service?"

Ruby nodded. She looked up at the other man, meeting him straight in the eye. "Thank you for coming, Dr. Shepherd."

Dr. Shepherd reached forward to touch Ruby's shoulder. I noticed that his voice cracked a bit as he replied, "Of course, Ruby."

"Throw him out," someone said again—but weakly this time. Everyone was sitting now. No one answered the protester.

His eyebrows raised, Mr. Wagner looked toward Paul, who simply shrugged at the funeral director. I stared at Paul, but he wouldn't meet my eye.

Mr. Wagner stood helplessly next to Henry's casket, his thin arms flapping at his sides, as if he wasn't sure what to do with them.

Dr. Shepherd took off his hat and stepped to the front of the room, glancing briefly at Henry's body. He gave Mr. Wagner a pointed look. The funeral director, abashed, left the front of the room, taking a seat on the opposite side of the aisle from us.

I put my hand on Paul's arm. "What's going on?" I whispered to him.

Instead of answering, he looked over my head at Ruby. I watched as their eyes met. He frowned, but Ruby tilted her head imploringly at him. He nodded ever so slightly, then bowed his head.

"Henry Glass," Dr. Shepherd said in a low voice, "was admired by many in this room."

I shifted in my seat. I uncrossed my legs, wrapped my arms more tightly around the baby, and stole a glance at Ruby. The girl's eyes were locked on Dr. Shepherd's face, her eyes dreamy, a small smile playing across her lips. Miss Wells, on the other side of Ruby, was sitting upright with her eyebrows knit together.

"But what happened to this man?" Dr. Shepherd said. "Certainly, his family suffered a tremendous loss. With the . . . the discovery of Mrs. Glass missing . . . Mr. Glass clearly experienced a shocking blow. It's one that many among us would have difficulty coming to terms with. And Mr. Glass reacted by taking his own life." The doctor shook his head. "It's tragic."

Here, Dr. Shepherd paused. No one said anything, and I thought the pause lasted a bit too long. Finally, PJ let out a long shriek, breaking the silence.

Dr. Shepherd smiled sadly. "Indeed, young man," he said, looking at the baby. "You have it exactly right. The only response to that is woe."

He looked around the room. "I'm not a minister." He glanced at Mr. Wagner. "Nor one who normally conducts funerals. I come from a Quaker tradition. In my heritage, no single person has more authority with God than another. All are welcome to speak." He raised his hands. "I encourage each of you— respectfully and in your turn—to stand and say whatever words you're moved to say." He nodded toward the left side of the room, then the right. "There is no requirement to speak, of course. You may recognize Henry Glass's life and passing silently, if that's your choice."

Dr. Shepherd put his head down, hands clasped in front of him. I peered behind myself. The mourners seemed uncomfortable, glancing apprehensively at one another. Finally, one man stood.

"Henry Glass was a true American," he said. "A patriot and a nationalist. He served his country and his God."

"Hear, hear," several voices murmured in agreement. The man nodded at those around him, clearly relieved at the approval of his speech. Then he sat down.

Another man got to his feet. "Henry was loyal," the man said, his voice hesitant. "He was the sort of man who kept his word." He looked around, then took his seat.

Dr. Shepherd slowly nodded, appearing to be deep in thought. He waited to see if others would stand, but no one did.

"Thank you, all." Dr. Shepherd glanced once more at the casket. Then he stepped over to Ruby and grasped her shoulder. Their eyes met, and I thought I detected a slight tear at the corner of Dr. Shepherd's eye.

Dr. Shepherd did not acknowledge anyone else. He unclenched Ruby's shoulder and, striding past us all, left the room.

24

Ruby

He leaves. He walks away and Ruby can't stop staring.

Is she in love with him? No. Nothing like that. Even if he were young—which he is not—Ruby wouldn't love him that way.

She loves him like a daughter loves a father. As a daughter *should* love a father, anyway.

Did she love her own father? She considers this. There was a time when she loved him—or thought she did. But she was very small then, and she didn't understand her father in those days.

She loved him because he cared for her. He took care of her after her grandmother died. He didn't abandon Ruby and her mother, the way her mother's father abandoned Grandma so long ago.

Perhaps, Ruby thinks, she should have loved her father only because of that. Imperfect as he was, at least he stuck around.

But in the end, she knows that was not a good thing for anybody.

But Shepherd loves her differently.

He didn't *have* to love her. Shepherd's love is chosen love. And his choice is Ruby.

For that, she will always love him more than she ever loved her own father.

She loves that she had the foresight to ask Shepherd if he'd perform her father's funeral service. She loves the words he spoke, the actions he took. Partly because she knows her father would have hated it. But also because Ruby herself adores it.

Some weeks ago, when Shepherd explained Quakerism to her, she thought it sounded brilliant. Ruby doesn't know much about religion, but if she was going to choose one, she'd choose to be a Friend like Shepherd. She'd love to be in a holy place where mostly it was quiet. Where no program or person told her when to sit and stand, what words to say, what songs to sing. She would only speak if there was something important to say. And her ears would hear others only if they truly had something significant to share.

"I want to go to Meeting with you someday," she told Shepherd recently. "I want to see what it's like at a Quaker Meeting."

"Well." He'd smiled. "That would be nice." He sighed and then went on, "A lot of things would be nice, wouldn't they? If only they could happen."

25

Angie

"We've got to get to the bottom of this," I said on the way to the cemetery. I shifted the baby on my lap and reached toward the floorboard for my purse. I pulled out a package of soda crackers and broke off small bits for PJ to gum. "We simply have to confront Ruby and ask her what's happening, Paul."

Only Paul, the baby, and I were traveling in the Ford. After Dr. Shepherd walked out of Henry's service, no one else seemed to know what to say. Finally Mr. Wagner stood, thanked everyone for coming, and, with the clipped precision of a teacher assigning last-minute homework, announced cemetery details.

We were the last to leave, and by the time we did, everyone else was already in their cars. Most of the mourners seemed in a hurry to leave; they tore out of the lot and onto the main road before Paul, Ruby, and I had even stepped out from under the porte cochere.

The few who remained avoided us. They got in their vehicles and waited, engines idling and lights on, heads bent over cigarette lighters or radio knobs. Several reporters were still hovering on the fringes of the parking lot, drifting about like butterflies on a warm spring day.

As we walked toward the rental car, Ruby asked Paul if she could ride with Miss Wells, and he grudgingly acquiesced. I watched as the teacher opened the passenger door of a battered Chevy—two-tone, butter yellow with a black top—then closed it after Ruby got in.

Now, driving slowly, Paul followed the hearse; Miss Wells trailed behind. Glancing over my shoulder, I saw several other cars following

with their headlights on, too. The few mourners who'd waited, I supposed—and likely some of those bothersome reporters, too.

"We need to get Ruby to explain it all," I persisted.

Paul stared at the hearse in front of him. "If Ruby doesn't want to
talk," he said, without turning his head, "then she's not going to talk."

"Well." I looked out the side window, then back toward Paul. "The
whole thing is just crazy, if you ask me. Who was that Dr. Shepherd
fellow? Who were the mourners? Half of them didn't even say hello to
you—much less accompany us to the cemetery or even stick around
to say good-bye before they left. I've never seen people act so rude at
a funeral."

I was aware that I was prattling, that I sounded like a fishwife. But
I didn't care. "Were they friends of Henry's?" I pressed. "Or Silja's?
Do you think any of them knows where Silja went?"

Paul glanced at me wordlessly and shrugged.

"You knew some of those people, didn't you?" I asked. "I could tell
you did, Paul."

He drummed his fingers against the steering wheel. "You ask a lot
of questions, Angel."

"And you don't ask enough," I replied. "This is your *family*, Paul.
How can you be so disinterested?"

"Angel, does it really matter?" Paul slowed as we approached an
intersection. A police officer standing next to his squad car waved us
through.

"Yes," I insisted. "It *does* matter. It's wacky." I shivered, though the
interior of the car felt warm and clammy. "I don't like all the secrecy.
How could Silja just up and leave her child like that? I don't understand it. I want to know what happened."

Paul sighed. "I don't see that you have much choice about this,
Angel." He put on his left blinker, following the signal on the hearse.
"The police are well aware of Silja's abandonment. But what more
can they do? They've checked the train stations and the airports. If
anyone matching Silja's description was seen, or if she was traveling
under her own name, they'd know it by now. But Silja is a grown
woman. She clearly wanted to leave—and leave with no trace.

"As for Ruby," Paul went on, "she'll open up when she's ready. Surely you can see that she's not ready yet." He executed his turn and approached the cemetery gate. "I think what makes the most sense," he said, "is for all of us—Ruby included—to go back to Wisconsin as soon as we can. Once we're away from here, perhaps Ruby will want to talk more." He accelerated, staying on the hearse's tail.

I breathed a sigh of relief. It was what I wanted—to go home. I couldn't believe I was going to get it this easily.

And Ruby needed to get away from Stonekill, too. The stark reality was that Henry was dead, Silja was gone and might never return—and Ruby was in shock. She needed to be somewhere she could safely mourn her father and come to terms with her mother's abandonment.

We would take her in; I would care for her. The girl obviously had no friends her own age and little support besides Miss Wells and that odd Dr. Shepherd at the funeral.

It would be better when all of us were away from Stonekill.

The burial was at a big, sprawling Catholic cemetery beside a highway. The grounds were filled with mausoleums, elaborate statues of saints and guardian angels, and a winding maze of roadways.

Wiping tears with his handkerchief and blowing his nose, Paul spoke a handful of words over the casket as it was lowered into the ground. His voice faint, Paul wished his brother well "on his journey to the other side." I didn't know what to make of that. Paul had been raised Catholic, just as I was—we would not have been able to get married at St. Mary of the Lake if it had been otherwise—but I knew that deep down he was a nonbeliever.

"I don't mind the rituals of the Church," he'd explained to me when we first began planning our wedding ceremony. "Communion, genuflecting, even confession. All of those things, frankly, are cleansing and restorative. But I don't believe in the specifics anymore. The finality of heaven and hell. The decision to canonize certain individuals. The all-knowing authority of the pope." He'd grinned. "But keep that under your hat, Angel, or they'll show us the door before we get a chance to say our vows."

I couldn't imagine anything worse than spending eternity surrounded by hellfire and demons. But then again, I'd never had so much as a passing thought about suicide. People like Henry, I thought, people who actually went through with it, must be so far gone—mentally—that hell didn't seem like the worst possible outcome.

The thought made me weep; it was the first time I'd done so since learning of Henry's death. Miss Wells stepped next to me and touched her gloved hand to the shoulder of my coat. I knew the teacher meant the gesture to be comforting, but it felt as unpleasant as if a stranger on the bus had touched me out of the blue. Was that because of her skin color? I wanted to think better of myself, wanted to believe I'd feel the same way if Miss Wells was white.

In any case, it would be rude to step away. So I stayed still, waiting. After a moment, Miss Wells removed her hand.

"I've got to get back to school," Miss Wells said as we walked toward the cars. "Ruby, you call me, okay?"

Ruby nodded and hugged her teacher. "Thank you for coming." Ruby's voice was barely more than a whisper, but I was glued to her speech, so few and far between were words from Ruby's mouth.

No one else had said a thing to Ruby or me. As gravediggers began shoveling dirt on top of Henry's casket, the few mourners who'd come to the cemetery shook Paul's hand or clasped his shoulder, then headed hastily toward their autos. Mr. Wagner had also left, along with the hearse driver. Strangers slowly drove the winding roadways; people placed flowers on far-off graves. But except for the gravediggers and a few reporters standing off in the distance, no one was near Henry's grave besides us.

The teacher nodded toward Paul and me. "It was nice to meet you both, Mr. and Mrs. Glass," she said. "Again, my condolences."

As she started to step away, I caught her coat sleeve. "Miss Wells," I said. "Would you come over this evening for dinner?"

Shocked at my impulsiveness, I put my hand over my mouth. The invitation had slipped out before I could give it much thought. But it seemed like the courteous thing to do, the neighborly thing. To pay back, even in a small way, this woman who had been so kind to Ruby.

Miss Wells seemed taken aback. "Thank you for your generous offer," she said. "But I'm afraid that my driving alone in the night—especially in the neighborhood where Ruby's family lives—wouldn't be a good idea, Mrs. Glass."

I was initially confused but then grasped Miss Wells's meaning. "Mr. Glass could pick you up and bring you home," I proposed. "Would that be all right?" I turned to Paul. "You'd do that, wouldn't you?"

His brow was furrowed and his mouth closed into a severe, thin line. Clearly, Paul would have preferred we'd discussed it beforehand.

After a moment, he said quietly, "I could do that."

"It's settled, then." I smiled brightly at the teacher. "Mr. Glass will pick you up at seven."

26

Silja

1947–1948

Silja's first view of Stonekill, New York, was from the backseat of a real estate agent's car. They'd driven through other Westchester towns—Ossining, Croton, Peekskill. The hamlet of Stonekill was smaller than but similar to those other places—downtowns with commercial districts and aging Victorians and Tudors, surrounded by newer developments on the outskirts of town.

When she thought of the suburbs, Silja had always pictured those developments. The ones the real estate section in the Sunday *Times* showed. Advertisement upon advertisement showcasing sparkling new homes in quaint, well-planned communities.

She'd told Henry it would be patriotic to buy a new house. "All those construction workers—they're all vets," she pointed out. "What better way to support them than by purchasing a brand-new house they've built?"

Hesitantly, almost under her breath, she added, "And you could be one of those workers, Henry."

But no. No to a construction job, and no to a new house, too. It was true that Henry wanted out of Brooklyn, out of the Alku, just as much as she did—he'd never taken to the place she'd called home her entire life. He said the Finnish customs and socialist views made him uncomfortable. "Like a fish out of water," he complained. "It doesn't feel like home to me, Silja."

But unlike Silja, Henry wanted to buy an older house. He told the agent as much on the drive to the suburbs. The man said, "I have just the place to show you, Henry."

Stonekill was on the banks of the Hudson, about an hour's train ride to Manhattan. As she stepped out of the agent's car on Lawrence Avenue, Silja looked up in dismay. Built in the late 1800s, when the village consisted of nothing more than a few shops and homes, a tiny harbor, and a depot, the Victorian house had ramshackle brown trim work and cream-colored wood siding. Two sleepy-looking, tall windows looked out on either side of the front door.

Henry took one look at the house's run-down facade and exclaimed, "I can make something of that."

For the first time since he'd come home from Europe, she saw real hope in his eyes. Well. He wouldn't be building other people's houses. But if he's fixing up ours, Silja thought, at least he's doing *something*.

So she nodded and they stepped inside. By the time they'd finished touring the house—Henry marveling at every nook and cranny, every original detail that, according to her husband, "only needed a little paint and patching to be good as new"—Silja understood that this was going to be their home.

They packed their things, said good-bye to the Alku, and settled into life in Stonekill. Silja memorized the train schedule to and from Grand Central Station. She knew how to time her brisk walk through Grand Central to the subway terminal, catching the Times Square shuttle and the exact Broadway line express train to put her at her desk at precisely 8:52 in the morning, Monday through Friday.

On the train ride home each evening, she sat contemplatively in the smoker car, lighting one Chesterfield after another, reading the *Times* and glancing at the river, its waves catching the setting sun's rays. Often she had to share a seat on the crowded train, but the men—nearly all the passengers were men—were solicitous, rising to offer her a window seat if she boarded too late to secure one before they were all filled.

At the Stonekill depot she watched as her fellow commuters—a sea of men in impeccable gray, black, and brown suits—got in their cars to drive home. Like the Glasses, these men and their wives had moved to Stonekill from the city after the war. With their education and their ambition, they started over. The couples bought two cars—one the husband drove to the depot, one the wife used to get around town. From their brand-new Colonials and split-levels and Cape Cods on the winding roads in the woods, the wives drove to the grocery store and the dry cleaner's. In summer they went to the village swimming pool in their station wagons full of kids. They had dinner parties and backyard bar-be-cues; they vacationed on Long Island Sound or at the Jersey shore.

Those transplants, those cutting-edge suburbanites, were supposed to be the Glasses. They were the people Silja had dreamed of being.

As the train rumbled north, its whistle fading in the distance, Silja stood on the sidewalk. She watched the men leave—Chevrolets following Dodges following Buicks, brake lights winking at her. Then she began her lonely walk up the hill—from Station Street to Lawrence Avenue, then one block south until she reached her house.

Lawrence Avenue was so different from those quaint new developments on the outskirts of Stonekill, they may as well have been separated by country borders rather than mere miles of winding wooded roads. The Glasses' neighbors on Lawrence had inhabited Stonekill for generations. Some had never in their lives been to New York City, less than fifty miles away—a fact that astounded Silja.

Walking home from the depot on warm evenings, she encountered hardscrabble children and laundry-hanging mothers. The children ignored her; the women nodded diffidently as Silja passed. Most were of Irish or Italian descent, their houses smelling of fried fish on Fridays during Lent. The men came home drunk on payday, staggering down the street singing love songs to the women who hollered from the windows for them to shut up already and get inside.

Silja passed dilapidated house after decrepit house. When she reached home, she sighed before heading up the walkway.

Henry, in carpenter pants and a work shirt, was gritty and smelled of sweat; he showered in the evenings after his day's work was done. Every day except the very coldest ones of winter, Henry was in and out of the house and the garage. Repairing. Gardening. Painting. Little Ruby followed him like a puppy dog, with the disheveled neighborhood children also joining Henry's Pied Piper parade. He patiently answered their questions, only shooing them away when he worked with power tools or other dangerous equipment. He and Ruby spent countless hours at the hardware store in town, becoming so closely acquainted with it that either of them could tell Silja the exact aisle and bin where one could find three-eighth-inch bibb washers, one-thirty-second-size drill bits, or stainless steel structural screws in ten different thicknesses.

Henry bought a Ford pickup truck and used it to haul all sorts of odds and ends home from the village dump. Discarded furniture—highboys and bookshelves and ladder-backed kitchen chairs that he sanded and refinished. Old newspapers that he used to add insulation to the house's thin walls. A lawn mower that he refurbished, adding new blades and repainting the handle with shiny red paint.

He taught Silja to drive, and said she could use the truck on the weekends to run errands if she liked. She loathed the truck but found she enjoyed driving, which provided a freedom she didn't experience when walking or taking public transportation. Henry adored his truck and drove it everywhere. She was lucky to get it for an hour on Saturday or Sunday.

The only cerebral work he insisted on was overseeing the household finances. Silja knew she could do a better job of it—for heaven's sake, she managed dozens of business transactions every day!—but she let it go. She understood that Henry needed to control something important—something they both knew she could easily handle, but he had to prove he could, too. Well, if it made him happy, that was easier on her in the long run.

She tried to do nice things for him. In the city, she shopped for him—buying elegant, fashionable suits from Brooks Brothers, stylish hats from Lord & Taylor, wing tips from the men's shoe department at Gimbels. Of course, he never wore any of the things she brought home for him—why would he, when all he needed around the house were dungarees, flannel shirts, and work boots? Nonetheless, she relished the orderly sight of the unused masculine attire lined up in the closet. When no one else was around, Silja would bury her nose in the closet and smell the new-clothes scent. She imagined Henry wearing the clothes she'd bought, tipping his hat at her before sauntering down the street toward the train depot. In her head, she heard the happy tune he'd whistle while she waved from the porch at his retreating figure.

He all but stopped drinking—once in a while he'd have a beer on a muggy afternoon, but more often he chose the hot tea he'd always so favored. He became stronger from his physical labor. His upper body muscles thickened; his legs had the lean, athletic quality of a long-distance runner's. His buttocks were firm and his limp was gone. He was more handsome than he'd ever been. Sometimes Silja stood outside the half-opened bathroom door, peering in as he showered, admiring his taut body through the steam.

It was as close as she got to him. Though they shared a bed, they kept to their own sides. He seldom touched her. They gave each other quick hello and good-bye pecks at the start and end of the day—but that was all.

She reminded herself how hurt he'd been, the times back in the Alku when she'd pressed the issue. She wouldn't make that mistake again.

Instead, she'd continue to be patient. Things still had the chance to get better—someday.

But at times the stark realization that this might be the hand she'd been dealt, forever, would hit Silja like a speeding train. She'd have to stop and catch her breath, trembling at the thought.

27

Ruby

At home after her father's burial, Ruby feels trapped but also like she shouldn't leave. Aunt Angie puts the baby down for a nap. Uncle Paul says he's going for a walk out back. He asks Ruby if she wants to come along, but she says no. She does want to get outside, she does want to walk through her family's forest. She'd like to wind her way toward the silent, secretive cemetery behind their property—so different from the crowded place where they buried her father. Ruby would like to walk among mossy, half-sunk gravestones and listen for the faint whispers of spirits.

But not with Uncle Paul.

Uncle Paul slips through the sliding door to the backyard. After he's gone, Aunt Angie steps to the front windows and glances out. Ruby follows her gaze and sees three cars parked by the curb. People sit in them, in the drivers' seats, doing nothing but watching the birdcage.

Aunt Angie frowns. "Reporters," she says. "Wish they'd go away." She turns toward Ruby. "Can I get you anything? Can I fix you some lunch?"

Ruby shakes her head. Aunt Angie stares at Ruby as if she wants to say something else. Then she says she's going to clean Ruby's mother's bedroom and bathroom.

Ruby nods. She completely understands why Aunt Angie would want to do that. Those rooms are a mess.

She goes in her own room and lies on the bed, staring at the posters on the walls. Her mother selected the posters. When she brought them home and asked if Ruby would like them hung in her room, Ruby just shrugged and said okay. Her mother bought her records and a record player, too, one that sits inside its own leather case. Her mother would come home from her day working in the city with 45's of the latest songs on the hit parade. "Have you heard this one yet?" she'd ask Ruby, holding up Elvis and Chuck Berry records in bright paper covers. Ruby would say no, and her mother would reply, "Well, it's all the rage. You should take a listen."

Sometimes Ruby would put the records on, although she doesn't really care for popular music. But she knew it pleased her mother to hear the music and see pictures of snazzy movie stars and heartthrob-inducing singers hanging in Ruby's room. The record player and the posters are the type of thing Ruby's mother would have wanted in her own room as a girl.

They're evidence, her mother would have told herself, that her daughter is just an ordinary teen girl.

The walls in Ruby's room are watery blue, almost the exact same color as the parlor was on Lawrence Avenue. Before they moved into the birdcage, when it was finished except for painting and a few small details, Ruby's mother allowed her to choose the paint color for her room. Ruby chose this color because it reminded her of the parlor, which was her favorite room in the old house.

The parlor was the first room in that house that Ruby's father remodeled, not long after they moved in. He started with the parlor because Ruby's mother liked to unwind there in the evenings, and her father wanted to do something nice for her mother, in hopes that she'd appreciate the house if he made it more to her liking.

That was long ago, when Ruby's parents still did nice things for each other.

Ruby was only four, and back then she did everything with her father. They poured pale blue paint into flat trays. He used a roller; she used a brush. He told her that when he was a kid there was no such thing as a paint roller. It was the handiest invention he'd ever seen. "Good old American ingenuity," he called it.

Years later, in her freshman history class—quite by accident while researching famous and not-so-famous twentieth-century Canadians for a term paper—Ruby learned that the paint roller was actually invented by a Canadian named Norman Breakey. She knew better than to share this discovery with her father.

In the parlor, her father stood on a ladder and worked the top section of the wall. Ruby crouched the way little kids do, with their bottoms sticking out, and painted the lower part of the wall. Her father had covered the floors with drop cloths so they wouldn't get paint on them, even though he said it was on his list to lay carpeting someday.

Ruby remembers the gloomy olive-green color the walls were before they started, and how the blue lit up the space. She remembers beaming at her father, who looked even taller on the ladder than he did when he stood on the ground.

"Your mother will love this," he said, standing back and admiring their work.

The next day, while Ruby napped, he painted the trim a sparkling white—so pure it almost blinded Ruby when she saw it, so pretty against the blue of the walls it made her weep.

After her father put away the paint supplies, they arranged the furniture. First, they laid down a Turkish rug her mother brought home from a Saturday shopping trip—something to brighten the place, she said. It looked like an oversize flying carpet, its edges fringed in creamy white, its pattern a riot of blues and reds and greens. They arranged Grandma's old sofa, side tables, and lamps facing the fireplace.

They moved in a plush, low armchair upholstered in turquoise-blue frieze fabric—a chair Ruby's mother selected at Wanamaker's Department Store in the city. Some years later, that chair was the only stick of furniture that made the move from Lawrence Avenue to the birdcage.

The day the chair arrived, brand-new, to Lawrence Avenue, it was brought by two sturdy young men in a truck filled with other deliveries. They asked Ruby's father what company he'd served in during the war. In those days, when the war was fresh on everyone's mind, men often asked each other such questions. *Where did you serve? What kind of action did you see?* Her father's response to the furniture deliverers—as it was to everyone who asked him this sort of thing— was monosyllabic, grunting. He just told the men to turn left and bring the chair into the parlor.

It made Ruby curious. Later, she asked her mother about it. Her mother said the men asked those questions to be friendly.

"Then why isn't Daddy friendly about it?"

Her mother shook her head and didn't reply.

Ruby's father set the new chair in a place of honor by the hearth. Her mother lounged there in the evenings. Her father might light a fire if it was chilly outside. Her mother would read to Ruby while she sat on her lap. After Ruby went to bed, her mother would have a cocktail and read the newspaper. She'd relax and unwind after her long day at the office.

It was an exquisite room. Who wouldn't be happy in a room like that? Who wouldn't appreciate a house like that?

Ruby's mother *should* have been happy. Ruby and her father were happy when they lived on Lawrence Avenue.

But that was a long time ago.

28

Silja

1948–1949

During their early years in Stonekill, Ruby was the single joyous thread in Henry and Silja's relationship, binding them together as a family. As she had when she was a baby, Ruby continued to adore Silja. She greeted her mother each evening with deep eyes that begged to be looked into—the way Silja had once stared dreamily into Henry's eyes.

Silja made small, gently teasing talk with Ruby at the dinner table, relating tales of her day in the big city and asking about Ruby's day at home. Afterward, the three of them would sometimes play a game. Ruby developed an affinity for Monopoly, which initially Silja thought the girl would be too young to understand. Silja expected the adults would need to go easy on Ruby, let the child win by making foolish moves of their own. She followed this tack in an attempt to make the game fun for her daughter—and for Henry, who would only play if he had the possibility of winning. He disagreed with Silja's pushover strategy; he said Ruby needed to learn that life wasn't a series of handouts. Henry's primary goal in Monopoly was to buy the most expensive properties, which he said were the only ones that had any value. He became frustrated when, by a toss of the dice, he missed landing on a desired property and had to pay a luxury tax or go to jail instead.

Ruby, it turned out, didn't need Silja's help and easily circumvented Henry's strategy. Ruby seemed to intuitively grasp the game's objective—stay out of jail and get rich. She quietly bought up the smaller properties, acquiring monopolies and installing houses and hotels. She purchased all the railroads, often trading what seemed to be more valuable property. By the end of the game—which might last several days—Ruby often controlled the board.

When that happened, Henry stood up wordlessly and headed to the kitchen to finish the dinner dishes. Silja and Ruby would put the game away, then snuggle together in the parlor, where Silja read to her daughter—*Stuart Little, The Secret Garden, Treasure Island*. At Ruby's bedtime, Silja gently helped the child off her lap, then stepped into the kitchen to ask Henry if he'd like her to put Ruby to bed. Or, she'd offer, could she fix him a drink? His response was always a polite no. Instead, he'd take the child upstairs himself. Silja, who no longer had coffee after dinner and had given up the beer of her youth—both rituals reminded her too much of Mikaela—returned to the parlor, where she read the newspaper and drank a martini.

Alone by the hearth, Silja remembered her dreams of a large family. Those sons she'd wanted—big boys, strong and lean like Henry. These fantasies, the life she'd envisioned, now felt like something that could only happen in a movie. One in which the blond beauty costars with the dark-haired dreamboat; yet another happy-ending romantic comedy.

Her actual life bore no resemblance to those dreams. It was unconventional, completely backward to the lives of other recent transplants to Stonekill. Nor did she have anything in common with the townies who lived in her neighborhood.

And yet, their neighbors felt sorry for the Glasses! The townies didn't mind the transplants—they brought money into the local economy, with their endless need for sacks of groceries, someone to hem their husbands' slacks, bountiful flower arrangements for their dinner parties. But the Glasses—neither lifelong residents like the townies themselves nor typical transplants like the customers in their businesses—were a mystery to most of Silja's neighbors.

The children got along all right, as young children will. Henry and Silja had a party on Ruby's sixth birthday, inviting the neighborhood children. Silja didn't know the families well, but Henry was familiar with them. He could name every child at the party, whereas Silja mixed up Billy with Bobby, Sarah with Sandy. One of the mothers—Sandy's mother or Sarah's, she wasn't sure which—attempted to strike up a conversation with Silja, but it quickly fizzled once they'd exhausted the topic of how quickly the children were growing up.

It was clear, Silja thought as she sipped her martini in the evening, that the mothers felt sorry for the Glasses. Mostly, they felt sorry for *her*. She could only imagine what they said behind her back.

29

Angie

It had been a stupid idea anyway, I fretted as I set the table for dinner. For one thing, there was nothing to cook. I'd purchased breakfast and lunch essentials at the market the day before, as well as a can of chicken noodle soup that I heated and served with grilled-cheese sandwiches that night for supper. But I hadn't thought through additional evening meals. And I certainly hadn't thought through having company.

If I'd been in Baileys Harbor, it wouldn't be a problem. At home when there's a death, that family's kitchen overflows with casseroles from neighbors and parish ladies. If Henry had died in Baileys Harbor, I could've simply removed a covered dish from the refrigerator, heated it in the oven, and called it good.

Silja's kitchen held few staples. I cobbled together marinara sauce from some cans of stewed tomatoes combined with a rather ancient-looking half of an onion I found in the refrigerator and a garlic clove that was so overripe the long, green interior stem was wider than the outside meat. There was a package of spaghetti noodles, too, and these I set to boil. I found a cookie sheet, spread butter on slices of Wonder Bread, then sprinkled on garlic powder. I turned the oven to three-fifty and set the sheet aside; I'd put the bread in to brown just before we ate. Perhaps I should have used garlic powder in the sauce, too, I thought; it would have been more flavorful than the elderly clove. I set a bright green canister of Parmesan cheese on the table.

Should I serve wine? Though their food supply was limited, Henry and Silja had an extensive liquor cabinet and an ample wine rack.

Across the big room, I eyed the bar area appreciatively. I didn't drink often, but a glass of wine would taste like a little tumbler of heaven after such a day.

But no, I decided. No wine with dinner. Not with a schoolteacher at the table. Better to stick to water and serve coffee afterward. Perhaps Paul and I could have a nightcap when he returned from bringing Miss Wells home.

I peered through the front windows, watching as Paul's rental car pulled into the driveway. Just before dusk the reporters had driven away from the house; it seemed they were calling it a day. They'd be back in the morning, I suspected.

With a burst of brisk air, Paul opened the front door. The house had no formal entryway; he and Miss Wells stepped directly into the large main room. Both were silent, and Paul seemed grim.

"Miss Wells." I stepped toward them. "How good to see you again." Miss Wells nodded. "And you as well, Mrs. Glass."

I offered a glass of water to our guest. Miss Wells said, "That would be lovely," at the same time as Paul suggested, "Let's open a bottle of wine."

His words were friendly, but I noted his subtly harsh tone. I recognized it from the times I'd heard him speak similarly to a customer at the Top Deck, if it was someone Paul had to serve but whom none of the staff liked. Guests like that—irritating as houseflies—were a standard at Gordon's. Blowhards who cast dirty boxer shorts and reeking socks all over their rooms for the cottage girls to vacuum around. Arrogant, queen-bee types who spoke to the front desk clerks in disdainful tones. People of both genders who littered the beach with cigarette butts and left grimy, sandy towels in a heap beside the pool. When such guests came into the Top Deck, Paul was always cordial to them, but if I were close by, I could hear how aggravated he was.

Though Miss Wells had been nothing short of pleasant, Paul was speaking the same way as he did to bothersome guests at Gordon's. I wondered if the teacher noticed.

"Wine. How lovely, Mr. Glass. Thank you." Miss Wells smiled in his direction.

Well, then. If the teacher *had* noticed his tone, she wasn't letting on.

I said nothing. I slunk away to the kitchen while Paul fetched a bottle from the wine rack.

Miss Wells looked around. "Where is your sweet little boy?" she asked, following me and seating herself at the counter.

I smiled; it was considerate of the teacher to ask after PJ. "He's in bed. He's had a big day for such a little one."

Miss Wells nodded. I glanced at her left hand; even though she was a *Miss*, anything was possible. "Do you have children, Miss Wells?"

The teacher shook her head. "Perhaps someday." She and I watched Paul as he crossed the dining area, wine bottle and stemware in hand. "I have two sisters who each have big families. So I'm a proud aunt to a passel of nieces and nephews. But none of my own."

I nodded. "Well, that's how it was for me until earlier this year."

"How is Ruby?" Miss Wells asked. "Will she be joining us for dinner?"

Paul inserted a corkscrew into the wine bottle. "She knows you were to be here. I'm sure she'll be out momentarily. If not, I'll check on her."

Miss Wells had a melancholy look about her eyes, the look of someone searching for light in a darkened space. "This whole thing has been a terrible shock for Ruby." She accepted the glass of red wine Paul held out to her. "Thank you, Mr. Glass."

Paul didn't answer. His eyes were on the bottle and wineglasses, pouring for himself and me.

I said, "Tell us, Miss Wells. What do you know of what happened? Ruby's said nothing to us."

Paul passed a glass to me and sat down at the end of the bar. I kept my gaze on the teacher, but out of the corner of my eye I saw Paul frowning at me.

"She hasn't told me much, either." Miss Wells took a sip of wine. "She said she came home late that day—I think she was doing homework in the library after school—and expected both of her parents to be here for dinner. But neither were at home, which Ruby found strange. After she discovered her mother's note, Ruby went out searching. She found Mr. Glass just a few steps into the woods." Miss Wells nodded toward the forest behind the house.

"That's right—Ruby found him," I said thoughtfully, remembering what I'd read in Jean Kellerman's article. "Whatever made her look out there?"

Miss Wells shrugged. "My understanding is that Mr. Glass enjoyed the woods. Mrs. Glass does, too—Ruby's told me that her mother goes out there most evenings in the twilight hours, to . . . I guess one would say reconnect with nature, after a long day away from it." She glanced around. "Look at this house. Mrs. Glass worked with an architect to design it, and it's as if they built it to bring the outside in." She set down her wine. "And Mr. Glass spent a lot of time working around the yard and in the garden, from what I understand."

I turned to Paul. "Goodness, I had no idea your brother had such a green thumb."

Paul glowered at me. "Well, you could hardly say you knew him, Angie. You only met him once." He took a long swallow of wine.

Stung, I retreated to the kitchen side of the counter. I turned my back on Paul and Miss Wells, stirred the noodles on the stove, and put the bread in the oven. Then, with resolve, I spun around, smiled warmly at the teacher, and asked, "I'm wondering, Miss Wells—do you know anything about this Dr. Shepherd who performed the service?"

Miss Wells tilted her head thoughtfully. "Ruby has mentioned some fellow she's been spending time with. I've been curious. And worried—she implied he was older, not a boy, though she never said that in so many words." Miss Wells met my eyes. "I asked around after I got back to school today. Turns out Dr. Shepherd is a professor at the New York Botanical Garden. Apparently they have a graduate study program at the garden; it's run in conjunction with the biology departments of several universities in the city. Dr. Shepherd is a leading researcher in the botany field."

"Impressive," I murmured. "He didn't seem like the professor type."

Miss Wells smiled. "Well, some academics can be like that, in my experience."

"How in the world did Ruby make his acquaintance?" I was aware that Paul was still glaring at me, but I ignored him, keeping my eyes on the teacher.

Miss Wells shrugged again. "Honestly, I have no idea." She stared into her wineglass. "Ruby only talks about what she wants to talk about—as you've probably noticed."

"She seems to keep to herself," I ventured. "No friends that she's mentioned, nor any that came to the funeral."

Miss Wells sighed. "She's tried—truly, she has," the teacher told me, looking up. "Not so much with boys—Ruby has never shown a keen interest in the boys at school. But I've seen her make overtures toward other girls, trying to join their conversations. They always shut her out." Her expression was wistful. "High school can be difficult for some kids—especially girls," she went on. "Often I find the students who have the easiest time with schoolwork have the most difficult time navigating the social waters."

I nodded. The timer on the stove went off, letting me know the spaghetti was done cooking. "Dinner in just a few minutes," I said.

Paul stood, setting down his glass. "I'll go get Ruby."

I felt it was my responsibility to keep the dinner conversation flowing, since I was the one who had invited Miss Wells in the first place. I asked where Miss Wells had grown up, where she went to college. She was from the Bronx and had gone to Hunter College. "It's Mrs. Glass's alma mater, too," Miss Wells told us. "We talked about it the first time we met, and she often mentions it when I see her."

"How nice for you," I said. "To have that in common." I selected a piece of garlic bread from the basket and asked Miss Wells, "And how did you end up in Stonekill?"

There was an underlying question, I knew, and I felt sorry for it, but I didn't know how to get around it. The underlying, add-on part of the question was—*this town seems like a strange place for a Negro woman to land a teaching job. Even if half the town is poor, they're still nearly all white.*

Miss Wells seemed to understand. She pressed her lips together and took a breath. "I applied," she said quietly. "I was the most qualified candidate. So they hired me."

Goodness. She sounded so *defensive*. I didn't understand it. I hadn't even *asked* the question. So why was Miss Wells feeling like she had to defend herself?

"Miss Wells is a wonderful teacher," Ruby said—the first words she'd spoken since we sat down. "My favorite teacher ever."

Paul smiled at the girl. "We can tell," he said. "We're glad—aren't we, Angie?—that Miss Wells has been so helpful during this time."

I nodded enthusiastically, relieved to hear Paul saying something pleasant about the teacher. "So glad," I said, turning back to Miss Wells. "So appreciative. Truly, we are."

Miss Wells nodded and delicately bit into a piece of bread. "And you?" she asked. "Where are you from, Mrs. Glass?"

I smiled. "A town called Baileys Harbor, in northeast Wisconsin right on Lake Michigan," I said. "I lived there my whole life. I went to the only high school in the area—it serves about a half-dozen small communities, including Baileys Harbor. Everyone knows everyone, all over the county. Mr. Glass and I live on North Bay now—a small settlement just up New Highway Q from Baileys Harbor. And *that* highway wasn't even there a few years ago. The gravel road where our cottage is used to be the 'highway'—its real name is North Bay Drive but folks sometimes call it Old Highway Q. I use the term loosely. A few years ago the state put in an actual highway, New Highway Q. It's not a big highway like here in New York, but we still call it a highway."

I realized I was babbling, and I knew it was because I missed home so much. Thinking about it, I felt my heart ache. I quickly changed the subject, asking Miss Wells the ages and names of each of her nieces and nephews.

After dinner, Ruby asked if she could speak to her teacher alone.

"Of course," Paul said, and I was thrilled to hear sincerity in his voice.

"I'll make coffee." I stood and began gathering plates.

"Thank you, but none for me," Miss Wells said. "I do need to get home soon. I'm sorry to make it an early evening."

Paul nodded. "Let me get your coat while you and Ruby talk." He turned to our niece. "Ruby, you may take Miss Wells in your room for a moment."

When they were gone, I faced Paul. "What do you suppose they're talking about?"

Paul shrugged. "It's none of our business, Angel." He put his hands on both my shoulders. "Stay out of it," he advised. "Stop questioning so much." He removed his hands and strode to the coat closet.

I stared at his back. "Fine," I said. "It's just that . . . well, I don't like it here, Paul." In my voice, I heard the little-girl tone I hated but sometimes was unable to control.

Paul turned to me. "I know, Angel." His voice was soft, compassionate. I was grateful he didn't bring up, or even imply, that it was my own fault I was there. "We'll go home as soon as arrangements can be made." He opened the coat closet door. "All four of us."

Yes, I agreed inside my head. Once we were back home, everything would be A-OK.

I pictured my father picking us up at the airport in Milwaukee. I thought about how we'd be weary travelers, our small posse that had been through such a terrible ordeal together. We would pile into my father's roomy Buick, with Paul sitting up front next to my father, and Ruby, the baby, and I settled into the back. I would doze off, baby in my arms, as we drove the highway north. It was a long drive, four hours—but before I knew it, I'd wake up and we'd be home.

I imagined myself showing Ruby around Door County. Taking her out on North Bay in the canoe. Driving with her on the roads that wind around the peninsula over to the west side, with its soft sand beaches and marinas. Hiking in Peninsula State Park, standing on the bluffs overlooking Green Bay. Bringing Ruby to my parents' home for Sunday dinner. Getting her registered at Gibraltar High School, my alma mater. Ruby would be classmates with some of my friends' younger siblings.

It would be my job to make Ruby feel at home. I welcomed the task; I'd make the girl feel like part of the family. Part of the community.

"Yes," I said to Paul. "All four of us. As soon as possible."

30

Ruby

Miss Wells wants to know if Ruby is all right, if they're treating her okay. "Your uncle," she says. "He seems to care for you, but . . . "

She says no more. She trails off and closes her mouth.

Ruby nods. There's not much more to say about that. Ruby is sorry Uncle Paul feels about Miss Wells as he does. She's sorry he doesn't like black people.

Ruby's father didn't like them, either.

"Your aunt is a nice lady," Miss Wells says, brightening.

Ruby nods again. Aunt Angie is more than nice. Ruby thinks she might be more clever than she lets on. Aunt Angie is like a cute little mouse that scampers around the baseboards. Nobody notices the mouse has been stealing earrings, loose change, bits of tinfoil—anything bright and shiny—and hiding them away in her mouse hole in some far corner of the house.

Ruby knows Aunt Angie was snooping in her mother's room yesterday. But if her aunt found anything worth finding, she would have been more inquisitive when she peeked into Ruby's room to check on her. Instead, she'd barely said anything, just talked about washing floors.

It was a misstep on Ruby's part, not taking care of things sooner. But it's all right now. Aunt Angie won't learn any more than Ruby wants her to.

Miss Wells says, "It wouldn't hurt you to trust your aunt, Ruby. I think she means well. I think she only wants to help."

Ruby considers this. Then she says, "I think so, too."

✿   ✿   ✿

After Miss Wells leaves, Ruby sneaks out of the birdcage and heads toward the Shelter.

When she gets there, she sits on the rock. It's just Ruby—no Shepherd and no snake tonight. She lights a Camel and looks out toward the cemetery. There's a waxing gibbous moon shining onto the tops of the old, sinking gravestones.

Everything is small in this cemetery. Everything is old and simple, like Shaker furniture or those samplers you see in museums, the stitching done by little girls a hundred years ago. There are no statues or mausoleums in this place; it's nothing like the big Catholic cemetery on a busy road where Ruby's father now lies.

She pulls her knees up to her chest and hugs them close, thinking about the different ways people house their dead. Personally, she likes the idea of a mausoleum or a tomb. A little bit of space, a little air. Even if you're dead, wouldn't it be more pleasant if you had some air around you?

She smokes slowly and contemplatively, resting her chin on her knees. She doesn't attempt to move the rock. She does not consider going down into the Shelter. But she imagines what it would look like if she did.

If she were down there, she would click on the flashlight that sits on the bookshelf. She'd shiver; the concrete walls always give the place a chill, like being inside a walk-in refrigerator. There would be a musty smell, as if something might be decaying. Her father was always laying traps down there for rats and mice.

The Shelter is about twelve feet by ten. Along the far wall are two sets of bunks, made up with plaid blankets and starched white pillowcases. Below the lower bunks are long pine storage containers, designed to hold clothes and bedding. Close to the entrance, the wall is outfitted with deep shelves upon which canned food items are arranged: soup, vegetables, Spam, beans. Large tins are labeled CEREAL FLAKES and CRACKERS in her father's blocky, chunky handwriting. Tall glass bottles of water are on the lowest shelf. The top shelf holds a tidy set of white ceramic dishes, paper napkins, and a wooden box filled with silverware.

In the far corner is a small area blocked off with a plywood door, where the toilet is. It's a big metal canister with a toilet seat on the top. There are dozens of rolls of toilet paper stacked on a shelf in there, as well as a supply of heavy-duty plastic bags for lining the canister. If they were forced to spend time in the Shelter, Ruby's father would remove the sewage bags and other debris after the transistor radio gave a CONELRAD signal—the radio's antennae rose through the roof and the ground above it, a slim spike sticking out near the boulder, one that nobody would notice without looking for it—that it was safe to be above ground again.

Her father was fastidious. He thought of everything. No one can argue that.

Between the toilet area and the table is a bookshelf. Ruby has read all the books on the shelf. There are novels by Ayn Rand—*The Fountainhead*; *Atlas Shrugged*. George Orwell's *1984*. *My Life and Work* by Henry Ford. *Brave New World* by Aldous Huxley; *We* by Yevgeny Zamyatin. The shelf also has games: a board for checkers and chess, Scrabble, a deck of cards, and a cribbage board.

That's nearly all that's in the Shelter. Nothing else down there to speak about.

Sitting on the rock, the Shelter deep below her, the gravestones to the east silent and knowing, Ruby pulls her mother's necklace from inside her blouse. She rubs her fingers on the sapphire. She does it over and over, the way a person might rub an oil lamp to bring out the genie.

One who could grant Ruby a wish. One who could help her fly far, far away.

Not just to another small town, like the one where Uncle Paul and Aunt Angie live. Tonight at dinner, hearing Aunt Angie talk about her home, Ruby realized there's little distinction. In the long run, another town anywhere in the country is going to be more similar to Stonekill than different.

Ruby's wish is to be truly and completely away. To be someplace where she can live a life as unlike this one as a bendy, twisted olive tree differs from the oaks and pines towering above her.

31

Silja

1949

The last week in August, Silja saw a sign posted near the train station for a folk concert to be held at a picnic grounds on the outskirts of Peekskill. The concert was sponsored by some group called People's Artists; Paul Robeson would be performing, and Pete Seeger and others. Silja knew that many considered Robeson a Communist—and perhaps he was, but playing music and gathering on a summer evening in support of the working man didn't seem like a bad proposition.

In fact, it sounded like the sort of thing her mother would have enjoyed. With the fourth anniversary of Mikaela's death approaching, Silja had been thinking a lot about her mother—and her past. Silja hadn't been back to Brooklyn, back to the Alku, in over a year. Sometimes it was hard to remember who she'd even been before they moved to Stonekill. Her links to her youth were dissolving; Dr. Franck had died a year ago, and Silja had lost touch with Johanna and most others from her school days.

When they'd first moved to Stonekill, she assumed she'd go back often, stay connected with her roots. She and Ruby went several times—paying respects at Mikaela's grave, visiting old neighbors at the Alku. But after those few visits, Silja didn't want to go again. Brooklyn wasn't the same without her mother. The last time she went, she left in tears and vowed never to return.

The concert, however, sounded fun—a welcome diversion and a fitting way to remember her mother. She mentioned it to Henry, who scoffed at the idea. "No, thanks," he said. "They say Robeson's a Communist; did you know that?"

"Of course I know that," she replied. "But it's just music, Henry. It's just a nice time."

"Well, I don't listen to Negro music," he replied. "Or any of that folksy stuff."

He lifted his shoulders, which were brown and bare, burnished and smooth as polished wood. He'd been mowing the lawn and had come in for a break. He poured himself a glass of water and, despite the heat, put on the kettle for yet another of his ceaseless cups of black tea.

Silja watched his Adam's apple as he drank. She wanted to touch it—touch any part of him, really. But she knew better.

"But you don't mind if I take the truck and go to the concert?" she asked. "And bring Ruby with me? I think she'd enjoy it."

Henry shrugged. "Do as you wish."

The early evening was clear, though humid. Silja drove Henry's pickup truck to the picnic grounds just east of Peekskill, arriving before dusk. The road was jammed with parked cars. Silja presumed it was because of the popularity of the concert, but she soon realized the cars belonged to protesters, not concertgoers. A crowd, mostly men and older boys, lined the roadway. They waved signs and shouted at those trying to make their way into the grounds.

"What foolishness," Silja muttered to Ruby, who sat small and upright beside her in the truck's cab.

Inside the picnic grounds, rows of wooden seats were set up facing the stage. A few dozen seats were occupied. Other small groups—some men but mostly women and children—picnicked on blankets spread beside the chairs. Silja was surprised at the low turnout, but she later learned that the entrance to the grounds had been blocked off shortly after she arrived.

She and Ruby found seats near the stage. Silja pulled fried chicken, deviled eggs, and apple pie from a basket—all made by Henry, and all delectable. He'd become quite the cook since they moved to Stonekill; often Silja came home from work to find him slaving in the kitchen, concocting something elaborate for supper. She was impressed by the variety of dishes he'd learned to make—fare as simply delicious as the picnic he'd packed for them tonight, up to and including extravagant dinners like braised short ribs with garlic potatoes *au gratin*.

As she and Ruby ate their picnic, she smiled apprehensively at those nearby. There was a low murmur as they waited for someone in authority to emerge, musicians to set up, something to happen. A cluster of teenagers, black and white, sat on the stage—legs dangling off the front of the stage as they chatted and flirted with one another. Silja was pleased at how the young people got along. No racial prejudices in this environment; it set a good example for Ruby.

Still, no one shooed the kids off the stage so the concert could begin. Silja saw no sign of Paul Robeson, nor anyone in charge.

A boy came running up the road from the entrance; Silja heard him shouting but couldn't catch what he said. Most of the men, and numerous teens—both boys and girls—followed the messenger up the road.

Silja and the other women stood around, staring toward the entrance, unsure what to do. Coming here was a mistake, Silja thought. Henry was right; I have no place here, and neither does Ruby.

But it would be impossible to leave now. Henry's truck was parked by the entrance, her access to it blocked by the protesters.

The teenage girls came running back down the road. "Listen, everyone!" a tall black girl shouted, her hands cupped around her mouth. "There could be trouble. Our men and boys are organizing to fight, but in order to stay safe down here, we need everyone on the stage. Come on, now."

Silja and Ruby were herded onstage with the other women and children. Silja clutched her purse and her picnic basket, and held Ruby's hand in hers.

It felt like they were there for hours—sitting ducks—but later Silja realized it was probably no more than thirty minutes. Darkness began to descend, and from the entrance there was yelling—it was impossible to tell what was said, or by whom. Silja gathered her daughter close to her body, cradling the child's head against her waist.

Shouts came from the hills to the sides of the concert grounds, and bobbling lights appeared through the trees. Someone on the stage said the mob was coming in from the sides; a few teenage girls took off up the road to alert the men. Soon several men appeared to defend the gathering of women and children on the stage. They locked arms and stood at the front of the stage. The immediate threat dissipated; no one came down from the hills once they saw the men.

"We'll stay here, in case they come back," said a man in front of Silja.

"Do you think they will?" She felt her body shake with fear.

He turned to look her in the eye. He wasn't tall, but he was sturdily built. He wore a plain button-down shirt and dark gray slacks. His hair was salt-and-pepper. "It will be all right," he said quietly, leaning toward her. "I don't want to alarm the group here, but I'll be honest, ma'am: there are a lot of hotheaded fellows up there. I still think our boys and men have the upper hand." His look was resolute. "We have composure on our side, something an angry mob never has. It's an advantage not to be overlooked."

They waited, listening. The floodlights were on the empty seats in front of them. Then the mob was upon them, descending from the entrance, along with the several dozen men trying to defend their space. The men on the stage sprang into action, swinging down and into the mob. Silja screamed and turned her back, with Ruby pressed against her stomach. The floodlights went out—someone must have cut the generator—and in the panicky darkness, everyone pushed against everyone else. Silja's eyeglasses went flying.

It was over within minutes. Somehow, the mob was pushed back, or lost its drive, or decided it wasn't worth it. Silja turned her head and with her fuzzy eyesight, saw the mob moving back over the hill.

"It's over now," someone next to her said. "They've gone."

They were told to wait in darkness—for how long and for what, Silja wasn't sure—but she stood patiently on the stage, Ruby beside her, until police cars arrived. "Everyone just clear out," a policeman called. "It's safe now. Go home." People started moving away from the stage, organizing into groups to go home together.

Searching the stage for her glasses, Silja felt a tap on her shoulder. "Are these yours?"

Gratefully, she took the glasses and placed them on her nose. She saw it was the same fellow who'd been defending the stage earlier.

"You should take your little girl and go home now, ma'am," he said softly. "Do you have a car?"

She nodded. "I drove here in my husband's truck."

"I'll walk you to it." The man lifted Ruby and began walking silently up the hill, Silja beside him. Ruby, wrapped around the man's torso, watched Silja. The girl's eyes were large, staring at her mother over the man's shoulder.

When they got to the truck, they found its tires slashed and windshield shattered. Silja winced at the sight. Henry was going to be furious.

"My car is here," the man said gruffly. He set Ruby on the ground beside a late-model black Plymouth coupe. "Where do you live? Can I take you home?"

"That's kind of you. We're in downtown Stonekill." She slid into the seat as he held the car door open for her. He handed Ruby onto her lap.

"Did you come by yourself?" Silja asked as he swung the car around and headed down the dirt road out of the picnic grounds. The mob had disappeared. Silja marveled that so much anger could simply dissolve, like bubbles in a pot after the stove is turned off.

"I did come alone," he said. "I just wanted to hear some good music and speeches."

Silja smiled. "Me, too."

"Me, too," Ruby echoed. "Why weren't there any musicians?"

The man tilted his head thoughtfully. "Because sometimes," he told Ruby, "it's not easy for people to see eye to eye."

Silja thought it generous of him to speak to the child so candidly, as if Ruby had the wisdom of one much older than her six years. Could he tell that just by looking into Ruby's solemn eyes?

He changed the subject, asking Ruby what grade she would be

starting in the fall, if she knew her teacher's name yet, the title and storyline of her favorite book. In the darkened, cozy car, Ruby readily answered all his questions, and even offered up information he hadn't asked for. "I know how to write in cursive already," Ruby told their driver. "My mother taught me."

Silja smiled. It was true; over the summer—noticing how neat and pretty the child's printing had become—Silja began giving her lessons in cursive. It was just in fun—another enjoyable pastime for their evenings together.

"Well, that's impressive," the man said. "Your teacher will be surprised."

"She sure will," Ruby agreed. "They don't teach cursive at school until third grade, so I bet nobody else in the first grade can do it besides me."

Silja wasn't accustomed to her daughter speaking so freely, especially to a stranger. She held Ruby close and gently rubbed the child's back through her cotton blouse. Ruby snuggled against Silja's shoulder, her arm draped around Silja's neck.

In the end, Silja let him drive to town but not to her house. She asked him to let them out near the station. "We live just a few blocks away. We can walk from here."

He nodded. "I understand, ma'am."

She took a long look at him. His down-turned eyes were brown; they had the devoted, amiable expression of a dog's eyes. In recent weeks, Silja and Ruby had been learning about dogs. Ruby was begging for a puppy, and they'd checked out a library book about different dog breeds. Paging through it, they discussed the pros and cons of each breed as seriously as one of Silja's negotiations at the office.

The man seated next to her in the Plymouth had the look of a Norwegian Elkhound, or perhaps a Newfoundland. Some loyal, brave companion who would never betray its loved ones.

"You're a knight in shining armor." Silja opened the car door and set Ruby on the sidewalk, then stepped out herself. "What's your name?"

He smiled at her—a kind and grateful smile, as if she'd been the one who delivered him from danger, instead of the other way around. "It's David, ma'am."

"David." She reached across the car seat and shook his hand. "I'm Silja, and this is Ruby."

He grasped her hand and shook it firmly, then let go. "I hope to see you again sometime, Silja." He nodded at the child. "And you, too, Ruby."

The girl leaned past Silja into the car, placing both hands on the passenger seat. "You're a good man," she said to David, her voice earnest, as only the very young can authentically be. "Thank you."

32

Angie

On Saturday morning after breakfast, Paul got on the phone, attempting to book an airline flight for all of us back to Wisconsin. When he'd reserved our flight to New York, he bought round-trip tickets but left the return date open-ended. But now he seemed determined that we all go back to Wisconsin as soon as possible. "There's stability there," he said to me. "Your parents can help out. And I want to get back to my painting."

I nodded, relieved. I knew it was selfish, but I didn't care if Silja came back to an empty house. She rather deserves it, I thought. A woman runs off and leaves her child—does she expect people to roll out the red carpet when she returns?

Unless Silja . . .

No. I still didn't believe that. I didn't know where Silja was, but I was sure she had nothing to do with Henry's death.

"We should be able to leave the day after tomorrow," Paul told me as he opened the telephone book on the kitchen counter. Whistling, he rifled through the business listings in the white pages, looking for a number for Northwest Orient Airlines. Stopping on a page, he ran his long fingers over the listings, then glanced up at me.

"I think it's best to start preparing," he said, picking up the receiver from the wall telephone. "See what you can do to close up the house. Go through the food in the refrigerator and the cabinets. Throw out anything you don't think we'll use." He looked around, phone wedged against his ear. "I don't know when we—or anyone—

will be back here. We don't want the place overrun with mice; best to close it up for now, and we'll think about it later, once we're settled back in Wisconsin."

I eavesdropped on his phone conversation while I cleared the breakfast dishes. "Yes, but you see, we need to get back—" There was a pause, and then Paul, sounding agitated, said, "Yes, I understand, but it doesn't seem *you* understand . . . no . . . yes, I see what you're saying. All right. Thank you."

He set the receiver in its cradle and looked at me. "They recommended I go to a travel agent." His brow furrowed, he opened the phone book again and resumed paging through it. "There's a travel agent in Yorktown—that's not far from here—with Saturday morning hours." He wrote something on a notepad on the counter. "Guess I'll pay them a visit."

He picked up the slip of paper and stuck it in his pants pocket. "Please, Angie," he pleaded with me. "While I'm gone, don't open the door for anyone." He thumped across the room to the front window; I followed him. There were no cars parked by the street—not yet, anyway.

Paul turned to face me. "Do not open that door for anyone," he repeated. "Especially reporters."

After Paul left, the house felt strangely silent—even more so than usual. The day was dark and overcast, threatening rain. I knew I should start on the project Paul had tasked me with—clearing out the kitchen—but I couldn't set my mind to it. I carried the baby to the living room and sat on the spread-out shawl with him, in front of the cold hearth. Absently, I stroked his silken hair, crooning softly.

"Daily, daily, sing to Mary, sing my soul, her praises due . . ."

I closed my mouth, distracted by my own thoughts. Ruby had come out for breakfast—which she'd eaten wordlessly, of course, although she did take a moment to pat PJ on the head, which pleased me. But after the meal was over she retreated to her room.

Was Ruby *ever* going to talk? Or leave the house? Did she ever go to the movies, go shopping—do things that normal teenage girls did? I wondered how Ruby usually spent her weekends. Weekends when her mother hadn't abandoned her and her father hadn't just killed himself, that is.

I grimaced and inwardly chided myself. I was failing at the job I'd given myself—mothering Ruby. By now, I should have figured out a way to break through to Ruby, to become the girl's confidante. With Silja gone, I'd assumed Ruby would welcome a little coddling and nurturing from me. But it hadn't been as easy as I'd expected. I hadn't counted on Ruby rejecting every advance I made.

Well, perhaps that would change once we got back to Wisconsin. When we were on my turf, not Silja's.

I heard a door open, and I looked up to see Ruby walking into the living room. The girl seated herself on the couch. On the floor beside the baby, I felt very small.

"I heard Uncle Paul go out," Ruby said, and I noticed that her voice was barely above a whisper. Why was she whispering? No one was in the house except the two of us and PJ.

"Yes, he's gone to make travel arrangements for us to go back to Wisconsin. All of us. We think it would be best to go home and await word from your mother there."

Ruby nodded. "Aunt Angie, I need to ask you a favor."

Finally, I thought. "What is it?" I asked hungrily. "What can I do for you, Ruby?"

Ruby hesitated a moment—probably put off by my eager-beaver tone. I scooted up onto the side chair so I could look her in the eye.

The girl seemed to consider a moment. Then she reached behind her back and pulled out a small book. "I was hoping you could keep this for me."

I looked at the item Ruby held up. It was about three inches tall and five wide. Its front and back covers were fashioned from thin, brownish-green leather, the hue reminding me of the wet, moss-covered stones back home in North Bay. The book's covers and pages were stitched together with a band of matching leather on the left side; there was a snap closure on the right. Engraved into the front cover was the word SNAPSHOTS. An etching in the center showed mountain peaks, behind them a setting sun.

"What is it?" I asked, my voice as anxious as if Ruby wanted to give me a suspiciously ticking clock.

"A photograph album." Ruby's tone was brisk. I half expected her to drop the album in my lap and brush her hands against one another, the way someone might when completing a job well done. "It's my mother's photographs. Mom enjoyed photographing the house . . . " She glanced around, then back at me. "But she didn't take many pictures of people, and she didn't like pictures of herself. But in here . . . " She trailed off, looking out into the woods through the back windows. "Well, in here are some photographs of people that she'd cherish."

I sat back, the baby nestled on my lap. I had no idea how to respond to this degree of disclosure from the normally monosyllabic girl.

Ruby held out the album toward me. When the baby reached for it, I gently pushed his hands away.

"I need you to keep this safe for me," Ruby said. "Please don't open it. Don't look at the photos. Just hide it, and don't show it to anyone, not even Uncle Paul." She glanced outside again, and then back at me. "Especially Uncle Paul." She leaned forward, pressing the album into my hands.

I studied the cover. I turned the small volume over, then looked back at Ruby. "You sure you don't want to keep it?" I asked. "It seems like it should . . . stay with you."

Ruby lowered her eyelids, then opened them again. "I think it would be . . . safer . . . if you kept it."

"Is there some kind of trouble, Ruby?" I asked. "Something that would be revealed in these photographs?"

Ruby paused, and then she said quietly, "I'm asking for a favor." She stood up. "I'm trusting you with it. I trust you to do the right thing with it."

She didn't come right out and state her meaning. But I heard it loud and clear: *I trust you not to open it.*

＊　　　＊　　　＊

After Ruby withdrew to her room, I set the baby back on the floor and studied the little album in my lap. The leather cover was smooth and unblemished. The binding strap wove through two holes and tied in the front. The snap, which closed a flap over the right side of the front cover, was tarnished gold. I ruffled the cellophane pages, which seemed to number about a dozen.

My fingers itched to undo the snap and glance inside—not through the entire thing, just at a photograph or two.

But no. I wouldn't do that. Ruby trusted me. She had entrusted me with this keepsake, instead of Paul or Miss Wells or anyone else. I had to honor that.

I rose, kissed PJ on the top of his head, and told him I'd be right back. Then I went down the hallway toward the master bedroom. Ruby's door was closed, and I could hear faint music from within. It sounded like it might be Elvis singing "It's Now or Never."

I peered into the master bedroom, looking at the suitcase Paul and I were sharing, the large valise I'd borrowed from my parents for the trip. Paul and I had been living out of the suitcase, reluctant to unpack and disturb Silja's things to make room for our own. Over the past few days, Paul had dug in that suitcase as often as I had. Our underthings and tops and my stockings and Paul's socks had become a jumbled mess. Just that morning, I had marveled at it, feeling syrupy and sentimental at the sight of my items intermingled with Paul's. It showed how closely coupled we were.

But clearly, I couldn't hide Silja's snapshot album in that bag. Paul would be sure to discover it the next time he was rummaging in there.

I went down the hall to the guest room. Here, too, PJ was living out of a suitcase—for PJ, I'd packed the battered old satchel Paul had brought into our marriage. It was small, barely more than eighteen inches across and perhaps fifteen inches deep. "How in the world did you carry your entire life's possessions in that little bag?" I'd asked when we moved into the cottage after our wedding. Paul had shrugged. "I don't need much," he said. "When I started painting, I bought a separate bag for my art supplies. Clothes . . . " He'd pulled two well-worn flannel work shirts from the bag and hung them in the closet. "I don't care much about clothes."

Paul's modest-size bag had worked well to pack PJ's tiny shirts, socks, and pants, as well as a supply of clean diapers and several diaper covers. I crossed the room and knelt in front of the bag. I thrust the photograph album into the neatly folded stack of soft cotton diapers. I was the only one who changed PJ. No one else would think to look for the album among the baby's things.

33

Ruby

It's important to intercept him before he returns to the house, so Ruby slips out the window and through the woods and circles back onto Stone Ridge Road. She walks all the way down to Route 202 and waits for him on the corner. When she sees the turquoise Fairlane, she waves and he slows to let her in.

"What are you doing here?" he asks.

"I needed to talk to you away from the house," she replies.

He pulls to the side of the road and switches off the engine. He keeps his hands on the wheel but turns his head to face her, waiting.

Ruby crosses her legs, with her knees pointing toward Uncle Paul. "It's bad," she tells him. "You're not going to like it."

He nods slowly. "Okay. Tell me anyway."

Ruby presses her lips together and watches his face carefully. "I have to know first," she says. "I have to know with one-hundred-percent certainty that you'll stand by me no matter what."

Uncle Paul doesn't say anything. He takes his hands off the steering wheel and slides his palms up and down along his thighs.

Ruby reaches into the neckline of her blouse and rubs her fingers on her mother's necklace. "You're the only one I can depend on." She leans toward him and whispers, "I have a lot of money."

"Money?" She can tell he's intrigued. "What do you mean, Ruby?"

"Well, I don't *have* money," she explains. "It's not like it's hiding under my mattress. But I know where to get it." She reaches forward and touches his shoulder. "But I need someone to help me. And there's no one but you, Uncle Paul."

He opens his mouth, and she knows he's on the verge of pointing out that this is not necessarily true. She knows he wants to ask her about Shepherd.

But more than that, he wants to know what she's willing to reveal to him.

"Ruby, you can trust me," he says. "Tell me anything, sweetheart, and know that you can trust me."

34

Angie

I was in the main room, reaching down to retrieve PJ so I could get him ready for his nap, when the telephone rang. I hesitated, unsure if Ruby would answer it. I waited until it had rung four times before deciding that, in contrast to my own teenage self only a few years ago, Ruby was unlikely to dash out of her room at the sound of a ringing telephone. Ruby was not the sort to dive headlong for the phone in hopes that it was one of her girlfriends, or her boyfriend *du jour*.

I scurried to the kitchen and picked up the receiver. "Glass residence."

"Angie?" the female caller asked.

"Yes?" It wasn't my mother, or one of my sisters or friends. Nor did it sound like the principal who'd called yesterday . . . Mrs. Hawke, wasn't that the name?

"Angie, this is Jean Kellerman." Before I could respond, Jean rushed on. "I just wanted to . . . I guess *apologize* would be the right word . . . for my article in yesterday's paper. I didn't think through how Paul would react to it." She paused, and then went on, "Did he see it?"

"He did." I tried to keep my voice neutral.

"Well, I hope he didn't get angry with you. I know Paul is a very private person."

I exhaled, then asked, "And how do you know that, Jean? You mentioned something the first night we were here—about how he must remember you. And he said he didn't." I crossed the kitchen, the telephone cord dangling behind me, and poured myself a cup of water from the kitchen sink. "But clearly, you know him and he knows you." I sipped my water. "I'd really like an explanation."

"Well, some of that was mentioned in the article," Jean said. There was a pause, and then Jean went on. "Did *you* read it, Angie?"

"Part of it." I was loath to admit Paul had snatched the paper out of my hands. "I didn't get a chance to read past the first page."

I looked around, wondering what had happened to the newspaper. I hadn't seen it since yesterday morning. Paul must have thrown it out. I opened the cabinet under the kitchen sink and glanced into the waste can stored there, but didn't see any newspapers.

Jean hadn't responded. I stood up, closing the cabinet, and asked Jean if she was still there.

"Yes," Jean said. I was sure I heard misgiving in her voice. I suspected Jean wished she hadn't called—or at the very least could figure out a way to hang up without being rude to me.

"So would you explain it, please?" I pressed.

Jean said quietly, "Have you asked Paul about this?"

I admitted I hadn't.

"Well." Jean sounded relieved. "I just don't feel right, straight-out revealing something . . . personal . . . that a man hasn't shared with his wife." She paused, then went on, "But, Angie, if you're not comfortable talking to Paul, there are copies of yesterday's paper—not to mention archives of past issues—here at the newspaper office. You're welcome to come in and look at them anytime."

I didn't reply. Instead, I asked, "Why aren't you here, Jean, camped outside the house? Why are there no reporters here?" I tapped my foot. "Yesterday we were mobbed by the press, and now they've disappeared."

Jean laughed. "News develops quickly," she said. "A story broke late yesterday, down county in Yonkers, about a massive narcotics ring that the police broke up. Everyone is on that story. I'm on my way there later this afternoon."

"Oh." I didn't know what to say. "Well, that's good news for us, I guess."

PJ chose that moment to begin wailing. I glanced at him and saw that he'd fallen over and couldn't right himself. "Jean," I said. "I'm sorry; I need to go."

"Certainly, Angie. But remember what I said. Stop in anytime."

When Paul returned around noon, I was standing on a step stool, clearing out the kitchen cabinets. I had taken down all the foodstuffs from the top shelves and was working on the middle row, setting items on the counter. I looked over my shoulder when Paul came in. "What should I do with all of this?" I asked. "The cans and jars—I guess we can leave those for the time being. But things like flour and sugar and crackers and cookies—we can't leave those things here if the house will be empty indefinitely." I shrugged. "But it seems like such a waste to throw them away."

Paul shook his head. "Just toss it, Angie," he said. "Toss it all." He looked out the back windows, toward the forest. "It doesn't matter."

I gave him a long look. I wanted—desperately—to confide in him. I wanted to tell him about Ruby's request. Show him the snapshot album. Open it and together view its secrets. Discuss it and dissect the photos—whatever they were—without caring what Ruby or anyone else thought. I wanted to tell him about Jean's call, have him confess . . . *whatever* it was he had to confess.

I wanted everything out in the open, so we could move on. So we could get past all this darkness, all this mystery in Stonekill.

But my instincts told me it wasn't a good idea. At least for now, at least until we got back home, it seemed wise to keep Ruby's secrets to myself. And confronting Paul about whatever Jean had insinuated would simply make him clam up. He'd become even more upset than he already was.

It was *not* what I wanted—secrets between Paul and me.

What I really wanted—as long as I was going for the impossible, I might as well go all the way—what I really wanted was for it to be last week. I wanted to be back on North Bay—just Paul, the baby, and me. I'd even be willing to return to that terrifying moment on the water just before I grabbed PJ and brought him safely back into the canoe.

I wanted to go back to the life I used to have. The life in which, for all intents and purposes, the other Glasses did not exist.

I sighed and climbed down from the stool, brushing my hands on a dishtowel.

Paul showed me our airplane tickets. "The best I could do is Tuesday," he said. "They had nothing for Monday." There were tickets for each of us except the baby, who would sit on my lap.

I studied the tickets. Paul Glass, Angela Glass, Ruby Glass. They were in a neat little stack inside a folder marked NORTHWEST ORIENT with the airline's logo in bright red on the front. I fingered the packet lovingly, as if it were the entry form for one of the never-ending stream of jingle and slogan contests favored by my mother, who was perpetually hopeful of becoming the next lucky thousand-dollar winner.

"Ruby will need to pack," Paul said. "She should be able to bring two bags."

I thought about Silja's album, nestled safely in the baby's bag. There would be no need for anyone besides me to open that bag between now and when we were home. Once we got to North Bay, I would return the album to Ruby, to keep in the attic room we'd fix up for her.

"Can you help Ruby with packing?" Paul asked. "Maybe give her a little direction." He shivered involuntarily. Last winter, I remembered, he had continually been cold; he was so lean, and he wasn't used to the harsh northern Wisconsin winters. "She'll need to bring her warmest things."

I headed down the hall. The baby was napping, the guest room door closed. I knocked on Ruby's door. "Ruby? Can I come in?"

There was a pause, and then a muffled yes. I opened the door and stepped inside.

Other than for a quick glance the first night we spent in the house, I had not been inside Ruby's room. The walls were painted a muted grayish-blue, like the sky on a partly cloudy day. My eyes were drawn to the big casement window on the far side of the room, which looked out on the forest. A maple tree not far from the house allowed dappled sunlight to filter in.

I glanced at the bookshelf next to the window. It was filled with required reading—books that I'd also read a few years ago, in my high school days: *The Scarlet Letter*, *Pride and Prejudice*, *Great Expectations*. I smiled, thinking of Miss Wells assigning these titles.

But in addition to classics there were more recent volumes that I guessed were not only discretionary for students but probably discouraged or even banned—if not by the seemingly open-minded Miss Wells then certainly by the school board. At least, that's how it had been when I was in school and someone was caught with something like *Lolita*, *Fahrenheit 451*, or *The Grapes of Wrath*—all books Ruby had on her shelves.

Ruby was lying on the bed holding a book titled *To Kill a Mockingbird*, with her thumb stuck in the pages to keep her place. She stared blankly at me.

I explained about the airline flight, the suitcases, the requisite warm clothes. "You can bring some of those books, too, if you like." I nodded toward the bookcase. "I know it can be helpful to have a few favorite books around." I smiled, hoping to appear generous and motherly. "My parents have an extensive library," I told Ruby. "We always had a lot of books in the house when I was growing up. In the cottage where Uncle Paul, PJ, and I live, we don't have room for many books. But you'll be able to borrow anything you like from my parents."

Ruby opened her book and cast her eyes back at its pages. "Okay," she said. "I'll start packing as soon as I finish this chapter."

"If you need any help," I said. "Maybe deciding what to bring . . . "

I faltered as Ruby looked up, her dark eyes leveled on mine.

"I've got it, Aunt Angie." Ruby turned her attention back to the book, her large rounded nose close to the pages.

I opened my mouth to speak, then thought better of it. I nodded and withdrew, quietly shutting the door behind me.

I hesitated a moment, then put my ear against the door's surface. I wasn't sure, but I thought I could hear Ruby snapping her book shut, rising from the bed, and beginning to bustle around the room.

35

Silja

Silja woke the morning after the riot feeling grateful to be safe at home. Without David's rescue, who knows what would have happened to her and Ruby?

The morning papers were full of articles about the riot. People had been bloodied and injured; one man was even stabbed, though it was unclear on which sides perpetrator and victim stood. A cross had been spotted burning on a nearby hillside, but no one knew who was responsible for that act.

Reading the reports—and later, when Silja admitted to him that his truck had been vandalized and would need to be towed—Henry was shocked. His outrage was not directed at the rioters, not even at the concert organizers, but at Silja.

"How could you bring our daughter to such an event?" he asked incredulously. "Burning crosses. Vandalized vehicles. No child should be exposed to such things!"

Silja attempted to keep her calm, but she was astounded at his misplaced blame. "*You* were the one who said it was fine with you if we went," she shot back. "Or have you forgotten that part?"

He didn't reply. Instead, he strode across the kitchen, pulling the telephone book from a drawer. "I hope I can find a tow truck driver willing to work on Sunday," he muttered. Snapping the pages as he hunted the listings, he glanced at her. "That's the last time you drive my truck anywhere."

"Fine." She crossed her arms over her chest. "I can buy my own car, Henry. I don't need your crummy truck anyway."

Shaking, she left the room. How could he be so nice one day—accommodating of her desire to go to the concert, even packing a picnic for her and Ruby—and the next, so harsh?

Since they'd moved to Stonekill, since Henry had the house to occupy his time, he only occasionally lost his temper with her. But she had to admit it was happening more often lately. Just last week he'd done it, she remembered now. It was the same sort of thing; they'd had a nice dinner, and not ten minutes after it was over, he was growling at her when he discovered she'd left the back gate open and raccoons had raided the garbage bin.

But things could be worse, Silja reminded herself. At least he didn't rant and curse at her daily, like some of the neighborhood men did to their wives.

That afternoon, the truck was towed to a mechanic's shop in downtown Stonekill. Henry rode along with the driver to pick up the truck, and when he returned, his demeanor was subdued.

He let out a low whistle. "That was quite a sight down there at the picnic grounds," he said. "At least two dozen vehicles in worse shape than my truck." He reached for the teakettle and set it on the stove. "Robeson's people must have been beyond hostile—why else would those outside the grounds become so ignited? Looks like a peaceful protest that got out of hand." He turned the stove's knob, then frowned at Silja. "Those Commies are always riling people up unnecessarily. Why did they need to come to Peekskill? Why couldn't they hold their concert in the city?"

Silja put her hands on her hips. "Because the cost to use such a space in New York would be astronomical." She raised one hand to fan herself. "Not to mention the weather, of course. Who wants to go to a concert in the city when it's this hot and humid?" She shook her head at him. "The People's Artists picked the perfect location. It was the mob outside the picnic grounds that was out of control—not the organizers or the concertgoers."

Henry gave her a long, skeptical look. "Those American Legion folks, they're reasonable men. They wouldn't have started something without provocation."

"Trust me," Silja said. "They did exactly that."

"Well, you'll never convince me," Henry said.

The kettle whistled and he shut off the burner. He poured boiling water into his cup, then turned back to Silja. "Either way, from the look of things you were damned lucky to get out of there with your necks," he observed. "How did you manage that, anyway? You never said."

A lie came easily to her. At the concert, she told Henry, she'd run into the beau of an old classmate from Hunter. "He gave us a ride home," she said. "Such a nice man." She turned to her daughter, who was seated at the kitchen table, eating a snack of grapes and a cookie. "Isn't that right, Ruby? A nice man Mother knew gave us a ride home."

Ruby nodded solemnly. Silja wasn't sure if it hadn't registered with the child that David was a stranger, or if she was well aware that he was, but was safeguarding Silja's lie.

A second concert was scheduled for the following weekend. Henry strictly forbade Silja from going, even without Ruby.

He needn't have worried. She had no intention of getting involved in that foolishness. In retrospect, she realized the reason for organizing the first concert hadn't been the music; calling it a concert merely provided a vehicle for the Robeson crowd to raise funds in a large country setting. She was disappointed but thankful she and Ruby had come to no harm.

Silja was no revolutionary; such activities didn't interest her. The day of the next scheduled concert, she went to the movies instead.

That fall they bought a car for Silja, a brand-new Buick sedan. It was large and clunky, with a nondescript gray body. She'd hoped for something sportier, but Henry insisted on the Buick. "It's dependable and well built," he said. "It's the kind of car I want you driving. If you and Ruby are going to be out on the roads, I want you both safe."

Silja sighed and gave in. She didn't expect to drive the car much, so it didn't really matter what it looked like. The Buick sat in the driveway all week long; she still walked to and from the train depot daily. But at least she no longer had to borrow Henry's ugly old truck on Saturdays and Sundays just to run errands or go to the movies.

In the spring of 1950, Henry's brother, Paul, sent word that he was coming for a visit. It was the first time he'd ever done so.

"How is it possible he's never visited us before?" Silja asked as they waited at the Stonekill depot for Paul's afternoon train from Manhattan. "I thought the two of you were so close."

Henry shrugged, the cool breeze off the river pulling at his hat. "Paul marches to the beat of his own drummer. You can't make him do anything he doesn't want to do." He pushed the hat back on and looked south down the tracks, his eyes on the arriving train. "And generally he only wants to do what suits his own needs."

As Paul stepped onto the platform, Silja was taken aback. "Are you sure you're not twins?" she asked after Henry introduced them. "Or am I seeing double? It *is* April Fool's Day. Are you two playing a trick on me?" She looked questioningly into Paul's dark eyes. The medal on a heavy chain around his neck—showing the image of a man carrying a child across a shallow body of water—caught the thin, late-day sunlight. Silja stepped away from its glare.

Paul's hearty laugh warmed the gusty afternoon. His smile reminded her of how Henry used to look when he laughed. It made her wistful, thinking about how seldom Henry laughed anymore.

Clasping Silja's hand, Paul assured her there was no trick. "Henry and I are our own men," he told her.

Nonetheless, Silja couldn't help marveling at the family resemblance. Even walking back from the station, the brothers sauntered next to each other with an identical stride. Ruby trotted back and forth between them and Silja, who walked briskly ahead. She kept turning around to see if they'd caught up, but each time she did, it seemed like they'd fallen farther behind.

✿   ✿   ✿

Henry's latest project was laying wall-to-wall carpeting over the wooden floors throughout the house, which had been scratched and worn since they'd moved in. Silja knew she complained excessively about the floors, but she couldn't stand how shabby they looked. "Let's just cover them up," she'd suggested time and again. "Let's just pick out some nice carpeting and be done with it."

Finally, Henry agreed—but only on *his* terms. Other people would simply go to a carpeting shop, select what they wanted, and arrange for delivery and installation. But not Henry. He bought remnants from a distributor; he said if each room had carpeting that fit baseboard to baseboard, and as long as the pieces complemented each other where they met in hallways and doorways, it would look fine. He would install the carpeting himself, with Paul's help.

Early the Monday after Paul's arrival, he and Henry climbed into the pickup truck, ready for a trip across the river to fetch the carpeting. Ruby, on vacation from school for Easter week, tagged along.

Silja watched as Henry turned the engine and the old truck roared to life. He reversed out of the driveway and drove into the dewy daylight—Ruby seated between the brothers on the bench in the truck's cab, Paul's arm thrown casually but possessively around her thin shoulder.

Silja saw Paul and Henry turn toward each other and laugh, and her first thought was that they were probably laughing at her.

In truth, however, she doubted it. Paul's gesture when they met had been warm, after all. And it was rare for Henry to be deliberately cruel to her. More often, he simply ignored her.

She turned away, biting her lip, and began her brisk ten-minute walk to the station.

Lately, Silja had begun to think about starting over.

She didn't know why it hadn't occurred to her before, but in truth she *could* leave if she wanted to. She could walk away from Henry and this gloomy little town. She could take Ruby and go west. Los Angeles. Silja imagined being warm all the time. Movie stars strolling down the street. Everyone driving a brand-new car. She'd enjoy living in a place where everyone had a brand-new car. She would get one herself, a convertible. On the weekends, she and Ruby would drive to the beach and swim in the Pacific Ocean. They'd get the dog they still talked about, but Henry didn't want. Nothing oversize or slobbery— just a small dog, a pug or a Yorkshire terrier.

Silja could take her daughter and leave. She truly could! She knew she had no grounds to divorce Henry. The only permissible reason she could use to get a divorce in New York State was adultery. And, of course, Henry being Henry, that was out of the question.

So if she did it—if she left—she would have to simply run. She'd have to leave without warning, taking Ruby, and running off in secret, hoping Henry wouldn't attempt to find them.

And would he? Silja wasn't sure. He always said marriage was forever, come hell or high water. And certainly he adored Ruby beyond all measure.

But sometimes she wondered if he had more affection for the house than he had for either of them. If he might just let them go and stay in Stonekill by himself. Alone in that awful old house—his mistress, that's how she'd come to think of the place.

So why not do it then? Why not run?

Well, she thought—maybe she would. Maybe one of these days that's exactly what she'd do.

36

Ruby

Ruby is waiting for them to go to bed. She opens her door and slips down the hall, watching Uncle Paul and Aunt Angie from the shadows. He's pacing the living room rapidly, nervous as a feral cat. Aunt Angie is sitting on the sofa watching television—*Bonanza*, it sounds like, or some other silly thing that has nothing to do with real life.

Ruby touches her toe to the carpeting, tracing the chevron pattern. She's never liked this carpeting, which is everywhere in this house. She despises its orderliness. There have been studies proving an overabundance of zigzags makes people feel unhinged. Ruby is certain this is true.

In their old house the carpeting was an array of patterns and colors—wild as a jungle, colorful as a collection of worldwide flags. The carpeting in Ruby's bedroom was blue-green; in the hallway it was burnt orange. Uncle Paul said those colors contrasted on the color wheel, and that's why they looked so good next to each other. The week Ruby's father laid the carpet remnants, Uncle Paul was visiting. It was his first time coming to Stonekill, and he helped her father with the carpeting.

Uncle Paul was the only person who could get her father to talk about certain things. Like the war. That week when Uncle Paul visited was one of the few times Ruby heard her father talk about it. He didn't go out for beers with the men around town, like the fathers of her classmates. They all went down to Murphy's Tavern in the evening, stumbling home late, because those who lived in that rickety neighborhood at least had the advantage of being able to walk to and from a bar. Ruby's father, who did appreciate a cold beer now and again but was hardly a drunk, scoffed at this. "Fools," he said when he saw them. "Can't control themselves."

Ruby's father was in control. He never let his emotions get the best of him.

Well, almost never.

She remembers their drive across the river to fetch the carpeting. They took Route 202 to the Bear Mountain Bridge and crossed there, then turned south toward Haverstraw.

With the long drive, there was plenty of time to talk. The men talked and Ruby listened, because that's what she's always been good at, listening. Uncle Paul told them about being an airman in the Pacific. He talked about his pilot training in Utah and Idaho—about how he thought he "knew the West like a well-worn suit"—but then he flew above it and learned a runoff-swollen river as seen from the sky covers thrice the land he thought it did when he stood on its banks.

There was a lot of waiting, he said. "People think of war like it is in the movies—action, action, action, all day long. But we sat around a lot of days, waiting for orders." Ruby's father nodded in agreement, and Uncle Paul continued. "Heck, some of the guys never saw action at all. One time up in Idaho, a training plane went down. Crashed right into the Kootenai River. Poor fellas died before leaving the US of A."

He contrasted the northwestern United States with the smoke-ruined islands of the South Pacific. "Surely, they must have once resembled a string of emeralds," he said. "But by the time I got there, most of them were nothing more than rubbled acres of burned-black trees and the carcasses of pigs and dogs. Not a bird to be seen in the sky or on the shores. They all died, or else flew off in search of safe haven. I'm not sure which."

Unlike when the men in town told their war stories, Ruby's father didn't criticize Uncle Paul for remembering the war. "He doesn't re-hash the same old things, just over a different beer, night after night," her father explained to her once. "He describes a different scene every time." Her father's eyes warmed as they only did when he spoke about his brother. "Paul," her father said, "is a different fellow entirely from those men in town."

In return for Uncle Paul's stories, her father opened up to Uncle Paul in ways he didn't with other people. On the drive to Haverstraw, he told Uncle Paul that when he was in France, he rubbed out a German by pushing him off a cliff. "The enemy was wounded and didn't have his gun," her father said. "But I had mine. I could have filled that Kraut bastard with lead, but there was something more satisfying in landing a solid kick in his gut and watching his body fall fifty feet. Fathead screamed until he hit the rocks below."

He paused, and then said, "Sometimes, I still feel guilty about it. As if it wasn't fair of me to kill an unarmed man that way."

Uncle Paul shrugged. "Bastard had it coming," he said. "And even if he didn't, it's a dog-eat-dog world." He looked at Ruby's father and said, "If the tides were turned, Henry, he would have rubbed *you* out. You always—*always*—have to look out for number one."

Finally, Aunt Angie turns off the television set and they head to Ruby's mother's bedroom. Ruby has long since retreated into her own room, so when Uncle Paul opens her door and checks on her, she's lying in bed reading. She looks up and tells him she's going to go to sleep soon.

"You do that," he says, opening the door a bit wider, like he wants to come in her room.

But he doesn't. From the doorway, his eyes meet hers. "It's going to be all right, sweetheart," he tells her. His voice is gentle and she's grateful for that.

She nods, and Uncle Paul says, "Get your rest, Ruby. I'll see you in the morning."

"I'll see you then," she says, making her voice sound sleepy. She turns off her bedside lamp and pulls the covers up to her chin, as if she's ready for sleep. Uncle Paul closes the door with a soft click.

But of course she's not ready for sleep. Once the house is dark and still, she slips through her window and out of the birdcage.

✿   ✿   ✿

Very late at night, when it's cloudy and darker out than it's been yet this autumn or any autumn in her memory and there's fits-and-starts drizzle falling, she finds her way back in the slick, rain-glistened woods until she gets to the rock. And there she meets Shepherd.

He's in a wool sweater over a collared shirt, with his hat low on his forehead like he always wears it. She takes out her Zippo, igniting it and holding the flame up to Shepherd's face. There's water on his cheeks and she doesn't know if it's rain or tears.

"Are you all right?" she asks him.

He nods and says, "Seeing you, Ruby, brings up so much emotion in me."

She closes the Zippo and puts it in her pocket. She shivers and he looks at her with concern. "This weather," he says. "You're freezing."

He pulls off the sweater and places it on her shoulders. She ties its sleeves across her collarbone, then wraps her arms around Shepherd's neck, laying her head against his chest. He puts his powerful arms around her back, and she lets herself rest there for a moment before stepping back and looking him in the eye.

"What did they mean at the funeral?" she asks. "When those people said you didn't belong there—what did they mean?" Her eyes search his. "I know what it *wasn't* about," she says.

He nods but doesn't speak.

"Is it about this, then?" Ruby reaches into her patchwork bag and pulls out a crumpled newspaper. She unfolds it and holds it up for Shepherd to see. Its date was a few weeks ago. The top of the page has the word OPIN-IONS in large, bold letters that become smudged as raindrops hit them. She can see Shepherd's eyes go right to the editorial letter titled, "What's Wrong with the John Birch Society? In a Word: Everything."

There is no need for him to read it. Surely, he's familiar with its contents.

"You wrote that, didn't you?" Ruby asks.

"Well, Ruby, it's my name right there at the end, in black and white." Shepherd's voice is subdued.

"My father was furious about this," Ruby says.

Shepherd nods. "I'm not at all surprised."

Ruby doesn't answer. She takes a step away from him.

He reaches out and touches her shoulder. "Ruby, I've never kept it secret who I am," he says. "Not from you. Not from . . . anyone."

She turns to look up at him. "You promise me?" she asks. "You promise me there were never any secrets?"

"There were things that were not discussed," he tells her. "But never any secrets and never any lies."

She believes him. She steps back into the circle of his warmth and puts her arms around his neck again. She feels like she could stay there forever, but of course she can't.

"Thank you for meeting me tonight," she tells him as they break apart.

"You know I'm here anytime you need me."

She explains about the airline tickets, the plan to leave for Wisconsin in a few days. She speaks of other things, too. Things Shepherd needs to know.

She goes on for a long time. She's talkative, in the way she is only with Shepherd.

Finally, it's time to part. She begins to untie the sweater from her shoulders, but he puts up his hand to stop her. "You keep it," he says softly.

Shepherd retreats over the stone wall to his car. Ruby hikes back through the woods to the birdcage.

37

Silja

August 1950 marked the one-year anniversary of the Peekskill riots. Reading newspaper articles commemorating the anniversary, Silja thought about David. What would have happened if he hadn't been there? She was loath to think about it.

Silja hadn't seen him since that night. She caught herself looking for him sometimes—at the train station, running errands on the weekend, going to concerts and performances at Ruby's school. She'd play out scenarios in her head, thinking about what it would be like if they caught each other's eyes across a crowded train platform or a busy street.

She knew that running into him was unlikely. She didn't know where he lived, his last name, or anything else about him. And yet she continued to daydream.

In October, Silja started a new job as manager of food operations at the Rutherford Hotel in midtown Manhattan. She was courted by the Rutherford. They knew her from Littleton Foods; she'd worked with the old manager for years. When he announced his impending retirement, the boss called Silja for an interview. The job was securely hers that afternoon.

Her position at the Rutherford paid better and was more prestigious than her work at Littleton had been, but it required longer hours. She began taking an earlier train to the city—6:36 a.m.—and often the 6:10 p.m. home. She rarely saw Ruby. But Ruby understood that a mother has to do what a mother has to do. Ruby was compliant, like Silja herself had been as a child. The life Silja had grown up living in the Alku—the life she shared with Mikaela—was simply her life. There were no choices offered, and even at a young age, Silja knew her best bet was to help her mother and to grow up as well as she could. Ruby was the same type of child.

Around the time Silja started working at the Rutherford, Henry sent away for information about a correspondence course in crime detection. The advertisement promised he could learn to be a private investigator "at home in his spare time"—a phrase that made Silja smile grimly when Henry showed it to her; spare time was something Henry had in spades. The correspondence school sent him a slim volume titled *The Blue Book of Crime*, which he pored over until it was dog-eared. He decided to enroll in the full course, which came in the mail one assignment at a time, along with a fingerprinting kit and other materials. After Henry finished and returned each assignment's exam, another assignment arrived. All told, there were sixty-eight assignments, which the school said could be completed in just over a year.

But Henry took much more time than that—performing the steps in each assignment several times, reviewing the exam until he felt sure it was perfect. He said if he was going to be slipshod about it, it wasn't worth doing at all.

Silja sighed, but didn't protest. In the city—in her new job, as she met colleagues and forged new professional relationships—she was vague when asked what her husband did for a living. She changed the subject as quickly as she could.

Two months after she started her new job, Paul returned for another visit, and he and Henry once again set about cavorting, tinkering, and in general acting like two retirees instead of two young men in their prime. Ruby gamboled happily around the two of them. Silja kept her mouth shut, her head down, and her feet walking toward the train depot. She spent as much time at work as she could.

And then, as she began to think Paul was wearing out his welcome, he announced that he'd be staying in Stonekill, but not with them. "I . . . um, someone else has offered hospitality," he stammered.

It turned out that the principal at Stonekill High School had been carrying on with Henry's brother. She was a divorcée in her mid-thirties. Paul told Henry and Silja that he and the principal had met last time he was in Stonekill, struck up an interest in one another, and stayed in touch.

Her name was Mrs. Hawke. What sort of name is *that*? Silja wondered. And if one was saddled with such a name, wouldn't one go back to one's maiden name after a divorce? Silja would.

Mrs. Hawke was short, plain, and dumpy. Silja couldn't understand what Paul saw in her. She had glimpsed Mrs. Hawke around town, and she knew the woman lived in a cottage toward the outskirts of town, not far from one of the new housing developments. She drove a dark green Studebaker that predated the war. She had a golden retriever; Silja had seen her walking it about town.

The night before Mother's Day, they had Paul and Mrs. Hawke over for dinner. When Paul introduced them, Silja called her Mrs. Hawke and she said, "Please—it's Kristina. With a *K*."

Silja raised her eyebrows, but said nothing.

Earlier in the day she'd suggested to Henry that he make something elegant—*coq au vin*, perhaps, or *sole meunière* with sautéed mushrooms and capers. He was perfectly capable of preparing such dishes, but for this meal Henry insisted on casual fare. He dragged the Weber grill from the garage onto the dilapidated brick patio out back. (Rebuilding the patio was on his endless list of "someday" household repairs.) He flipped hamburgers and served them with potato salad and grilled vegetables. Silja scowled but let it go, opening one of her best bottles of Cabernet and passing generously poured wineglasses around the rusty metal table—the table that wobbled on the bricks no matter which way Henry turned it

"Do you cook, Silja?" Kristina asked. Although not yet six o'clock, it was dark under the two oak trees that dominated the backyard; they were already leafed out due to an unusually warm spring. Mosquitoes nipped the women's bare arms; Henry lit a thick candle to chase them away.

Silja shook her head. "I'm in the food business, but I don't cook often," she admitted. "Henry is the chef in the family."

Kristina nodded. "Well, it's certainly delicious."

It actually wasn't his best. The distraction of someone new at the table seemed to cause Henry difficulty timing the meal. The burgers were past well done and the vegetables were nearly raw. Yet, no one lifted a finger to help Henry—which, Silja realized later, was rather ungenerous of them.

Picking at her meal, she wondered: When did she become so critical of her husband? Now that she'd all but given up the dream that Henry would ever do anything meaningful with his life, did that suggest she'd settle for nothing less than househusband perfection?

Over the course of the evening, Silja drank more wine than she normally would. But so did Kristina. With a loosened tongue, Kristina told Silja all about herself. She'd graduated from Barnard—the college Silja had dreamed of attending but couldn't afford, having been turned down for a scholarship there. Kristina graduated several years before Silja finished at Hunter. She, too, had married during the war—but the marriage was childless. Mr. Hawke returned from Europe and they had remained together for a few years before going their separate ways.

Kristina shrugged. "Not meant to be," was all she said. "Guess I was waiting for this fine gent instead." She shone her eyes at Paul.

Silja found this amusing—more, she was sure, due to the wine than the actual entertainment value. She felt herself becoming more generous in her opinions. Perhaps it wouldn't be so bad after all, Paul shacking up here in Stonekill.

Kristina and Silja compared favorite actors and movies—Kristina was a Gary Cooper fan, and Silja still adored Cary Grant. They agreed that some weekend afternoon they would see a matinee together.

The evening ended late, long after Henry put Ruby to bed. After

Paul and Kristina drove away, Henry and Silja silently climbed the stairs. She felt dizzy and tired, and fell into bed without saying good night to her husband.

The next day was Mother's Day. "I don't understand the reasoning behind a 'holiday' like this," Henry said as he began washing the breakfast dishes. "Especially for someone like you, Silja. You already have a nice dinner waiting for you every night. You already spend your weekends relaxing. Every day is Mother's Day, isn't it?"

Silja sighed and picked up the Sunday *Times* from the kitchen table. Wordlessly, she headed to the parlor.

At least Ruby made her a card at school, which Silja placed on the mantel and looked at frequently throughout the rest of the day. *Happy Mother's Day to the best mother in the world.* Did Ruby decide on that wording herself, Silja wondered, or did the teacher encourage every child to write such a sentiment?

Thinking back on the evening with Kristina Hawke, Silja had mixed emotions. It was fun at the time, but now she felt embarrassed to have actually hit it off with a divorced high school principal living in sin with her frivolous brother-in-law. Wasn't such a relationship beneath her? Surely she could find someone more suitable with whom to strike up a friendship.

But who? Mentally, Silja scanned the names of women she knew in town—from the blue-collar mothers in her neighborhood to the snooty members of the local country club. She shook her head. She didn't have anything in common with any of them. At least Kristina liked movies.

In June, she and Kristina were finally able to arrange a movie date. They saw *The Prowler*, with Van Heflin and Evelyn Keyes. It was a dark story about a cop who fell in love with a married woman and went on to kill her husband, falsely proclaiming self-defense. He married the woman and they ran off together, but then she found out he was actually her first husband's killer. To complicate matters, she was expecting the cop's baby. It all ended rather gloomily, with the pair split up and the cop shot by a sheriff's deputy as he tried to escape his past and his own crimes.

Kristina watched silently, munching on popcorn, while Silja nibbled licorice. After the credits rolled by, they turned to one another. "Well," Kristina said. "Every man certainly has his dirty little secrets."

Silja gave her a look that Kristina must have thought odd, because she smiled and told Silja it was all right. She patted Silja's hand. "Dirty little secrets are not the end of the world," she assured Silja. "If you consider how many people there are on this planet, living most of their lives behind closed doors with who-knows-what going on behind them—if you think about that, you realize your own secrets might be rather tame in comparison."

Was that true? Silja often thought of her own situation as being a no-win predicament. But perhaps everyone else had worse problems than her own.

They saw a few other movies after that, and several times that summer Kristina and Paul came for dinner. But by October, Silja sensed a cooling in Kristina's attitude toward her. She didn't return Silja's calls and never initiated contact with Silja herself. When Silja swallowed her pride and asked Henry to ask Paul about it, Henry reported that Paul told him Kristina was buried in work since the start of the school year.

How humiliating, Silja thought. How humiliating to have attempted to form a friendship, and to be rejected—moreover, by someone who was nearly as much of an oddball in this town as Silja was herself.

She tried to shrug it off, but it made her feel lonelier than ever.

On the blustery, cold afternoon of New Year's Eve, 1951—the day before Ruby's ninth birthday—Paul showed up on their doorstep. He was there, he said, to tell them good-bye. "I have to move on," he said as he stood on the porch with a suitcase at his feet. "My train leaves in twenty minutes. I'm not welcome here anymore."

"Paul." Henry moved forward and clasped his brother on the shoulder. "You know you're always welcome here with us."

Paul shrugged. "I made a mistake," he said quietly. "I shouldn't have . . . gotten involved here. I wanted Stonekill to be somewhere I could come back to anytime. And now . . . " He looked around helplessly. "Tell Ruby I said good-bye, won't you?"

Silja felt her lips press into a severe line. "She and Sarah went to the O'Briens' place to play with their girls." She nodded over her right shoulder. "It's just at the end of the block. You could go say good-bye yourself."

Paul's face held alarm. "No, that wouldn't . . . I don't want to interrupt her playtime." He looked away. "And I don't want to knock on a stranger's door."

"Don't be silly," Silja pressed. "You know who the O'Briens are. They're the family with all those girls. Didn't Kristina pay their oldest daughter to walk her dog a couple of times?"

Paul shook his head. "I don't know anything about that. And besides, I need to head out. I don't have time to go down there right now."

How unkind of him! Silja couldn't believe it. She looked at Henry, who shrugged and held out his hand to Paul.

"Best of luck to you," he said. "Stay in touch, old pal."

Paul nodded. "I'll do that." He picked up his suitcase and stepped off the porch into the dim, frosty afternoon.

Henry went back to his project—sanding the newel posts and stair railings in preparation for restaining—but Silja stood in the doorway, watching Paul hurry down Lawrence Avenue and disappear around the corner toward the train station.

She was in shock. That he couldn't even say good-bye to Ruby—and on the day before her birthday—was beyond Silja's comprehension. It was the ultimate in selfishness.

Something must have happened, she thought—something more serious than the garden-variety breakup of a romance. But she didn't know what it could be. Did Henry know? She couldn't tell whether he did or not.

✢　　✢　　✢

Later that evening, after Ruby was in bed—crying herself to sleep over Paul leaving—Silja sat Henry down and told him that she wanted to start searching for a new house. "We can't stay here," she said. "I cannot stay in this house, in this little town, for one more second. I want what *I* want, Henry. I've worked hard and I've earned it. And Ruby has, too."

His eyes were downcast, and she was sure he'd caught her insinuation—she and Ruby had earned it. But he had not.

But was that fair? He had paid dues that she'd never understand. He'd fought in a war. He almost lost his life. He lost parts of himself— inside and out—that he could never get back.

So she gentled her voice. "It's for *all* of us," she said. "It will be a fresh start for the three of us. You'll see."

He looked up then, and she could see the musing in his eye. "Can I *build* you a house?" he asked. "Would you let me build your dream house for you, Silja?"

She remembered how she'd wanted him to get into construction work years ago, when they first moved to Stonekill. She was touched by his sentiment, but things had changed since then. She didn't want a prefab house that looked like everyone else's. Nor—though she appreciated his homegrown skills—did she want Henry to spend years fiddling around, building her some shabby version of what he thought a "modern" house should look like.

So she shook her head firmly. "No," she said. "No, I would not let you do that." She took a breath, and then went on, "If you want to get a job, Henry, and *pay* for the house to be built—fine. But you can't build it yourself. I want it done right."

His eyes registered shock, then anger. He stood and left the room without another word.

38

Angie

The knock on the front door was so insistent that I was sure Paul and Ruby, who were both still sleeping, would awaken. PJ had had an atypically fussy night, and at six-thirty in the morning, I rose for the third time, put on my dressing gown, and fetched the baby from his makeshift crib in the guest room. I warmed a bottle and sat with PJ in one of the low-slung easy chairs by the hearth, the blue and green shawl wrapped around my shoulders. With my back to the front windows, I watched dawn break on the trees behind the house.

When I heard the knock, I turned my head and stood. I shrugged off the shawl, pulled my robe tightly around my middle, and stepped to the front door, babe in arms. I peered through the big glass windows. Over the expanse of lawn, I spotted two police cars, both with New York State Troopers emblems on their side doors, parked in the driveway.

Silja, I thought instantly. They've found Silja.

My heart creeping into my throat, I opened the door. Two officers stood on the flagstone step. "We're sorry to bother you so early, miss," one of them said. "Is there a grown-up at home?"

I raised my eyebrows at him. "I'm a grown-up." They were the first words I'd uttered since rising from bed; much to my dismay, they came out as squeaky as if Minnie Mouse had spoken. I cleared my throat and added, "I'm twenty-one."

The officer nodded. "Okay. Can we come inside?"

"What's this about?" I snuggled the baby closer to my chest. "Have you found Mrs. Glass?"

The officer shifted uncomfortably. His gold name tag was etched B. HILL. "That's not why we're here." He paused, then went on, "We're here to bring in Miss Ruby Glass. We want to question her about the death of her father."

"Ruby . . . ? What?" I shook my head. "I'm sorry; I don't understand."

"Miss, could we come in?"

I eyed Officer Hill. "It's Missus," I told him. "Mrs. Paul Glass."

He opened his mouth to say something, and then closed it, his lips making a thin, firm line across the horizon of his face.

The other officer—younger, appearing not much older than me—stepped forward. "Please understand, Mrs. Glass," he said gently. "Miss Glass is not being accused of anything. We just want to ask her some questions."

I glanced at his name tag, too: R. BRENNAN. "Didn't you question her right away?" I asked. "When Henry died, didn't you talk to her then?"

Officer Brennan nodded. "We did," he said. "But circumstances . . . the situation . . . has been altered." He looked upward, then back at me. "Further information has come to light, and we'd like to talk to Miss Glass about it."

"You *have* found Silja!" I heard the relief in my own voice. "Thank God."

Hill glared, and Brennan turned red. "Ma'am, we can't say anything more," Brennan stammered. "Would you let us in, and let Miss Glass know we're here?"

I stood still for a moment, and then I stepped aside and let the officers into the house.

I went to the master bedroom. Leaning over my husband, I whispered fiercely in his ear, "Paul. Wake up." I gently nudged him on the shoulder. "I need to tell you something."

He opened his eyes, staring at me fuzzily.

"Paul," I said urgently. "The police are here. They want to talk to Ruby."

Paul sat up, instantly alert. "Tell me everything."

After I told him, Paul rose from the bed, pushing me aside. He slipped into a pair of trousers and buttoned a shirt, making me feel half-naked in my cotton robe and thin nylon nightgown. I set the baby carefully in the center of the bed and quickly dressed, putting on stockings, hooking myself into a bra and girdle, and topping my underthings with a wool skirt and a beige sweater. I stepped into a pair of black flats. Paul was right: being dressed was better. I already felt more in control.

"I'll get Ruby," Paul said. "You better offer them coffee."

Hill and Brennan refused the coffee, though they did sit in the living room when I asked them to. Paul conferred with them quietly, the three men seated around the hearth, while I, still holding the baby, hung in the shadows near the kitchen. Ruby was yet to emerge from her bedroom when all three stood up.

Paul walked over to me. "I'm going with them," he told me. "I'll call you as soon as . . . whenever I know anything."

"What about Silja?" I whispered. "Do they know anything more? Did they tell you anything?"

Paul looked away from me, toward the sliding door to the woods. "There's no news on that front, Angel." He glanced at the officers again. "Let me check on my niece," he called to them across the room. "I'm sure she's almost ready to go."

Paul returned with Ruby, who shuffled out in a pair of baggy slacks and a too-large gray pullover sweater that I was sure must have belonged to Henry. Her hair was drawn into a messy ponytail.

Paul gave me a long look, one that I had trouble deciphering. Was he trying to tell me something? I shook my head at him and frowned. If he was trying to say something nonverbally, I wasn't getting the message. I was more frustrated with myself for not getting it than I was at Paul for attempting to convey it.

Then, after the others were outside and I was starting to breathe a sigh of relief, Officer Brennan turned around to face me.

"Is it all right if I have a look around, ma'am?"

"A . . . look around?"

"Yes, I'd like to look in Miss Glass's room, and just around the house a bit."

"Do you . . . is there a search warrant?" I didn't know much about scenarios like this, but I'd seen enough episodes of *Dragnet* to know that the officer should have a warrant.

He reached into his pocket and produced a paper, holding it out for my inspection. I glanced at it, then looked at him. "All right," I said softly. "Let me show you the way."

Brennan was courteous. Although he looked through Ruby's dresser drawers and the books on her shelf, he did so respectfully, moving items aside methodically and placing them back exactly as he'd found them. He glanced in the girl's messy closet, shaking his head. "Teenagers," he said. Watching from the doorway with PJ on my hip, I did not reply.

After searching under the bed, the officer stood and asked, "Okay if I take a quick gander at the rest of the house?"

I saw no alternative, so I shrugged and stepped aside.

He went back to the main room first. Looking up at the tall ceilings, he let out a long whistle. "Didn't want to say so in front of my superior . . ." He smiled at me, as if we were in collusion. "But this is quite the place."

His grin was so infectious, I couldn't help smiling back. "Yes, it took me by surprise, too, when I first saw it." I lifted PJ higher onto my hip. "My understanding is that my sister-in-law designed it, or at least worked with an architect who shared her vision for it."

Brennan nodded. "Well, I don't know about you, but *I* sure didn't grow up in digs like this."

"Me, neither." I glanced around. "This whole world is foreign to me."

He was pacing the front room, walking the perimeter and looking inward toward the furniture around the hearth, as if gauging something. "Where are you from?" he asked.

"Wisconsin. A peninsula called Door County, on Lake Michigan."

I held up my right hand, palm facing the officer. "If my hand was Wisconsin, my thumb would be where Door is. It's a tourist area, and we have lots of fruit orchards, too."

"Sound like a pretty place," Brennan said.

I smiled again, despite myself. Officer Brennan reminded me of the boys I grew up with. He would have fit right in, back home in Baileys Harbor.

The baby started to fuss, and I grabbed the shawl from where I'd left it draped over the chair. I placed the shawl and the baby on the carpet with the measuring cups and bowls.

I turned back toward Brennan. Pleasant as the officer was, I was ready for him to leave. "Are you about done?"

"Yes, of course." He started for the front door, then glanced down the hallway. "Wait—I almost forgot the other bedrooms," he said, and then added, apologetically, "Sorry, ma'am. I'm kind of new at this."

My heart thudded. I followed Brennan down the hall to the master bedroom. He began by opening the closet door and poking his nose inside. "Quite a full closet here." He didn't say anything about all the items in the closet being a woman's clothes.

My eyes darted toward the dresser where Silja's jewelry box sat, with the envelope inside it containing who-knows-what.

Heavens, Angela, I scolded myself—you may as well have shouted and pointed it out to him. But the officer was still going through the closet, sliding the hangers one after the other from right to left.

He moved on to the dresser, but he didn't touch the jewelry box. After a few minutes, he turned on his heel and went into the guest room. "Baby sleeps in here?" he asked, seeing the bed set up with the dining room chairs around it.

"Yes. We have nowhere else to put him. We're going home on Tuesday, so it's okay."

It struck me that perhaps we would *not* be going home on Tuesday. What was going on at the police station? I wished I could be a fly on the wall there.

Brennan opened the closet door to reveal Henry's clothes. He turned toward me. "You have any idea if Henry Glass had been sleeping in this room?"

I shrugged and didn't reply.

The officer glanced at the baby's suitcase. "Baby's bag?"

I nodded, thinking of the little snapshot album snuggled between the clean folds of cotton diapers. But Brennan just chuckled. "For such little people, they sure need a lot of stuff." He passed out of the room, and I followed him back to the main part of the house.

"Thanks for letting me look around," he said.

He peered at me almost shyly. His innocent look made my heart ache. *Why* in heaven's name had I decided none of the nice boys in Baileys Harbor were good enough for me?

Because, I sternly reminded myself—because I'd held out for the man of my dreams. And he'd appeared, just as I knew he would.

We'd be fine, I told myself. Paul and I would be fine, once we were able to leave this house forever.

"Sure," I said softly to the officer. "Anytime."

I desperately wanted to ask him to reveal any tiny detail about Silja that he might have. But after Hill's silent rebuke earlier, I knew Brennan wouldn't comply.

"If you need anything, Mrs. Glass, please let me know. You can reach me at the State Troopers' station in Hawthorne."

I nodded. "Thank you, officer," I said, ushering him out the front door.

I closed the door and leaned against it. I glanced across the room at PJ, who was watching me from where he sat squarely in the middle of the spread-out shawl. "Well, *that* was a close call," I said to him. He babbled in response.

I went to the kitchen, finally able to make the coffee no one else had wanted. Pouring a cup, I looked around, wondering what I was supposed to do while I waited for Paul and Ruby to return. Clean some more? There was ample opportunity; the house presented a seemingly unlimited buildup of dirt and grime.

But what was in that snapshot album?

No, I told myself firmly, sipping coffee. No, it was not mine to know.

Not under normal circumstances, I argued back. But these are hardly normal circumstances.

I set my cup on the counter. I'd just go check on it, I thought. Just make sure it was still there, was still in the baby's suitcase.

I held the small leather book in my hands. Turning it over, I ran my fingers over the soft spine. How many times had Silja opened this album? How many times had she looked fondly at these photographs—whatever they showed?

"No, Angie," I chided myself—aloud, as if I'd be more convinced by the hum of my own voice than by thoughts alone. "You have no right." I reached forward, determined to nestle the album back into the suitcase.

Then I stopped, reconsidering.

What if the photos revealed information that would help? Who would I be, if I didn't even look for clues? Didn't even try to help?

Glancing furtively around, I went back to the main room, the little album clasped in my fingers. The baby was still playing happily on the shawl.

I picked up my coffee cup from the counter, sat down on the davenport, and slid my finger under the album's flap. I held my breath as the snap came undone with a tiny, almost inaudible click.

39

Ruby

They all sit in a little windowless room, just like on television. There's a table and chairs and the cops offer coffee or water to Ruby and Uncle Paul, and they both say no. A chunky ceramic ashtray, brown as a pile of dung, sits in the center of the table. It's the kind of thing kids make in shop class in seventh grade. Ruby wonders if some officer's kid made it, and the officer brought it to work and said he didn't want that ugly thing on his desk, the department could have it, and some secretary didn't know what else to do with it, so she put it in the interrogation room. Does the officer's kid know where it ended up?

Ruby asks if she can smoke. But they say no, she can't, because she's a minor.

On the other side of the table is Officer Hill, and seated next to him is another man who introduces himself as Detective Slater. He wears a suit, not a uniform. Ruby keeps her eyes on Hill's name tag. She doesn't like Hill, but she likes his name, because it's a real word. Hill is almost as good a name as Glass.

Hill doesn't talk; he just sits there. Slater does all the talking. He's chain-smoking Viceroys, stubbing them out in the ceramic ashtray. Ruby watches him with envy.

Slater starts off by saying, "Ruby, I see in these notes from Detective Duffy, who you talked to a few days ago, that you've been asked a number of questions already."

He looks up from the piece of paper in front of him. Like he's just reading it casually. Like it's a newspaper article or a magazine he picked up at the drugstore, something to read while he waits for the train, the way Ruby's mother used to do. *Life. Harper's. Architectural Digest* (her favorite). She'd bring them home and give them to Ruby when she was done with them.

Slater seems to be waiting for Ruby to say something, but she's not sure what, so she just nods. She pulls her sweater—Shepherd's sweater—tighter around her body. She wraps her hands inside the sweater's cuffs, gathering the wool in bunches.

"I just want to go over it one more time," Slater says.

He's looking at Uncle Paul when he says this. But then he turns to Ruby and takes the cigarette out of his mouth. He smiles briefly, like he's trying to encourage her. Befriend her.

And she can't blame him. That's his job, right? His job is to get her to trust him.

"So tell us again, Ruby," Slater says, "exactly how you came to find your father's body."

"The house was dark when I got home," Ruby explains. "Neither of my parents were there."

"No sign of your mother? Any indication she'd come home from work?"

Ruby pulls her hands out of her sleeves. She wants to reach inside Shepherd's sweater and bring out her mother's necklace; her fingers long to play with it. But revealing the necklace is a bad idea, so instead she twirls her ponytail in her fingers. "I checked the garage, and my mother's car wasn't there. That seemed strange and I started to worry."

"I see," Slater says. "And then?"

"Then I went to the kitchen." Ruby looks at the wall above Slater's head. "And found my mother's note on the counter."

Slater shuffles his papers. "According to this report," he says, "the note read as follows. 'Dearest Henry and Ruby, I'm sorry for how this must happen, but I'm leaving you both. Life is too short to wait any longer. Henry, take care of our daughter. Ruby, be a good girl for your father. I love you both.'"

Uncle Paul exhales. This is the first time he's heard these exact words. Ruby wants to look at him but she forces herself to turn her eyes back to the detective.

Slater says, "Is that the note you found, Ruby?"

She nods, and Slater asks, "What happened next?"

"Well, my father liked the forest. So it made sense to look for him there."

Slater says, "It must have been quite dark out there."

Ruby agrees.

"So how did you find your father in the dark?"

"He wasn't very far into the woods," Ruby points out. "It wasn't difficult."

"And when you found him?" Slater asks. "What happened then?"

"Then I came inside and called the police," Ruby says. "And I waited inside for them to show up, which they did pretty quickly."

Slater nods slowly. "I see," he says. And then he asks, "So at no time after you got home from school did you leave the property? At no time did you walk or drive anywhere?"

Ruby opens her mouth and then closes it. She does this a few times. She puts her hands on her knees and gives them a little squeeze.

Uncle Paul holds up his hand. "Excuse me," he says. "Where is this going? What are you trying to get from this young girl?"

Slater gives Uncle Paul a long, steely look. "We want to make sure we have everything right, Mr. Glass," he says. Ruby can tell he's trying very hard to keep his voice even and emotionless. "We just want to make sure we have the facts."

Uncle Paul half rises in his seat. "She's not saying anything more without a lawyer present."

Slater and Hill glance at each other. Slater stubs out the third cigarette he's had since they sat down.

"That's within her rights," he says. "Is there someone you'd like to call?"

Uncle Paul seems to flounder for a moment, and then he says, "Yes, I can figure it out. Just give me a telephone book and a quiet place to make a call."

Slater shrugs. "As you wish."

All three men rise, and Ruby rises with them.

Slater says, "You need to stay where you are, Ruby."

She sits back down. Uncle Paul touches her shoulder. "You sit tight," he says. "I'll be back soon. If anyone comes in, just keep silent."

Ruby nods and doesn't reply.

But she's thinking: surely, Uncle Paul, you know that staying silent is my specialty.

40

Silja

1952–1953

They looked at every available parcel anywhere nearby. Silja soon grew tired of tramping through muddy lots—all of them either too small, too remote—or not remote enough, as was one lot that sat right on Route 6, with traffic whizzing by at lightning speed. She arrived at each appointment hopeful and left each discouraged.

The home-design process itself was agonizing, too, but only because of Henry. He fought every aspect, every step of the way. Eventually Silja took to meeting with Fred, the architect, in secret—because at the first few meetings, when Henry was there, everything Silja said she wanted in the house, Henry contradicted. One story or two? Basement or crawl space? How many bedrooms? How many bathrooms? They couldn't agree on any of it.

Finally, she lied to Fred outright. "Henry doesn't really care," she said when she met with Fred after work; she caught an early train home, unknown to Henry, and from the station went in a taxi to meet Fred at his office in downtown Tarrytown. "Henry said you and I should just go over everything, and if you have any questions I can't answer, I'll relay them to him." She gave Fred as warm a smile as she could muster. "And I believe we owe you an installment," she said, handing him a check. "Let's get that out of the way."

But none of it mattered without a plot of land. He could design, Fred told her, but until there was a site to work with, anything could change.

❀   ❀   ❀

In June, they walked a plot of land that had just come back on the market; it had been spoken for when they first started their search, but the deal fell through. It was three acres on Stone Ridge Road, in the woods on the outskirts of Stonekill. Silja had hoped to move to another community; the plot, while secluded, was still within the town limits. That meant Ruby would still be attending Stonekill schools, and Silja would still take the train from the Stonekill station.

It was a compromise, but perhaps it would be worth it.

Silja was struck by how deep and still it felt; she heard nothing but birds, the soft rustle in the underbrush of squirrels and chipmunks and—she shuddered to think of it, but it was probably true—snakes. Well, she told herself, that comes with country living.

There were homes on either side, but not too close. A tract at the front of the property had been cleared to make way for a house. Thick woods stretched behind the muddy, cleared tract; rays of sunlight glittered through the branches of towering oaks and elms. The real estate agent, Jim, told Henry and Silja that an old Dutch cemetery, rarely used anymore, bordered the back of the property.

Henry adored it. "This is perfect," he said. "You can build any type of house you want here, Silja, as long as there are still plenty of woods for me to wander."

Silja turned to Ruby. "What do you think?"

"It's so pretty," the girl said. "So quiet and far away from everything." She stared into the woods. "You could disappear, if you wanted to."

Silja laughed. "Well, honey, please don't disappear."

Impulsively, Ruby took Henry's hand. "Come on, Daddy—let's go explore."

Silja watched them crash through the underbrush. Jim had been inspecting the sewer line that was recently put into the property in anticipation of a house on the land. He stepped beside Silja, watching Henry's and Ruby's figures growing smaller until they were swallowed in the thickets.

"They certainly are two peas in a pod," Jim murmured.

Silja didn't answer. Instead, she turned to him and asked, "What would it take for us to get this property?"

One day in early fall, with construction well under way, Silja had an odd encounter with one of the builders. He was reading the plans, going over them with the foreman, when she walked up. They finished their conversation and the foreman walked away.

"Glass, huh?" the worker asked her.

"Excuse me?"

"Last name is Glass, I saw on the plans. 'Glass Residence,' it said." He wiped sweat from his brow and regarded her closely. "Any relation to Paul Glass?"

Silja was so startled, she didn't reply for a moment. Finally, she said, "You know Paul?"

The worker picked up a few lengths of board and dragged them across the yard. "Oh, I know him all right."

She had no idea what he meant. "Well, I'm sure you're aware he doesn't live in Stonekill anymore."

The man gripped the wood so hard his hands turned red. "Yeah, I'm aware. And good riddance." He slammed the boards into a pile he was creating.

Well, Silja thought, at least we're in agreement about that.

Driving back to Lawrence Avenue, she resolutely put it out of her mind, letting her thoughts wander instead to what her finished house would be like. She dreamed of the big windows, of morning sunlight filtering into the house past the treetops to the east. She imagined a blazing fire in the massive stone fireplace, on winter nights when snow flew outside the floor-to-ceiling panes on either side of the living room.

She had hoped they would move in before winter came, but delay after delay occurred—first it was something with the soil, and then the septic, and then they were waiting on the mill. And on and on.

Silja had no choice but to grin and bear it, keeping her eyes on the prize.

❁   ❁   ❁

But what that worker said continued to haunt her. She ran into him a few more times, and nothing else was said. Finally, she asked Henry about it.

He was—so typical of him!—evasive.

"Paul lived in Stonekill for almost a year." Henry fetched the mail from the front hall table and walked back toward the kitchen. Silja followed him. "And he didn't live in our house, Silja. There's no way to know who he associated with or where he went every day."

"I know, but . . ." She shrugged helplessly. "I wish you'd been there," she said. "I wish you could have seen that construction man's face. How . . . angry he looked."

Henry threw several advertisements in the trash can, leaving two bills and a letter on the kitchen counter. The letter, addressed to Henry, was from Paul. Nothing surprising in that; Paul frequently sent a quick post to let Henry know where he was.

"Do you think Paul will ever come back here?" she asked.

Henry was studying the postmark on the envelope, and she glanced at it, too. Cedar Rapids, Iowa. She had no idea where that was. She would not be able to place Cedar Rapids on a map of Iowa, if such a map were presented to her with no city names on it.

Henry hadn't responded. "Did you hear me?" she asked.

He was still studying the envelope, turning it over in his hand. Silja knew he was waiting until she left the room to open it. "I'm sorry—what?" he asked.

"Paul. Do you think he'll return to Stonekill someday?"

Henry gave her a long look. "Would you come back here, if you were him?"

One blustery winter Saturday, Silja drove to White Plains to shop for furniture and accessories for the new house. With the car, she could pick up a few small items—lamps and throw rugs, maybe—and put everything else on order for delivery when the house was completed.

She wanted everything new—sofa and tables, a dining room set, bedroom ensembles for the master bedroom and Ruby's room. Abstract prints for the walls—Henry would like that. Brass plant stands with hairpin legs. Thick ceramic vases in an array of colors, which she would fill with flowers she bought in the city. A fine, sleek desk for the third bedroom, which Silja planned to use as both guest room and office. With such a desk, she'd welcome the opportunity to catch up on work in the evenings. The only furnishing from Lawrence Avenue she planned to keep was her beloved aqua, frieze-upholstered chair. Combined with a contemporary sofa, side tables, and a second, complementing chair, it would look perfect in the living room of the new house.

As she strolled through an aisle of dining room tables at B. Altman, Silja heard a woman laughing. She looked up, stopping in her tracks. Not twenty feet away, among the kitchen sets, she spied David.

And a woman.

She was smiling, holding his arm. She wore gloves, a navy coat, and a matching hat. She had an elegant, well-groomed appearance, though her face was lightly lined; she looked to be in her forties. She was tall and narrow, and Silja thought her build seemed out of place beside David's short, solid physique.

The woman's hand brushed the surface of a kitchen table. She asked David a question Silja couldn't catch. He nodded and responded, his voice too low for Silja to hear.

Then he glanced across the space and saw Silja—motionless among the tables and chairs, her handbag clutched in both hands in front of her.

David raised his eyebrows, and she knew he remembered her. He tipped his hat at Silja, then leaned toward the woman, whispered something, and gently steered her away.

As the pair walked toward the escalator, David turned back to look at Silja. She felt her hands shaking as his eyes locked upon hers. His lips twitched into a small smile that seemed to Silja almost regretful.

What did it mean? There was no opportunity to find out. Seconds later, the tops of both David's head and the woman's had disappeared as they descended the escalator to the floor below.

She thought about it for weeks afterward. That was that, she told herself. He had someone else. Even if Silja were unattached, it wouldn't matter; David clearly was spoken for. And why should she care? She was being silly. They'd only met one time; he was nobody to her, after all.

But she couldn't stop thinking about him. Couldn't stop her mind's eye from seeing that gloved hand on David's arm. Couldn't get the picture of his seemingly apologetic smile out of her head.

To console herself, she bought herself a present: a Brownie camera, the latest model, in a beautiful leather case. She'd never been one for taking many pictures—there was a woeful photographic void of Ruby's infancy and young childhood—but now she began taking photo after photo of the house construction, documenting the project inside and out as the walls went up, the finishing touches went in, and the furniture was arranged.

The elegant, glass-walled house was completed in March. Silja couldn't stop admiring it. The house looked exactly like something you'd see in Southern California. Instead of moving there, she'd brought Los Angeles right here to Stonekill, New York.

She knew what her mother would have thought of such a sumptuous home for one small family. But Silja was enthralled. She'd earned it, she told herself. She'd worked hard all her life and finally got what she wanted.

Not bad for a working girl from Brooklyn.

Ruby loved the big windows and the woods; she was constantly outside. Silja hoped Ruby would make new friends, not like the kids in downtown Stonekill. But she didn't hold out much hope for the neighbors on Stone Ridge Road, either. They weren't what she'd expected, all those years she'd lived on Lawrence Avenue and envied those who lived out here. Their houses were repulsive raised ranches or cheap Colonials, covered in pink, yellow, or white siding. The women, if they contributed any income to their families, did so by hosting Tupperware parties or being Avon ladies. Everyone drove station wagons—a necessity, because most families had at least four children. Silja kept telling herself that with so many children about, perhaps some precocious child—some anomaly—would become Ruby's new best friend.

As for Henry, she knew the house was not to his liking. Admittedly, there wasn't much work to be done; the house was perfect. But he loved the land, and there was plenty of room for a garden. Once they'd settled in, he went back to his crime detection correspondence course, which over the years he'd fiddled with but never seemed to be able to complete. He also started picking up the occasional handyman job—found mostly via word of mouth through folks he knew from hanging around the hardware store in town.

It pained Silja to watch Henry whistle cheerfully as he packed his toolbox and backed his decrepit truck from the garage of their magnificent house in the early mornings, heading out to do some grubby little task. It wasn't the image she'd ever had in her head of a working husband.

Still, it was better than nothing. Henry seemed content, and that was what mattered.

He's fine, she thought. They all were. Henry had something to do. Silja had her gorgeous glass house. Ruby had books to read and a forest to run in—and over time, she would surely make some friends on Stone Ridge Road.

Silja remembered her fantasies about leaving Henry. She didn't think that way anymore. There was no need to upset the apple cart. They'd finally arrived at their destination, and they were *all* happy.

On a warm June night just before sundown, the Rosenbergs were executed. It happened not far from Stonekill—in Ossining, at Sing Sing prison.

Silja knew what they were accused of. She knew that Ethel and Julius Rosenberg had been tried and convicted as spies who provided top secret military information to the Soviets. She knew that Julius was accused of being a courier, and Ethel of typing notes and performing other auxiliary tasks.

Whether they actually did what they were convicted of, Silja couldn't say. But either way, she didn't believe the Rosenbergs—particularly Ethel, a mother of two young boys—deserved to die. Not that way. Silja couldn't imagine what that much electricity flowing through the body would feel like.

But she had to imagine it. Because she had to explain to ten-year-old Ruby why her father would get in his truck, drive down the highway, and stand as close to the prison as he could get, bearing witness.

"Why would he want to be there?" Ruby asked Silja.

Silja wasn't sure herself. When Henry mentioned it, he said he was going "with friends." She'd asked him what friends, and he'd only shrugged and said a couple of fellows from town. No one she knew, he told her.

It was odd—since when did Henry have friends? Were they people he had met through his handyman jobs? Silja had no idea.

"I don't know why he wants to be there, actually," she admitted to Ruby. "It doesn't seem like the kind of thing most people would want to be anywhere near, does it?"

"Maybe he's hoping to somehow get the Rosenbergs out alive," Ruby suggested.

Silja laughed bitterly. "No, that's not it. He doesn't want them out." She paused, and then added, "He thinks they should die. He's there to support the executioners."

Ruby shuddered, and Silja instantly regretted her truthfulness. Why hadn't she simply lied to the child?

"Why would Daddy think that?" Ruby asked. "Did they do it? Did they spy?"

"Well, lots of people think they did. At their trial, it was determined that they did." Silja didn't know what else to say except, "The courts decide these things, Ruby. The government. We have to trust our government to make the right decisions, even if we don't agree."

Ruby looked at Silja with dark eyes like her father's. "So *you* don't agree?" she asked Silja. "You don't think they should die?"

"No," Silja said. "I think it's barbaric. I think killing someone for a crime like that is something that only a barbaric society would do."

"Are we barbaric, then?" Ruby persisted. "Are you saying our government is barbaric?"

"Ruby, I don't know." Silja sighed. "All I mean is, I don't think this is right."

Ruby apparently relayed their conversation to Henry, because the next afternoon he stormed into the house from the garden—slamming the sliding glass door until it shuddered—to accuse Silja of being a Rosenberg sympathizer.

"That's not what I said at all," Silja told him. "I just said I thought it was barbaric, executing them that way."

"It was by no means barbaric," Henry said. "It was patriotic. You should have been there. I should have taken Ruby. It was silent. Dignified. There was none of that squawking, protesting nonsense, like all the lefties in New York and Washington did."

Silja rolled her eyes and said nothing. But her stomach flipped, wondering if David had been at a protest in the city. It was possible, wasn't it? She knew that many people—many of them Communists, she reminded herself; no sense beating around the bush—had protested the Rosenbergs' executions at demonstrations in New York, Washington, and other cities. Even though all those years back David had told her he was at the People's Artists concert just for the music, not for the speeches, she didn't know that for certain.

Well, who cared a fig if David *did* protest? Who cared what he thought and did? David had a woman in his life. He wasn't someone Silja should concern herself with in the least.

In any case, Henry didn't notice her eye roll. "Everyone there knew we were doing the right thing," he said. "Everyone wanted to support the United States government. As well you should, Silja." He stomped his feet, getting mud on her kitchen floor. "You of all people."

"Me of all people? Why is that?"

"Because this country has done so much for you. For immigrants. Welcomed you and gave you a home when you had nothing."

"Henry, I was born here," she reminded him. "I'm not an immigrant."

"Maybe so," he conceded. "But you came from nothing, and look what you have now." He wiped sweat from his brow. "You should be grateful, Silja, for everything you have. You should be thankful, instead of always wanting more and more."

"What more and more do I want? What are you talking about?"

He swept his arm toward the glass-walled living room. "You call this less and less?"

"I don't see you complaining about it, though," Silja shot back. "It's okay with you—isn't it?—to hang around this 'more and more' every day. Living the life of Riley while *my* income pays the bills."

He stared at her with cold eyes.

"*Your* income? What about my handyman jobs?"

She laughed bitterly. "Really, Henry, let's not kid ourselves."

The minute she said it, she realized how cruel it sounded. She opened her mouth to apologize, but he turned on his heel, slid the door open, and closed it with deliberate calm. She watched through the glass as he tramped into the garden and picked up a hoe, raking it across the weeds with brisk, savage strokes.

41

Ruby

Nobody is in the little room anymore to say Ruby can't smoke, so she takes out her father's Zippo and lights a Camel. She smokes it slowly, relishing every puff. Then she has another, and after that she has one more.

Eventually she grows weary of sitting there smoking. So she gets up and starts pacing the room's perimeter. She sticks as close to the wall as she can, the fingers of her right hand scraping along the wall, the nails digging into the flesh-colored paint.

Ruby notices that if she digs hard enough, she can scratch faint lines into the wall with her index, middle, and ring fingers. So she keeps going, round and round the room. She digs in, deeper and deeper, creating three thin, parallel lines a few feet above the floor.

It feels like everyone has been gone for hours. There's no clock in the windowless room and Ruby is not wearing a watch. She has no idea how much time has passed—an hour, three hours, the entire day.

They can't leave her here forever, right? It's not a jail cell. It feels sort of like one but Ruby isn't stupid, she has at least some sense of what a real jail cell would be like, and this isn't it.

Usually she doesn't mind being alone, but she's starting to feel lonely and she's starting to miss Uncle Paul and she's even a little bit beginning to doubt he's coming back at all.

Maybe he's left her here.

✿　　✿　　✿

Back in elementary school, kids used to say things about Uncle Paul. Everyone knew he'd lived with Mrs. Hawke. Ruby was young and Mrs. Hawke wasn't her principal yet when that was going on, but Ruby knew what was said.

Harry Lister, who is ugly as sin and thin as a mangy weed, once told Ruby that her uncle hit on young girls, and that's why he had to leave Stonekill.

"That's bunk," Ruby said, and turned away.

"You're walking away because you know it's true," Harry called after her.

"Shut up, dipstick!" she said. He laughed at her back.

"Asshole!" Ruby screamed, turning to face him. She took two giant steps toward him and swung her fist hard against his jawbone. Harry stumbled in surprise.

Before he could catch his breath, Ruby ran. She could outrun anyone at school—and besides, Harry wasn't about to tell anybody that he'd been hit by a girl. It would be too humiliating.

Harry Lister's father was one of the guys building the birdcage. Back then, Ruby hated that man, even though it was Harry who'd said those things about Uncle Paul—not his father. But Harry must have heard that somewhere, right?

Now, though, it makes more sense. Ruby is older now, and she understands Uncle Paul much better than she did when she was a kid.

42

Silja

1954–1957

Less than a year after they took up residence in the new house, Henry suggested he move from the master bedroom into the guest room. "This house is so big," he said. "We could spread out. Have our own space."

So is this how it finally ends? Silja wondered. Is this how a marriage that never really was a marriage comes to its conclusion? Surely, this was the first step toward the two of them parting ways.

"Do you want a divorce, Henry?" she asked hopefully. She looked him in the eye. "We could go to Reno. It would only take a month or two. It's not—" She continued speaking, her voice low. "It's not impossible. Not if we agree about it."

He gave her a quizzical look, as if he thought she might not be right in the head.

"Are you crazy?" he growled. "No—of course I don't want a divorce." He took a step toward her, towering over her but not touching her. "Marriage is forever, Silja," he went on. "You don't walk away from marriage vows. No matter how fate changes your expectations, when you make a promise like a marriage vow, it's for keeps."

It was what he'd said all along—in his letters from the front, when he first came home from the war. Always, he'd proclaimed they would be together for the rest of their lives.

For years, that was also what she'd wanted. But long ago she'd stopped holding out hope for their marriage to succeed. Instead, she'd begun to hope that Henry, too, would realize they were better off apart. That he'd agree they should call it quits—amicably and without strife.

Why in heaven's name would he dig in his heels about this? Because of some silly ideal about "for better or for worse"?

Apparently so. She was speechless, as the implications of what he'd said began to sink in.

In all honesty, though, he had a good point about the bedrooms. She disliked sleeping next to him, had disliked it for a long time. At night she tossed and turned—her body tense, her mind prowling its farthest corners of brooding and speculation like a cat kept inside after dark. She stayed on her own side of the bed, knowing he didn't want her anywhere nearby. Her longing to touch him never truly subsided— but she knew he'd recoil if she laid a hand on him. Even in the new house, sharing a king-size bed, she still felt his presence and never fully relaxed.

They made the move over a weekend. They transferred the desk— Silja had selected it to go with her beautiful house, and she wasn't about to surrender it to Henry—from the guest room into the master bedroom. She spent several hours setting it up, trying it in different corners. She organized file folders and sharpened pencils.

As they moved Henry's clothes to the guest room closet, Ruby watched wordlessly. Passing her daughter in the hallway as she brought a load of Henry's shoes to the guest room, Silja gave the girl a brave smile. "It doesn't mean anything, honey," she assured Ruby. "Daddy and I just need more space, that's all."

Ruby didn't respond. She brushed past Silja, heading for the back door and the woods.

Once Henry's clothes were removed, Silja filled his side of the master bedroom closet by spreading out her wardrobe. Sorting through her clothes made her wistful. She still wore a lot of green—Henry had been right all those years ago; green *did* bring out the color in her eyes. In the city, shopping on her lunch hour, she bought herself green dresses and suits in the latest styles.

Henry sometimes bought her green things, too—mostly with money she earned, of course; his handyman jobs brought in a pittance. At the little shops in downtown Stonekill and other nearby towns, he'd pick up emerald earrings, a printed scarf in a pattern of kelly and jade, a felt hat or pair of gloves in forest green. Buying things for her was a kindness, she knew—but to Silja it felt like a forced kindness. When she wore something he'd purchased, Henry looked at her not with admiration but instead with smug satisfaction.

It was similar, in its way, to the elaborate dinners he cooked. He cooked for her, of course, for their family—but as with everything he did, cooking was more for his own gratification than for anyone else.

An effect of Henry's move, one that Silja hadn't seen coming, was that he stopped cleaning the master bedroom and bath. He'd always been the family housekeeper, ever since they moved to Stonekill—heck, even at the Alku, Silja remembered, when she was at Hunter and her mother was working all the time, Henry took over the cleaning chores. He'd done a commendable job of it, too; she had to admit it. Once, when she'd complimented how spick-and-span the house was, he said it was residual from being in the army. "Everything in tip-top condition," he told her.

But now he told her that "her room" was private and he wasn't going to enter it anymore, even to clean. "You can manage," he said, handing her a can of Ajax and a sponge one Saturday morning.

"Or we could get a cleaning woman," she proposed.

"Over my dead body," he said, walking away. "No strangers in my house, thank you very much."

Silja detested cleaning. She put it off as long as possible, rarely giving her room the attention it deserved.

It was a ridiculously hot and humid Sunday in July—the warmest Silja could remember in a long time. How is it possible, Silja thought, that a girl who grew up in Brooklyn, where the temperature and humidity soar as early as May and as late as October, is now affected by such circumstances? Perhaps, she mused, she was getting less tolerant at her ripe old age of thirty-five.

At midafternoon, she announced to Henry and Ruby that she was going to the picture show—both for the movie itself and to enjoy the air-conditioned theater. She invited Ruby along, but the girl declined; she was lounging in the living room, fanning herself with a copy of *The Catcher in the Rye*. Henry was in the kitchen, making sauce from the season's first ripe tomatoes; Silja didn't bother to invite him because she knew he'd say no. The oxblood-colored cover of Ruby's book and the half-chopped tomatoes on the kitchen counter—an assortment ranging from rose-colored to scarlet—stood out in stark contrast to the stylish neutral tones of Silja's beautifully decorated home.

"Well, I'll be back in time for dinner," Silja told them. Neither responded.

The picture was *An Affair to Remember*, starring Deborah Kerr and Silja's proverbial heartthrob, Cary Grant. The actor was getting older, too, just like real people. Whenever she saw Grant's image these days—on a movie poster, in a magazine, at the theater—she was reminded that even in Hollywood, eventually laugh lines and graying hair take over.

The theater was crowded, given the hot weather and the popularity of the newly released movie. After the house lights dimmed, a solitary gentleman took the seat two down from Silja. There was no one between them. She found at movies, particularly romances, that many men—presumably dragged along by women—fussed and squirmed the entire time. She couldn't make out the face of the man two seats away, but during the show she noticed he was content and well mannered. He was contemplative through the middle of the film and seemed relaxed as they watched the sentimental ending.

When the house lights went up, he turned toward her, and Silja saw his face for the first time. He broke into a smile. "Well, if it isn't Silja from Stonekill."

"David," she said, unable to hide the shock in her voice. "My knight in shining armor." She uncrossed and then recrossed her legs, leaning toward him. "I've never forgotten your kindness that night."

"And I've never forgotten you or your little girl. Ruby, isn't it?"

"That's right. You have a good memory."

He smiled again. "For some things, yes." He glanced toward the darkened screen, then back at Silja. "What did you think of the picture?"

"It was wonderful," Silja replied. "A roller-coaster ride, but optimistic at the end. I'm glad it turned out the way it did."

"Refreshing to see a happy ending," he said. "Not every story has one."

"Indeed not," Silja agreed. They were both silent. Neither got up, though the other patrons were filing out. It seemed to Silja as if David was waiting for her to say more, so she ventured another comment. "The acting was wonderful. I've always been a fan of Cary Grant. And Miss Kerr is a delight."

David nodded. "Do you see many movies?" He turned so he could look her in the eye, leaning his torso over the seat between them. Silja fiddled with her eyeglasses and curved her body closer to the empty seat.

"I do go to the movies quite a bit, actually," she said. "Nearly every weekend—even if I have to see the same picture over and over." She shrugged. "That's country living for you. Slim pickings, unless one wants to venture to the city. And I already do that every weekday for work."

She realized she was babbling, and she shut her mouth. The woman she'd seen him with at B. Altman a few years ago hadn't been a yapper. Clearly, he preferred women who didn't run at the mouth.

But David seemed unaffected by her chatter. "I enjoy the pictures as well," he said. "Perhaps we'll meet here again next Sunday." He stood, put on his hat, and tipped it at her. "It's good to see you again, Silja."

"And you." She watched his sturdy, retreating back as he walked out of the theater.

✿   ✿   ✿

Well, she told herself as the week wore on—who *wouldn't* go back the next Sunday?

Silja arrived early, intending to sit in the same seat. She found David had beat her to it—almost as if they had a planned engagement.

He stood when she arrived. "Would you like your same seat, madam?"

Silja smiled. "Yes, I'd love that." She patted the seat next to her. "You can come over here, if you like."

He did so. "We're both early."

"Yes." Silja stole a glimpse at his left hand. It was bare. No wedding ring. So he wasn't married to the woman with whom she'd seen him shopping.

But still, there was only one way to know for sure where things stood. Her voice hesitant, she asked, "Did you find . . . what you were looking for?" She took a breath, and then went on. "That day at the department store. Did you and your . . . friend . . . find the kitchen set you wanted?"

He laughed heartily. "Ah, that day." He smiled. "Mrs. Murray is my father's caregiver. He's elderly and lives with me, but he needs someone to check on him while I'm at work. Our kitchen table and chairs were badly in need of replacement, and Mrs. Murray was kind enough to give up her Saturday afternoon to help me select something new. We found nothing there, but at Macy's we picked out a very nice set."

Silja could feel her entire face grinning. "Well, I'm glad to hear that," she said. Then she added, "Overjoyed, one might say."

"*Overjoyed*. That's quite a strong word." He raised his eyebrows. "Truly, Silja?"

She nodded. "Absolutely."

David's eyes were brown, but lighter than Henry's. And David didn't have that odd hooded appearance that always made Henry seem to be glowering even when he wasn't angry. David's expression was friendly, Silja thought, as if he wanted to know everything about everyone around him.

She sounded smitten, she scolded herself. She sounded like a schoolgirl with a crush.

The lights dimmed and she settled in, leaning her left shoulder just the slightest bit toward David's side.

It wasn't long before she was seeing him every weekend. Their movie dates in Westchester morphed into meeting in the city, evenings when she told Henry she had to work late.

It started innocently enough. Movies, theater, dinner. Just spending time with a friend, she told herself. She was allowed to have friends, wasn't she?

But she couldn't deny the growing attraction between them. No, not *growing*, she corrected herself. The allure had always been there. Ever since the night of the forestalled concert in Peekskill, David had been unforgettable.

His smile overflowed with warmth. He smelled of chicory and leather. Sitting next to him in darkened Manhattan theaters, she would inhale deeply, slowly—memorizing the scent of him so she could recall it during her late-night train ride home.

At Grand Central he would face her, giving both her shoulders a tight squeeze. Not quite an embrace—but more than a handshake, certainly. He whispered her name, then good-bye. He tipped his hat and said, "Until next time. I'll call you." She watched him stride off, her heart beating, her palms sweaty, anxious that he'd change his mind about her, that she'd never see him again.

But he *did* call. He always did—at the office, of course. Was she free that evening to meet him? Yes, certainly she was!

One night after dinner at Sardi's, they stepped outside. It was a chilly November evening with drizzle falling, and Silja shivered in her raincoat. David pulled her close, and she turned into his embrace— naturally, as if she'd been doing so her entire life.

Their lips met in a deep, hungry kiss. When they broke apart,

David said, "I've wanted to do that, Silja, since I first laid eyes on you." He kissed her again. "I can't tell you the number of times I've thought about it."

"Me, too." She hesitated, and then added, "And more than that, as well."

He smiled gently. "Is that so? Makes two of us."

Now it was up to her, Silja knew. David was a gentleman; he wouldn't push her.

She nodded over her shoulder. "The Hotel Piccadilly is two blocks away," she murmured softly, pressing her face into his coat collar.

He stepped back so he could look into her eye. "Are you sure, Silja? You're absolutely sure this is what you want?"

She didn't hesitate. Instead, she nodded and took his arm. "Come," she said firmly. "Come with me, David."

43

Ruby

The scratches along the wall are so deep now, Ruby has paint under her fingernails. She turns and goes in the other direction so that her left-hand fingernails will be painted underneath, too. She starts humming, because there's nothing else to do.

Eventually she gets tired of fingernailing a line around the room at waist height. A straight line is as dull as a pair of socks that's been washed too many times. So she starts strolling around the room, scratching out curlicues and random letters and nonsense words.

She's very careful to use her own handwriting. She wouldn't want it to look like she was forging anyone else's.

Finally, she sinks down to the floor in a corner of the room. She grazes her nails into the old linoleum and finds that even if it's worn out from chairs being moved around and people's shoes and who knows what, it doesn't give as easily as the paint on the wall does. The floor is scratched, but she can't make it any worse.

There is nothing else to do but close her eyes and imagine being somewhere else.

Ruby pretends she's in the woods with Shepherd. She'd like to be anywhere except this room, but in particular she'd like to be with Shepherd. She closes her eyes, and it's as if the skin on her eyelids is Prince Hussain's flying carpet, a thousand and one nights of whisking her to places before and beyond this suffocating chamber.

In her mind, she can be anywhere she wants to be. She can smell the tree bark and the earth, she can feel Shepherd's hand in hers, reassuring as a thick rope anchoring the small, drifting watercraft that's Ruby.

Since she started meeting Shepherd in her family's woods, everything has been better—not only her free time but even her school days. *I have a secret, I have a secret*, Ruby chants to herself while she walks the high school halls alone, while she sits on the school bus—near the front, where nobody bothers her but nobody talks to her, either. But it doesn't matter that other kids shun her, because she has a secret.

Shepherd has been meeting her for the past couple of weeks. It was risky—incredibly risky—but no one knew about it. Not Ruby's parents and not anyone else.

The first time was coincidental. He was driving near the high school just after dismissal bell, and Ruby saw his car and waved. He pulled to the curb and rolled down the passenger-side window, leaning over to ask if she wanted a lift. Ruby said she usually took the school bus home, but a ride would be nice.

She explained how to get to her family's property the back way, through the cemetery. She showed him a thicket of trees beside the crumbling old road winding through the cemetery. From there, you could tell if there was any activity in her family's forest—any reason not to hop over the stone wall onto their land. Ruby warned Shepherd that if he saw activity, he should never step over the wall. But if all was clear, it was fine to come over.

He furrowed his brow. "Maybe it would be easier if you'd just call when you want me to visit."

"I could do that," Ruby conceded. Shepherd gave her his telephone number, which has come in handy many times since.

Ruby waited such a long time to have a friend. And now she has one. She smiles, thinking about seeing him the night before. About everything she told him.

And then she frowns. She doesn't want to admit it, even to herself, but she's just a tiny bit worried. She's made some bold decisions in the past twenty-four hours. She hopes she doesn't regret them later on.

If Shepherd were here, he'd tell her in his gentle, low voice that it would be all right. "You can't control everything, Ruby," he'd say. "But you can control your own state of mind. Close your eyes and let your mind be free of worry. Let it go, and it *will* go, Ruby. Trust me."

That's what Shepherd would tell her. She wishes she was with him now.

44

Silja

1958–1959

Silja drove the long way home from the station. She was still getting used to the speed and agility of her new car, an MGA roadster convertible. The car—an absolute indulgence, she knew, but she deserved it—gave her a thrill every time she revved up around the curvy Stonekill roads. I should have traded in that awful Buick a million years ago, she thought. What in the world was I waiting for?

Her mind wandered to thoughts of David. Only two days until she'd see him again. She hummed as she drove, a mindless tune, enjoying the crispness of the early-fall evening.

It was with reluctance that she pulled into the driveway. She hopped out of the car, opener key in hand. She inserted and turned the key in a keyhole attached to the side of the garage, and the door magically rose on its tracks. There was no need to push the door up and pull it down by hand.

She slipped the MGA into the garage, next to Henry's truck—more faded and rusty every year, like an old coffee can left in the yard. She returned to the keyhole and turned it the other direction, ducking back into the garage under the closing door.

Inside the house, she changed into dungarees for her customary early evening walk in the woods. Henry was nowhere to be seen, and Ruby was doing homework at the kitchen bar. Silja waved to her daughter as she opened the sliding door to the backyard.

"Make sure to stop in and say hello to Dad while you're out there," Ruby told her.

Silja stopped and turned. "What do you mean, honey? Where's Dad?"

Ruby shrugged. "Take your walk. You'll see." She turned to her books and, without looking up, added, "Make sure to go all the way to the back."

Silja walked into woods bright with autumn foliage. She wandered past tall trees, squat bushes, thorny vines. Over the years, Henry had created a maze of faint pathways throughout their three acres. Unlike Henry and Ruby, who both knew their way around seemingly by instinct, Silja never really understood the rhyme or reason of the paths. But she made sure to never go in the woods after dark. As long as there was a bit of lingering light, as long as she could look to the west and see the zigzagged roofline of her house, she could find her way out.

Toward the back of their property, near the sagging stone wall that separated their lot from the old Dutch cemetery, she came across Henry. He was digging vigorously in a small clearing. He had a space approximately ten foot square roped off, and he was entrenched two feet deep.

"What are you doing?" she asked.

His head came up and he wiped sweat from his brow. "Bomb shelter," he said simply.

Silja was speechless. "Why in the world would you do such a thing?" she asked. "Do you really, truly believe the Russians might drop the bomb on us?"

He gave her a long look before answering, as if he couldn't believe she was asking the question. Then he said, "Everyone believes that, Silja." He gripped the handle of the shovel more tightly. "Everyone with any sense, anyway."

She shook her head and turned on her heel. She went back to the house, stepped inside, and began fixing herself a martini.

A bomb shelter. It was the most preposterous thing she'd ever heard.

Ruby was still sitting at the bar, doing her math homework. "How long has Dad been out there?" Silja asked.

Her daughter shrugged. "All day, I suppose. He started right after you left this morning, and he was still at it when I got off the school bus this afternoon." She turned the page of her math textbook and chewed thoughtfully on her pencil's eraser tip.

Silja shook her drink, poured it, and took a deep, satisfying sip. "What do *you* think?" she asked. "Do we need a bomb shelter?"

Ruby looked up from her book. "Well, it can't hurt to be prepared," she said. "And besides, Dad needs something to do."

Silja tilted her head, curious. "Dad needs something to do?"

Ruby stared at Silja, as if she couldn't believe the question. "Of course," she said. "You see—don't you, Mom?—how restless he is. Sure, he has his odd jobs and his correspondence course. But they don't take up enough of his time or his energy. He's like a prowler, always skulking around. Except he has nothing to steal, so he has to invent other business to keep himself sharp."

Her words took Silja by surprise. Certainly, Silja was aware of Henry's hang-ups and quirks. But she hadn't realized Ruby noticed such things.

Silja took a long look at the slender girl—her daughter who had none of Silja's curves but instead had been blessed with a strong, lithe body. Ruby got straight A's in every subject, although English was her favorite. She didn't have many friends—no, Silja corrected herself, ever since they'd moved to Stone Ridge Road, Ruby didn't have *any* friends. She was quiet and obedient at home. She still liked board games, though she had outgrown Monopoly. She preferred chess, with one or the other of her parents as her opponent. Ruby enjoyed winning, of course—who doesn't?—but she didn't gloat. She was a gracious winner. A respectful daughter. She never gave a hint of trouble.

In that moment, Silja realized something: her only child was nearly grown, and she had spent more hours of Ruby's childhood away from her than Silja cared to count. It seemed just yesterday that Ruby had been a solemn child—the little girl Silja read to by the hearth in the old house on Lawrence Avenue, in those treasured moments she shared with her daughter. And now look at her, Silja thought—fifteen years old, a sophomore in high school.

It hadn't worked out the way Silja once expected it to. Ruby was supposed to be the eldest daughter in a large family. A family that Silja was meant to be home with, a family she was meant to take care of while Henry provided for them.

In a few years, Ruby would be off to college. And then, Silja wondered—then what would she do? She'd be stuck here with Henry—living alone with the man who wouldn't grant her a divorce, her husband who wouldn't release her to be with another.

She looked up and saw Henry coming back through the woods. He was shirtless, covered in dirt. His muscular, tanned body gleamed with a fine sheen of sweat.

Silja felt a faint longing deep within her. But—attractive though he still was—her desire was not for Henry.

Not anymore.

She called Kristina, whom she hadn't seen in several years, and asked her to coffee. "It's about Ruby," Silja told Kristina over the telephone.

They met on a Saturday morning at a diner on Route 9, some miles south of Stonekill. Kristina suggested it, and Silja didn't protest. She knew Kristina didn't want to be seen around town with Silja any more than she wanted to be seen with Kristina.

"I'll get right to the point." Silja poured creamer into her coffee and stirred. "I'm worried about Ruby. She seems fine, on the surface. And yet . . . "

She trailed off. Kristina dropped a lump of sugar into her coffee. "And yet?" Kristina prompted. Her eyes met Silja's.

"I don't know." Silja put up her hands helplessly. "I guess I just hoped . . . I thought maybe she would develop some interests. Cheerleading, or a sport. Or playing an instrument. Something." She drummed her fingers on the tabletop. "She comes home every day and does her homework. She gets good grades. She doesn't ask for much. But . . . "

"But she must want *something*," Kristina finished, nodding. "Of course she does. All high school kids do." She took a gulp of coffee.

"See here, Silja—I don't have kids, but I know teens. Some of them figure it out on their own. Some need a little direction. Ruby is a smart girl. A capable girl. But capability isn't the same thing as understanding one's own needs. Ruby needs someone to look up to. Someone to help her fill in the blanks."

"You mean me."

"Well," Kristina said. "You are her mother, after all."

They were both silent, drinking their coffee. The waitress came by and asked if they wanted to order anything to eat, but both refused.

"How are you, in general?" Kristina asked. "It's been . . . a long time."

Silja nodded. "I'm well. Work is going well. I love my house."

Kristina asked, "Do you still go to the movies?"

Silja could feel her mouth curving into a smile. "Not much around here," she admitted. "I used to, but . . . " She ducked her head, feeling suddenly shy. "Now I just go in the city sometimes. With . . . friends there."

She was dying to confide in someone. She wanted to gush about David, to testify her love. Talk about how sublime it felt to be enfolded in his embrace. How much she relished twisting her wedding ring off her finger and tossing it on a hotel nightstand before climbing into bed with David. How she longed to take the damned thing off forever, maybe throw it into the river, accompanied by a joyful, satisfied laugh.

How, for the first time in years—at least for a few hours each week—she was fulfilled. The way a married woman should be.

But she couldn't say such things to Kristina. She couldn't say them to anyone. "Thanks for the advice about Ruby." She finished her coffee and stood, leaving a couple of dollar bills on the table to cover her own coffee and Kristina's.

Throughout the fall, Henry continued to dig. He said he wouldn't be able to complete the bomb shelter before snow flew, but he wanted to have the space laid out. By the middle of October, he'd deemed the hole nearly big enough. He put the project aside for the winter, planning to rent a small concrete mixer in the spring to pour the floor and walls.

In the meantime, he created a makeshift drafting table in his room, using milk crates and a wide, worn-out board. Silja hated how it looked; she averted her eyes every time she passed the doorway to his room. He spent endless hours there, poring over a little government-issued pamphlet he'd sent away for, entitled *The Family Fallout Shelter.* He drew up plans. He consulted how-to books for ventilation advice and dry-cell battery power usage.

"Fifteen feet down," he said, spreading a drawing on the kitchen counter to show her. "That's overkill—the recommendation is ten—but better safe than sorry. The space itself will have a ten-by-twelve footprint, not counting the entrance. You see," he went on—his voice earnest, his finger pointing at a partition on the drawing, "you have to have at least one right-angle separating the entrance. That prevents most of the radiation from entering the main space."

"Does it now," Silja murmured, sipping her martini. "Fascinating."

She went out to take a look one frosty evening just before it began being too dark for her evening walks after work. In the last rays of sunlight, Henry stood beside the hole, wearing a wool plaid jacket and dungarees. His breath was visible in the cold. Silja wrapped her arms around herself and stepped closer to the hole.

"Eight-inch-thick walls," he told her proudly, sweeping his hand across the hole. "And the roof will be steel beams and concrete blocks. No one—nothing—will be able to penetrate it."

Silja could feel a small smile playing on her lips.

"You think this is funny, Silja?" he asked.

She shook her head. "No, of course not," she replied. "It's very serious business, Henry." She stepped closer and inspected the hole. "I appreciate you taking these steps to protect our family. Truly, I do."

Of course, she was lying. The whole thing was absurd.

Henry didn't answer; at first she thought he believed her. But then he said, "This doesn't worry you at all, does it?"

"No," she told him. "It doesn't worry me. Because it's not going to happen. We will never need a bomb shelter. No one is dropping a bomb on us, Henry. It's just propaganda. It's just fear-mongering."

"Oh, really? And on what authority do you have this information?" He began hauling long two-by-eights across the shorter sides of the hole—they would keep out animals, he'd said, over the winter. "What do you know, with your swanky dealings in the city all day long? Who provides you with inside information on what the Soviet government may or may not be planning?"

"For heaven's sake, Henry," she snapped. "I don't need an inside authority. I read the newspaper."

Henry gave her a withering look, as if he were not convinced that the *New York Times*—the most prestigious paper in the nation— could contain information of any value. It shouldn't surprise her, she knew. Henry's idea of keeping up with current events was to occasion- ally read the White Plains paper, *The Reporter Dispatch*, and to pore over the local rag—that silly *Stonekill Gazette* that arrived each Fri- day. "Written"—Silja used the term loosely—not by true journalists, but by a bunch of townie hacks.

"You know big newspapers are run by Communists," Henry said. His voice was low, as if someone might overhear him giving away na- tional security secrets.

Silja couldn't help it; she laughed aloud. "Now you are completely off your rocker."

"Goddamn it!" Red-faced, he picked up a plank and raised it above his head. He adjusted his stance and choked his grip, as though the plank were a baseball bat and he was setting up to hit a home run. He glared at her and took aim—it was as if she were a baseball coming toward him, as if he planned to hit her squarely across the jaw with enough force to knock her backward into the forest. She stepped away and put up her hands to protect her face.

Her actions seemed to give him pause—enough to come to his senses. He thrust the plank onto the ground, sliding it across the hole's opening next to its neighbor. She breathed a sigh of relief.

He regarded her fiercely. "You do what you need to do," he said, his voice chilly and even. "But remember that I'm keeping my eye on you, Silja."

After dinner one night in early April, during the first thaw of the spring, there was a telephone call that Henry answered. Silja heard him exclaiming joyfully. Without a word, he jumped into his truck and tore off.

"Whatever was that about?" she asked Ruby, who was helping her load the dishwasher. Ruby shrugged.

Ruby continued to do well in school. At her last parent-teacher conference, all of her teachers, including the nice new English teacher, Miss Wells—thank goodness Henry hadn't been there to see that Miss Wells was black; he would have thrown a fit—gushed about Ruby's smarts. They mentioned how well-thought-out her papers and assignments were, how she consistently raised her hand in class. "A model student," the teachers told Silja, and she beamed with pride.

But still she worried. She'd tried, more than once, to talk to Ruby about finding a hobby or a club. The school play? Debate team? Track and field, with those long legs of hers? To each idea, Ruby shrugged and said it wasn't her thing. After one too many rebukes, Silja gave up. At least Ruby wasn't a delinquent. And she wasn't fast; Silja needn't worry about that. In fact, Ruby showed no interest in boys whatsoever.

Of course, neither had Silja, as a girl. Not until she met Henry.

A half hour after he left, while Ruby and Silja were settled in the living room reading, Henry returned. And he brought the biggest surprise Silja had seen in years: Paul.

They came in together through the heavy slab front door, breathless and bustling—arms around each other's shoulders, looking every bit the matched set they'd always been. Paul set down his small leather satchel and whistled, looking around. "Well, you've certainly come up in the world," he said, meeting Silja's eye as she rose from her chair.

She crossed the room to the entryway. "Paul. What a surprise."

From behind her, a thin figure with a flash of long blond hair barreled forward and wrapped itself around Paul's lean frame, almost toppling him over.

He laughed and put his arms around Ruby's back. "Hey, there," he said. "Be careful or you'll knock your wobbly old uncle on the floor."

Ruby buried her head against his neck. "You're back," she whispered. "Finally, you came back."

He gently pried her away from himself. "Let me get a look at you." He held her at arm's length. "You're practically grown up," he said. "So tall and pretty. You look like—"

Paul glanced at Henry, who nodded. "Like Mother," Henry said. "I see it, too, especially around the eyes. Just like Mother."

This was news to Silja. She'd never so much as seen a photograph of her mother-in-law; she'd no idea Ruby bore any resemblance to her.

Besides, people always said Ruby looked like Silja. And she couldn't imagine that she looked anything like Henry's mother. She'd never met the woman, who'd died a few years ago. Was it 1955 or 1956?— Silja wasn't sure. She remembered Henry had received a telegram telling him that his mother had passed. Pneumonia, it was; she'd been stricken suddenly and was unable to make a recovery.

"Goodness," Silja had said to Henry. "Do you need to go to California?"

Henry sighed. "I suppose I do," he said. "She'll have left little in the way of an estate. But God knows Paul wouldn't be capable of settling her affairs without me there, too."

"Well, you'll get no argument from me on that score," Silja agreed. But she couldn't help adding, "Practical matters aside, though—you want to pay your respects, don't you? Even if Paul *could* handle it himself, you belong there, Henry."

He narrowed his eyes at her. "What do you mean by that?"

"For heaven's sake," she said. "Even if you weren't close, she was your *mother*. You were her elder son. Of course you want to be there to attend to her last wishes. Perhaps Ruby and I should go, too."

Henry had glared at her. "There is absolutely no need for you and Ruby to go," he barked. "And I'll thank you to mind your own business, Silja. It has nothing to do with you."

Before she could say anything else, he stomped out of the room.

She'd let it go, and he made the trip himself, traveling cross-country by train and returning two weeks later. She asked him how it went, and his only reply was that it went as expected. "There's nothing more to say about the matter," he told her. "It's a closed chapter."

Now, seeing Ruby for the first time in years, Paul asked the girl, "Do you forgive me?" He gave her an imploring look. "For leaving all those years ago—and on the night before your birthday, no less! Can you forgive me for that unforgivable sin?"

She nodded and said, "You're back. Nothing else matters."

Paul, Silja learned, was there to help with the next stages of the bomb shelter construction. It seemed that getting the roof done alone was too much even for Henry.

"I'm surprised to see you," she told Paul from the doorway as she watched him unpack his things in Henry's room; he was to sleep on the couch in the living room, but Henry said Paul could store his things in Henry's dresser.

The house had a celebratory air; Ruby was fixing Paul a snack, and Henry was pouring a beer for him. At Henry's insistence, Silja had taken Paul down the hallway so he could settle in. "I thought you said you were never coming back here," Silja went on, crossing her arms over her chest.

Without turning around, he continued to move shirts and socks from his battered satchel into an empty dresser drawer. "Henry wrote to me. He needs my help."

Silja bit her tongue to keep from mentioning Kristina. Instead, she said, "Yes, building a steel beam, concrete block roof is pretty important stuff. Not a project to attempt on one's own."

"Henry told me you think this is a joke," Paul said. "That doesn't shock me." He placed several pairs of boxer shorts into the drawer, then closed it firmly. "But unlike you, Silja, I have my priorities in order." He turned to face her. "I make sacrifices to do what's right."

"*You* make sacrifices?" she said, a bemused smile playing around her lips. "You? What sacrifices have you made, exactly, Paul?"

Paul gave her a cold stare. "Thanks for showing me to the room," he said. "You can go now, Silja."

She nodded toward the drawer he'd filled. "Just don't get too comfortable," she said. "You're already wearing out your welcome, as far as I'm concerned."

She turned and left without another word.

Both Paul and Henry assured her the visit was temporary, just a week or two. "And then what?" she asked Paul. "Where are you off to next?"

He shrugged. "I'm not sure," he said. "Somewhere I can continue to paint. That's all I know at this point."

Paul had taken up a hobby—painting watercolors—and his art supplies were all over the dining room table. Twice she'd cleaned up spills on the carpeting. Really, she thought—this couldn't be taken somewhere else? Perhaps outside?

"You should think about painting nature," she suggested to Paul one evening after she got home from work. "The woods are lovely this time of year. You could go out in the woods and paint."

He gazed through the plate-glass window in the dining room toward the forest. "I can see the woods just fine from here. I can paint what I see from here, without getting cold or rained on." He winced. "Or bit by mosquitoes. I hate mosquitoes."

Oh, for heaven's sake. Silja turned away. With a tiny smirk in Paul's general direction, she opened the sliding glass door and stepped into the forest for her evening walk.

45

Ruby

Before Shepherd started meeting her there, Ruby had walked in her family's woods alone.

She remembers when Uncle Paul came to help her father with the Shelter. She remembers sneaking up on them one afternoon when she got home from school. Stealing quietly through the woods, in the way only Ruby knew.

Her father and Uncle Paul were laying the roof beams. Steel beams, ten feet across, that they'd brought home in her father's pickup, a few at a time, and then hauled through the woods. They did the hauling after dark, when no one was watching. Ruby's father said the Shelter had to be a secret, because if the neighbors knew about it, when the bomb dropped they would all come knocking and want their place inside. "And there's only room for family," her father said. "Only blood matters, Ruby."

After she crept up on them, she crouched down behind a rock and watched. She didn't have to hide; Uncle Paul and her father always welcomed her presence. But she wanted to hear what they'd say if they didn't know she was listening.

Uncle Paul was talking about why he left, the last time he was in Stonekill. "You remember the fallout, Henry," he said. And then he grinned and added, "Metaphorically speaking, of course. Not the fallout we're creating protection from here."

Ruby's father did not return Uncle Paul's grin. His look was stern. "You left an awful mess behind," he told Uncle Paul. "You left a lot of unanswered questions." He stood up and stretched. "I would've had a hell of a time keeping all that from Silja if she hadn't been so obsessed at the time with finding a plot of land for the house." He shook his head. "That damn reporter, that Kellerman woman. Her questions could easily have been resolved, had you'd stayed and told the truth."

"Mrs. Kellerman wouldn't have believed me," Uncle Paul said. "No one would." He took hold of one end of the beam, waiting for Ruby's father to lift the other side. "It was my word against hers," he said. "Against *theirs*. Kristina was on that girl's side. Not that I blame Kristina for that; her job was on the line."

Ruby's father lifted his end. "But you didn't do it. You told me you never laid a hand on that girl."

"Never did," Uncle Paul agreed. "But it could have been read more ways than one. That's the trouble." He shrugged. "Did that girl kiss me? Yes, she did. Did I kiss her back?" Uncle Paul shook his head. "Not in a million years," he told Ruby's father. "I pushed her away."

"But you'd befriended her in the first place."

"Not intentionally," Uncle Paul explained. "More than once, she came to Kristina's house. *Our* house. Kristina hired her to walk the dog when I was busy putting in new kitchen cabinets."

They set the beam carefully into place and Uncle Paul bent down to pack dirt around his end. "Kristina wanted it all," he said. "A cheap dog walker. Free labor for her house. Not to mention a toss in the hay whenever she wanted it." He scoffed. "Old bag. What did she think? That she'd put a pretty girl in front of me—that she'd send a pretty girl to our house *alone*—when I was there by myself? And Kristina thought I wasn't going to react when that girl came on to me?"

"So you *did* do it." Her father said exactly the words Ruby was thinking.

Uncle Paul stood up, reaching for another beam, and told Ruby's father he'd done nothing.

Ruby breathed slowly, in and out, listening to the calm in Uncle Paul's voice. She knew he was upset, but he wasn't losing his cool. She knew then, and she knows now, that she can learn things from Uncle Paul.

"I did nothing," Uncle Paul repeated. "She was pretty, yes. She was young, yes. Do I like young, pretty girls? I'm only human, Henry—only a man. So what do *you* think?"

Uncle Paul picked up the next beam. Sweat stood out on his brow when he lifted it, but Ruby knew that was from physical exertion, not from the conversation.

"I have needs and desires like any man," Uncle Paul said. "But that doesn't mean I act on them when it's inappropriate."

Ruby's father—the man who had been sleeping alone for years—held his mouth in a straight, bitter line.

"And now?" her father finally asked. "These days—do you have a woman, Paul?"

Uncle Paul stepped to the side, bringing the beam beside its partner in the roof they were creating. "Well, there have been lots of women," he said. "Lots of women over lots of years." He grinned. "Who knows what I've left behind? There could be little Paul Juniors all over the goddamn country, for all I know and for all I care."

"But now?" Ruby's father persisted. "Is there anyone specific? Any special woman in your life?"

Uncle Paul grimaced and told her father that no, at the moment there was not.

Her father leaned over and patted down dirt. "Here's my advice," he said. "Whether you want it or not. Finish helping me here. We only need a few more days. And then hit the road, Paul. Move on and find somewhere to settle down. Somewhere far from here."

Ruby's father stood up and pulled a red bandanna from his back pocket. "And look for a pretty girl to settle down with," he added. "There are plenty of girls out there who'd fall all over a guy like you, Paul."

He wiped his forehead and told Uncle Paul not to be a fool. He placed the bandanna back in his pocket. "There are plenty of fish in the sea," he went on. "And if you choose wisely, you'll find one who can keep you out of trouble."

46

Silja

With so much of his attention on the bomb shelter, Henry had begun to neglect cooking and housekeeping. His own room was neat, and once a week he cleaned the hall bathroom, which he shared with Ruby. But other than a cursory wiping of countertops and stacking the dishes in the dishwasher after meals, he stopped tidying up the kitchen. They still enjoyed garden-fresh vegetables, but Henry's elaborate main courses gave way to meat loaf, tuna salad sandwiches, or frozen fish sticks. He rarely ran the vacuum cleaner or washed the floors. Silja couldn't remember the last time she saw him dust.

Silja didn't mind the meals so much; being in the restaurant business, she enjoyed gourmet lunches daily in the city, and several nights a week she had dinner with David. But the dirty house began to affect her. Yet again, she ventured the idea of a cleaning lady. They could afford it, and there was no reason the house should not be washed and disinfected on a regular basis. Silja dreamed of coming home to a spick-and-span, sweet-smelling home.

But Henry would have none of it. "You send a cleaning lady here, and I'll throw her out on her ear," he barked. "No strangers in this house, Silja, and that's final." He glared at her. "You want it clean, you clean it yourself."

"Well, fine," she told him. "You're being asinine, Henry—but I see I'm not going to win this battle."

She reserved all of a warm Saturday in mid-May for clearing out clutter. Much as she abhorred cleaning, it had to be done. With Paul finally gone and summer on its way, every room in the house needed airing.

She started by organizing her own bedroom, followed by Ruby's. She hauled out old papers, out-of-date magazines, bent hairpins. She tossed earrings with their back clasps broken off, slips with stretched-out elastics, shoes with heels broken beyond repair. She even dusted a little, slowly and deliberately pushing a rag across the horizontal surfaces in both rooms. She hated the way rising dust made her eyes water, but she knew dusting was good for the house, in the same way swallowing castor oil was good for the digestive tract.

Dust rag in hand, she passed the door to Henry's room. She hesitated, then ventured inside. Clean is clean, she told herself—she may as well do all of it while she was on a roll.

The air in Henry's room was stale; she pushed open the casement window, letting in a mild spring breeze. She tied her apron more tightly around her waist and began humming a cheerful, made-up tune.

Tomorrow was Sunday. She'd see David in less than twenty-four hours.

Smiling and humming as she dusted Henry's nightstand, Silja came across a stack of pamphlets.

How to Recognize a Communist in Your Midst
The Importance of Being Prepared
Do You REALLY Know Your Loved Ones?

For heaven's sake, Silja thought—is he serious? She opened one of the pamphlets and read:

> Its not how they look, its what they do! COMMUNISTS can be any body. Your mechanic. Your grocer. The woman next to you on the train.
> So how do you know?
> Look at his reading material. Do NOT let him see you do this. COMMUNISTS are SNEAKY.

Listen to what he says. Does he make SNIDE remarks about YOUR United States Government? COMMUNIST

Is he ATTRACTED to men? COMMUNIST

Is she suspected of REJECTING her wedding vows? COM-MUNIST

Silja stomped down the hall to the kitchen. "Where did these come from?" she asked, holding out the pamphlets toward Henry.

He looked at her steadily and didn't take them from her.

"There are groups," he said. "There's a group right here in Stonekill."

"Groups? What groups?"

He tilted his head. "It's beneficial," he went on, "for me to associate with like-minded people."

"Beneficial? Like-minded people?" She shook her head. "What are you talking about, Henry?"

He shrugged. "I wouldn't expect you to understand this." He looked at Silja calmly. "*You*, especially, I don't expect to understand."

"What does that mean?" She crossed her arms over her chest. "Are you saying you think I'm a Communist?"

He didn't answer for a moment. Then he said, "I don't feel like I know you very well, Silja. I'm not sure I ever have." He turned away and busied himself at the kitchen counter, chopping asparagus with a heavy butcher's knife.

"We've been married for seventeen years, Henry," Silja said. "How can you say you don't know me, you never knew me?"

"I don't know what you do all day." He took a sip of tea from the cup beside him. "I don't know who you associate with."

"For God's sake!" she burst out. "I *work* all day! That's what I do. I work all day so we can have this nice house and you can sit around here brooding and building bomb shelters and planning how you will live through Doomsday. *That's* what I do."

She looked down toward her feet. Yes, she *did* work hard. But she also spent her free time—almost all the free time she could—with

David. It was what she was looking forward to on Sunday; she and David had plans to meet at Pound Ridge Reservation for a hike.

But Henry didn't need to know that.

"Your work is exactly the problem," Henry complained. "You're gone all day. No other wives do that."

He raised the knife and brought it down soundly across a row of asparagus. Chop, chop, chop.

"And whose fault is that, Henry?" Her voice was wobbly, which infuriated her; they were in their situation because of Henry, not because of her. "Whose fault is it that your wife supports this family? Whose fault is it that we're so abnormal?"

"I never asked you to carry that load," Henry said. "You wanted to do it. If you hadn't, I would have gone to college. I would be supporting us, like a man is supposed to do."

What was he talking about? He'd never shown the slightest hint of motivation to go to college after he returned from the war. The closest he came was that silly crime detection correspondence course he never even finished.

"So go ahead and do it!" she said, her hands pressed onto the edge of the counter, leaning toward him. "Ruby is sixteen. She doesn't need you around all day long. Get an education, Henry. Figure out what you want to do with your life. You're not even middle-aged yet. You have plenty of years left."

"No." One-handed, he scooped up asparagus ends and tossed them in the trash.

Then he turned to face her, knife raised, handle gripped in his right hand. "No, Silja, it's too late for college. And besides . . . " He glanced at the pamphlets in her hand. "I've found my work. I know now why things turned out the way they did. I was meant to do this."

"What does that mean? What are you meant to do?"

He held the knife aloft, its blade gleaming in the sunlight. He pointed it toward her, inches from her chest.

"Egads, Henry," she said. "Get that thing away from me." She stepped back and asked again, "What do you mean?"

He persisted, reaching across the countertop toward her—knife in hand, knuckles red.

"Stop," she said. "Stop that and answer the question. Please."

Was it because she said *please*? She wasn't sure. Either way, he seemed to reconsider his behavior. He set down the knife and looked her in the eye.

"I'm not just reading those pamphlets, Silja," he said. "I'm the one who wrote them."

The next day, thinking about it as she drove east on Route 35 to meet David, Silja felt more apprehensive than furious. The way Henry messed around with the knife had certainly been disturbing. Good thing Ruby hadn't been present to witness something like that.

And those pamphlets worried her—no doubt about it. She could only imagine what Henry would think of David, were he ever to find out the kind of man Silja was involved with.

Not that David had anything to hide—not really. While he had sympathy for the plight of the working man—and what kindhearted person didn't?—David wasn't involved with any Communist crowd. Yes, he was outspoken in his beliefs—but he wasn't involved in any subversive actions, for heaven's sake.

Henry wouldn't see it that way, though. Henry would be furious with her—not just for having an affair, but also for who the affair was with.

Well, Henry would never find out. She and David were careful. She needn't worry about it.

Beyond that, Henry's pamphlets had made her wistful. They were awful, not just because of their ridiculous content, but also because of how poorly they were written. It was like the writing of a child who hadn't been tutored in proper grammar and syntax. She remembered Henry's letters from the war. They'd always been short and to the point, containing errors here and there. Not the greatest prose, but at the time she'd chalked it up to stress over his situation, lack of time to write a proper letter.

She remembered her mother's socialist pamphlets and signs, re-membered what a skilled writer and dedicated steward Mikaela had been. Silja thought about how she had learned at Mikaela's knee—about not only socialism, but also how to turn a phrase. It was a skill she used at her job, in both written and spoken communication.

How much better, Silja thought, she herself could have worded Henry's pamphlets—if she shared his beliefs, of course. He could have supplied the ideas and she could have made the words shine.

What a great team she and Henry would make, Silja thought. If only they were on the same side.

Well, if there had ever been a chance for that—and she doubted there had been—it was too late now.

If she hadn't started her silly cleaning project in the first place, she'd never have found those awful things he wrote. It would have been better *not* to know. She'd learned her lesson. She'd stay out of his room—and out of his life, as much as possible—from now on.

By June, the bomb shelter was finished. Silja couldn't imagine a more asinine waste of time and money. But Henry was thrilled. "Come down and let me show you," he entreated.

She truly didn't want to. The ladder—a series of iron rungs bolted to the concrete wall—unsettled her as she made her way down step by cautious step. At the bottom, she had to leap off the ladder, landing with a thud in the darkness. Slowly, with her hands pressed to the hard, cold walls on either side of a narrow corridor, she stepped toward a dim light ahead of her. Around the corner from the entrance she found herself in the main part of the bomb shelter.

Henry, going down ahead of her, had lit a battery-powered lamp on the bookshelf. In the low light, she took a look around. She had to admit the bomb shelter was spacious, all things considered; she could stand up fully, could turn around. She needed to take four long steps to cross from one side of the room to the other.

Still, the space felt constrictive, like it might swallow her whole.

She went back around the corner and looked nervously at the blue sky above her, through the hole fifteen feet above her head.

"We could last down here for a month," Henry said confidently, coming up behind her and tapping the concrete walls. "Nothing could get in. We'd be safe and snug as bugs."

And then what? Silja wanted to ask. And then we emerge, and the world is gone, and it's just us—what happens then?

Honestly, if a bomb did fall from the sky—and of course such a thing would never happen—she wouldn't want to be one of the only people left on the planet. Let that bomb blow me to bits, she thought. I'd rather die.

That's probably what Henry would prefer, too. He likely hoped that if a bomb dropped, Silja would be far away from Stonekill and his beloved bomb shelter.

But thinking about Ruby, Silja became remorseful. What if such a thing truly did happen, and Silja wasn't at home, but was in the city, or off somewhere with David? Her daughter would be left to fend for herself, with only her father to care for her.

It was a sobering thought.

In August, they received news from Paul: he was to be married. In a million years, Silja could not have predicted such a thing.

Paul, it turned out, had spent the summer in Wisconsin, in some resort area called Door County. (What an odd name for a county, Silja thought.) There was something about Paul's watercolors, about how Door County was an up-and-coming artists' community, and tourists paid handsome sums for watercolors of Lake Michigan and the local scenery. According to Paul, the painting was going well, but not well enough to afford a room in Baileys Harbor, the little town in which he'd planted himself. So he began working as a bartender. He'd met a girl with whom he was now quite madly in love, he said—and she with him.

They were to be married in a few weeks. Paul wanted his brother's family to come to Wisconsin, so Henry could be the best man at his wedding.

"How in the world would we get there?" Silja asked Henry, after scanning Paul's letter.

He gave her a scornful look. "There are airplanes, Silja," he said. "Or hadn't you heard?"

Silja felt rather foolish. She'd never thought about airplanes flying somewhere as remote as Wisconsin.

It turned out they could fly to Milwaukee, then rent a car and drive several hours to Door County, which was in the northeastern part of the state. The only way Silja knew this was by looking in the atlas.

Silja bought Ruby a pair of low heels and a blue taffeta dress for the wedding, which Ruby glanced at but refused to try on, saying it was too much bother. All Silja could do was cross her fingers that the clothes would fit.

"I don't care what I wear to some silly wedding," Ruby said. "But I can't wait for the trip. I just want to get on that plane and *go*."

When Silja asked why she was so eager, Ruby said, "Because we never go anywhere."

It gave Silja pause. Ruby was right. They certainly could travel if they wanted to. They had the money and time. And Ruby was a big girl, not some baby who needed constant care.

Of course, if Silja were to travel, she'd prefer to travel with David, not Henry.

She let herself imagine it. Seeing the world with David. Bringing Ruby along.

It would be a dream come true.

It took an entire day to get to Baileys Harbor. They went in a taxi to LaGuardia, flew to Milwaukee, then stopped at the Avis Rent-a-Car desk to acquire an automobile. They journeyed north on Highway 41, through towns with odd names—Menomonee Falls, Fond du Lac, Neenah. In Green Bay, they headed northeast. Finally, nearing nightfall, they drove through the little town of Baileys Harbor, then went a few miles farther north on the highway and turned off at a place called Gordon Lodge.

After they'd checked into the lodge—there were some cottages on the property, closed up for the winter, and the lodge, which was still open—they walked across the lawn to the bar where Paul worked. The bar was in a separate building right on the lakeshore. The Top Deck, it was called, and it was indeed the upper level of a boathouse-like structure facing the water.

With the tourist season over, few other people were around—neither guests nor workers. Paul ran the bar as if he owned it, setting up glasses and pouring drinks with a flourish. He told them that if it were the season, they never would have been able to use the space for the wedding; it would have been booked by tourists. But since hardly anyone else was there, and since he and the bride were both Gordon's employees, the owner gave them a break.

Paul told them about the bride. "Comes from a big Catholic family," he said. "They're among the few Catholics in Baileys Harbor; the service will be at the only Catholic church in town. Most folks around here are Lutheran—Norwegians or Swedes; the joint is chock-full of Lutheran churches." He sipped his drink. "But the Doyles are well-off and respected. Dr. Doyle has a family practice. There are six kids; Angie's the youngest. All the rest married and living nearby." He set down his half-empty glass and added ice to refresh it. "So many nieces and nephews, I can't keep track." His eyes twinkled at Ruby. "But don't worry, sweetheart—you'll always be my number one."

She smiled back at him and slurped her Coca-Cola.

Paul and Angie planned to live in a cottage that had once been her grandparents' vacation home, Paul explained. It was in a settlement just up the road, a place called North Bay. "It's not even a town," Paul said. "Mostly just summer cottages. Really pretty, though, especially where the Doyles' place is, right along the bay." He ran his fingers through his thick hair. "Angie's dad's people were from Chicago, but they spent their summers up here. Her mother was a local girl. They met at a dance one summer about a million years ago."

Reaching across the bar, Paul clapped Henry on the shoulder. "I wish you could stick around, old pal," he said. "I'm going to spend the next few months winterizing the cottage. Insulation, new windows, and I have to figure out a way to keep the well water from freezing. I could sure use your expertise, Henry."

Silja's heart leaped at the notion—Paul was more than welcome to Henry's help, if he wanted it. Heck, Henry could stay here indefinitely. If he never came back to New York, she'd be thrilled.

But Henry shook his head, saying he had work and commitments of his own back in Stonekill.

Silja laughed. "What work?" she asked. "What commitments? Building bomb shelters? The occasional hour spent replacing the hinges on someone's squeaky front door?"

Henry glared at her. "My business is my own," he said. "I stay out of your business, Silja, and I'll thank you to stay out of mine."

She rolled her eyes. "Okay, Henry. Fine." She finished her martini and stood. "Come on, Ruby. Let's turn in."

Ruby followed her back to the lodge. Henry stayed at the bar; he and Paul were up half the night, Henry seated on a barstool and Paul behind the bar. Silja knew about it because when Henry hadn't returned to their room by two in the morning, she got up, put on her dressing gown, and glided across the chilly lawn toward the Top Deck. Peering in the window, she saw the two of them, identical heads bent toward one another, laughing and talking quietly.

No one else was about. She turned and ran back to the lodge before they could see her.

The next day was the wedding. Silja'd had no idea Paul could pass himself off as even remotely religious, but she had to admit he did a fine job. He looked every bit the reverent bridegroom—and Henry, standing beside him, also knew all the right moments to kneel, to cross himself, to murmur words of worship and praise. The pages in the small book in their pew—which, apparently, one was meant to consult during the service—were confusing and appeared to be out of order. The book was of no help to Silja and Ruby.

Silja thought of her own wedding at the courthouse in Manhattan, and how little was required of Henry and herself. Names, birth dates, current places of residence. Say these words after me. Sign here, please. And that was it; they were pronounced husband and wife.

Silja could tell—by the warm wishes bestowed on her parents, the way guest after guest heartily clasped Angie's father's hand and affectionately kissed her mother's cheek—that what Paul had said last night was true: he was marrying into an admired, stable family. Who would have guessed such a thing could happen? Not Silja. She was surprised Angie's parents—particularly the father—didn't see through Paul's facade. What man would want a ne'er-do-well like Paul as a son-in-law? Perhaps they were simply grateful that their daughter was married— and had married a Catholic.

At the reception there was much dancing, much drinking of beer and eating of sausages, and many toasts to the health of the bride and groom. The poor girl looked exhausted by the end of it all, and Silja hoped Paul would have the sense to take her off to bed earlier rather than later. When Silja whispered as much to Henry, he said, "Paul knows how to handle these people. Look how well he's doing."

Silja felt her lips pursing together. "He's not doing well enough to know what his wife needs, that's for sure."

Henry glared at her. "Leave it be, Silja. For once in your life, just leave it be."

The bride was a cute, just-blossomed thing—not a lick like Kristina—with wavy brown hair and bright blue eyes. Freckles across the girl's nose only added to her youthful appearance. Her sisters looked so much alike, and dressed as they were in identical bridesmaid dresses, Silja would not have known one from the other, had one not had short hair and the other a longer, fuller style. Both women sported little gold cross necklaces, as did Angie. When Paul loosened his tie at the reception, Silja saw the glint of the chain holding his St. Christopher medal.

The irony was not lost on her: in an area filled with Lutherans, Paul had somehow found the one available Catholic girl to marry. Looking around at the tall, blond, Nordic-faced guests, Silja almost felt as if she were back at the Alku. These people looked as if they could be related to everyone she'd grown up with. Heck, her own father could be one of those balding old men sitting at the bar, laughing and sharing stories over pints of beer. But she wouldn't know him.

The notion made her melancholy, and she spent a good deal of time smoking and staring out the windows at the lake, deep in thought.

More than once during the wedding reception, Silja caught Henry and Paul huddled together, glancing her way. She tried to pass it off as a silly paranoia, but she couldn't deny what she saw. She couldn't even say they were trying to hide it.

What in the world is that about? Silja wondered that night as she tossed in bed restlessly, careful to keep to her side. She didn't want to disturb Ruby, with whom she was sharing; Henry slept alone in the room's other bed.

As always, she wondered if Henry had any inkling at all about David. But no; she knew he didn't. She and David had always been discreet.

The next day, she chose not to confront Henry about his odd behavior at the reception. On the long drive back to the airport, the wait in the terminal, the ride on the plane—through all that, through gathering their luggage at LaGuardia, hailing a cab, and riding home to Stonekill, getting in long after dark and dragging themselves to bed—she said nothing to Henry. They talked about how vast and treeless the scenery was along Lake Michigan. They discussed the pros and cons of airplane travel, and speculated about what the weather would be like when they landed in New York. Safe topics that Ruby could converse with them about.

They did not talk about those glances, those shared words between the brothers.

Because if Henry *did* suspect? Well, on the one hand, Silja didn't want to know.

But on the other hand, she wished he did. Sometimes she wished the whole thing could finally come to a head. Could be resolved once and for all.

No matter the consequences.

47

Angie

Perched on the davenport, my half-finished cup of coffee growing cold on the side table next to me, I scanned the black-and-white photographs in Silja's album.

All the photographs seemed to have been taken on the same day, in the same location—on a small motorboat, it looked like, similar to the one my parents had at home on Lake Michigan. I could tell, by the vastness of it, that the water I saw in the background must be the Hudson River. There was some mass in the distance on the water; I squinted to make it out, and realized it was the fleet of unused ships I'd seen when we drove to the funeral home the other day.

The first group of photos showed Silja and Ruby. They were recent; Ruby looked as she did now, and Silja seemed about the same as I remembered from my wedding day. Both mother and daughter were in casual weekend wear—Silja in a pair of slacks and a sleeveless blouse with ballerina flats; Ruby in pedal pushers, a short-sleeved top, and sandals.

There were four photos of mother and daughter. In each one, Silja and Ruby sat close together on the motorboat's bench. The first showed their heads bent toward one another, as if sharing a joke. In another, they looked straight at the camera, smiles on both their faces. Yet another was profiles—Silja and Ruby facing each other with their large noses touching.

I turned to the next photograph. They had switched photographers. Now the person holding the camera must have been Silja, because she was no longer shown.

Instead, the photograph showed Ruby with a man. A sleepy-eyed, stocky man with a kind expression. He sat next to Ruby in the spot Silja had vacated.

It was Dr. Shepherd.

He wore chinos, a golf shirt, a tweed cap. His hands rested lightly on his knees. His cap was pulled down over his brow, but both he and Ruby looked directly into the camera, smiles on their faces. It was unmistakably the same man who had been at Henry's funeral.

There were four photographs of Ruby and Dr. Shepherd. In the second picture, Ruby was pointing across the water at a sailboat in the distance. In the last two, they seemed to be in friendly conversation.

Holding my breath, I turned the album's pages once more.

The last set of photographs—three this time—showed Silja and Dr. Shepherd.

In the first photo, Dr. Shepherd had a hand on Silja's arm, but at a slight distance; between their bodies, I could make out the side of the boat and the river in the background. In the second, they sat closer together, and Dr. Shepherd looked at Silja while she smiled at the camera.

The final photo showed Dr. Shepherd's arm around Silja's shoulder, and her head nestled against his collarbone.

PJ let out a long, lonely-sounding wail. With a start, I realized I'd been completely ignoring the baby; he'd rolled himself under a side chair and couldn't get free. The chair, with a sleek wooden frame and aqua-colored fabric, was almost big enough for me to crawl underneath myself. It must have been frightening for PJ to look up and see the dark underside of the chair, instead of the beamed ceiling the baby had become accustomed to in the past few days.

I set down the photograph album and picked up PJ, holding him close. "It's all right, little one," I murmured. "Mommy is here. You're fine."

PJ was covered in dust. When I had vacuumed the other day, I'd given it a lick and a promise, ignoring the furniture's undersides. I should have been more thorough, I scolded myself—but then again, *I* wasn't the one living in a filthy house.

"Disgusting," I muttered, carrying the baby to the kitchen and wiping his face and hair with a damp dishtowel.

What kind of homemaker was Silja, anyway, to let her house get into this kind of shape? Paul said that Silja lived opulently—well then, why didn't she have help? Even if Silja refused to clean her house herself, she must be able to afford a cleaning woman.

I took PJ to the guest room and changed his clothes. I smoothed his hair and studied his face. He looked back at me with dark, sparkling eyes. I pulled him close and kissed the sweet-smelling top of his head.

I put PJ down for a nap and returned to the living room. I looked through the album's pages one by one. I studied the nuances of each photograph. Traced my index finger around the three faces, puzzling over their connection.

Dr. Shepherd was not Ruby's father—of that, I was certain. Ruby's eyes were an exact replica of Henry's. And her long, lean body was all Glass. The short, stocky professor with the down-turned eyes looked nothing like her.

But clearly, something had been going on between Dr. Shepherd and Silja—something that Silja had drawn her daughter into.

Abruptly, I tossed the album on the couch and hurried down the hall. In the master bedroom, I rushed to the dresser, fumbling with the clasp on Silja's jewelry box and lifting out the necklace tray.

I stood back in shock. The jewelry was all there. Silja's fine bracelets and rings and earrings. All the expensive pieces.

But no envelope.

I pushed everything aside, looked for a false compartment on the bottom. I looked under the jewelry box and rifled through Silja's dresser drawers.

As I did so, I caught sight of myself in the mirror over Silja's dresser. For just a moment, I thought I saw someone else in the mirror: a woman taller than me, older, with blond, elegant upswept hair and deep hazel eyes.

I backed away, slamming the dresser drawers closed. Then I took a breath and smiled at my own foolishness. It was just my mind playing tricks on me.

As I looked around the room, the desk in the corner caught my eye. Long and sleek, its surface was supported by spindly metal legs. Its only two drawers were on the right-hand side, below the desk's surface. I opened the drawers and began pillaging the contents. The lower drawer contained hanging files; I pulled out a few folders and saw that they appeared to be related to Silja's work. In the upper drawer, a plastic desk organizer held paper clips, rubber bands, a stapler.

Avoiding the mirror over the dresser—looking anywhere but there—I continued searching the room. I rummaged through Silja's closet racks and shelves, but all I found were the fancy clothes and stacks of shoe boxes I'd already seen. I looked under the bed, coughing at the dust and filth. There was nothing there but grime. I wondered if anyone had vacuumed under that bed since the house was built. I doubted it.

Fifteen minutes later, I'd torn the room apart. But if the envelope was there, I failed to find it.

Carefully, I put everything in Silja's room back as it had been before my search. And then I went into the hallway and stood still, considering.

I was certain the envelope contained a clue of some sort. Did Ruby take it? She *must* have. Thinking it through, that made more sense than the envelope being in Silja's room anyway. Why would Ruby move it from the jewelry box to another location in Silja's room? She wouldn't, of course; she would take it to her own room. If I hadn't been so rattled by the figment in the mirror, I'd have realized that sooner.

I was wasting time.

I sprinted down the hall to Ruby's room. I opened every drawer in the dresser and nightstand. I shuffled through the books on the bookshelf. Thrusting open the closet door, I plowed through mounds of clothes on the closet floor. A cardboard box of hairpins and barrettes. A loose stack of 45's, their slippery black surfaces escaping my grip as I pushed them aside. A sloppy pile of school papers that I skimmed through. Ruby got all A's, which didn't surprise me. I glanced at the girl's English essays and history papers, her math homework done in a neat, spidery hand.

And then, at the bottom of the stack, I found some papers that made me pause. I pulled them out of the closet and sat back on my heels, studying them in the light from the window.

They were construction plans of some sort. Not of this house, but of a smaller structure. The dimensions were noted—eight-inch-thick walls, an interior space twelve feet by ten. One drawing showed a tidy layout of shelving, bunks, a table, and a small closet-like space marked "WC."

I turned to the next page. SITE PLAN was written across the top in block-shaped letters. The page showed the small structure and the area around it. I could plainly see where the structure stood in relation to Henry and Silja's home—in the woods, at the far end of the property line.

Whatever could this thing be? Had it ever been built, or was it just on paper?

If it *had* been built, did Paul know about it?

And why did Ruby have construction drawings of it?

I dug back into the closet. If those drawings were there, perhaps the envelope was, too. I just had to look more carefully. I went back through the class work stack, and then took the clothing items, one by one, shaking them out before tossing them aside.

The first few items revealed nothing. And then, turning a denim jacket right-side out, I came across an envelope stuffed into the sleeve. Finally, I thought, here it is.

But it wasn't. Unlike the envelope in Silja's jewelry box, this one was not blank.

It was addressed from Paul to Ruby.

The postmark was from several weeks ago. I had no idea Paul exchanged mail with Ruby. She did not, to my knowledge, write back.

Perhaps this was the first time he'd written her. Perhaps he was wait-ing for a reply.

I wanted to read his words, but doing so felt wrong. I placed the envelope carefully where I'd found it, turning the jacket back inside-out and inserting the envelope in the jacket sleeve.

I stood. I moved about the room, carefully restoring everything to the chaotic condition it had been in before I began my search. I hadn't made it much worse; everything had been in a jumble when I'd opened the door to Ruby's room. But I attempted to leave the jumble as close to its original state as I could.

I turned on my heel and went out, closing the door.

I heard PJ awaken, and went to the guest room to fetch him. Sit-ting on the bed, I regarded my son, taking in his small features—his soft hair, his round cheeks and fair skin. And, of course, those dark eyes. PJ returned my gaze with an open and sociable expression, as if I were an old friend he'd run into on the street.

I picked him up and held him close, rocking him against my breast. "Sweet little man," I murmured. "I love you so much."

The telephone rang, and I scurried to the kitchen. "Glass resi-dence."

"Angel, it's me." Paul's voice sounded tense, exhausted.

"How are you? How's Ruby? What's going on there?" I swayed PJ, his back pressed against my stomach. "I've been so worried."

Paul sighed. "I can't go into details. But we'll be here for a while yet, I think."

I glanced at the wall clock; it was not quite noon. "Is there anything I can do? Any way I can help?"

"You just sit tight, Angel." Paul's voice was low and soothing, reminding me of my father's when I was a child and a nighttime thunderstorm would rouse my sisters and me. "It will be over soon."

48

Ruby

Ruby is very, very tired by now of being in the little room. The wall is full of her scratches, barely a spot she can reach that hasn't been gouged. She stands back in satisfaction. It's a job well done. Her father always said no job was worth doing if you weren't going to give it your all.

When will they return? Where is Uncle Paul? He didn't abandon her here, did he? No, Uncle Paul wouldn't do that. He'll be back.

In theory, this room should feel solid, like the Shelter. It has no windows, just like the Shelter. It's dark, just like the Shelter.

But it does not feel indestructible. Unlike the Shelter, this room feels like a place that could cave in.

Finally, the door opens, and Slater and Hill enter, followed by Uncle Paul and another man. Hill is carrying an extra chair, which he arranges at the table. Everyone sits.

Slater looks around. "I see you've been busy, Ruby."

Ruby doesn't answer, which is the right thing to do because the new man growls at Slater. "Please don't address my client without addressing me first, Detective."

The man turns to her. "Ruby," he says. "My name is Mr. Kurtz, and your uncle has hired me to represent you. I want you to know you don't need to answer any questions at this time. You're not being charged with anything. You're free to go whenever you want. And my suggestion is that you leave right now." He glances at Uncle Paul. "Your uncle agrees with me."

Uncle Paul says, "We can go to Mr. Kurtz's office and speak further with him, Ruby."

Ruby nods because she knows that's the only way she's getting out of this room, although she has zero intention of saying anything to this Kurtz character. She dislikes him even more than she dislikes Slater, which isn't saying a lot.

Kurtz stands and tips his hat at the cops. "Gentlemen."

Slater stands too, and you can tell he's angry. "We'll be in touch," he tells Kurtz.

Kurtz ushers Ruby and Uncle Paul toward the door. "I'm sure you will."

Outside the cop shop, in the parking lot, Kurtz tries to persuade Uncle Paul to bring Ruby to his office right then and there. "I want you to tell me everything, Ruby," Kurtz says, turning to her. He touches her shoulder, and she flinches.

"I'm sorry," he says, drawing his hand away. "I have a daughter just about your age." He tilts his head, looking at her. "Ruby, do you know what attorney-client privilege is?"

Of course she does. Does this flake think Ruby doesn't read? That she's never seen *Perry Mason*?

But Ruby doesn't say that aloud; she just nods. No reason to be rude, especially if she wants to get out of here.

"Well, then you know you can trust me. I'm your lawyer and I'm here to help."

She turns to Uncle Paul. "Can we go now?"

Uncle Paul looks at Kurtz. "Let me talk to her. I'll call you as soon as possible."

Kurtz sighs. "The sooner the better," he tells Uncle Paul. "This thing is a ticking time bomb."

❖   ❖   ❖

Uncle Paul holds the car door open for Ruby. He's being very supportive, all things considered.

She slides in and pushes the cigarette lighter. Uncle Paul gets in the driver's side just as the lighter pops out and Ruby reaches for it, Camel in her other hand. He watches her wordlessly, then takes out his Luckies and lights one.

They both sit silently, smoking. Ruby looks out through the front windshield at the parking lot and the road beyond it, watching the traffic buzz by.

Uncle Paul finishes his Lucky, then opens his window and tosses the butt onto the pavement. "Want to go for a drive?"

"What about Aunt Angie?" Ruby asks. "She's got to be frantic by now."

He smiles, but his look is grim. "It's nice of you to think of her. But she'll be fine."

Ruby shrugs. "Okay, then. Let's go for a drive."

49

Silja

1959–1960

The truth came out in October, a few weeks after they got back from Wisconsin. It made so much sense, Silja had no idea how she'd missed it. The girl, Angie, was pregnant, expecting a baby in March. No wonder there was such haste.

Henry said Paul had told him while they were in Wisconsin. When Silja asked why Henry didn't share the information with her, Henry said, "Because Paul told me in confidence. If he'd wanted you to know, he'd have told both of us."

"But you're telling me now." She walked across the living room to the bar and began fixing herself a drink.

He smirked. "It's not like you wouldn't have found out."

Silja knew she should let it go, but she couldn't resist. "You're the one who wants us to stay married, Henry," she reminded him, adding ice and vermouth to her martini shaker. "Aren't husbands and wives supposed to share this type of information with one another?"

Eyebrows raised, she glanced back to where he stood at the kitchen counter, thinning pork chops with a meat tenderizer. A pot of green beans simmered on the stove. It was an anomaly these days, Henry making a substantial meal like this.

Across the big room, he gave her a long, hardened look. "There are all kinds of marriages," he said, raising the tenderizer and bringing it down with a solid thwack, flattening the meat under it. "Let's hope Paul fares better at it than we have, shall we?"

He hit the chops viciously—over and over, as if he intended flattening them to the thinness of paper. Watching him silently, Silja shook her drink and poured it into a glass.

"Can't see how any two people could do worse," she mumbled, adding an olive to the glass and sucking juice from her fingers.

As he opened his mouth to respond, Ruby walked in from the hallway. Silja took her drink and stepped outside onto the patio. She stared through the glass as Ruby sat down at the kitchen counter, leaning forward to chat with Henry. He relaxed his brutish stance, set down the tenderizer, and gave their daughter a beatific smile.

Silja consulted a lawyer in the city, asking if there was any way to force Henry into granting her a divorce. She did not mention David.

The lawyer, a fellow named Barnes, said divorce was possible only if Henry agreed to it—and even if that happened, the lawyer said, Henry would surely take her to the cleaners. "You and Mr. Glass could argue over the specifics tooth and nail, but at the end of the day I'd put money on him getting your house and your child," Barnes told her. "Yours is an unusual case, Mrs. Glass. There aren't many women who come here in your position. Generally, we can't get a wife out of a marriage if her husband is unwilling, unless there's absolute proof of adultery."

"What about abuse?" Silja asked. "He says terrible things to me. He's threatened me."

Barnes raised his eyebrows. "Ever laid a hand on you?"

Silja thought about that long-ago night at the Alku. Just a little prod, she'd told herself then. It meant nothing. And it happened ages ago. In another lifetime, it felt like.

"No," she admitted. "Not really. Once, early in our marriage, he pushed my shoulder a bit."

"Documented bruises? Any kind of scar?"

"No," Silja said. "Nothing like that."

The lawyer shrugged. "A little pushing between spouses is not uncommon, ma'am. Has he ever done anything more combative?"

"No," she said, for a third time. "On a few occasions, he's acted like he might get . . . physically aggressive. But he controls himself."

"Well, Mrs. Glass. That doesn't sound like abuse to me. And even if it was, in New York State abuse is invalid as grounds for divorce. I'm sorry to inform you that you don't have a case." Barnes pursed his lips. "My advice would be to make the best of your situation." The lawyer pushed a stack of papers neatly together on his desk. "Try to find the good in your husband, ma'am. Every man has it, you know."

With winter on the way, Henry was busy outfitting the bomb shelter in case they should be ensconced there during the cold months. He piled more blankets on the cots and added a portable heater, one he rigged up to be battery-powered.

"With Paul a married man, will we need to make room for his bride and the baby, too?" Silja watched Henry stack cans of Campbell's soup on the kitchen counter, preparing to transfer them to the shelter.

He presented her with a long, withering look. "Paul is thinking about building his own." He added a can of tomato soup to the stack. "But yes, if it came to that and they were here, we would make room."

Silja laughed. "And who would we push out to make room, Henry?"

He didn't answer. He didn't have to. He wouldn't readily grant her a divorce; she knew that much. But she also knew exactly who he would push out of their family, their home—and his preposterous bomb shelter—if he could figure out a way to do it.

She still saw David nearly every Sunday. In the winter they went to the movies, but in warmer weather, she met him in natural places—his favorites. State parks, riverfronts, hiking trails. They saw each other whenever they could manage it during the week, too—after work in the city, where they would have dinner and then get a hotel room.

It reminded Silja of those early days with Henry, except now it was better. So much better.

David was a patient and accommodating lover. His kisses were indulgent, never aggressive. He caressed her skin, head to toe, his fingers slowly tracing the small hairs on her arm as if he had all the time in the world, instead of an hour or two. He entered her only when she was ready, wet and warm, her skin alive with the heat of his touch. He pulled her on top of him so he could look her in the eye as their bodies joined. Sometimes they lay side by side—her lower hip pressed against the sheets, her upper leg wrapped around him. "Silja, Silja, Silja" he murmured as he thrust into her, chanting her name over and over like he was praying.

Afterward they lay together for as long as they could, until the hour grew late and she knew she had to rise, dress, and make her way home. During those times, Silja thought about how she longed to stay with him all night. Just once.

No, *not* just once, she corrected herself. Forever. Every night, for the rest of her life. She'd never—not with Henry, not with David—slept all night in a lover's arms. She had no idea what it would feel like to wake up warm in David's embrace, the rising sun filtering through the curtains, birds outside singing a morning tune.

Unlike with Henry before the war, she was careful now. She saw a doctor in the city, acquired a diaphragm, and used it faithfully. There would be no unintended pregnancy. Not that she wouldn't adore having David's baby. She fantasized about the child they might have created together, if circumstances had been different. She thought about the kindhearted, gentle soul who would have come from her union with the man she'd been destined for all along.

He'd never been to Stone Ridge Road. There was no opportunity to show him her beautiful glass house; Henry was always there.

David lived in White Plains, in a spacious apartment he shared with his elderly father. David had married young, but his wife died of pneumonia a year or two into their marriage. There had been no children. He never remarried; after his wife's death he lived alone for many years. "It broke my heart to lose her," he told Silja. "I thought she was my one true love. I thought I'd never again care for anyone so much." He looked deeply into Silja's eyes. "I was wrong about that, Silja."

After his mother passed, David moved his father into his apartment, where he could better care for the old man as his health began to decline. Once, early in their relationship, David took her to his apartment. It was late at night; they'd been out to dinner in White Plains. He suggested bringing her home, "just to show you my place." He smiled shyly when he said it, and her cheeks glowed. "You know my father lives with me," David stammered. "He'll be sleeping when we get there. We'll have to be quiet and we can't stay long. But if you want to see it . . . "

She'd nodded. "Of course. I'd love that."

She admired the tidy, cozy kitchen, the comfortable living room and dining room, the large oil paintings of flowers and landscapes. David said his mother had been the artist.

Standing in the doorway of David's office, Silja smiled fondly. The room, overflowing with textbooks, microscopes, and dozens of potted plants, was so completely perfect for him. It was the exact home office she would have imagined him to have.

"What's this?" she asked him, touching the leaves of a shimmering green-and-white plant in a brass pot.

"*Pteris argyraea*," he replied. "Otherwise known as a silver brake fern. Pretty to look at and easy to grow. I'll get you one."

"I'd like that. It's beautiful."

"Yes," David whispered, turning her toward him. "Beautiful, just like you."

She stepped away from the plant and into his embrace. *Beautiful*, he'd said. Not just sexy, as Henry called her back in the day. Not his baby doll. David made Silja feel like the person she'd always wanted to be. Someone beautiful.

They heard a hacking cough from the back of the apartment. David sighed and released her. "Let me check on him," he said. "And then I'll drive you to the train station."

He'd replaced the Plymouth coupe he took Silja and Ruby home in when he rescued them from the riot in 1949. He now drove a '56 Mercury Montclair, dark blue with a hard top. Most days, he left the car at home and took the train from White Plains to his lab at NYU, or else to the New York Botanical Garden in the Bronx, where he conducted research. Other days, he did fieldwork, driving the Mercury to bucolic locations throughout Westchester.

An only child like Silja, David had grown up in Brooklyn Heights, not far from Silja's own girlhood home. It took some months into their relationship for Silja to see it, but eventually she realized how much David reminded her of the Finntown boys. Not in looks; David was as dark-complected as Henry. And not in age, either; David, now in his early fifties, had been too young to serve in World War I but too old for World War II. Nonetheless—in his easy confidence, his work ethic, his earnestness—he resembled those fair-haired Finnish lads of her youth.

He was a smart man, an unselfish man. A man living an honorable, uncomplicated life.

She longed—would have given anything—to kick Henry out. She fantasized about inviting David to move into her wonderful house. They could build out the back—there was certainly room for an addition—creating space for his father, too. They would remove Henry's silly homemade desk from the guest room. David would fill it up, floor to ceiling, with bookshelves. She could imagine him there, working diligently in the evenings, then coming late to join her for a nightcap, cozy in front of the hearth in the living room, the glowing darkness of the glass walls surrounding them. Retreating together to the master bedroom—the room where she'd slumbered alone for years, but where she would now sleep wrapped in David's warmth night after night. Just before they fell into dreams, he would whisper that he loved her and she'd respond in kind. When they woke in the morning, his expression would tell her he couldn't believe his good fortune to have her as his mate for all time.

David would—David *did*—love her.

Loving her was something Henry had never done enough of. Even in those first weeks of their courtship and marriage, before he left for the war—looking back, she realized that it wasn't *her* specifically, but rather the idea of a woman who was completely under his thumb, that appealed to Henry.

Sexually and in every other way, Henry had gotten his kicks from controlling her, not from loving her.

Well. Those days were gone. She'd never live like that again. She'd never let herself be reined in by anything but love.

50

Angie

I returned to the guest room and looked around. Where to search here? And for what? I wasn't sure, but I was compelled to look around. I set the baby on the bed and opened the closet to explore. I found nothing there except Henry's clothes. Those dated, unworn suits beside his shabby work clothes. Muddy boots and plaid shirts and dungarees.

I turned back to the room. There was a desk here, but it was nothing like Silja's—just a board held up by stacked milk crates on either end. Upon the board's surface sat an ancient Smith-Corona typewriter, neatly centered. A file box was in the back right corner of the desk; I opened it to find household bills—filed by date and marked PAID at the top of each one in blocky handwriting. In one of the upper milk crates was a metal office tray containing drawing tools: mechanical pencils, rulers, a protractor. There were several nubs of pink erasers and a box of lead sticks for the pencils. The crate below it held blank typewriter paper. The crates on the other side were empty.

My eyes fell on the nightstand next to Henry's bed. I opened the drawer and found a wooden box and a few pamphlets. I turned the pamphlets over in my hand, reading the titles and glancing at the text. Anti-Communist rhetoric. Well, that didn't surprise me. Paul, too, scoffed at anything resembling Communist ideals. "Look how well that's worked out in East Germany and Russia," he'd say, his voice laced with sarcasm. "Good thing we've got J. Edgar Hoover making sure it doesn't happen here."

When he said such things, I would nod and murmur assent. This type of talk had nothing to do with me; I had no opinion on it. Paul knew and accepted that I was a Kennedy Democrat; it came with the territory of marrying a Catholic girl, he said, smiling indulgently at me. "Any president is all right in my book, as long as he leaves Hoover right where he is, in charge of the FBI," Paul opined. "If he does that, I don't care what else the president does."

I put the pamphlets back in the nightstand drawer and set the wooden box on the bed. Seating myself and leaning the baby against my hip, I opened the box.

It contained letters. Each one was addressed to Henry. Each one was from Paul. They didn't go back far—just the past year or so. It seemed likely that Paul had written to Henry before then, but if Henry had kept other letters, they were somewhere else. This batch started about when Paul had arrived in Door County.

I scanned the first few pages, and smiled as I read about myself. Dated June 10, 1959:

You were right, Henry. I've met a girl, quite a pleasant girl. Cute as a button and worships the ground I walk on. A willing sexual partner; seducing her was effortless. All in all, it's very satisfying.

And on August 25:

We're so thankful you'll be here for the wedding. Angie is anxious to meet you—and Ruby, too.

Another from November:

I'm nearly done insulating the cottage. Just in time, too, as the cold comes early in this part of the world. Married life treats me well. Angie is a sweet girl. She's handling pregnancy like a champ. She's built for it; you can tell. When I heard she had five siblings, I knew she came from hardy breeding stock!

I grimaced; it certainly wasn't the nicest thing I'd ever heard about myself. But men are apt to use crude words when speaking—or writing—to other men.

I read about PJ's birth in March:

I'm the father of a son, Paul William Glass Junior. Rest assured the name was not my choice; Angie insisted on it. She came through the birth with no troubles, and she and the baby are both doing well.

I knit my eyebrows, feeling defeated as I read Paul's words. I remembered how Paul had not wanted the baby to be his namesake. "He should have his own name," Paul said when I suggested Paul Junior. "He shouldn't be burdened with someone else's." But I pleaded my case. My oldest brother was named after my father, and my father after my grandfather. It meant something, I told Paul, to pass a name from father to son. It represented continuity and connection between the generations.

Paul carried on his protests, but eventually he gave in.

I opened his next letter, dated from May:

The watercoloring goes well, but living here is limiting—I must admit it. It's as if my world has shrunk, Henry. I know you'd say that's normal, that any man would feel that way once he's saddled with a wife and child. But I no longer recognize myself. It's as though someone else is living this life. Not me.

His words made me wince. Did Paul truly feel that way when he wrote this letter? I wondered if he *still* felt that way. If so, he'd never let on. I wished he would have shared his feelings with me. I'd have to talk with him about it, I resolved, once we got back home.

On another subject, in a letter from early June:

Yes, I am loath to say it, but I do believe your wife is dangerous, Henry. I agree with your precautionary steps of the separate bank account, as well as passports for you and Ruby. I would be

happy to hold some of your money here, too, if you'd like. Let me
know.

Be watchful, brother. Stand firm, and be always on your guard.

Dangerous? I shuddered, considering Henry's letters *to* Paul. Unlike Paul's possible correspondence with Ruby, I was well aware that the brothers regularly exchanged letters. Paul kept Henry's letters in his studio, neatly stacked in a metal bin on a work bench in the corner of the room. I'd never had a shred of curiosity about them. When a letter arrived from Henry, I simply placed it on the desk for Paul to read when he came in from his work. The letters disappeared to the studio, and I never gave them another thought. I'd assumed their content was typical men-talk—sports, I would have speculated, had I speculated at all.

How foolish I'd been.

From a letter to Henry late in the summer:

I've made a huge mistake. The truth is that I'm stifled here, Henry.
The sexual part is gratifying; I admit that. I find the girl irresistible
sexually. But I can get that anywhere, without all this liability.

I don't know how much more I can take. This tiny house and this
tiny life—it's not for me at all.

With trembling fingers, I picked up the last letter. It was dated only a few weeks ago—September 18, 1960.

My husband had written:

Dear Henry,

I am in receipt of your letter of Tuesday last.

We have just returned from church. What a ruse that is, as you
well know, or at least must remember. So clever of you to marry a
girl who doesn't care for religion the way Angie does. Of course, we
know now where that's led you, so maybe it's not so clever after all.

I appreciate your continued suggestions to build a bomb shelter
of my own. Yes—perhaps it would give me some direction. Something to do beyond sitting here, painting and brooding.

*It would mean staying here, though. And I'll be honest, Henry—
staying is something I'm not at all convinced is the right thing for
me to do.*

*But I'm trapped here. Trapped in a marriage to a girl I don't love
and a life I don't want.*

*I wish I knew what to do, but I'm at a loss. I'm sorry to burden
you with this, Henry, but it's true.*

Kindly, your brother,
Paul

"Holy Mother of God," I breathed.

I leaned back against the headboard. Who was this man? This
didn't sound like the Paul I knew. This didn't sound like the man
who—just a few days ago—snapped at me, then immediately gave me
a soft, loving look and apologized.

How could Paul say to Henry that he didn't love me? How could
he call me *Angel* and then tell his brother he wasn't in love with me?

I glanced at PJ, nestled peacefully against my thigh. I thought
about Paul—the stranger with whom I'd created this sweet child.

What in heaven's name could I have been thinking? What compelled me to take that kind of risk? To have sex with—and wind up
having a baby with—someone I barely knew?

And now I might be carrying another child of his. I felt a surge of
nausea at the thought.

I put the box back in the nightstand. Letters in one hand, I carried
PJ to the kitchen. Holding him on one hip, I mixed and began heating
a bottle.

After I fed him, I set him back on the shawl with his toys. I went
back to Ruby's room and retrieved Paul's letter from her jacket sleeve.

I took a deep breath, then drew the single-page letter from its
envelope.

Dearest Ruby,

*I think about you all the time. I know I shouldn't write to you. I
know I should be content to just talk on the phone. I love hearing*

your voice. It reminds me of my mother's voice. Of how it sounded when she was happy. So pretty and lilting, so full of life.

A man should not think about a world where there's only himself and his niece. I know that, Ruby.

And yet I do think about it. About what it would be like if everyone else was out of the picture. If there was no one but the two of us, without a care in the world.

Please know I say this with all the love in my heart. I want to give you the world, Ruby. I want to experience everything with you, and with you only.

I know this cannot be. I know I shouldn't put such thoughts in writing.

And yet here it is. I can't help myself. I feel better having said it.

If only it could come to pass.

Love,

Paul

The breath ran out of me. I let the letter slip from my fingers as fat tears rolled down my cheeks.

Eventually, I composed myself. Sniffling, I took Paul's letter and the construction drawings to the living room. I patted PJ's head, then sat on the davenport. I studied everything carefully—letters, drawings, photographs. Then I stood, took the items with me, and tucked everything into PJ's suitcase in the guest room.

On my way back to the living room, I glanced through the big windows. The day had turned foggy and dark; looking out at the weather sent an involuntary shiver through my body. I returned to the guest room and found PJ's blue wool jacket and hat. I grabbed my own tweed car coat from the front hall closet, slipping it on as I crossed the living room.

Baby dressed in his outerwear and in my arms, I opened the sliding glass door that led to the backyard. Taking a deep breath, I descended the deck. I crossed the yard and looked around. Sure enough, at the back edge of the yard, there was a faint dirt path—barely discernible—leading into the forest. I stepped onto the path and followed it.

I wound through thick, dark trees—so much denser and taller than the spindly, new-growth pines that dotted my forest property on North Bay. I lost my way several times—there were numerous small trails throughout the woods, some that ended abruptly, some that seemed to circle back onto a trail I'd already passed.

The forest here frightened me—and the fear was an uncomfortable, unfamiliar sensation. Never in my life had I been afraid of unknown places. Never in my life had there *been* many unknown places. I knew every corner of Baileys Harbor. I knew my way through not only my parents' property and house, but also all the others on their street, and the next street, and the next. On North Bay, at my grandmother's cottage that was now mine, I could find my way around every nook and cranny with my eyes closed on a moonless night.

Everything in my life, until I met Paul, had been comfortable and familiar.

How had I become the only girl from my town who took a risk? The girl who did what no one else was willing to do. Married a stranger. Took a chance on a different sort of life.

At the time, I'd felt plucky, dauntless. Even a bit rebellious. People looked at me with new eyes when I walked around town with my handsome husband and my big belly sticking out. My belly that showed the world who I truly was—a grown-up woman with grown-up desires. My pregnancy told the world what he'd done to me. What he'd done with my permission.

Look at me! I'd shouted—without ever saying a word. *Do you see me—sweet little Angie Doyle? Ha! Now you know what I'm capable of.*

Those times had been among the most self-satisfying in my life. But now I saw that taking a chance on Paul may have been the biggest mistake I'd ever made.

I went in circles, holding the baby against my chest to protect him from the spitting rain. I looked over my shoulder, apprehensive as an escaping prisoner.

Fearful of—what? An owl? A fox?

Paul?

Spotting the hill-and-valley-shaped roof of Silja's house above the tree line, I got my bearings and found a path heading east. I breathed a sigh of relief and walked with determination along the faint path. The rain began coming down more heavily. It pelted the yellow, orange, and red leaves clinging to branches, making them look like vibrant shards of stained glass.

Toward the back of the property—precisely where I would have expected to find the structure from Henry's drawings—I came into a clearing with a low stone wall nearby, separating it from an ancient cemetery.

I shook, brushing raindrops from my brow and covering the baby's head with one hand. I looked around, up and down. There was nothing in the clearing except a flat-topped boulder. There was no structure. Clearly, it had never been built. Some grand plan Henry had; a grand plan for—something. I wasn't sure what. But whatever it was, it hadn't been built.

Holding PJ against my chest, I stared at the space and the crumbling tombstones beyond it. A low rumble of thunder in the distance made PJ whimper. I ran my hand over his back, soothing my child and trying to decide what to do next.

51

Ruby

Rain is pouring down as Ruby and Uncle Paul pull into the driveway on Stone Ridge Road. She thinks about how the house looks the same as always. If you didn't know better, you'd think her parents still lived there.

It certainly doesn't look like a crime scene.

They dash through the raindrops and into the house. Aunt Angie is nowhere to be found. Uncle Paul frowns. "Strange," he says. He goes down the hall to check the bedrooms.

Ruby shakes off Shepherd's sweater, sits at the counter, and waits. The birdcage is very still—the only sounds the rainfall outside, Uncle Paul's footsteps, and the click of doors opening and closing. Ruby sees her grandmother's shawl on the floor in front of the hearth. The plastic cups and bowls Aunt Angie has been letting the baby play with are scattered on the shawl. There's a single coffee cup set on a coaster on the side table next to the sofa.

Other than that, nothing in the birdcage—nothing Ruby can see, anyway—is out of place.

Uncle Paul strides back down the hall and crosses the kitchen. He opens the sliding door to the backyard, looking around for Aunt Angie.

He turns to stare at Ruby, his eyes wild. She's never seen him look like that before.

Without a word to her, he runs outside. Ruby watches as he crashes into the rain-glazed woods, calling for Aunt Angie. His voice overflows with more panic than she's ever heard from it.

52

Angie

I turned out of the drenched, muddy clearing and into semiprotection under the trees. I was about to make my way back to the house when I heard my name shouted—loud and clear across the woods. Paul's voice.

My heart pounding, I turned to my right and scrambled through the forest. Pushing aside branches, I wound through the woods, turning west when I estimated I was out of the Glasses' property and behind the house to the north. Over my left shoulder, I could hear Paul calling for me. Thunderclaps and rainfall masked the noises I made crashing through the narrow passages among trees, and I said a silent prayer of thanks to the Virgin Mother—or maybe Mother Nature, or whoever was listening—for the deafening cover.

My instincts sent me in the right direction, and I found myself in the neighbor's backyard. I glanced around quickly, then crept toward the far side of the neighbor's house. I emerged onto Stone Ridge Road.

Walking briskly up the road, I heard something jangling. I stopped and reached into my coat pocket. What I felt made me pause and lean against the back of a wide oak, where I wouldn't be seen from the Glass house. I pulled the item out, dangling it in front of my eyes. PJ reached for it and I let him hold it.

It was a set of keys. Gently, I turned it over in PJ's hands. A car key was riveted onto a narrow, looped swath of navy leather, embossed with MG in an octagon on one side and the words REAL ENGLISH

LEATHER IS USED IN THIS UPHOLSTERY on the other. Two house keys and another, smaller key were attached to a metal ring at the other end of the looped leather.

They must be Silja's keys, I thought. Jean Kellerman's article had mentioned Silja drove an MGA, which I knew was built by the MG Motor Company. But why were Silja's keys in my coat pocket?

I frowned and pulled the collar close to my nose, inhaling deeply. The coat had an unfamiliar smell—something strong and fragrant like perfume, a scent I couldn't pinpoint.

With PJ cradled in my right arm, I let my left arm dangle. The coat sleeve hung off me, well below my fingertips. The coat's shoulders, too, I realized, were cut much broader than I needed for my small frame.

This must be Silja's coat. Did Silja and I own the same tweed car coat? Or at least something so similar, I hadn't noticed the difference when I grabbed the coat from the front hall closet. I shuddered, suddenly hating the scratchy feel of Silja's coat collar against the bare skin of my neck.

Why were the keys in Silja's coat pocket? Silja had left her car at the train station. Wouldn't she have taken her keys with her, or at least left them in the car's ignition, or the glove box? Why would her keys be in a coat Silja hadn't even been wearing when she ran away? It had to be a duplicate set.

Gently, I pried the keys from PJ's hand and slipped them back into the coat pocket. I hurried up the road to Silja's house and turned into the drive.

53

Ruby

In a few minutes, Uncle Paul is back. "Not out there," he says. He shakes rain from his head as he steps inside. "I can't imagine where she would have gone. It's not like her to run off."

Ruby just shrugs again, because what does she know?

The front door opens and Aunt Angie comes in, carrying the baby. Her head is drenched and Ruby notices there's a small evergreen branch trapped in her hair on the left-hand side. Aunt Angie must notice, too, because she runs her hand through her hair. The little twig falls to the floor.

Uncle Paul comes forward and takes PJ, pulling off his little blue coat and hat. Aunt Angie hands him over silently. She has her lips pressed together in a thin line. It reminds Ruby of a look her mother often gave her father.

"Where were you?" Uncle Paul asks.

"I . . . I was just taking a walk. To pass the time." Aunt Angie doesn't look at him when she says this. She stares at Ruby, who stares back but doesn't say anything. "It was only cloudy when we went out. Then the rain started and we got caught in it." Aunt Angie opens the hall closet and hangs up her car coat, which is similar to one of Ruby's mother's coats.

"Well, I'm glad you're back," Uncle Paul says. He sets the baby down on Grandma's shawl in front of the fireplace. "Is anyone hungry?" he asks. "I can go out and get a pizza."

Ruby knows that Uncle Paul and Aunt Angie probably expect her to go to her room, but instead she crosses the living room and sits next to PJ. She fingers the fringes of the shawl and looks up at Aunt Angie. "This was my grandmother's," Ruby tells her.

"I didn't know," Aunt Angie says, and her voice sounds defensive. "I'm sorry. I saw it in the hall closet the other day and just grabbed it. The carpeting is sort of rough, and I wanted something soft for PJ to sit on."

Ruby meets her gaze. "It's okay," she tells Aunt Angie. "I want him to use it. It's nice to see it getting used."

She brushes a bit of the shawl's fringe against PJ's face and he giggles. Leaning toward him, Ruby takes in his honest, simple scent. "He smells so good," she says. "Like soap, but even better."

"Well," Aunt Angie says. "He certainly seems to enjoy your company."

Ruby nods. "We'll take the shawl with us to Wisconsin," she tells Aunt Angie. "He can use it there, too."

Aunt Angie is still staring at Ruby. It might be that she's just surprised Ruby is talking so much.

"I mean it," Ruby says. "We'll pack it up and bring it along. It's a nice memento to have."

Angie nods. She comes forward and scoops up the baby from the shawl. Without looking at Uncle Paul, she says, "Maybe you should go for that pizza now."

"Sure thing," he replies. "There's a place downtown, if it's still there. Ruby, is Dinardo's still downtown?"

Ruby nods and stands up.

"You want anything else?" he asks. "Garlic bread, soda pop?"

Ruby shakes her head. "I'm not very hungry. Just get what you want."

After he leaves, Ruby expects Aunt Angie to say something to her. To ask what happened at the cop shop. To ask what's going on.

Looking at her—standing next to the dining room table with the baby in her arms and a confused look on her face—Ruby can tell Aunt Angie opened her mother's photograph album.

It's okay if she did. It's what Ruby expected would happen.

"Ruby, I—" Aunt Angie starts to say.

Before she can go on, Ruby turns away and heads down the hall. "You and Uncle Paul eat the pizza. Save me a piece for later."

She goes to her room and closes the door.

54

Angie

I knocked on Ruby's door. "Ruby? Please open up."

There was no response. I tried the handle, but it wouldn't give. Ruby had locked it from the inside.

I wasn't sure what to do. Did Ruby assume I'd looked at the photograph album? Moreover, did she suspect me of snooping? What if she found out I'd taken the letter Paul wrote to her, and the construction drawings? If she looked for them in her closet, she'd know that I took them—or she'd think the police did.

Well. She'd talk to me then, I was sure. If she wasn't going to let me in now, I'd simply wait for her to come to me.

I brought the baby to the guest room for his afternoon nap. After he was down, I went back to the living room and looked out through the front windows. Rain spattered lightly outside, but for the most part the storm had passed. I walked across the room and turned on the television set. The New York Yankees were playing the Boston Red Sox in what the announcers said was the last game of the regular season, before the Yankees headed into the World Series later that week. I had no interest in baseball, but I watched mindlessly for a while, then turned off the television set and instead switched on a small transistor radio sitting on the kitchen counter. I fiddled around with the stations until I heard a newscast, then sat down on one of the barstools to listen. There was mention of the narcotics sting in Yonkers, the one Jean had told me about. Five men had been arrested; two more, plus a woman, had fled the scene and were still at large.

There was no news about Senator Kennedy; apparently, he hadn't been campaigning over the weekend. I became wistful as I remembered how excited I'd been—less than a week ago, though it seemed like a lifetime—by the debate between Senator Kennedy and Vice President Nixon. With no television in our cottage, Paul and I had spent the evening at my parents' house, watching the debate on my parents' set. The baby asleep on my lap, I sat on my parents' davenport and held Paul's hand. All of us were mesmerized by the engaging, handsome senator from Massachusetts. Jack Kennedy's good looks reminded me of Paul's. They didn't look exactly alike, not the way Paul looked like Cary Grant, but the senator had the same sort of thick dark hair and warmth in his smile as my husband.

That night—the night of the debate—my world consisted of my family, Paul, PJ, and thinking about the first time I'd step into a voting booth. Now, everything had been turned upside down.

The door opened and Paul entered, pizza box in hand. He met my gaze and said hello. Without responding, I rose from the barstool and turned off the radio.

Paul set the pizza on the kitchen counter. He crossed the room and made drinks, while I got out plates and napkins for the two of us. He brought the drinks to the counter and handed one to me. I sipped my Scotch, not quite believing that we were drinking at this time of day. But then again, nothing was what it had been before.

He took a swallow of his own drink. "Where's Ruby?"

"In her room. She says she'll eat later."

He sat down heavily on a barstool. "They wanted to question her," he said, and his voice was barely above a whisper. "But she's not being charged with anything. So I got her a lawyer and that scared them off—for now. But, Angel, the lawyer says the cops think . . . " He bit his lip. "They think Silja killed Henry. They want to know what Ruby might know about it." He took a bite of pizza, his eyes averted from mine.

I put my hand to my mouth. The horror of what he was saying sunk in. It was true—based on the photographs—that Silja likely would've been happy to see Henry disappear.

But to actually have *killed* him? Was that even possible? How would Silja have done that? And if she had, would she have taken her young daughter into her confidence?

"Why would the police think that?" I asked Paul. "I thought the coroner ruled it a suicide. What's changed to make them suspect Silja?"

He shook his head. "I don't know for sure," he told me. "But some-one must have planted that idea in their heads."

What did he mean? Was he referring to Jean Kellerman? I frowned and took a bite of cheese pizza. "What about the note?" I asked. "The note Silja wrote, saying she was abandoning her family. What about that?"

Paul shrugged. "The lawyer thinks the cops probably suspect it's a red herring. Silja planted it so she could get away."

"But what about Ruby? Silja wouldn't just leave Ruby on her own after doing a thing like that, would she?"

Paul shrugged again. "I don't have any answers, Angel."

"What does Ruby say?" I pressed. "What did she tell the cops?"

"She didn't tell them anything. The lawyer—name is Mr. Kurtz—advised her not to speak. Kurtz tried to get her to go to his office. Get all her cards on the table and figure out what to do. But she was hav-ing none of it. She wanted to come home."

I sat quietly, thinking about everything he'd said.

Then I asked, "What do *you* think happened, Paul? Do you think Silja . . . could do a thing like that?"

He looked at me slowly, evenly, with a look of bewilderment.

And I finally saw it—what I hadn't been willing to see in all the time I'd known him.

He was arranging his features for me. Putting on an expression for me.

In this moment, his look made him appear puzzled. And yet, I was sure he wasn't puzzled at all. He had a strong opinion about what had happened, and perhaps even facts to support it. But he wasn't going to share that with me.

How often had he done that in the past? How often had he painted love, gentleness—even lust—on his face?

How often had he donned a mask, and I hadn't been willing to see it?

"I don't know, Angel," he said. "I really don't know what to think."

I pressed my lips together and didn't respond. He wasn't going to be honest with me—that was clear. Of course he wasn't—why should he be? For heaven's sake, the man was in love with his own *niece*!

She could be in danger from this man. So could I. So could PJ.

I needed time; I needed to figure out what to do. And the only way to buy that time was to do to him what he'd been doing to me.

I'd have to stop being myself.

Ruby hadn't come out by the time we went to bed, and although I wanted to check on her, Paul said it was best to leave her alone. As we settled in for the night, I moved as far away from Paul as possible, to the edge of Silja's king-size bed. When he reached for me, I told him I was tired. "It's all just too much," I said. "It's overwhelming."

In the darkness, he squeezed my shoulder. "It will be over soon," he said. "We'll get back to Wisconsin as soon as this is all cleared up."

And then what? Even if the lawyer could somehow get the police to let the girl go—then what would happen? We'd all go back to Wisconsin, and Paul would continue to live with me—with Ruby there too, and PJ, and possibly a new baby—in a loveless marriage?

Or would he abandon me? Would he leave, taking Ruby along?

Would she go with him?

I closed my eyes. My mind raced around, trying to hatch a plan. But fatigue overtook me and eventually I fell into a deep sleep.

55

Ruby

She watches from the doorway to her mother's room, and when she hears Aunt Angie snoring softly, she steps in, quietly like a cat, and comes up to the bed on Uncle Paul's side. He's sleeping on her mother's side of the bed, and this feels like a violation, but Ruby tries to ignore that.

It hardly matters now.

She touches his shoulder and as soon as he opens his eyes she puts her finger to her lips and then slips from the room, knowing he'll follow her.

In her bedroom she closes the door behind them and she tells him what was hidden in her closet and now is missing.

"It was here," she says, and she points at the pile of clothes on her closet floor.

"When?" he asks. "When did you last see it?"

She shakes her head. "I think a week or so ago." She lowers her voice and whispers—though they are the only ones there, "Before my father died. He may have . . . it's possible he took it."

Uncle Paul pauses, then says, "If he did, it would be in his room. Or in the bomb shelter."

"Maybe," Ruby says. "One of us has to check, I guess." She gives him an imploring look. "I don't want to. Will you do it?"

He reaches to hug her and she lets him. "Of course, sweetheart," he says softly into her hair. "You climb back into bed. I'll go check his room, and if I don't find it, I'll . . . I can go out to the bomb shelter."

"There's something else," Ruby says, and she tells him about the Shelter drawings. "They were here, too." She shrugs. "I don't know why I took them, but I did. And now they're gone."

Uncle Paul nods. "I'll find them," he says. "Don't worry, Ruby."

He slips from her room. She knows she won't sleep, so she waits in the dark, eyes open. He's so stealthy, Uncle Paul. She can hear him slipping almost soundlessly into the room where the baby sleeps, then coming out a few moments later. His footsteps are a bit more urgent now; she can tell his strides are longer as he crosses the hallway. She hopes Aunt Angie doesn't wake and hear him stepping outside.

He's gone a long time. When he comes back, she's still awake and she stares at him, wide-eyed. He shakes his head.

"Thank you for looking, though." She smiles tentatively at him. "That was brave of you."

He brushes off this comment. "Did your father have hiding places in the house? Anywhere you can think of?"

She stares at him helplessly. "Probably, but I can't guess where they would be. He was secretive . . . you know that."

Uncle Paul nods. His forehead breaks out in a sweat and for the first time in her memory, his shoulders shake. "This is bad, Ruby," he says. "This is really, really bad." He balls his hands into fists. "Jesus, this is bad."

She calms him down by laying a hand on his arm and making him sit on the bed.

She stands in front of him. No way will she sit next to him, though she knows he wants her to.

"Let me think this through," he says. "I'm going to the living room to have a drink. You stay here. Close your door and don't open it unless you hear two knocks. If you do, that's me and it means I have a plan."

56

Silja

1960

On a warm springtime Sunday, Silja had plans to spend the afternoon with David at Croton Point Park. It was a parcel of land jutting out into the river from the town of Croton. David and Silja were fond of meeting there; it was too far from Stonekill for anyone to recognize Silja and too far from White Plains for anyone to recognize David.

As she paid her fee at the park entrance, Silja glanced in her rear-view mirror, looking for David's Mercury. She smiled when she saw it in the line behind her, a few cars back.

And then she froze.

Several vehicles behind David's, she made out an ancient, battered Ford truck.

No, she thought, shaking her head—it couldn't be. Henry wouldn't have followed her. When she left the house, he was vehemently turning over garden beds in preparation for planting. Or had that been a ruse? Was he just waiting for her to leave, and then jumping in the truck and tailing her, staying just far enough out of sight that she wouldn't notice?

Her hands trembling, Silja turned her head side to side, trying to figure out what to do. There was no way to signal David. They should have had a plan in place for this type of thing long ago. What was she thinking, not expecting it to ever happen?

Well, she'd park her car, rendezvous with David, and hope for the best. Maybe it was time, after all. It was hardly the place she would have chosen—but perhaps it was time for it all to come to a head.

❖   ❖   ❖

David pulled in next to her and came toward her with opened arms. Silja put her hand out as if to hold him at bay. With her other hand, she put her finger to her lips and nodded toward the parking lot entrance. The truck pulled in and Silja could finally make out the driver.

It was Ruby.

"Good heavens," she said to David, her voice awash with relief. "It's my daughter." She waved Ruby over.

The girl was graceless behind the wheel. She'd only had her license for a few months and rarely drove; Henry was the one who'd insisted she learn. She parked the truck crookedly next to Silja's MGA. Silja and David watched silently as Ruby emerged from the driver's side.

"You followed me," Silja said simply.

"You're gone every Sunday," Ruby replied. "You used to ask me to go to the movies with you. But you never ask anymore." She shrugged. "I started to wonder."

Silja looked from her daughter to David, and then back again. "Perhaps you remember Dr. Shepherd," she said. "You were very small. It was a long time ago."

Ruby nodded. "I remember," she replied softly.

Silja watched as his eyes met her daughter's. "Ruby," he said. "It's my pleasure to see you again, after all these years."

To Silja's surprise, Ruby—her girl of few words—responded to David. "It's nice to see you again, too." Then she looked at Silja. "Would you walk with me, Mom?"

"I—of course," Silja said. "Dr. Shepherd and I were going to have a picnic." Her voice was wobbly. "Maybe we still can—and maybe you can join us, Ruby."

"Maybe." Ruby took off across the parking lot toward the riverbank, and Silja sprinted after her.

The girl halted at the edge of the parking lot; Silja stopped next to her, chest heaving, catching her breath. "I'm so sorry you had to find out this way," she said between breaths.

In front of them was a grassy area, with a gravel path leading to the river. Standing on the retaining wall that separated the land from the water, fathers and their kids fished, more likely to reel in a squirming eel than the catfish they probably hoped for. A group of down-on-their-luck old-timers—no doubt they'd walked into the park; it was improbable that they had a car—hovered nearby. Perhaps they were hoping the fishers would share their catch, whatever it turned out to be.

Ruby shielded her eyes from the sun and looked back across the parking lot toward David, who was still rooted in place, near the three vehicles. "Is he your lover?"

Silja hesitated, and then nodded.

Ruby didn't say anything. She seemed to be digesting the information. Then she said, "Well, I guess I'd find a lover, too, if I were married to Dad." The girl tilted her head at David. "Have you been seeing him ever since that night when I was a little kid? That's a long time to have a lover."

Silja explained how she and David had become reacquainted by chance a few years ago.

Ruby picked up a flat stone and skimmed it across the water. "He's a nice man," she observed. "I remember his kindness."

"He *is* kind," Silja agreed. "I've never known anyone kinder."

Her breathing had returned to normal, but she felt compelled to take a deep swallow of air before asking Ruby, "Will you give him a chance? Will you keep this from your father—will you keep my secret—and take some time to get to know him? I think if you do . . . you'll see why this means so much to me."

Ruby shrugged. "Well, let's have that picnic and see how it goes."

David had taken picnic fixings from his own car and Silja's, spreading them on a table under a just-budding elm tree. "Plenty for everyone," he said as they approached.

Ruby met his eye. "What should I call you?"

He tilted his head. "Hmm. Dr. Shepherd seems too formal, doesn't it?"

"And David too informal," Silja interjected—hearing her mother's voice in her head, admonishing her to treat elders with respect. Immediately, she chided herself; she should let Ruby call David by his first name. It would ease the awkwardness.

But before Silja could say anything else, Ruby suggested, "What about just Shepherd? Would that be all right?" Her look was almost shy. "You look a bit like a German shepherd," she added.

David laughed. "Shepherd it is, then."

They ate their picnic. Two of the old men who had been near the water stepped closer, eyeing the feast. When Silja, Ruby, and David had finished eating, David gave the men the leftovers, then reached in his pocket and handed them his loose change.

Silja, with determination, foraged in her pocketbook, brought out her wallet, and gave each man a five-dollar bill. "For dinner," she said. "Or tomorrow's meals if you're not hungry the rest of today."

Ruby watched the interaction with a bemused smile. "I like this version of you, Mom."

Silja sighed with relief. She'd hadn't given the men money in order to impress Ruby. She'd given it because it was a generous thing to do. Still, she was pleased with the turn of events.

After that, she began inviting Ruby on their Sunday outings. She missed being alone with David, but she saw him often enough during the week to make up for it.

She felt guilty about the situation. What kind of mother shares the secret of her affair with her teenage daughter? What mother would condone a child lying to her father about her whereabouts? Nonetheless, Silja loved the charade she shared with Ruby. She relished giving the girl meaningful looks over the dinner table on Saturday night, slipping into Ruby's room after the meal to let her know what was planned for the following day. Silja and Ruby waved good-bye to Henry—off to the movies, they assured him—climbing into the MGA to head out for their latest adventure with David.

Perhaps it was her imagination, but Silja noticed Ruby begin to blossom in more ways than one. Her carriage was more graceful, her laugh more genuine. That was David's influence, Silja told herself; it had to be.

She knew it would be better if Ruby had friends. Real friends, girls her own age. It was unnatural for a seventeen-year-old girl to spend weekends with her mother and her mother's lover. But Silja was willing to look past it, to embrace the rekindled closeness between herself and her daughter. To cherish the time she spent with David and Ruby.

He shared his work with Ruby, who took an interest in all he knew. She'd never realized there were so many varieties of plants, Ruby told Silja and David one day as the trio hiked at a small Putnam County forest preserve, one of David's favorite, remote areas to explore. "So many growing things, so many green things," Ruby said. "I've always just walked past and on top of them and didn't even look. Never thought about their details, their purpose. There are plants that do everything. Food for us, food for animals. Shelter. Protection."

David chuckled. "You'd be amazed to learn all that plants can do. They're amazingly versatile, and endlessly educational." He stepped into a boggy area. "Look here, Ruby—see this one? It's *Cicuta maculata.* Common name, spotted water hemlock. Poisonous in the root, and to a lesser degree throughout the plant. Steer clear."

"Wow." Ruby regarded the plant with admiration.

On a hot, humid Sunday in early July, David borrowed a motorboat from a fellow professor at NYU. Silja and Ruby met him at the Tarrytown Yacht Club, where its owner docked his boat. Once aboard the sturdy little craft, they made their way north through the choppy waters of the Hudson.

Ruby leaned over the windscreen, the breeze blowing her long hair back from her face. "This is incredible," she said. "This must be what it feels like to fly."

David gunned the motor and the boat sped up.

Silja felt liberated. Is this what being on the water is always like? she wondered. If so, I should do this more often.

It was freedom. It was pretending she didn't have a care in the world.

They approached the Mothball Fleet, the ships anchored on the west side of the river by Jones Point. "Ooh, I've always wondered what it would look like in there, among those ships," Ruby said.

"Let's find out." David slowed down and steered between two tall freighters.

With almost no breeze to whip it up, the water between the ships was smooth as glass. Silja was amazed; it was as if the fleet had somehow tamed the unruly river. David guided the boat effortlessly among the ships, weaving from one lane to the next. Other power-boats whizzed by, some of them towing water skiers. Ruby and Silja waved at the skiers, who took one hand off their crossbars to wave back.

"I've always heard the wind didn't get in here," Silja said. "I never quite believed it, but it's true."

They pulled north of the fleet, into a small bay. They were almost directly across the river from Stonekill, and Silja thought about Henry, back at home deep in the forest. Doing whatever it was he did all day long when she and Ruby weren't there.

David cut the engine and lowered the anchor. "Let's stop and enjoy the view." They drifted gently, the waves languid in the bay.

Silja had brought her Brownie camera, loaded with a fresh twelve-shot roll of film. "Take some photos of Ruby and me," she suggested to David, handing the camera to him.

After he'd taken a few shots, he gave the camera back to Silja. She hesitated, and then asked Ruby, "Can I take some of the two of you?"

Ruby looked at her long and silently, the wind lapping waves behind her. Silja knew what she was thinking: If there were photos of David, what would happen if Henry ever saw them?

"It's all right," Silja said gently. "It's worth the risk."

And it was. She'd come to treasure those photos—and others Ruby took that day of Silja and David—for as long as she possessed them.

Ruby agreed. "These are wonderful," she said, a week after their day on the river, as she paged through the little album in which Silja had placed the photos. "A perfect memento of a perfect day."

She looked up at Silja, then back at the photographs. "We look just like a family," Ruby said. "Just like a regular mom and dad and their kid." She gently traced her index finger over a photo of herself and David. "I wish Shepherd was my father," she confessed. "I know it's terrible to say, Mom, but I do."

It would be wrong, Silja knew, to agree with Ruby. Instead, she replied, "I understand that you feel that way, Ruby."

"Well." Ruby handed the album back to Silja. "I guess we have to be grateful for what we have. We have to be grateful, at least, that nothing can tear us apart."

57

Angie

In the morning, while I put coffee on, Paul knocked on Ruby's door.

"Ruby," he said. "Come out. You need to eat, and then we need to go see Mr. Kurtz."

He tried the door, but it was locked. He frowned. "Strange," he said. "Angie, do you have a hairpin? This lock shouldn't be too hard to pick."

It took only moments for Paul to use my hairpin to jimmy the lock. He turned the handle and opened the door. I wasn't surprised that the room was empty.

Paul didn't seem surprised, either—but really, I thought, how could I tell? I had no idea what he truly thought about anything.

"We should have kept a better eye on her." He sighed. "Stay here, Angel—I'm going to check the woods."

I kept my mouth shut and watched him disappear down the narrow path.

When he returned, he looked distressed. "Not out there," he said, glancing back toward the woods. "I'm sure she could hide herself pretty well out there—all those thick trees, and she knows those woods like the back of her hand. But I looked around, and . . ." He shrugged. "I just get a sense that's not where she is."

"What are you going to do?"

He looked a bit lost, and for a minute my heart melted for him. And then I remembered that, for all I knew, he wasn't the least bit confused.

There was no way to know, really, when he was being authentic and when he wasn't.

The telephone rang, and Paul dove for it. He listened, then replied, "Yes, I understand. Of course . . . yes, we're happy to cooperate. Thank you. We'll be on our way shortly."

He hung up and turned to me. "That was the police," he said. "They want us to move out. Everything around here is evidence, all of the sudden. They want us to go to a hotel for a few days while they sweep the place." He took a sip of coffee, then set down his cup. "We'll have to call your parents," he said. "Let them know we can't come home tomorrow, that we probably need to stay a few more days at least. We need to be here for Ruby, Angel. The police won't let her go, and we can't just leave her alone to handle this by herself. Who knows what they're looking for?"

"But that's—why?" I asked. "Can the police do that? Just come in and go through everything?"

He shrugged. "Apparently, they can. I'll check with the lawyer—I don't know any more about this kind of thing than you do, Angel. But in the meantime, we may as well go." He nodded toward the hallway to the bedrooms. "You go pack," he said. "I can help, if you like. I could take care of the baby's things—"

"No!" I heard the sharpness in my voice and immediately toned it down. "No, I mean—you don't need to do that. I have it . . . " My voice trailed off, and then I said, "It's all organized just as I want it. I need to pack it so that I can find things."

Paul smiled. "Well, I should know to leave the woman's work for the woman," he said. "Just be efficient, would you, Angel? I'll call Mr. Kurtz and your parents. Then I'll go throw a few things in a bag for Ruby."

"They said we were to go to a nearby motor inn—it's just down the highway," Paul told me as he loaded the suitcases into the trunk of the rental car. "They're expecting us. The county is putting us up. The cops said to relax and rest, and they'll let us know as soon as we can go back to the house."

"And Mr. Kurtz said it was okay?"

Paul nodded. "He said if they have a warrant, there's nothing else we can do." As we pulled away from the house, Paul's look turned to scorn. "I can't fathom what they're looking for. And even if they did find anything, would it hold up in court? I doubt it. The whole place has been compromised. How long has it been—almost a week since they found Henry's body? Can't imagine a jury would believe any evidence in that house is clean."

Though I could tell he was trying to sound confident, I caught the hint of hesitation in his voice. But as he warmed up, he seemed more genuinely certain. "How many people have been in and out of there since September twenty-sixth?" he asked. "You, me, Ruby, the baby, those cops yesterday morning." His expression turned bitter. "Even that Negro, for God's sake."

"Heavens, Paul," I snapped. "You can't tell me you'd in any way involve that lovely woman!"

"Lovely?" Paul scoffed. "She had knowledge written all over her face. She's the type that knows things but stays quiet until it suits her. Sneaky. She was a sneaky type. I could tell from the moment I met her. I wish I hadn't agreed to have her over. I wish I hadn't let her be alone with Ruby."

What nonsense. I looked out the window.

Paul reached across and touched my shoulder. "I'm sorry, Angel," he said, and I turned back to see what appeared to be a sincerely contrite expression on his face. "This is all so stressful," he went on. "This is . . . I've never had to do anything like this before. And all I want to do is go home and grieve Henry, and get back to my painting . . ." He drifted off.

He played his part so skillfully, I thought. Well, I could do that, too.

I reached up to my shoulder and tightened my hand around his. "It's okay," I said softly. "It's okay, Paul. I'm here for you." I glanced again out the window, then turned back to him, putting a smile on my face. "We're in this together."

As soon as we'd settled in our first-floor motel room, Paul put his jacket back on. "I'm going to look for Ruby," he said. "I have a feeling I know where she is."

"Where?"

He frowned. "I shouldn't say," he told me. "Just trust me, okay?"

I didn't answer. Silently, I watched him back up the Fairlane and leave the motel's parking lot.

I took Jean Kellerman's business card from my purse and traced my fingers over the office address for the *Stonekill Gazette*. Then I picked up the telephone and called for a taxi.

The newspaper office was in tiny downtown Stonekill. A bell over the door jangled as I entered. The building was small, with a reception desk and a few other desks in a main room. From somewhere in back, I heard machinery running. Printing press, I decided.

The receptionist greeted me and asked how she could help, but before I could answer, Jean Kellerman stood up from her desk in the back of the room. "Angie," she said, coming forward. "So good to see you again." She patted PJ's head.

I nodded and asked if I could see last Friday's edition of the *Stonekill Gazette*.

After giving me the paper, Jean went back to her desk and resumed her work. I sat in the reception area, baby on my lap, paper spread out on the chair next to me. I skimmed Jean's article on the front page, then turned to page 3, as instructed.

So Violent . . .

[continued from page 1]

Glass, a transient who has spent time off and on in Stonekill over the years, was accused of putting a Stonekill High School female student in a compromising position. No charges were filed in the incident, but according to the student's account, Mr. Glass made advances toward her when she went to the home of Mrs. Kristina Hawke, Stonekill High School's principal, to walk Mrs. Hawke's dog as requested by the principal. At the time, Mr. Glass was living with Mrs. Hawke in her home, though the pair was not married. After the incident, Mr. Glass left Stonekill. It is unknown whether he has returned here in the interim.

Upon learning that Mr. Paul Glass was again in Stonekill in the wake of his brother's death and his sister-in-law's disappearance—this time properly accompanied by a wife and infant son—this reporter attempted to contact the family of the student involved in the 1951 incident. The family refused to comment.

In a statement, Mrs. Hawke said only, "We at Stonekill High School are saddened to learn of the death of a student's father. We mourn together as a community, and we pray for healing for the student and her family in the coming weeks."

There are many unanswered questions in this mysterious case, and many riddles that the police—not to mention innocent young Mrs. Angie Glass—must solve.

I carefully folded the newspaper and placed it on a side table. Jean stopped typing. She met my eyes, then came over and sat next to me.

"Is there anything I can do for you?" she asked. Her voice was surprisingly gentle. She didn't sound like a reporter chasing after a story. She sounded like a friend. She spoke to me like Joyce or Alice might, and I had to blink back tears.

"Thank you, Jean. But no." I stood, hoisting the baby onto my hip.

Jean also stood. She seemed to hesitate a moment, and then she leaned toward me. "I heard the police brought Ruby in for questioning."

I nodded. "Yes, but she's not been charged with anything." I shifted my purse strap higher on my shoulder. "I suppose you already know that, too."

"I do." Jean looked through the newspaper office's storefront windows. Few people moved about the quiet old downtown. She turned back toward me. "Angie, you know Ruby wasn't brought in because of my article, don't you? The police won't investigate based on a reporter's speculation." She shook her head. "Something else must have happened to make them suspect Silja."

I shrugged. "Well, I don't know what that is. Paul says he doesn't, either."

I closed my mouth. There was no need to tell her I didn't believe Paul.

Jean was silent, too, as if considering how to respond. PJ burbled happily and grabbed my earlobe. I tenderly extracted it from his fingers.

"You know," Jean said. "You might want to go see Kristina Hawke. She and Silja . . . well, they were friends at one time. Don't hold what happened with Kristina and your husband against Kristina. She can come off rather brash, but deep down she means well."

I asked for directions to the high school; Jean told me it was only a few blocks away. Then she put her hand on my arm. "Here . . ." She reached for one of her cards from the business card holder on the receptionist's desk and scribbled a number on the back. "That's my home number. You call me anytime, Angie. Anytime at all."

The high school was just past the main part of town, on a sloping hillside. After catching my breath from walking uphill with a baby in my arms, I went inside and found the front office.

"Mrs. Hawke expecting you?" the secretary asked, when I inquired whether or not the principal was in, and if so, if I could have a few minutes of the woman's time.

"No, she . . . well, it's a personal matter. I only need a moment with her." I tried to sound grown-up, and I stood as tall as I could. I was aware of my button nose and the headband I wore. Except for the baby in my arms, I looked more like a student here than an adult.

"Well, have a seat, miss, and I'll see if she's available."

"Ma'am," I said. "It's ma'am." But the secretary was already facing away from me, speaking into an intercom, and she either didn't hear or simply ignored what I said.

58

Ruby

Early in the morning, Ruby walks down to Route 202 to the drugstore on the corner. She slips a dime into the pay phone outside the store. The call she makes is brief.

Afterward, she slips back the long way, through the cemetery. She hides in her family's woods—not too far in, close enough to see the birdcage, to see and hear anything that happens, but far enough that she can't be seen from inside.

In a short while Uncle Paul and Aunt Angie drive off, just as she expects them to.

Still, she waits. There doesn't seem to be much reason to go anywhere else. She sits on the rock and hugs her knees and smokes. Warm sunshine is beginning to dry out the soggy woods, making everything around her sparkle.

Eventually Ruby heads back to the birdcage and to her room. She takes a good look around. She feels bad about the books she's leaving behind, but not about much else. She grabs *To Kill a Mockingbird* and stuffs it in her pocketbook.

In her mother's room, Ruby takes a few other items, slipping them deep into her patchwork bag. She heads to the living room and stuffs her grandmother's shawl in the bag, too.

After that, she goes back to the woods. Back into hiding.

Back to playing her part.

59

Angie

Mrs. Hawke looked like her name. She had a large, hooked nose, and although she wasn't tall, she was buxom and solid in her figure. She shook my hand firmly and didn't flinch when I gave my name.

"Mrs. Glass," she said as we sat down. A wry smile played across the principal's lips. "What a delight to meet you. And your little boy." She glanced at PJ, perched on my lap.

I fished a rattle from my purse for the baby to play with. "Thank you for . . . taking the time to meet with me," I said softly, and was immediately annoyed by the hesitancy in my own voice.

"And what can I do for you, Mrs. Glass?"

I didn't know how to begin. I'd expected condolences on the family's loss, or questions about how Ruby was doing. But Mrs. Hawke simply leaned back and waited.

"I . . . well, I came to see you about . . ." I looked down, my face flushed, and then looked back up. This was ridiculous. I needed to gather my resolve. I took a breath and said, "I just wondered what you might know about the Glass family." I looked toward the window, then back again. "What you know of Henry and Silja. What you think may have happened to them."

Mrs. Hawke grimaced. "My understanding is that Henry took poison. There's an assumption that it was suicide." She fiddled with some papers on her desk. "Tragic. Must be terrible for Paul. And for Ruby."

There was sympathy in her voice, but it felt false to me. Clearly, this woman did not feel the least bit sorry for Paul—or even for Ruby.

Did that mean she thought Ruby was aware Silja had killed Henry? If that was even true, that is.

"And Silja?" I asked. "Where do you think she is?"

The principal shook her head. "Ah, Silja." She smiled, looking down at her desk. "She could be anywhere, couldn't she?" Mrs. Hawke looked up at me, as if waiting for confirmation.

"Ruby was questioned yesterday," I blurted out. "The police wonder what she knows about her father's death. They . . ." I paused, and then went on. "They suspect Silja of killing Henry."

Mrs. Hawke seemed to be composing her thoughts. "And do you believe that, Mrs. Glass?" she finally asked. "Do you think Silja could have done such a thing?"

"I don't know," I said. "That's why I'm here. I thought you might . . ." My eyes met Mrs. Hawke's. "You know Silja, don't you?" I looked down, then back again. "You're friends, or at least you were."

Mrs. Hawke regarded me carefully, and then said, "Yes, it's true Silja and I were friends at one time."

"You didn't come to her husband's funeral." I gave the principal what I hoped was a stern, grown-up look. "Even if you knew Silja wouldn't be there, you could have come to be supportive. You could have supported Ruby."

"Miss Wells did that," the principal pointed out. "We agreed that was more appropriate."

"Because you had an affair with my husband?" I said boldly. "I read the article in last Friday's newspaper, you know."

Mrs. Hawke chuckled. "I'm sure you did." The older woman looked out the window, then back at me. "Look, Mrs. Glass, in not attending the funeral, I was trying to show compassion toward your husband. I didn't think he'd want me there." She leaned forward. "In recent years, Paul developed a distaste for me, as you probably know," she said. "As a matter of fact, so did Henry. I was not a favorite of either Glass brother."

"Why?" I asked. "I understand about Paul, but why Henry?"

Mrs. Hawke snorted. "Henry Glass believed I'm a Communist," she said. "He wasn't the first to make that accusation, either. It doesn't take much, in a little town—even one that falsely thinks of itself as oh-so-modern as this one—to be accused of such a thing. Hire a Negro to teach literature—of all things!—to a group of mostly white teen-agers." Her arm swept across the desk. "Do that, and you've pretty much sealed your fate."

"Miss Wells."

"Yes. Miss Wells. I fought the school board long and hard to get her hired, because she was—she is—the best of the best. But they didn't see it that way, and neither did Henry. He saw me as friend of the Negroes. Friend of the socialists and the Jews. Friend of everyone outside the establishment. So, clearly, a Communist. Is that not so, Mrs. Glass?"

I didn't know what to think, or how to respond. PJ let out a loud laugh and tugged at my hair.

"And now here you are," the principal went on. "Here you are, seated in my office, on your lap this child who is the spitting image of his father—my ex-lover." I cringed at the words, but Mrs. Hawke didn't seem to notice. "And you are accusing me of—what, exactly?"

"I'm not accusing you at all!" I cried. "I'm just trying to get some answers."

"Does Paul know you're here?"

I shook my head, my curls bouncing around my cheeks.

"Well, *Mrs.* Glass," she said, and I could again hear that mocking tone in her voice. "Here's what I can tell you. Silja didn't have an easy situation, not by a long shot. And Henry was a madman."

"A madman?" It seemed a harsh description, even from this se-vere, brutish woman.

Mrs. Hawke laughed scornfully. "Family heritage, right?"

I shook my head again. "I'm sorry; I'm not following you."

The older woman stared at me for an unbearably protracted mo-ment. Finally, she said, "Tell me, Mrs. Glass—how long have you known Paul?"

I shifted uncomfortably and tightened my grip around PJ's waist. "About fifteen months," I said. "We met last summer when we were working at the same resort."

"Ah. I see." Mrs. Hawke nodded. "And how much has he told you about his origins?"

"His . . . origins?"

"Yes, where he comes from."

"He comes from California," I said with authority. "He and Henry were raised in wine country."

Mrs. Hawke nodded again. "So they were. And you know about their parents, don't you?"

"Just that they've both passed," I replied. "What else is there to know?"

The principal's look was incredulous. "You *don't* know," she said softly. She shook her head. "You poor child."

"Mrs. Hawke." I pressed my lips together. "With all due respect, ma'am, I'm not a child."

Mrs. Hawke's lips curled into a slow smile. "No, of course you're not." She leaned forward and shuffled some papers on her desk. "And as an adult—as the man's wife—you deserve to know about Paul's family. He hasn't told you, so I shall."

She settled back into her seat. "Paul isn't generally a heavy drinker; I'm sure you know that." I nodded, and she went on. "But one night, he had a few too many—he did that every now and again, at least back in those days. And that night, he told me everything about his family." Her expression was amused. "Everything he hasn't told *you*, it seems."

I opened my mouth and then immediately closed it again—afraid to say anything, for fear she'd change her mind and refuse to continue.

But continue she did. She told me that Paul and Henry had been raised by parents who fought constantly. "Whatever there was to disagree about, they disagreed," she said. "Their father bellowed; their mother became upset. They made each other miserable, but despite their mutual disdain, they were churchgoing Catholics, so divorce was not an option. Paul said his mother could be sweet and affectionate when his father wasn't around, but when he was . . ." Mrs. Hawke shook her head. "Every day of his childhood, Paul's parents found something to differ on, from the starch in the sheets to the flavor of jam on their breakfast toast to the unpaid gas meter bill."

And they didn't just use words, Mrs. Hawke said. It was also physical. "The fistfights went both ways, according to Paul," Mrs. Hawke said. "The mother was a good-size woman—tall, sturdy. Had a mean left hook." She shook her head. "But in the end, she didn't use her fist when she attempted to kill the man."

"Attempted to . . . what?"

"This is what Paul told me," Mrs. Hawke said. "He told me his mother got ahold of a Japanese pistol called a Nambu that she bought from some fellow working the vineyards. Took the Nambu to the local tavern one night, knowing she'd find her husband and sons there. Fortunately, she hadn't practiced much, and wasn't much of a shot. She grazed the old man's ear, but otherwise, no one was hurt. The place wasn't too crowded that night, or she might have killed someone else by mistake." She raised, then lowered her eyebrows. "Alas, the story doesn't end there. The senior Mr. Glass couldn't withstand the shock of this incident. He had a heart attack and keeled over on the barroom floor. Right in front of his wife, his sons, and a room full of others."

"How awful." My voice was barely above a whisper.

Mrs. Hawke nodded. "Police came and hauled her away. She was tried for attempted murder, but her lawyer got her off on an insanity plea. They locked her up in the loony bin." She grimaced at me. "Broke Paul's heart; he adored his mother. Said if their father had been kinder to their mother, she never would have taken such a drastic step."

"But it sounds like she wasn't all that kind to him, either," I observed.

"I guess for Paul, it was neither here nor there," Mrs. Hawke replied. "He left because he couldn't stand to see his mother locked up. I don't know why Henry left. I suppose he'd simply had enough of the situation. I'm not sure either of them ever went back."

"Paul did—when his mother died," I said. "He told me he traveled to California. I don't know if Henry went or not. That was before Paul and I met. He didn't say anything else about it—just that she'd passed."

"Well," Mrs. Hawke said. "Now you have the whole story."

"I had no idea." I held PJ tightly and looked down at my lap. "I don't know what to do."

Mrs. Hawke picked up a pencil and tapped it on her desk. "Look, Mrs. Glass. I don't see how I can help you. All I can say is, the more you know the better you can prepare. Right?"

I looked up, eyeing the principal cautiously. "Prepare for . . . what, exactly?"

"Mrs. Glass." The principal stood. "I've taken enough of your time," she said. "You should get back before anyone misses you."

I rose. "Well, thank you."

Mrs. Hawke nodded. "There's one more thing, Mrs. Glass," she said. "The Glass family is chock-full of secrets. Everyone in Stonekill knows that, and it's one of the reasons few people here care for them." She crossed her arms, looking down her nose at me. "But you should know that Paul is—always has been—well aware of everything that goes on in that glass fortress out in the woods."

As I was leaving the school office, the bell began to ring, signifying the end of one class hour and the start of the next. The sound took me back. It was only a few years ago that I was walking the halls of a high school, books instead of a baby pressed to the front of my sweater.

I was heading toward the school's entrance when I heard my name. "Mrs. Glass? Is that you?"

I wheeled around and saw Miss Wells standing at the doorway of a nearby classroom. Briskly but reluctantly—I needed to get back to the motel before Paul did, but I didn't want to be rude to Miss Wells—I walked over.

"How nice to see you again." The teacher stepped aside to let one student out and two in. All three greeted her as they passed; she said good morning to the incoming pair and told the parting student to have a great day. Then she turned back to me. "What brings you to school, Mrs. Glass?"

"I . . . I came to see Mrs. Hawke . . . about . . . " A lie came quickly to me. "Mr. Glass wanted to make sure it's all right if Ruby continues to take some time off from school. He sent me to discuss it with Mrs. Hawke."

"That was wise," Miss Wells said. "I can put together a work packet so Ruby doesn't fall behind. I'm sure her other teachers would be happy to do the same. I'll speak with Mrs. Hawke about it."

I nodded, knowing that meant I'd be caught in my lie. But there was nothing I could do about it.

"How is Ruby?" Miss Wells asked.

The baby wiggled in my arms, and I shifted him to my other side. "She's managing."

Miss Wells regarded me silently. And then she put her hand on my arm. "Mrs. Glass," she said. "Ruby needs a mother, you know."

"She *has* a mother," I said. "I'm sure Silja will come to her senses and return for Ruby." As soon as I said it, I realized how unlikely it might be.

The teacher nodded slowly. "I'm praying for that," she replied. "But Ruby needs someone to care for her right now. Not in the same way this child does . . ." She smiled at PJ. "But Ruby does need a mother's care."

I didn't know what to say. I realized, quickly and uncomfortably, that although Miss Wells was a *Miss*, she was likely several years older than me.

I nodded at the teacher and stepped back. "Thank you," I said. "I'll keep that in mind."

60

Silja

1960

It would be fine, Silja told herself nervously, one muggy night in July when she returned home from the city late. Getting ready for bed, she'd removed her diaphragm and noticed immediately that it didn't seem as if she'd inserted it correctly. What a silly, amateur mistake, she told herself, shaking her head.

But it would be fine. She was thirty-eight years old. It was only once. The likelihood of conception was very, very small.

And if it happened? Well, she'd cross that bridge if and when she came to it.

"We have to find a way out of this," Silja told David toward the end of August. "I can't live like this anymore. Especially now that I've seen how happy you make Ruby. And now that . . ." She trailed off, a small smile playing around her lips. Then she sighed. "It breaks my heart, knowing that we can't simply be together. It kills me that Henry stands in the way of . . . everything."

She was driving her MGA toward the Bear Mountain Bridge. Ruby had declined to join them; she was engrossed in a novel by a new author, someone named Harper Lee. Though she'd already read it cover to cover, Ruby said she wanted to stay home and read it again.

It was risky being so close to Stonekill—and to Henry—but the road was one of Silja's favorites to drive when she didn't have a destination in mind. She loved the curves, the way Route 202 rose higher and higher from the riverbed until it crossed the river on the suspension bridge 150 feet above the water.

But today, she had to admit the sharp turns in the road were getting to her. Nausea came over her in a sudden wave, like an unexpected last hill on a roller-coaster ride you thought was almost over. She slowed down and took in a gulp of fresh air. The queasiness diminished.

David, in the passenger seat, watched her carefully. "Are you all right?" he asked softly.

She nodded. "It's passing," she assured him.

"Should I drive?"

Silja shook her head. "No, it's better driving than being a passenger." She smiled valiantly at him. "This way I know when the curves are coming up."

They reached the turnoff for the bridge and followed a sporadic line of other Sunday drivers across. The day was clear and warm, but a breeze off the river put a chill in the air. She looked down and saw the *Alexander Hamilton*, the large, side-wheeled sightseeing steamship that came up from the city every Saturday and Sunday, heading north just past the bridge. Tourists were waving upward from the open-air deck. Silja and David waved back, though they knew they were too high up to be seen from the ship.

David put his hand through his graying hair, ruffled by the wind whipping through the opened top of the convertible. "Pull over when you get across," he said. "I have something for you."

She obeyed, passing through the roundabout on the west side of the bridge and stopping on the shoulder near the entrance to Bear Mountain State Park. David reached into his coat pocket and pulled out a light blue, sateen jewelry box.

Eyebrows raised, her eyes met his as he handed it over. "Open it," he urged.

Inside was a teardrop-shaped sapphire on a silver chain. Silja held it up in the afternoon sunlight. "It's beautiful," she whispered. "I love the color."

David nodded. "I knew you would."

She turned toward him. "But why . . . " He'd never bought her an expensive present before. He paid for their dates and hotel rooms, and he frequently gave her flowers—often ones he'd grown himself in his laboratory's greenhouse. But he'd never given her anything like this.

He took the necklace from its box and unclasped it, placing it around her neck. "I thought . . . what we have together, and what we have to look forward to . . . well." He shrugged. "It's worth celebrating."

Silja glanced at her reflection in the rearview mirror, admiring the dazzling stone. Then she reached across the seat and entwined her arms around his neck. "I love you so much," she said hoarsely. "I want to be with you always, David."

"Silja. My love." He gently removed her eyeglasses before kissing her neck, her cheeks, her mouth.

She sighed, eyes closed, wanting to stay right where she was. Stay there for all time.

If only she could figure out a way.

61

Angie

The baby jiggling against my thigh, I walked frantically down the steep hill toward town, searching for a pay phone so I could call a taxi. I couldn't stop thinking about everything I'd learned.

What else was Paul hiding from me? What other secrets did he have?

If only I hadn't been so smitten. If only I hadn't been so damn trusting.

I furrowed my brow. It was my mother's words drilled into me—my sisters', too, though of course they had also learned at our mother's knee. Trust your man. Find a man you can trust, and then let him handle all the big problems.

Raise your babies, and forget about everything else.

I glanced at PJ. He was so small, so innocent. He had his whole life ahead of him. Who knew what life would bring for him? I was thankful for his maleness. Things would be easier for him because he's a boy.

That's the way it's always been. Life is easier for boys.

And yet, I reminded myself, Senator Kennedy has a young wife, not much older than me, with opinions and interests of her own. Recently I'd read in the papers that before she was married, Mrs. Kennedy was a photojournalist—interviewing people on the street and taking their photographs. It seemed so brave—but terrifically fun as well. I was sure that I'd love doing something like that.

And what about Miss Wells? True, she was only a teacher—

anybody could become a teacher, it was the most accessible path for women into the working world.

But Miss Wells had broken barriers. She could've worked in a Negro school district, but she chose to apply for a more well-paying position. I thought about my implication the other night at dinner—how I'd wondered, but hadn't asked, why Miss Wells would want to work in Stonekill.

Remembering the moment, I felt my face redden with shame. It was no wonder Miss Wells had felt defensive. She probably spent half her life defending herself for doing what any smart person would try to do: become the most successful person she could be.

Look at Miss Wells now. She was respected—maybe not by everyone, but by her students and her boss. And they were the people who mattered the most.

Could I do that? Could I become respected? Could I be a woman who did brave, adventurous things?

Or was it too late?

The rental car was parked at the motel when my taxi pulled in. "Damn," I said softly to myself. "Damn, damn, damn." I tapped the driver on the shoulder. "Please, just let me out around the corner," I said. "Behind the building."

When I came around the motel and unlocked our room door, Paul stood up from the chair he'd been seated in. "Angel," he said. "Where were you? Why would you go off like that?"

"I . . . I just needed some fresh air. I couldn't sit around in a motel room all day. So PJ and I went for a walk."

The lies were becoming easier and easier, the more of them I told.

Paul frowned. "Well, all's well that ends well, I guess. But please don't do anything like that again—at least without leaving me a note." He shook his head. "I was so worried about you," he said, gathering the baby and me in his arms. "You and PJ."

I smiled, slipping from his grasp. He picked up the phone and ordered a room service meal. But before it arrived, he took his car keys off the dresser. "I haven't found Ruby yet. I'm really starting to worry," he said, jangling the keys. "I need to go out and keep looking. You sit tight, okay? Turn on the television or something. I promise to be back as soon as I can."

I didn't answer. I watched the door close behind him, then peered through the curtains as he got into the rental car, parked just outside our room, and drove away.

I wanted to call someone—Carol Ann or Joyce or Alice—and tell them everything. But I had no idea if I could do that from a motel room. How would that get charged? Would the county pay for that, too? And besides, it was all so far-fetched by now, I didn't even know how I'd explain it to someone back home. I wouldn't know where to start.

Should I call Jean Kellerman? I took Jean's card from my purse and looked at the handwritten telephone number on the back.

No, that was silly. Sympathetic as Jean had seemed at the newspaper office, at the end of the day she *was* a reporter hungry for a story. She wasn't a friend.

I answered the door when room service arrived. I ate one of the three sandwiches, leaving the other two for Paul and Ruby. After settling the baby into the crib that had been brought in for him, I sang softly to him, rubbing his back until he went to sleep. Sitting in the chair next to his crib, I dozed off.

The sharpness of car headlights outside the room's window woke me. I straightened my back and turned to see Paul and Ruby entering the room. I held a finger to my lips and pointed to the baby. Paul closed the door softly behind them.

I took Ruby awkwardly in my arms. "Are you all right?" I asked.

Quietly—so quietly that I almost didn't hear her—she whispered, "I trust you, Aunt Angie." Then she pulled back from me and nodded. "I'm all right," she said, loud enough for Paul to hear.

"Ruby, you should sleep," Paul said, rubbing his own eyes. "I brought you a suitcase with some clothes. And your toothbrush. I'm sorry if I didn't know what else you'd need; maybe you can borrow makeup and all that from Angie."

Ruby and I glanced at each other. I wore makeup, but Ruby didn't;

we could tell that about each other just by looking. But Paul wouldn't know such a thing. Men didn't know such things—even men who proclaimed to be artists, men who were supposed to notice beauty and details.

We all settled into bed—Paul and I in the bed by the door, Ruby in the one next to the bathroom. Paul took me in his arms and kissed me chastely on the cheek. "I can't wait to be home with you," he said, taking one of my breasts in his hand. He rubbed my nipple and murmured, "Can't wait . . . "

Despite myself, I felt my body responding. My nipple hardened in his fingertips, and I felt a tingling between my legs.

How can it be, I wondered, that the body can want what the mind knows is wrong?

"We'll be there soon," I whispered to Paul. I slipped out of his grasp and turned onto my side, facing away from him. He slung his arm around my waist and kissed my neck. Soon I heard him snoring deeply in my right ear.

But I couldn't get to sleep. I tried lying still and breathing evenly, hoping sleep would find me. But every time I closed my eyes, they popped open again.

I gingerly unfolded myself from Paul's embrace and sat upright. Turning toward Ruby's bed, I saw the girl staring at me.

We locked gazes but said not a word. I gave her the slightest nod of my head, and she silently rose from her bed. Her grandmother's shawl was spread across her bed, and she draped it around her shoulders, on top of the baggy sweater she wore over her nightgown.

Rising and slipping on my robe, I motioned toward the door. Ruby followed me outside. We sat in two lawn chairs outside the room, leaving the door ajar. The night was clear and crisp, the October air chilly. Both of us sat cross-legged, our feet under ourselves in our chairs. We pulled our outer layers more tightly toward our chins. We could see the baby in his crib, but not Paul.

"So you couldn't sleep either, huh?" I asked.

Ruby shook her head. "I'm glad you were awake. I need to talk to you." She leaned in close.

62

Ruby

"What is it, Ruby?" Aunt Angie asks. "Tell me."

Ruby glances around the corner into the motel room, then back at Aunt Angie. "You need to get Uncle Paul to send you home tomorrow," she whispers. "You and PJ. He still has the airplane tickets for tomorrow afternoon. You need to convince him to put you and PJ on that plane."

And then Ruby closes her mouth and blinks. She almost never cries. She barely recognizes the feeling of tears for what they are. She reaches into the neckline of her nightgown and fingers her mother's sapphire necklace.

"What about you?" Aunt Angie asks. "Where will you be?"

Ruby looks at Uncle Paul's car, parked in front of them. Its bumper gleams in the moonlight. "I'll be here," she lies. "Waiting to see what else the police want from me."

Aunt Angie doesn't say anything. Then she asks, "Wouldn't it be better if I stayed, too? I think you need the support, Ruby. I think you need . . . " She looks up at the starry sky, then back at Ruby. "You need a mother nearby, Ruby."

If only it were that easy. Ruby shakes her head.

"It's going to get tricky," she says. "Please, Aunt Angie." She recognizes desperation in her own voice. "If you can't get on that plane for yourself—or for me—will you do it for PJ?"

Ruby tilts her head toward the crib just inside the motel room. "You got a beautiful baby out of all this, Aunt Angie. The most important thing is to keep your beautiful baby safe."

She hesitates, then goes on. "My mother and Dr. Shepherd were expecting a child. But not anymore. That baby won't ever have life."

Aunt Angie stares at her and asks why not.

Ruby shakes her head. "It doesn't matter. It won't happen, that's all. I don't want to talk about it." She looks away, then back at Aunt Angie. "You have some things that are mine," she says quietly. "My mother's photographs. My father's letters from Uncle Paul, and his drawings. You have those things, don't you?"

Aunt Angie nods. "I'll give them back to you," she tells Ruby, starting to rise. "They're in the baby's suitcase."

Ruby puts her hand on Aunt Angie's arm, and she stops and sits back down. "No," Ruby tells her. "Leave them where they are. That's actually a perfect place for them." She thinks about it for a minute, and then adds, "If you can do it without Uncle Paul noticing, move the photo album to your pocketbook. But leave the other things where they are."

Aunt Angie tilts her head, looking at Ruby curiously. "Why would I do that?"

"Because I'm asking you to."

Aunt Angie breathes in and out slowly. "There was an envelope in your mother's jewelry box," she says. "I wanted to open it, but I didn't. Now it's gone."

Ruby nods. "My mother's photograph album was in that envelope. I took it. And then I gave the album to you, because I knew it would be safe with you."

Aunt Angie takes this in and doesn't reply.

Ruby shifts in her seat, leaning closer to Aunt Angie. "Do you have . . . there was another letter, too."

Aunt Angie gives her a long, level look. "I have that one," she says, and Ruby can tell she's trying to keep her voice even. "And that letter is exactly why I don't think it's a good idea to leave you here alone with Paul."

Ruby understands why Aunt Angie feels this way. But she says, "I've trusted you, Aunt Angie. Now you have to trust *me*. I know how to handle Paul." She leans in and goes on, "That letter, it's evidence.

It implicates Uncle Paul, or at least raises suspicion. Uncle Paul thinks my father found it. He thinks it's somewhere in the house." She gives Aunt Angie a beseeching look. "Please—you cannot tell him you have it."

Aunt Angie's mouth puckers into a frown. "I have no intention of trusting Paul with anything right now."

"Well, that's wise," Ruby replies.

She doesn't tell Aunt Angie what Uncle Paul suggested when he told Ruby his plan. Uncle Paul said they would get out of this whole mess a lot easier if they didn't have to worry about Aunt Angie.

"What about PJ?" Ruby had asked him.

Uncle Paul shrugged. "We'd keep PJ with us. You could pretend he's yours."

Ruby admits she was tempted. It was an appealing notion, after everything that's happened.

But it wouldn't be right. So she told Uncle Paul they shouldn't do that. "PJ belongs to Aunt Angie," she insisted. "They need to stay together, and they need to stay safe." She put her hand on his arm. "Please, Uncle Paul."

He frowned. "I'll think about it," he said. "*I* need to make the plan, Ruby. Let me handle it."

She nodded, not because she agreed but because she knew arguing with him would get her nowhere. She felt chilled, touching his arm. She drew her hand away.

Now, next to Aunt Angie in the darkness, her body so close Ruby can feel everything about it—its vibrancy, its innocence—her heart is heavy for Aunt Angie. If she gets safely back to Wisconsin with PJ, Aunt Angie will have to live with the knowledge of what's happened.

Ruby knows a lot, but one thing she doesn't know is what it's like to believe someone loves you and then learn he doesn't. Whatever else Ruby might not have, she knows from which corners of her world love finds its way to her.

So she tells Aunt Angie she's sorry. Truly sorry.

Aunt Angie is silent for a moment, and then she says, "Ruby, you know where your mother is—don't you?"

Slowly, Ruby nods.

"Will you tell me?"

Ruby ponders the question, though she already knows the answer. Before Uncle Paul told her his plan, she wouldn't have considered it. When Ruby gave Aunt Angie the photograph album, when she let Aunt Angie in on even the smallest detail, she had no plans to tell Aunt Angie everything. Not then and not ever.

But now Ruby knows it's the right thing to do. There is something about trusting Aunt Angie completely that makes everything that was terribly wrong start to feel absolutely right.

So she leans toward her aunt. Their heads together, whispering in the cold October evening, Ruby speaks.

When Ruby is finished, Aunt Angie sits back and stares at her. "Holy Mother of God," she says softly. She clasps her hands together, making a fist in her lap. "We need to go to the police. You can tell them bits and pieces, Ruby. You don't have to tell them everything. They're already searching the house—"

"No, they're not," Ruby says. "Uncle Paul made that up. To get you to leave. It was me on the phone, pretending to be the cops."

Aunt Angie grimaces. Then she says, "Even so—the police can help us, Ruby."

Ruby shakes her head. "We don't need the police. What we need to do is convince Uncle Paul to let you get on that plane. And we need to pretend we never had this talk."

"Ruby—"

Ruby stops her by putting her hand on Aunt Angie's arm. "Aunt Angie," she says earnestly. "Please believe me when I tell you I'm not in danger. But you and PJ are. That's the important thing."

She takes her grandmother's shawl from around her shoulders and places it in Aunt Angie's lap. "I want you to have this. Take it home with you. Keep it safe for me."

"Ruby." Aunt Angie looks her in the eye. "Thank you. That's sweet of you, honey." She looks up at the stars overhead, her fingers playing with the shawl's fringe.

Ruby smiles, but she also shivers, chilled without the shawl despite the warmth inside Shepherd's sweater. Aunt Angie rises and takes her hand. "Let's get you back inside," she suggests. "I'll try to sleep, too, but mostly I need to think about all this."

63

Silja

Silja's second pregnancy made her not only nauseated at odd hours, but also as emotional as a teenager. She reminded herself of some melodramatic young star Natalie Wood's Judy in *Rebel Without a Cause*, maybe, weeping at the drop of a hat over the despair that had become her life.

Alone in her bedroom at night, Silja cried hot, fat tears of frustration. She wrapped soft sheets around her body, leaned back against the pillows she'd so carefully selected for their advertised promise of maximum comfort. She blubbered into tissue after tissue, her nose itching and her eyes spidered red.

She wished she could run—take Ruby and David, take her body with David's child growing inside it. Just disappear, like she used to dream of doing before she had her house, before she loved David. But even if it were possible—and she knew it wasn't—she would lose everything if she left. Her home, her job—everything she'd worked so hard for. It wouldn't be fair.

Henry was the one who deserved to lose. Not Silja.

One night as she lay sobbing, willing her flip-flopping stomach to calm down, there was a light tap on her door. She wiped her eyes and put her glasses on. She rose from the bed, drawing her robe around her body. She wasn't showing, not yet, but it was only a matter of time.

She opened the door to find Ruby standing in the darkened hallway. "What is it, honey?" Silja asked. "Are you all right?"

Ruby nodded. "Yes. But are *you*?"

Silja glanced behind the girl. Henry was nowhere in sight—probably out in the woods, out in his silly bomb shelter. She drew Ruby into her room and closed the door.

"I thought I heard something in here, so I came to check on you." Ruby regarded Silja carefully. "Have you been crying, Mom?"

"Oh, Ruby." Silja sat on the side of the bed. Tears streamed down her cheeks.

Ruby put her arm around Silja's shoulder. "Remember when we used to snuggle up together?" she asked. "Back in the parlor on Lawrence Avenue?" She squeezed Silja's shoulder. "You always made me feel better if I was sad," she said softly, coaxingly. "Maybe I can make *you* feel better now."

"That's sweet, Ruby. Thank you." Silja sniffed, and then broke out in fresh sobs. "I just don't know what to do!" she wailed. "I'm at the end of my rope, Ruby, I—"

She cut herself off, shaking her head. "You should go," she told the girl. "I appreciate your concern, honey, truly I do. But I can't burden you with this. You don't need or deserve to hear about adult troubles."

"Mom. Look at me." Ruby tilted Silja's chin so they were eye to eye. "Tell me what's going on. Maybe I can help."

"You can't. There's no help. There's no solution."

"Just *tell* me, okay?"

Silja couldn't stop herself. Like faulty car brakes too long unattended and finally giving out entirely, Silja's heart rolled past the point of control. She took Ruby's hand in hers and spilled everything. She told her teenage daughter about her lover's baby, who would be born the following spring—unless Silja did something about it soon. She knew there were places she could go, a doctor she could see. Her own physician was the premier gynecologist in the city. He would, she was sure, be able to recommend someone reputable for a woman of means like Silja. She couldn't be the first woman in his practice who'd been in such a predicament.

It was possible, of course. But Silja couldn't bear the idea. Aborting David's child was the last thing she wanted to do. But she didn't see any other options.

"I only wish David and I could get married," Silja said. "I wish Dad would grant me a divorce, so I could marry David. But he won't." She bit her bottom lip, feeling bitterness rise in her throat.

Ruby sat quietly, her hand still in Silja's, appearing deep in thought. "There has to be a way," she said finally.

Silja shook her head. "There's no way. There's no solution. At least, none that I can see."

Ruby squeezed her hand. "Mom, I don't want you to worry," she said. "Try not to worry, okay?"

64

Angie

We all rose early, unable to sleep soundly in the small, unfamiliar space. After we'd eaten breakfast, again brought by room service, Paul wiped his mouth with his napkin, pushed himself back from the table, and stood. He looked down at me and said, "I need you to come with me to the house. I forgot some things." He nodded toward his niece. "Ruby can stay here and keep an eye on PJ."

I was so startled I didn't know what to say. Finally, I asked, "What about the police? Won't they be there, searching?"

Paul shrugged. "We'll have to take that chance. There's something I need from there. If the police are there, I hope they'll let me in and let me . . . take it."

I asked why he needed me to come along.

"Because I do," he said. "Just trust me, Angel, that's all."

He gave me the soft, dreamy-eyed gaze I knew so well. Or thought I'd known, anyway.

I pressed my lips together. "I have a different idea," I said. "You still have those plane tickets, right? Why don't you put PJ and me on that plane today back to Wisconsin?" I put my fingers on his hand, splayed on the table, and let them rest there. "There's so much to think about here," I said gently, massaging his hand. "You could focus better if PJ and I were out of your hair."

He closed his eyes, then opened them. "I don't want to be separated from the two of you." He put his other hand on top of mine, so my one hand was sandwiched between his two. "I'd be lost without you, Angel."

If only it were true. If only I believed him.

"Paul," I pleaded, my voice as gentle as I could make it. "I'll feel so much better at home, away from all of this. And I have faith in you. I *know* you can clear everything up if only you can concentrate on it. Then you and Ruby can join the baby and me back in Door County— you'll be there in no time at all. I'm sure of it." I gave him my best big-eyed, cajoling look. "Please, Paul."

I waited, my eyes locked with his. He stared at me, then turned toward Ruby, who seemed intent on her half-finished eggs and toast. She must have felt his eyes on her, because she lifted her head. For just the smallest moment, their eyes met. Neither spoke. Then she went back to her meal.

He turned back to me. "All right," he said. "I'll phone your parents and let them know you're coming home today after all. Go pack your things and the baby's in one bag. You can use the big one—I'll take my small case back."

I focused on packing, hunched on my heels with my back to Paul while I removed his things from the larger bag and transferred PJ's items in. The packet of letters and drawings was safely wrapped in a layer of clean cotton diapers that I buried at the bottom of the bag I'd take home with me. I slipped Silja's photograph album into my purse.

Ruby asked if she could take a walk while she waited for us. "I won't go far," she promised Paul. "No farther than the motel office. I'll just enjoy the view of the river." She smiled at him. "Okay?"

He grimaced but acquiesced. Only a few minutes later she returned. And then we were on our way, my things and PJ's in the suitcase placed in the Ford's trunk.

"I still need to go back to the house," Paul said nonchalantly as we drove away from the motel. "Remember, I said I left something there."

"What is it?" I asked.

Paul said, "I can't tell you, Angel. I'm sorry, but some things are personal."

I didn't press the issue. When he pulled into the driveway on Stone

Ridge Road, no cars were there. "Ah," Paul said. "No cops. We're lucky, it seems."

Lucky. It was a word that meant nothing. I leaned back in the seat, baby in my arms.

"Come in with me," he said, reaching for my hand. "Please, Angel."

I glanced at Ruby, in the backseat. She shook her head slightly.

"The baby is almost asleep," I whispered—and it was true; he was drowsy in my embrace. I didn't shift to take Paul's hand. Instead, I said, "I can't move; I'd disturb PJ. You go get what you need, Paul, and we can be on our way."

He seemed to waver, as if deciding whether or not to pressure me further. I kept my eyes locked on his, letting him know I wasn't going to change my mind.

Ruby watched our exchange. Paul turned and met her gaze. Neither of them said anything, but their eyes were fixed on one another.

Finally, he stepped away from the car. He hurried up to the house, unlocked it, and went inside.

I looked back at Ruby. "Smart," she said.

Paul was gone only moments, and when he returned, his hands were empty. He strolled calmly, whistling. It was as if he'd gone inside for a missing tie or pair of cuff links.

He sat in the driver's seat and shifted to look at Ruby. "Here," he said, reaching over to hand her a shiny object. "I found this inside. I think it belongs to you."

As Ruby took the item from him, I saw that it was a battered, tarnished Zippo lighter.

Paul reversed out of the drive and drove away. None of us looked back.

At the airplane gate, I settled into a seat with the baby on my lap. Ruby watched me, then glanced at a nearby clock.

"You have a good fifteen minutes until you board, Aunt Angie," she said. "I'm going to take a walk." She turned toward Paul. "Want to come with me, Uncle Paul?" she entreated. "Please?"

Standing near the window, watching planes arriving and departing, he turned to face us. He jiggled his hands in his pockets. He looked uncomfortable—as if he wanted not just to walk, but also to break into a run and flee the scene.

"A walk," he replied. "Okay, sure."

Ruby leaned toward me. "Don't say anything," she whispered. "This is good-bye and good luck." She kissed the baby on the top of his head. "I'll be in touch when I can." She stood up and motioned to Paul.

He patted the baby's head, then ran two fingers across my cheek. Smiling his white-toothed, movie-star smile, he said, "Back before you know it, Angel."

I kept my eyes down and didn't say anything. I watched them stroll away side by side, looking as if they didn't have a care in the world. Two identically tall, lean figures. Both of them wily as foxes, uncontrollable as birds.

PJ began to fuss, and I reached over him into my handbag, to retrieve the bottle I'd prepared at the motel. Once I arrived at the airport in Milwaukee, I'd have little to do. My mother, always organized and ready for every situation, would have everything PJ needed. I would be able to sit back and enjoy the drive to Door County, with PJ safe in my mother's arms.

My mother would take over. And I could stop being the grown-up.

I stuck the bottle in the baby's mouth and closed my eyes, lost in thought. When I opened them, someone was seating himself next to me. I glanced to my right, and then gave a small cry of shock.

It was Dr. Shepherd.

"Mrs. Glass." Dr. Shepherd extended his hand. "I'm glad to see you again." He had on a dark gray fedora, a gray suit, and a modest blue button-down shirt. He looked ordinary. Like he could be anybody. A man who would blend in with a crowd.

"How . . . why . . ." I stammered. "What are you doing here?" I glanced around. "Did you follow me?"

He nodded slightly.

"Why would you do that? What do you want from me?"

PJ turned his face toward the doctor, causing the bottle to slip from his mouth and formula to dribble down his chin. He let out a loud cry; I turned his head gently and put the bottle back between his lips. He reached both chubby hands up to clutch it, his gaze on Dr. Shepherd. I dabbed the spilled liquid from PJ's chin.

Dr. Shepherd met the child's eyes. "Certainly his father's son, despite that fair hair of his."

I nodded. There's no denying Paul's genes in our child. He has the mousy brown Doyle hair, but other than that he's the spitting image of Paul.

"What will you tell him, as he grows?" Dr. Shepherd shifted in his seat, leaning toward me.

"What will I tell him about what?"

"About his father."

I pressed my lips together and didn't answer. Instead, I asked, "Did Ruby tell you I'd be here? Did she get Paul to walk away before my flight left, so he wouldn't see you?"

Dr. Shepherd nodded again. "She did."

We sat silently as the baby finished his bottle. I hoisted him to my shoulder to burp him, then looked at the doctor over the top of PJ's head.

"Dr. Shepherd." I took a breath. "I'm so sorry about Silja." I hesitated, then put my hand on his arm. "And your child."

65

Ruby

None of them looked back at the birdcage as they drove away. And Ruby was glad, because she knew what she'd see and she didn't want Aunt Angie to see it. Or maybe Aunt Angie wouldn't have seen it, because the spark was so tiny.

On Sunday night when he told her the plan, Uncle Paul told Ruby how he was going to set it up. And he's so smart, Uncle Paul—his plan was to lay it out in her father's bedroom, using kerosene and a string. He'd drill a small hole in the door, thread the string to the front entryway of the house, where he'd light it just before he left.

It would all work, Uncle Paul said, in such a way that he could start it slowly, with just a flick of Ruby's Zippo.

Just a tiny flicker and then he was outside and they were gone before anyone could notice. Not the neighbors, and certainly not Aunt Angie.

Uncle Paul said that the birdcage would explode—the birdcage and everything in it, including the evidence Ruby told him was somewhere inside. Her father's fastidious drawings of the Shelter. And the letter Uncle Paul had written to her, expressing his desire to be with Ruby and no one else.

Evidence that Ruby insisted she'd searched and searched for, but never found. Evidence that Uncle Paul also tore the house apart looking for, after he took Aunt Angie to the motel.

Uncle Paul said it would look like a meteor hit from the inside. It would be too late for anyone to do anything except watch the birdcage go up in a massive cloud of smoke and flames.

Where did he learn to do something like that? The war, maybe, or somewhere in all his travels. Who knows?

When it comes down to it, Ruby doesn't know much about Uncle Paul.

She supposes she should stop calling him Uncle now. She knows that's not how he wants her to think of him.

What she *does* know about Paul is that he's clever. He knows how to get out of a situation and disappear. And that's a skill Ruby needs right now. Like a magician, Paul can make her vanish.

Later, if necessary, Ruby can make *him* vanish. She's quite capable of that.

It wouldn't be the first time, would it?

66

Silja

1960

When she got home on Monday evening, she felt nauseated—again. She ran for her room and dropped her pocketbook on the bed. She dashed into the bathroom and knelt in front of the toilet. It was only after she'd flushed and stood up that she saw Henry standing in the doorway.

"What the hell?" he asked.

"Stomach bug," she said simply. "Going to lie down for a bit." She tried to brush past him.

He held out his arm, blocking her way. "Stomach bug, my ass." He pushed forward, forcing her toward a corner. "I came in here today looking for a bar of soap. We ran out in the other bathroom. And what did I find?" He thrust open her vanity drawer and shook her diaphragm case at her. "What the hell is *this*, Silja? No, don't tell me— don't say a goddamn thing. I know what it is. And apparently it didn't work as well as you'd expected it to." He shook his head. "You must be quite the Fertile Myrtle, *Mrs*. Glass," he said. "Two unplanned pregnancies in a lifetime. And how many lovers?" His eyes narrowed. "Or maybe this isn't the first one."

She shook her head. "He's the first," she said. "The one and only." She gripped the edge of the vanity. "Henry, I want to be with him, and he with me."

"Who the hell is it?"

"No one you'd know."

"Tell me his goddamn name, Silja!"

Silja sighed. "His name is David Shepherd. He's a good man, Henry, a gentle soul—"

"David Shepherd?" Henry's eyes narrowed. "I've heard that name. He's that smart aleck who writes letters to newspaper editors. Goes around libeling patriotic Americans. And *why* does that punk Shepherd write those letters? Because he's a goddamn Communist, that's why!" Henry's face was red from hairline to neck. "For Chrissake, Silja!"

Silja shook her head. "That's simply not true," she said, trying to keep her voice even. "He's just a good man who loves me, and I love him back."

"I don't give a goddamn who you love, Silja. You're *my* wife. You're married to *me*."

"But this isn't a marriage," she pleaded. "It hasn't been one for a long time. Even you'd have to admit that, Henry. Please," she went on hastily. "Please, Henry, be reasonable. Grant me a divorce and move on." She mustered a smile as a desperate plan came to her. "I'll set you up," she proposed. "I'll buy you a big old house like the one we had on Lawrence Avenue. You can fix it up. You can live as you like, do as you like."

His expression was stark and stony-eyed. "You have got to be kidding me," he said slowly, enunciating each word. "Not in a million years, Silja, is that how this will play out."

He stepped toward her, and she backed up. In the small space, she had nowhere to go.

He hit her hard on the left cheek. The blow knocked her down, into the corner by the toilet. Her eyeglasses flew from her face and onto the tiles.

"You goddamn whore!" Henry hit her again. She flinched, making herself as small as she could against the cold porcelain.

He grabbed her arm and pulled her roughly until she stood. "Get moving."

"Henry, stop," Silja cried. "Please, just stop and let me go."

"Fuck you, Silja." He pushed her the length of the hall ahead of him. Tears streaming down her face, she wobbled on her heels as they made their way toward the sliding door to the backyard.

He kicked the back of her knees. "Take your shoes off."

She looked at him questioningly.

"Just do it, dammit!"

Obediently, she bent down and slipped one high heel, then the other, off her feet. She tried to swing around with the second one, aiming for his eye, but without her eyeglasses she missed by a mile, batting the air next to his shoulder instead.

Henry laughed cruelly. "Nice try," he said, easily knocking the shoe out of her hand. He prodded her back. "Go."

He held fast to her elbow as they wound along the dirt pathways through the forest. "Henry, please," she pleaded. "Please let me go."

He didn't reply. They came to the clearing where the bomb shelter was.

Silja looked around. "What are you going to do?" she whispered.

He glared at her. "I'm going to put you down there," he said. "I'm going to put you down there and lock you in and you see how long you last without anyone knowing where you are." He shook his head. "Honestly, I don't know what I'm going to do after that," he said, and his voice was conversational, almost confessional. "So how handy is it to have someplace to store you while I figure it out?"

"Please," she whispered again.

He didn't reply. He gripped her arm as he rolled away the boulder that half-covered the opening. One handed, he leaned down to twist open the round metal door. Only someone with his strength and know-how would be able to do that, Silja thought.

She'd underestimated him. How could she have been so foolish? So blind?

As he turned to guide her down the ladder, she tried one more time to pull away. It was her last chance and she almost made it. She slipped through his grip, but he was faster than she. He grabbed her again, this time around the waist.

"Get the hell down there!" he yelled, pushing her from behind.

They were the last words Silja heard. She fell headfirst into the darkness.

67

Ruby

So many times in the past week Ruby has tried to imagine what it was like for her mother in those last few moments. How terrified she must have been. How myopic she must have felt as he marched her outside—without her eyeglasses, his grip on her arm tight, able to see only a few inches in front of her.

Did she try to run? Try to escape? Ruby suspects she did. But he would have given her no chance.

"I didn't mean to kill her," Ruby's father said when he told her what happened. "I just meant to put her down there for a while, until I could come up with a plan. But she . . . " His dark eyes transformed to narrow slits as he looked past Ruby, through the sliding glass door into the opaque, unruly woods. "Well, let's just say she got what she had coming."

"How?" Ruby whispered. "How is it possible she had it coming?"

Her father turned toward Ruby. "Her activities were questionable. That's all I'm going to say about it, Ruby. It was business between your mother and me." He opened a kitchen drawer, taking out a pad of paper and a pen. "But the police wouldn't see it that way."

He thrust the pad and pen toward Ruby. "You need to help me cover this up," he demanded. "We need to make it seem like she ran away."

He looked at Ruby with that hooded, blunt expression of his—and, for the first time in her memory, she was afraid of him. Usually she thought of him as just a lonely, mildly crazed man, like someone out of an Albert Camus novel—more a character in a made-up story than an actual person. Frightening in theory, but ultimately harmless.

But now she realized she hadn't seen him for who he truly was. He was more predictable than that. He was like a plant adapting to changing conditions. Growing longer roots, maybe, or sturdier seeds. If conditions changed—if he felt his world was threatened—he wouldn't hesitate to make changes to remove the threat.

She should have seen it sooner. Her mother should have seen it, too. But Ruby couldn't blame her mother; she was blinded, after all.

Ruby could try to outwit him, but what if she failed? Would he do to her what he'd done to her mother?

"Here's what you need to do, Ruby," he said. Then he explained what he wanted from her.

She needed more time. But in order to stall, first she had to ensure his trust. She had to demonstrate loyalty to him.

So she did what he said.

She forged a note from her mother. That part was easy; she'd known for years how to replicate her mother's handwriting. Once, long ago, her father had told her—he learned this through his crime detection course—that people generally imitate the handwriting of the first person who teaches them to write in cursive. Ruby had learned first from her mother, not from the teachers at school. So it was little surprise that Ruby's handwriting was so similar to her mother's.

The cops hadn't figured that out when Ruby was questioned the other day. If they suspected it, they'd have asked Ruby to produce a handwriting sample. But it was probably just a matter of time before they went down that path.

After writing the note, Ruby put on her mother's car coat—her father didn't ask her to do that; Ruby wanted to wear it—and drove her mother's car to the train station, with her father following in his truck. In cover of darkness Ruby parked the MGA in her mother's usual spot in the depot parking lot.

She got out and glanced around, and she was pretty sure no one except her father was watching her.

She dropped her mother's keys into the coat pocket. In the dark, desolate evening Ruby walked up the hill as if she were going to the old house on Lawrence Avenue. But of course she didn't go to that house, because that's not where her family lived anymore. When the truck pulled up to the curb, she hopped in.

Her father's hands shook on the steering wheel. "You really want to know what happened?" he asked. "You want to know why she deserved it? I'll show you when we get home. I have a newspaper in my room, from a week or two ago. I saved it to show some of my friends. Letter to the editor, written by one of those Commie freaks. It's all about how the things people like me say are hateful, how our message is extreme. Nothing could be further from the truth—we just want our country back, that's all." His eyes narrowed. "Goddamn Commies. And you know who *that* goddamn Commie was, the one who wrote the letter?" He hit the brakes sharply at a red light and turned to Ruby. "You know who?"

"No," Ruby replied. "Who?"

"Your mother's lover, that's who. Your mother was cheating on me. I know I said earlier that it was none of your business—but I've thought about it, and it *is* your business. You have a right to know that your mother was unfaithful to your father—and with a goddamn Commie lowlife." The light turned and Ruby's father pressed down the gas pedal. "If I ever get my hands on that bastard, I'll tear him from limb to limb."

Ruby didn't answer. They sat in silence the rest of the way back to the birdcage.

Inside, she hung her mother's coat in the closet and asked her father if he'd like some tea.

"Yes," he said wearily, sitting on the sofa. "I'd like that a lot, Ruby."

So she made him a cup. But before she brewed it, she slipped into her room and retrieved something she wished she'd had the foresight to put to use much sooner.

Afterward, she called Shepherd.

When he arrived—parking in the cemetery and finding his way through the darkened woods to the birdcage—she enfolded herself in his arms and in a low voice and in the way she could bare her soul only to him, she told Shepherd everything.

As she spoke, he stared at her father's body in the living room—lying motionless on the floor in front of the hearth, coffee table askew from her father kicking it as he convulsed, as Ruby watched him die. Viewing the tableau—it looked like the final scene in a box-office thriller, something Ruby's mother would have appreciated—Shepherd's shoulders began to shake and his expression crumbled.

"It's all right," Ruby told him. "It's not *right*—she's gone, and that means it can never be right again—but we can fix things up." She stepped back and took both of Shepherd's hands in hers. "I have a plan. I just need your help."

Shepherd did what she asked of him. He put on the work gloves Ruby gave him and easily hauled her father's body onto his big shoulders. He carried the body to the woods and pushed it around under the oak tree Ruby pointed to, leaving marks in the dirt and fallen leaves that would indicate convulsions. Then Shepherd slumped the body at the base of the tree.

Ruby's father had taught her all about fingerprinting. He'd emphasized that carelessly left fingerprints were the simplest way to detect a criminal. So Ruby was scrupulous. She donned gloves, then used a handkerchief to wipe her fingerprints from her father's empty teacup. She braced it in his hand and pressed his stiffening fingers around the handle. Then she unwrapped his hand from the cup and placed it by her father's side.

The setup was good. It looked like something a heartsick man might do.

Ruby stepped back. "We should go see about her now."

In the darkness, Shepherd gave her a long look. "Are you sure?" He glanced up at the tangled treetops, then back at Ruby. "You could leave her where she is. *How* she is. You could tell the police that it happened almost the way it did: he killed her in a fit of rage, and then killed himself in remorse."

Ruby had already thought through the same scenario. But she shook her head. "No. I want to see her. I want to make sure she looks all right." She blinked. "I don't want anyone to know she's down there. I don't want anyone messing around with her." Her eyes meeting Shepherd's, she added, "Please."

He hesitated a moment, and then he agreed.

She brought her mother's eyeglasses, pocketbook, and high heels along; the Shelter was the safest place to store them. It was a slow, dark walk through her family's forest until Shepherd and Ruby reached the Shelter.

They rolled back the boulder and Ruby opened the metal door. She started down the ladder, then saw that Shepherd was standing still, watching her in the half-light of the moon.

She went back up and poked her head through the opening. "Aren't you coming?"

He bent down next to her and touched her shoulder. "I just . . . I don't think I can." He looked toward the cemetery, then back at Ruby. "I'm sorry, Ruby. I just can't see her like that."

Ruby stared into his dog-kind eyes. He'd done so much for her; she wouldn't push him about this.

She reached across to put her hand over his, on her opposite shoulder. "It's okay," she said. "I understand. Wait for me; I won't be long."

At the bottom of the iron ladder, Ruby stumbled onto something bulky and knew what it was. She stepped over it and entered the main room, grabbing a flashlight from the shelf. She turned back to the entrance and saw that she'd been right: her mother's body lay motionless on the concrete floor near the lowest ladder rung. Seeing her that way brought a sob to Ruby's throat. It was the only time in the past week, except for last night outside the motel room with Aunt Angie, that Ruby has cried.

Her face flushed and her eyes stinging with tears, Ruby went to work. She set her mother up properly—as properly, anyway, as you can for a person who died by such violent means. Ruby dragged her body—it was too heavy to lift—and laid it on the floor between the bunks. As best she could, she straightened her mother's broken neck. She spread her mother's hair on a pillow and made sure her clothes were in place—her skirt smooth, the collar of her blouse straight.

There was some blood; not a lot. Ruby thought her mother's body must have started miscarrying the baby, probably when she landed. She used a wool blanket to cover her lower half. She folded her mother's hands into one another, across her belly where Ruby's baby brother or sister was.

It sounds creepy but it actually made Ruby feel better—making sure her mother looked so dignified.

Ruby remembered her grandmother's funeral. She unclasped her mother's sapphire necklace, just like the Finnish pastor did with Grandma's locket, and fastened it around her own neck.

When there was nothing else to do, she stood back and looked at her mother. She didn't know what to say. She tried to remember how to say "Rest in peace" in Finnish, but the words weren't there. So she said it in English, and then she touched her mother's cheek and then she backed away.

She climbed out of the Shelter and closed it up. Shepherd was sitting on the cemetery wall, waiting for her. Together they rolled the boulder on top of the metal door, then sat side by side on the wall.

Shepherd didn't ask, but even so, Ruby told him, "She looks all right now. She looks peaceful." Ruby stared up at the glove of the sky, holding a handful of stars. "She's not where she should be, but she's at peace."

"Thank you for . . . attending to her," Shepherd said. "I couldn't have done it." His face darkened, and he added, "But I *could* have done what you did to him. I wish I'd had the chance. Bastard, that's what he was. I'm sorry, Ruby, but it's true."

She nodded, because it *was* true.

"Ruby, I'm astonished by you," Shepherd said quietly. "By what you're capable of." He turned toward her. "You got the water hemlock yourself? Boiled the roots yourself? Where did you learn to do that?"

"The library. I've been reading up on it ever since you mentioned it."

"I see." Shepherd stood. "Do you want me to walk you back to the house?"

Ruby rose from her seat and shook her head.

"You have someone to call?" he said. "The police, of course, but is there anyone else? Someone you can stay with tonight?"

She thought of Miss Wells and told him that yes, she could call her English teacher.

Shepherd touched her shoulder. "I don't know what to do now," he whispered, and his eyes filled with tears.

Ruby was heartbroken for him. She put her arms around his neck, her head resting against his jacket collar. "There's nothing else *to* be done now," she told him. "Nothing except miss her."

68

Angie

His mouth tightly drawn, Dr. Shepherd looked away. He glanced around the crowded airport gate, then back at me. "Ruby told you everything, then?"

I nodded. "Except for this: I've been wondering about one thing." I adjusted PJ on my lap, sitting him upright so he could look out the big windows to my left, watching airplanes come and go. "What made the police suspect Silja?"

"I don't know," Dr. Shepherd said. "Perhaps some commuter came forward and said he'd seen Silja leave the Stonekill station after work that night. Or maybe someone saw Ruby leave Silja's car at the station later in the evening, and thought it was Silja. Ruby said she thought no one saw that, but . . . "

Dr. Shepherd shrugged. "There's another potential explanation," he said. "I didn't ask Ruby about this, but when I think about it, I believe it's possible. Ruby might have called the cops herself and gave them that tip anonymously."

I stared at him. "Why would she do such a risky thing?"

"It was risky, all right. But she wanted to leave. And she had to make sure Paul was scared enough that he'd be convinced he had to take her away."

"She wanted to leave with Paul." I bit my lip. "She wanted to be with my husband."

Dr. Shepherd shook his head. "That's not it—not quite. She had to get away—as far away as possible, and she knows he's the only one who has the means to take her. He has her passport. He has plenty of money; she told me he drained her father's savings account yesterday. She knew I couldn't take her, because I have other obligations here . . . my father . . . " He looked over my head and PJ's, toward the airplane parked outside my gate. "Ruby couldn't run the bigger risk of being caged up," he said. "Not for a second."

I thought about that. "You're an accessory to this crime, doctor. I could turn you in, you know."

He glanced at me, eyebrows raised. "You certainly could. But I don't think you will."

"What makes you think that?"

He smiled. "Because you, my dear, understand love. I can tell, just by seeing you with this child—you understand that love transcends justice."

I didn't answer. I snuggled my son closer. My beautiful, wonderful son.

Dr. Shepherd stood. "I think we've talked enough. I wish you all the best, Mrs. Glass."

"Wait." I fished in my purse until I found the little photograph album. "You should have this."

Dr. Shepherd took the album. "Well, I'll be," he said softly. "Did Ruby give you this?"

I nodded. "She said to make sure it was in my purse, not my luggage."

Dr. Shepherd laughed aloud. "I'm going to miss that girl."

Safely on the ground in Milwaukee, I stepped off the plane and looked around. I was at the top of the stairway leading down to the tarmac.

The wind blew. The plane had come in over Lake Michigan; the airport is only a few miles from the shoreline. I could feel the lake's effects, and they spoke of home to me. The water, the air, was different from what I'd experienced in New York. What was the difference? I couldn't put my finger on it, but somehow—even though I was at a busy metropolitan airport in Wisconsin, and I'd come from a remote wooded area in New York—the atmosphere felt purer to me.

Like there was nothing here to hide.

I held the baby on my hip and stepped down. "Careful, ma'am," a porter said as I reached the last stair tread. He pointed toward the doorway to the airport.

From here, I would make my way inside and find my parents. I would go home and start my life over.

I clutched PJ tighter. I thought about how I could—almost—turn the trip to New York into an invented story. It felt like something that hadn't actually happened.

Not just that. If not for the babe in my arms, I could make up the entire experience of being married to Paul Glass in the first place.

But here was my son—soft and real and every bit mine.

I nestled PJ against my chest and went inside. I stepped into the warmth, the familiarity, of home.

69

Ruby

Ruby and Paul return the rental car and take a shuttle bus from La-Guardia to Idlewild, the airport from which most international flights leave New York. He has their passports and a lot of cash. It wasn't difficult for Paul to pretend to be her father and close out the account her father kept in a bank in Ossining.

Paul even had identification that showed who he was. Henry Glass, with his photograph right there in the passport. Clear as day.

Ruby is thinking about how Shepherd once asked her, "If you could go anywhere in the world, Ruby, where would you go?" And she told him she'd always wanted to see the Greek islands.

It's a shame she has to leave Shepherd. She'll miss him and she knows he'll miss her. But there was no other option.

"I still think it was a mistake, letting her go like that," Paul says on the shuttle bus.

Ruby shakes her head. "It will be fine," she tells him. "She's not going to say anything, Paul." She shifts in her seat and looks out the window at the office and government buildings, the diners and filling stations, lining Grand Central Parkway. "Aunt Angie just wants to get on with her life and forget about all of this."

"Well," Paul says. "I would have preferred the insurance of knowing she couldn't ever speak up."

"She won't," Ruby says. "And even if she does, it won't matter. No one will find us."

"Let's hope not." Paul frowns, and then goes on. "That doctor, too. How do we know *he* won't speak up?"

"Because he doesn't know anything," Ruby lies. "He's just somebody I met. Somebody who told me a little bit about plants—and that's what gave me the idea of what to do." She rubs her fingers on her mother's sapphire necklace, which is around her neck as always. She wraps her arms around herself, cozy in Shepherd's sweater. "He isn't anybody, Paul. Trust me."

Paul mumbles something under his breath, then changes the subject. "I'm sorry you don't have your suitcase," he says. "We can buy a few necessities at the airport, and anything else you need once we reach our destination."

Ruby nods, patting her pocketbook. It has *To Kill a Mockingbird*. It has her grandmother's locket. It has one photo of her mother and Shepherd from the day they went boating on the river—one she took out of the album before she gave it to Aunt Angie.

She also took some photographs from the shoe box in her mother's closet—pictures of her mother and grandmother when they were young, pictures of Ruby herself as a baby.

She glanced at the pictures of the birdcage. She picked up her father's army picture, the one he sent her mother when she was pregnant with Ruby. But in the end, Ruby didn't take those photographs.

Let them burn.

The other day, when he told her his plan, Paul ventured that the river would be a good place for a body. "Or, if that isn't to your liking," he said, "there's extra space in that deep grave out in the forest."

His grin was callous, almost sinister, and Ruby knew Paul was being his truest self in that moment.

But he was right—there was plenty of room in the Shelter. And no one would ever know. Or perhaps they would, but by the time they did, Ruby and Paul would be long gone.

She tried to talk him out of it. But she knew he wasn't easily letting go of the idea. When he tried to bring Aunt Angie inside the house this morning, Ruby knew exactly why. She's thankful Aunt Angie stood up to him.

Still, all of this helps her understand Paul better. She understands what he's capable of.

She hopes he doesn't—prematurely—realize the same about her.

"Where to?" Paul asks as they walk up to the Pan Am ticket counter. "Anywhere you want, Ruby."

Ruby thinks about it. There's Greece, of course, but that's better saved for another day. So she glances at the list of departing flights to see which one leaves soonest.

Then she says, "I've heard Spain is beautiful this time of year."

EPILOGUE

Angie

1962

It was the first truly chilly morning of the fall, but at least it wasn't windy. I wore a heavy cardigan and dungarees. I left my son—now an active toddler—in my mother's care, saying only that I wished to borrow my parents' boat and take it out on the lake alone.

"Suit yourself," my mother said. "Willie and I will be fine—won't we, buddy?" The boy nodded and asked his grandmother for a cookie.

I kissed my son, staring into his gorgeous dark eyes, my hands gently squeezing his tiny shoulders. Even when my mother or another trusted adult is watching him, I find it difficult to pull away.

I'm not an overprotective mother—I have no reason to be. My child has a brigade of parental figures; even without a father in the picture, he wants for nothing. So it's not that I worry about his well-being. The reason I gaze so deeply at him is that I'm looking for indications of the type of man he'll become. Fortunately, thus far I've seen nothing resembling his father's demeanor.

It's hard to remember calling him anything besides Willie. Not long after my return from New York, I told my family I could no longer think of my son as Paul Junior. "He needs his own name," I said. "We can call him by his middle name, William."

After reluctantly pulling away and waving good-bye to my mother and Willie, I walked down the wooden steps—these much sturdier than the stairs leading from my cottage to North Bay—to the dock where my parents keep their motorboat.

I looked back at the clapboard-sided, dormered house. I took in the manicured lawn and the tidy pots of gold and purple mums on the porch. Everything so genuine, so familiar.

I'd been tempted, when I returned from New York, to move back home. It would have been so easy. Between my parents living there and my sisters coming over daily, there would have been plenty of people to rock my baby, feed him, find him clothes to wear.

But I couldn't do it. After a few days resting up at my parents', the baby and I moved back to the cottage on North Bay. The first night there, alone under a quilt in the old-fashioned, iron-framed bed that had once belonged to my grandparents—and for a year had been my marriage bed—I slept soundly and solidly. A deep, dreamless sleep.

For days, I did nothing but play with the baby, clean, and organize. I scrubbed everything, though it was already spotless. I removed Paul's meager wardrobe from the closet and dresser, packing his clothes in an old hatbox I found in the attic. In the studio, I crated Paul's supplies and stored his paintings in shallow cardboard boxes with sheets of tissue paper in between each piece.

One night when the baby was sound asleep in his crib, I took out the packet of Henry's letters to Paul. With the shawl that had belonged to Silja's mother wrapped around my shoulders, I sat by lamplight in my tiny living room, reading each letter word for word.

They didn't tell me anything I didn't already know. All they did was make me sorely regret not reading them sooner. If I had, maybe Silja would still be alive.

The next morning I took those letters, plus the items Ruby had given me, and sealed everything in a wooden box I bought at the hardware store in town. I wound twine around the box and double-knotted it.

Once I had it all boxed up, I hauled every bit of Paul's presence to the attic. I stacked it in a corner and didn't look at it again.

After that, I wasn't sure what to do. Before I could make any real decisions, I needed to know what my immediate future held. There was no answer for that except to wait until a few weeks had passed.

My family monitored me carefully and anxiously. I told them the barest of facts about what had happened in New York—just enough so that they wouldn't push me to alert the authorities. "It doesn't matter," I said. "If the only way to get Paul to return to me is by force, then I don't want him back anyway."

I received a telephone call from New York a few days after I got home—regrettably from Officer Hill, rather than Brennan. He wanted to know any details I could provide. "They're gone, is all I know," I told him. "They have passports and cash. They could be anywhere."

The next day, a local cop—a boy I *do* know from school, actually—showed up at my doorstep with a warrant. I let him look around, but it was clear Paul and Ruby weren't there and hadn't been there. After that, the police left me alone.

My mother and father stopped by the cottage daily. I didn't tell them what truly concerned me, but I assured them that the baby and I would be fine. "We just need time," I told my parents. "Time to figure out the next chapter of our lives."

Ten days after I got home, my period arrived. I cried tears of joy and relief. There wouldn't be a second child, at least. That was a blessing.

In the spring, after the last thaw, I celebrated Willie's first birthday by reading him the listings in the Sturgeon Bay Vocational School catalog. "Secretary?" I asked him. "Teacher's aide? Or maybe Mommy should get really crazy and learn accounting." He looked at me with that curious, amiable expression of his, then reached for the catalog, crumpling it in his chubby hands.

In the end, I chose a business administration path—remembering that it had been Silja's path, too, or something akin to that. Despite everything else that had happened, no one could say Silja hadn't provided for her family. I needed to do that, too.

Less than a year into the program, I began dating a boy I met on campus. Jack is my age and hails from Little Sturgeon, in the southern part of Door. I've made no promises to him, but I enjoy his wide-eyed grin, his closeness with his parents and siblings, how easily he's welcomed not only me but also Willie into his life.

All along I've known I could get my marriage to Paul annulled. It might be a long, tedious process, but it was possible, given my youth when I'd married and my parents' good standing in the Church. Not to mention the fact that I'd had not a word from Paul in almost two years.

"Maybe," I told Jack not long ago, when he asked me if I'd ever consider getting hitched. "Maybe, Jack, but don't rush me." I wrapped my arms around his neck. "We've got all the time in the world," I whispered in his ear. "No need to move fast."

And then one day last week, I received a letter from Ruby.

It was postmarked Karavostásis, Greece. I looked it up on a map, and found the Greek island that was home to the town of Karavostásis.

The death certificate fell out of the envelope first. Paul had died in Barcelona six months before. I studied the official seal. It was in Spanish, but I could decipher Paul's name, date of birth, date of death. And the words in Spanish: *Causa de muerte : caída accidental*.

The next day in the college library, I looked up *caída* in an English-Spanish dictionary. It means "fall."

Dear Aunt Angie,

I put something in this envelope that might be useful. I don't know if you've thought about marrying somebody else. If you did, it seems like having a first husband's death certificate would come in handy.

Long ago, Paul and I gave up the names we traveled under. If you have money, it's not at all difficult to acquire documentation saying you're somebody else. So Paul's actual death certificate is under a different name, and it's with that name on the tombstone that he lies in a Spanish graveyard. But I figured the extra step of obtaining a death certificate with his real name on it might be helpful to you.

It's an unfortunate way to die, a fall. The body often contorts in all sorts of ways you wouldn't think possible if you didn't see it with your own eyes. For Paul, though, it happened quickly and maybe not too painfully. But still quite sad, as I'm sure you'll agree.

Paul and I flew to Madrid, but we didn't stay there. He was afraid we'd be tailed. We moved around for a few months, then settled in Barcelona. It was not only scenic, but also an effective place to hide because it's a big city where no one knew us and by then we were pretty sure no one cared. We had plenty of money—thousands from my father's account. Since he earned barely a dime the entire time I knew him, my assumption is he'd been siphoning my mother's earnings for years.

So money wasn't a problem. What was a problem was Paul. He turned out to be so controlling. He wanted to decide what I wore, where I went, the books I read.

And other things, too. Everything, really.

I tried to run away from him a few times, but he always found me and brought me back. I put up with that as long as I could.

His death means those days are finally over. I have to say I'm glad of it.

My life is better now. I came here because I missed living in a small town. Isn't that ironic? I left Stonekill because I thought it was too tiny to contain me. And I wasn't even willing to come to your small town, Aunt Angie. I thought I'd had enough of small-town life. But after Barcelona, I realized it wasn't the size of Stonekill that was the problem. The problem was being kooky high schooler Ruby Glass.

There's an open-air café in Karavostásis, and I'm a waitress. I rent a room in town and go to the beach every day. Locals call me Chrysi. That's short for chrysafénios, which means "golden."

Once I got here and settled in, I wrote to Shepherd. I was afraid to write to him from Barcelona—I was worried he'd write back and I knew how Paul would react to that. Like I said, he controlled everything. I couldn't even get to the post box without Paul beating me to it.

But now Shepherd and I write regularly. He can't visit me—he still has his father to care for—but he says someday he hopes to.

Here's a story for you, Aunt Angie. I thought you might like a story:

Today, a woman with blond, upswept hair and cat-eye glasses walked into my café. She wore a green linen dress that was tight at *the waist, full in the skirt, capped in the sleeves. The whole shebang accentuated her full figure in all the right places.*

I was in my usual getup—sandals on my dusty feet, cutoff shorts, and a gauzy top because it's hot here even this time of year, when most of the tourists are gone and business is slowing down.

The woman took a seat in the back of our outdoor café. After she'd ordered and I brought her food, I watched her from the corner of my eye.

She wasn't my mother, of course. I don't want you to get the wrong idea, Aunt Angie. I wish she'd been my mother, of course. But what is, is.

When she finished her meal, she came to the counter to pay. "Delicious," she said to me in English, because she could tell I'm not Greek. One look at my hair and it's obvious I'm not Greek. "Best spanakopita I've had since I've been in Greece."

I nodded but didn't answer.

"I'm just passing through Karavostásis," she went on. "The ferry made a stop here. I was hungry, so I got off for lunch."

"It leaves in twenty minutes," I told her. "Don't miss it or you'll be stuck here until Friday."

She smiled at me. "Doesn't seem like such a bad place to be stuck."

Well. She's right about that.

As I watched that stranger walk toward the dock, I thought about my mother.

I hope the things I've done, the place I've landed, would please her. I couldn't give my mother peace, Aunt Angie. I couldn't help her live the life of her dreams. And for that I'll always be sorry.

But I can give myself peace. I hope she'd be happy for me. I think she would.

Take care of yourself, Aunt Angie—and your sweet son, too.

Love,
Ruby

I started the engine, pulled the lines from the dock, and maneuvered onto Lake Michigan. The breezes moved my hair back, and I stood, one knee on the seat, gunning the motor as the boat sped onto the lake.

The eighteen-foot craft, powerful beneath me as it zipped over the water—as powerful as my young, strong body—made me feel fearless.

I thought about the youthfulness of my body and mind. About how much I'm capable of.

I'm twenty-three years old. I have my whole life ahead of me.

I drove northeast into the swells of Lake Michigan. I passed Toft Point, Moonlight Bay, the Cana Island Lighthouse. I pushed the throttle until I was at full speed. The boat jolted over the waves, but I held fast to the throttle and looked straight ahead with clear, open eyes.

Despite its depth, nothing about this lake frightens me. Once, when my son was only a baby, my quick thinking saved him from drowning in these waters. I know I can handle anything the lake—or life—puts in my path.

Looking back toward the shore, I could see Gordon Lodge. The resort is thriving. The original wood-beam lodge has been replaced with a larger, modern building, but the Top Deck looks the same as always. I drove far from the shore, until Gordon's and the cottages on North Bay were mere specks on the forested land in the distance.

Finally, I killed the engine and let the boat drift. From a leather satchel I'd brought along, I took out the wooden box. Once it was sealed, I'd never opened it again. But I knew everything was there. Paul's letters to Henry, and Henry's letters in return. The packet of bomb shelter drawings. And the horrible, confessional love letter Paul wrote to his niece.

Under the string binding, I added the letter Ruby sent me.

The letter that, more or less, implicated the girl. For the second and—I hoped—the last time in her life.

On top of the box, I placed a heavy stone I'd found near my parents' dock. I wound a rope tightly around everything and tied it fast.

I tossed the weighted packet over the side of the boat. It landed on the water's surface with a plunk and slowly sank into the depths of the lake. I knew that soon it would be covered with sand, and in a short while, it would be indistinguishable from the rocks around it.

Not once did I doubt my actions. Not once did I wonder whether I was doing the right thing.

I turned over the boat's engine and looked across the lake. I pressed down the throttle and steered toward the shoreline, heading for home.

ACKNOWLEDGMENTS

So much gratitude is due. To Tara Parsons, thank you for your re-
lentless passion and razor-sharp edits. Much appreciation to Susan
Moldow for the opportunity to join the Touchstone team. Thanks to
Isabella Betita, Courtney Brach, Kelsey Manning, Sydney Morris,
Jessica Roth, and everyone else at Touchstone. Agent extraordinaire
Susanna Einstein and foreign rights maven Sandy Hodgman have my
gratitude and friendship.

A second novel rides the coattails of a debut's patronage. To the
dedicated booksellers and librarians, book clubs, friends and fans who
attend readings and events for *The Bookseller*, gracious radio hosts,
journalists, and book bloggers who help get the word out—thank you,
from the bottom of my heart.

Details make the story, especially in historical fiction. Clare Miller
Wood (1936–2016) was the resident expert on North Bay; I'm grateful she shared her memories with me. Thanks also to Lynn Corriveau
for help with Door County specifics. Mary Hauser and Jerry Randall
open their North Bay home to my family every summer; their gift of
unplugged, imaginative time together is one for which I'm grateful.
Thank you to Peter Bracichowicz of Corcoran Group Real Estate,
who gave me an extensive tour of the Alku and illuminated the history
of Sunset Park, Brooklyn (a.k.a. Finntown). *Kiitos* to Annette Lyon
and Arlo Pelegrin for help with the Finnish language, and *gracias* to
Grethel Van Epps for the Spanish. Although Stonekill is fictional, it
wouldn't feel genuine without details of the sights, sounds, and scents

of northern Westchester that still resonate with me. I drew on my own childhood memories, those of my sister Susan Wright, and stories and photos shared by natives of Peekskill, our hometown. Thank you.

Standout research materials include *The GI's War* by Edwin P. Hoyt; the 1946 John Huston documentary *Let There Be Light*; Howard Fast's *Peekskill USA: Inside the Infamous 1949 Riots*; and Amy Stewart's *Wicked Plants*. (I also appreciated Amy's input when I had deeper questions.) Two slim volumes provided authentic details: *The Blue Book of Crime* (1948), which Henry would have received as part of his correspondence course, and the 1959 government booklet *The Family Fallout Shelter*. Note the booklet's copyright date; I hope readers grant me poetic license in allowing Henry to pore over this booklet a year before its publication. Any other historical inaccuracies are either my mistakes or intentional in the interest of story.

Kudos to Jennifer Kincheloe and Gary Schanbacher for insightful early reads. Pat Mulcahy, thank you for helping me see the forest through the trees (pun intended). For standing by me every step of the way, I thank Gillian Braun, Mary Elliott, Robin Filipczak, Shana Kelly, Jocelyn Scheirer, Sandra Theunick, Maura Weiler, my book club members, everyone at Lighthouse Writers, and my multifarious online tribes.

Thanks to Daphne du Maurier—who, by penning *Rebecca*, gave birth to the contemporary literary thriller, and to Richard Yates—who, in writing *Revolutionary Road*, put into beautiful words postwar suburban angst.

Finally, I'm grateful to my family. Thank you, Sammy, Dennis, Jane, and Charlie—for your commitment, your smiles, and your love. I'm a better person, and a better writer, because of you.

ABOUT THE AUTHOR

Cynthia Swanson is the *New York Times* and *USA Today* bestselling author of *The Bookseller*. An Indie Next selection and the winner of the 2016 WILLA Award for historical fiction, *The Bookseller* is being translated into more than a dozen languages. Cynthia has published short fiction in numerous journals and was a Pushcart Prize nominee. She lives with her family in Denver, Colorado.

1/2018